Kris Longknife
BOLD

Mike Shepherd

ACE
New York

ACE
Published by Berkley
An imprint of Penguin Random House LLC
375 Hudson Street, New York, New York 10014

Copyright © 2016 by Mike Moscoe

ISBN: 9780425277386

First Edition: November 2016

Printed in the United States of America
1   3   5   7   9   10   8   6   4   2

Cover illustration by Scott Grimando
Cover design by Katie Anderson
Book design by Kristin del Rosario

Acknowledgments

As Kris finishes up her first midlife crisis, I'm also hitting the twenty-fifth anniversary of my first short story publication. It's been a wild ride, and now seems like a good time to thank all the people who helped me along the way.

I will always be grateful to Sheila Simonson and the group at the Novel Writing class at Clark College. They helped me through those first stumbling efforts, taught me how to do dialogue (you know, Mike, that stuff in quotes), and gave me the discipline to write ten whole pages a week. Mary Rosenblum and her writers group helped polish me. Mary also gave me the benefit of her Clarion experience.

Thank you, Stan Schmidt of *Analog*. You were the first to see the writing potential in me and give me the approval I desperately needed. Like with all writers, that approval came in the form of a check.

Jenn Jackson has been the best agent that I could ask for. She's given me all I needed and kept out of my way when I needed that. My longtime editor at Ace, Ginjer Buchanan, picked me up and gave me a second chance when others might not have. She was a perfect match for twenty years. I hope she enjoys a long and fun retirement; she richly deserves it. I appreciate Diana Gill's contributions to *Kris Longknife: Bold* and my other latest books. I'm grateful to the whole gang at Ace for the work they've put into the production that turns my manuscript into the finished product you readers enjoy. Oh, and I do love Scott's cover art.

The folks at Lincoln City, both at the Historic Anchor

Inn and the Sunday brunch bunch, have supported me through a lot and helped me keep going. I'm sure you will keep me going for a long time to come.

My first readers also really deserve a very special thank-you. Lisa Müller and Edee Lemonier do a great job of cleaning up my all-too-frequent typos and nits. Oh, and occasionally they back up my wife's "You really need to fix that section."

Around the house, Nikki and Danny, my grandkids, are not only interesting sources for inspiration, but they've also come to understand what it's like to have a writer for a grandpa. They've learned to enjoy the ups and put up with the downs. They also love going to cons with me.

Then there's Ellen. She's devoted years to learning how to be the best first reader that a writing husband could hope for. Thank you, honey, for everything.

1

Admiral, Her Royal Highness Kris Longknife did her best to cut her corners as she'd been taught in those long-ago days at Officer Candidate School. But then, Gunny had never suggested how you managed the correct military entry with a bundle such as Kris cradled in her left arm.

The unholy trinity were waiting for her.

Kris came to a halt before the middle one, Field Marshal McMorrison, Chief of Staff for the entire military of the United Society. She saluted, bringing her hand right up her gig line—as much as she could without bopping that tiny bundle.

"Admiral Kris Longknife reporting as ordered," she said, more to her great-grandfather Ray, King Raymond I to most, seated in the guest's chair to the right of Mac's desk. The last member of the unholy trinity, Admiral Crossenshield, Crossie to most, had a chair to Mac's left.

"Now, what was the all-fired hurry?" Kris failed to avoid adding.

"What is *that*!" the King said, pointing at the bundle cradled in Kris's left arm.

Is he so locked up in his own little bubble that he didn't get the word? Kris removed the blanket that had protected her infant daughter's face, keeping her warm from the crisp autumn weather during the drive from the space-elevator station to Main Navy. "This is Ruthie Marie. Jack and my first-born," she said.

She pointed Ruthie's gummy smile at the two couples who stood by the bookcase to the left of the unholy three. They didn't look at all surprised to see her bundle. Indeed, if they hadn't known of tiny Ruthie, they would never have been here.

"Can I see the baby?" Kris's mother, Brenda, squeed. At her elbow, Great-grandmother Ruth Tordon, more commonly known as Mrs. Trouble, held back. Brenda was so rarely happy after the kidnapping and death of her third child, Eddy, that any moment of joy was not to be denied her.

Kris met her mother halfway and most gently and carefully managed the transfer. Mother must have been getting practice with Honovi's three; Kris had to do little to get Mother's arms just right.

You will *get this just right. This is* my *baby,* Kris thought but did not say.

Ruthie gave Brenda a toothless grin. Brenda grinned back, enraptured. Gramma Trouble stood at one elbow, Kris at the other. Brenda could not have dropped Ruthie if she wanted to.

"Her full name," Kris provided, "is Ruth Maria Brenda Anne."

"Hi there, my little Brenda," Brenda said.

Great-grampa Trouble, trouble to his enemies, trouble to his superiors, and just flat trouble to everyone, including himself, stood well out of range of any spit-up with Billy Long-knife, Man of the People, Prime Minister of Wardhaven, and Kris's occasional father.

"What's her last name?" Grampa Ray asked, coming to stand by his longtime friend, General Trouble, ret.

"Haven't decided," Kris said. "Probably we'll have to do it before she starts school, but we can wait."

"You're married to Jack, here," the King said, no part question at all.

Lieutenant General Jack Montoya nodded, as did Kris.

"When did that happen?" was as gruff as a man could manage under Ruthie's gummy grin.

"While I was out of any chain of command," Kris said. "Just

before you issued orders making me God Almighty in the Alwa system."

That got a snort from Ray and a chuckle from everyone else paying attention.

"I'll bet you any amount of money Rita was at the bottom of this," the King growled.

"She officiated," Kris said, beaming happily.

"That woman keeps everyone wrapped around her little finger," Ray muttered.

Kris considered how much Great-grandfather Ray had pulled the strings that damn near wrapped her in a spiderweb of conflicting duties on Alwa but said nothing. Ray was what he was, and there was little she could do to change him at his present age, with 120-plus years disappearing in the rearview mirror.

Grampa Trouble laid a nearly affectionate hand on Ray's shoulder. "Ray, you knew those two were going to tie the knot, it was only a question of when and where."

Kris let out a sigh. This was going smoother than she had expected.

The *Wasp* had jumped into the Wardhaven system, finally slowed down enough to hit it at under fifty thousand kilometers an hour. Kris had expected an immediate message from Mac or Ray. After all, they were the ones who had had Grand Admiral Sandy Santiago relieve her of her command and order her home "soonest."

No message.

The *Wasp* docked at High Wardhaven Station as smoothly as if Captain Drago were still at the conn. Kris had expected a message as soon as they opened their locks and plugged into the station's landline, air, water, and sewer.

Nothing.

Jack had to order up transport for Kris and a two-squad Marine Honor Guard—fully locked and loaded. A chief bosun's mate, a fatherly type, had followed along, a diaper bag slung over his shoulder with such aplomb that none would dare gainsay him.

Only when they had dropped down to the main beanstalk terminal in Wardhaven had the necessary transport been waiting for them. They'd been whisked from the terminal to Main

Navy and led by a very silent lieutenant colonel to Mac's inner sanctum.

The colonel had passed them to Mac's secretary, who smiled, and said, "You are expected," and held open the door to Mac's inner office.

Kris had taken a deep breath and reported in.

She still had no idea where the fire was that required her to leave the fleet she had built up, the people she had sworn to protect, and the industrial base she'd grown and overseen.

I've had enough of being the visiting fireman. Especially enough of being ordered from pillar to post with no idea of what I'm supposed to do or how to do it.

Still, Kris held her tongue as Ruthie smiled and did her best to wrap around her tiny finger all of Kris's problem people, the Troubles excepted . . . sometimes.

Even Ray finally tried his hand at holding Ruthie. That was when disaster struck.

Ruthie scrunched up her face and let out a yowl. Then she spat up.

Good girl. I've wanted to do that so many times, Kris thought.

But "diaper bag" was what Kris called for. The Marines and the chief had been able to avoid Kris's little family reunion. *Lucky them.* These were usually a disaster, and there was no need for the Marines to know just how bad it got the higher up you went. Smart Jack, he'd grabbed the bag, not considering it beneath a three-star to pack the necessities for his tiny daughter. Now he handed the bag to Kris, already opened and with a cleaning cloth, half–pulled out. Kris flashed Jack a smile; whether they were fighting off bug-eyed monsters or close family, she could always count on him.

Kris traded the cloth to Grampa Ray for Ruthie. Jack had another cloth in hand, so Kris could clean up the tiny one. It was clear, however, that Ruthie had had enough of being nice for family. She still hadn't quite figured out what her lungs were for, but she already knew how to make with her own little war cry.

"How long's it been since she was fed?" Gramma Ruth asked.

"Just before we headed down," Kris answered as she checked to see that the diaper was neither wet nor messy. "I think this is an 'I'm hungry, where's lunch' howler," Kris agreed, only too happy to use Ruth for an excuse to get a break from all this family attention.

"Can I feed her?" Brenda asked eagerly. "Do you have a bottle?"

"We were not prepared for children on Alwa Station," Kris explained. "We've had to do everything the old-fashioned way."

"Body birth and breast nursing, huh?" Gramma Trouble provided when Brenda frowned blankly.

"Yep," Kris said. "Do you have a room where I could nurse Ruthie?"

"How did you come to have a baby on the front line?" Grampa Ray asked, with a lot of royal command behind it.

Kris had been waiting for that one. "Someone sabotaged my new birth-control implants, figuring that a pregger admiral couldn't command. I dumped his ass in the bird-guano mines and commanded very well, thank you. By the way, thanks for those beam ships. We would have been toast when six alien hordes hit us all at the same time. With them, *they* were toast, slathered with marmalade. We did get the first two on our own, thank you very much. Anyway, Ruthie and I need to commune with motherhood just now. Jack can explain more if you need it. Where do we go?"

Ruthie emphasized the urgency of Kris's request with a bawl that was only three on the baby Richter scale but threatened to go higher if not appeased.

"Erwin," Mac commanded urgently on his intercom. The secretary appeared at the door. "Show the admiral to Admiral Ballo's office. He's taken leave today."

Erwin led Kris out of the office, into the hall, and to the next door down. It opened to a very standard set of senior flag officer's spaces. The walls were a deep mahogany. The outer wall had large picture windows with drapes that could be pulled shut. There were a desk, a meeting table, and a discussion pit, all standard-issue. The large armchair in the discussion pit was the one thing out of military step. It was a rocker.

"Admiral Ballo has a bad back," Erwin explained.

"He's not in today?"

Erwin glanced at the wall that the admiral shared with Mac's office. "He didn't say so, but I think he wanted to stay out of range of the collateral damage."

"Smart man," Kris said, and began to loosen the coat of her dress blues.

Erwin got the message and left.

"So it's just you and me, babe," Kris said, and settled Ruthie at her right breast, which, to be honest, was starting to ache. If Ruthie hadn't called for a chow break, Kris might have had to.

Kris began to relax as Ruthie suckled hungrily. She had a good view from her seat of blue sky and white clouds. That scene could match hundreds of worlds humanity had settled on.

Kris chose to let that thought wander on its way and smiled down at the miracle at her breast. "It is just you and me, little one."

2

"Kris, we're going to stay," had become an all-too-frequent refrain in her last days on Canopus Station.

Penny had been the first.

"Kris, would you mind terribly if Masao and I stayed?"

"No," Kris had said, as cheerfully as she could manage. "Of course not."

But Penny went on talking, as if an explanation might make it hurt less.

"Admiral Santiago has offered us both a place on her staff. I'm to head up her intelligence section. She says it will mean captain stripes."

"How will Masao feel about you outranking him that much?" Kris asked.

"He won't. Santiago has authorization to create a staff drawing in officers from all the Alliance we have out here on Alwa Station. And she can promote them, too. Masao is overdue for lieutenant commander, and commander as soon as she can find an excuse for it."

"I wonder why I never got that authority," Kris grouched.

"I don't know, but it's nice she has it. I've also talked with Taussig. We're going to go in on a farm along that big river in

Rooster territory. We've asked for a young colonial couple to go in with us. They'll cover the place all the time, and we'll rotate being home."

Penny paused. "Home. Strange to call this place all the way across the galaxy home."

"If it's where your and Masao's roots are, then it's home," Kris had said.

"I've got to get past losing Tommy," Penny said, suddenly. She still choked when she said the name of her husband of three days, who gave his life so that she might live.

"Yes, you do," Kris said, softly. She suppressed a shiver at the memory of ordering the dumb metal of her ship to seal all the holes in its hull . . . and seal Tommy's fate.

"I know, Kris. I will. Masao is the man I want to do it with."

Their conversation meandered along for a while longer before Penny finally left, leaving Kris to contemplate the changes that life brought your way.

Captain, no, Vice Admiral Drago was next.

"Commander Pett do okay by you?" he asked Kris after he had smiled at Ruthie Anne and assured Kris that she was a perfect baby.

"I'm alive, and the *Wasp* isn't even in line for the body and fender shop."

"Any landing you can walk away from."

"So, what really brings you around?" Kris had finally asked.

"Do you trust Commander Pett to get you and this cute little one back across the galaxy without a problem?"

"I do. Why?"

"I'm thinking of hanging around here for a while."

"Lots of people are," Kris allowed.

"I mean, it's not like admirals around here spend all their time trapped behind a desk. Everybody fights from four stars down to an Ostrich seaman recruit."

"It seems to go that way," Kris said, and paused to see if there was more to his hankering.

"And there's this colonial woman. She's buried two husbands and claims she can put me in the ground. I told her my wedding gift to her will be her very own burial plot," Drago said, grinning.

"Whatever floats your boat," Kris answered.

They talked for a bit longer, Kris praising Drago's handling of Fourth Fleet in the last battle. They left with promises to get together when next they shared the same space and share a beer and bring each other up to date.

There must have been something wrong with the air-recycling system; Kris needed a tissue to blow her nose.

Amanda and Jacques were no surprise.

They dropped by to gush to Kris that Prime Minister Ada of the colonials had set up a Science Advisory Committee and invited both of them to fill slots on it.

"We'll have an entire budding economy to work on," Amanda said.

"She's in hog heaven," Jacques growled.

"And you aren't?" Amanda growled right back. "You've got all kinds of bird cultures to work with, and I've heard you say the humans have many divergent cultures among themselves, what with the colonials and the Navy and the industrial types."

"Oink, oink," Jacques said through a happy grin.

"And we've also been asked to establish Alwa's first university," said Amanda, getting even more enthusiastic. "They haven't agreed on a name. Rita U just doesn't carry, and she's had so many other last names."

"Rita suggested we name it after her father, Nuu U," Jacques put in.

The two of them talked nonstop for most of the time they visited with Kris and only took a few moments out to fuss over Ruthie Anne before leaving to collect the last of their belongings still on the *Wasp*.

It took Kris a half hour of nursing Ruthie to calm down from that whirlwind.

She found herself wondering when Abby would come calling and what her own decision would be. They were only a few days shy of departure when Kris's maid, bodyguard, and so much more came into the *Wasp*'s wardroom at lunch, went down the steam tables, then casually settled into the chair across from Kris.

"How are things going?" Abby asked, buttering a roll.

"I would give half my trust fund to sleep through the night just once," Kris said.

"I hear that youngsters are death on sleep. What did Shakespeare say? 'Babes doth murder sleep.'"

"You may have that wrong," Nelly provided from Kris's collarbone.

"Whatever."

"Did you snap up some of that free land down among the Ostriches?" Kris asked, kind of sidling up to the big question.

"No, General Bruce and I have signed for some land along that nice, long river in Rooster territory. We've got the homestead between your Penny and Commodore Taussig and my boss Pipra."

"I figured Pipra would have you and Bruce as part of her farm crew," Kris said.

"She did, too," Abby said, "but I set her straight. Steve and I will be teaming with four fab supervisors and another brigade commander. We got two colonial couples signed up to help us. It shouldn't be too hard, and if Pipra tries anything too friendly with my Steve, well, I still know how to shoot."

Kris took a long drink of milk. "I don't blame you for not wanting to go back. You were just a maid there. You've really soared out here."

"I was never 'just a maid,' and you never treated me as if I were."

"Not after you saved my neck once or twice," Kris admitted.

"Even before I did," Abby put in. "Kris, you good people, and I'm so glad I met up with you."

"I'm glad you've been a major part of my life for the last six years," Kris allowed.

"If I don't get out of here, I'm gonna start blubbering," Abby said, and suddenly, her place across from Kris was empty.

Kris would have happily left her lunch right there, too, but she was feeding Ruthie as well as herself. After dabbing at her eyes with a linen napkin, she resolutely finished her lunch, but ship food was never so lacking in taste as it was that day.

Kris found herself blinking her eyes as she stared out the window at the sky over Wardhaven. She borrowed one of

Ruthie's cloths and dabbed away the moisture threatening to run down her cheek.

"Would I have stayed there if we could?" she asked Ruthie. Like all infants, Ruthie had no answers, only needs.

There was a knock at the door.

"I'm not decent," Kris called.

"I don't care," came in Jack's voice, and the door opened to let him in. He covered the distance with a few long steps, then traced Ruthie's busy cheeks with a gentle touch that also just happened to make feathery strokes on the breast the babe was busy draining dry.

Kris shivered at the pleasure.

"How are things back there?" Kris asked a minute or so later, motioning to Mac's office with her chin.

"No blood on the carpet."

"Yet."

"I don't know. I think Ruthie has kind of secured a temporary truce. Ray hasn't asked Billy a single political question, and vice versa. The two women are talking maternity and sharing pictures of the latest grandkid or great-grand tyke. I won't bet money on it, but I think your mother might just be softening a bit."

"That would be nice. Maybe we can find peace at last."

"You both know what it's like to be a mother now."

Kris nodded, then changed the subject. "Has anyone told you what's so on fire that they needed to haul me all the way back here to put it out?"

"No, but I think Ray's about to split a gut to get it out for you. You weren't nearly as close to popping with Ruthie Marie as Ray is with his secret."

"Speak for yourself, husband. I'll decide how close I was to popping and who gets to claim they're worse."

"My mistake," Jack said quickly, but with a fond grin.

Kris assumed the grin was for her breasts hanging out while she tried to return Ruthie's logistics to the properly hidden place polite society demanded.

Jack might be grinning, but he was also reaching for Ruthie, pulling her to his chest, and giving Kris two free hands. With that bit of help, she was able to get properly uniformed without dripping milk down her dress blues. *Hurray for our side.*

"Well, let's go see what sneaky mess Grampa Ray wants to get me into this time," Kris said, and led the way, letting Jack provide the rear guard, with Ruthie in his arms for the moment.

3

By the time Kris, Jack, and Ruthie got back, the room had changed. Gramma Trouble and Brenda were on a couch, eagerly awaiting Ruthie. Kris took in the rest. The King sat at the head of a conference table. Crossie and Mac were at his elbows.

There was an empty chair at the foot of the table, with Billy and Trouble sitting at its elbows. Kris expected that chair was for her. What she didn't much care for was that the two empty chairs, one of which would have to be Jack's, were too far from her.

"Father, would you mind letting Jack have that chair?" Kris said.

Billy looked surprised, but he sheepishly rose and took the next chair down. Kris hoped that didn't put him too close to the other side. She'd hate to see him back Ray if it came to that.

Nope, the two of them were too much alike to agree on much of anything.

Seated, Kris let the silence in the room stretch for only a bit, then said, "Okay, why am I here and not out there where you said I was indispensable, Your Majesty?"

"Do you remember Vicky Peterwald?" the King said without preamble.

"How could I forget her? I saved her neck when the aliens wanted us dead, and she stabbed me in the back the first time she could get her lovely, ivory boobs in front of a camera."

"You don't like her?" Ray said.

"I didn't say that. I pity the kid, growing up in that gutter that passes for Imperial Harry's Palace. What's she up to that makes you ask?" Kris said, still no more informed about where this was going and getting less and less patient for Ray to get there.

Grampa Trouble must have sensed Kris's mood; he jumped in. "Greenfeld is going to hell in a handbasket. The Empress has made several attempts to kill Vicky and they are the two leaders of a civil war that threatens to tear Greenfeld apart."

"And that matters to me how?" Kris asked.

"The Emperor has asked you to mediate between the two women," King Ray said. "Since you once saved his life, he thinks you'd be fair. For some reason, Vicky has also accepted you as mediator."

"And the stepmother?" Kris asked.

"We haven't heard from her," Crossie admitted.

"But if we did?" Kris asked the intelligence honcho.

Crossie scratched his left ear. "I have no idea if she'd say something positive, but she hasn't said anything negative."

Kris let all that she'd been told run around in her head for a few moments. Her mouth started talking long before she wanted it to. "Are you folks crazy? I'd have to be dumb . . . or insane . . . or the boldest person in human space . . . to get between the three of them. The only reason I saved Henry's worthless skin was because his death would have had my fingerprints faked all over his body, and there would have likely been a war."

Kris shook her head. "As for him and Vicky, you can't trust either of them to agree to anything and keep to it for more than five seconds. I hear the Empress is even worse."

Crossie had the good sense to nod along with Kris.

"So why are you trying to send me into this valley of death? You know, Ray, your last idea, setting us up for a stalking horse out on Alwa, was really dumb. There is no way anyone could look at our DNA and the DNA of the rest of the animals on Alwa and think we were from there. No way."

"We kind of figured that out," Mac said. "Fortunately, we came up with the beam weapons. How were they?"

"Horrible. Wonderful. They just barely saved our asses. They were one mad scientist's wild science project, and we just barely managed to duct tape them into something like a warship. You really need to do better next time."

"We're working on that," Ray said. "Maybe after you do this little favor for the Emperor, you can help us."

"You mean maybe if I survive this little suicide mission," Kris said dryly.

"We plan to send you with a fleet of the new frigates," Mac said.

"Battlecruisers," Kris corrected.

"Rita has you call them battlecruisers," Ray said, his face clouding up.

"No, *I'm* calling them battlecruisers," Kris snapped. "What with twenty 22-inch guns, they can stand up against any battle line we've got."

"But they can't fight in a battle line. Their lasers all point fore and aft." Admiral Crossie, who'd never commanded a ship, provided the Navy input.

Kris's growled "Who in here has the most experience commanding a battle line?" was hardly a question.

The room fell silent, as if a guillotine blade had slashed through further comment.

Kris waited a long minute before going on. "Besides, if I'm going to become the mediator hunting for any peace that can be found between these two crazies, I'll need to impress them. I expect to keep these admiral stripes, and I intend to lead a battle line. I'll also likely need a whole hell of a lot more, but that, at least, is a start."

"It's no big thing to change the manuals to say battlecruiser instead of frigate," Mac offered.

"You like those stripes," Ray said.

"You want to send a commander, or what am I, a captain, out there to patch together something between those three huge egos?"

"I see you made your husband a lieutenant general," Ray said, eyeing Jack.

"He commanded a corps dirtside with three Colonial Guard

divisions and attached Alwan auxiliaries as well as the Fleet
Marine Force afloat. I see no reason the people risking their
lives shouldn't have the rank to show for it. There was damn
little pay."

Grampa Trouble wetted a finger and made two marks in
the air.

Grampa Ray scowled at him but said nothing.

"Well, if that's settled," Mac said, "I think we can call this
meeting done and move on to other things. Admiral," he said,
looking at Kris, "I've had several of my staff examining what
a mediation mission might look like."

"Fine, but one more thing, Your Royal Majesty, before we
go," Kris said.

"Yes, Your Royal Highness?" Ray said, returning formality for formality.

"When this mad job is done, no more. No more wild jobs.
I want a job with a desk in Main Navy. I want Jack to have a
desk, too. Maybe we share the same office, maybe he's on a
different floor. But I want us to have lunch together without
anyone trying to blow us to hell, and I want to go home at 1700
to the kids. Yes, I said 'kids,' as in two at least. You hear me?"

"Message received and understood," the King said. "But
I'll bet you any amount of money that you won't last a month."

"And you'll lose," Kris said. Retrieving Ruthie from where
Gramma Trouble was doing her best to settle her down after
Mother had gotten her sputtering and spitting up, Kris led Jack
from Mac's office.

"Take me to Nuu House," she almost begged Jack.

4

Nuu House seemed somehow smaller, Kris reflected, as they drove up to the portico. It couldn't be that she was taller: She'd lived here through university. She'd thought herself fully grown to womanhood back then.

Maybe it wasn't so much a case of size as perspective. She'd seen an alien raider's base ship up close and personal.

After you've seen one of those puppies, everything looks tiny.

Kris smiled at that reflection.

A Marine from the escort opened the door for Kris. Jack preceded them in, as he usually did, to do one quick check for security. Strange to see him apply that standard procedure to Nuu House, but habit was habit, and Kris loved him for the way he looked out for her and Ruthie.

Kris walked into the foyer, with its spiraling black-and-white tiles . . . and came to a halt.

On the staircase where Abby had once stood, there was a matronly figure in some sort of gray-and-white civilian uniform backed up by four younger women in the same attire, each a stair step higher than the last. At the foot of the stairs, echeloned out from them, stood four hard-faced people, three men and one woman, who, even if they wore suits, were cut from same identical mold.

The older one looked familiar.

"You are . . . ?" Kris started.

"The guy who yelled for you to stop the elevator before you let yourselves out on a Sarin-gas-filled floor."

"Ah, yes. I believe I thanked you for that when you visited me on the *Mutsu*."

"Yes, you did, Your Highness."

"And I asked you to answer a question for me."

"You did that, Your Highness," he said with the hint of a gleam in his eyes.

"You must have answered it. When I got the message on where the trading fleet was, I knew you'd gotten to the bottom of Grampa Al's suicidal plan. Was it too much of a problem?"

"Not at all, Your Highness," he said with a gentle smile.

"Ha!" That was from the young woman of the group. "He nearly got himself killed, and he *was* kidnapped."

"Yes," said a young male. "We have pictures, all unsuitable for work."

Kris raised an eyebrow.

"Well, it may have been a tad tight for a bit," the senior lawman allowed.

"What brings you to Nuu House? Last I heard, you were a senior chief agent in charge for the Bureau of Investigations."

"I will likely be so again, Your Highness, but I and my talkative colleagues here have been seconded to the Secret Service to head up your protection detail."

Beside Kris, Jack cleared his throat. "We have several platoons of Marines to do that."

"No doubt, sir, but you will allow that we may be more informed as to matters here locally. You did quite well leading me a merry chase, but that was a bit over two years ago."

"He has a point," Kris allowed.

Jack considered that for a moment, then said, "I will coordinate my Marine guard with your people. I'm a belt-and-suspenders man where the safety of my wife and daughter are concerned."

"I couldn't agree with you more. Now, Your Highness, as you may recall, I am Senior Chief Agent in Charge Taylor

Foile; these are the people who will be heading up one of your around-the-clock shifts. Mahomet Debot," was a dark-haired man of swarthy complexion, as dark as Jack. "Rick Sanchez," was only slightly lighter than Jack, "and Leslie Chu," was a milk-skinned redhead who hardly looked the part of her surname. "One of these three or I will be on duty at all times, leading a team to protect you that will rarely be less than twenty strong. Please let us know thirty minutes in advance of your plans to leave the house, so we can get a police escort."

"Someone must consider us a high risk," Jack said.

"I have not been told anything except to apply this level of protection," the agent said evenly. If he knew more, he was not telling.

"Does my father have this much in the way of his going out for a drink?" Kris asked, eyes narrowing.

"No, ma'am," Agent Foile said evenly.

"Hmm," was all Jack had to add to Kris's thoughts.

"We must talk about this later, Agent Foile," Kris said, and turned to the five women arrayed up the stairs. "And you are?"

"We will provide twenty-four hours a day, seven days a week, care for your infant," the matronly woman answered.

"What weapons are you qualified with, and when did you last shoot?" Kris snapped.

"Weapons? Shoot?" the older woman said. If possible, the placid faces on her and her subordinates might have shown a hint of surprise.

"Who hired you?" Kris asked, trying not to sound snappish.

"Your mother, although I think there was another, older woman involved in vetting us," the spokeswoman said.

"Not an old, ramrod-straight military-type guy?"

"No, Your Highness. Although the older woman did have that kind of clipped way of speaking."

"It comes from cohabitating with Grampa Trouble," Kris allowed. "Okay, you are not weapons-qualified. We'll have to see about changing that. Do you have a bag packed so you can run for the beanstalk if I suddenly decide to take off for space?"

Now the women's faces did drop. "Ah, er, ah, we weren't told we would have to leave Wardhaven City," the older woman answered. "And I, for one, have no desire to touch a gun, much less shoot one." Two of the other women nodded agreement. The other two exchanged looks that seemed to say "I told you so," but they didn't join in the others' open refusal.

"Once again, my mother has done for me what I did not want or need. The three of you are dismissed. I will arrange for you to get two weeks' severance pay. Special Agent Foile, please see that full background checks are made on the other two. There is a pistol range in the basement. General, detail two Marines to begin their introduction to weapons. By the way, ladies, if you have friends who are qualified as nannies and sharpshooters, or willing to learn, you may invite them to come in for an interview tomorrow."

"Yes, Your Highness," the two said with a bit of a curtsy.

"Come with me," said a new voice.

Kris turned to find a young woman in Navy blues with the single stripe of an ensign on her sleeves and a gold aiguillette of staff on her right shoulder. "And you are?" Kris asked.

"I am Ensign Megan Longknife, your *aide-de-camp*, secretary, and general dog robber, Your Highness. I qualified with several weapons at OCS last month, but you'll likely want me to get better. Now, I'll see that these three woman are properly taken care of and their access to the grounds revoked. May I borrow one of your Marines, General, to escort them to the front gate?"

"Certainly. Carry on," Jack said, and she turned smartly to follow her orders.

"Just a moment, Ensign Longknife." The young woman turned back to Kris. "I've never met you."

"No, ma'am. I'm from Santa Maria. The Alnaba side of the family."

"Ray's daughter?"

"Is my grandmother," Meg supplied.

Kris nodded. "Okay, carry on, and we'll talk later. Nelly, help her with the paperwork."

"I think I already am, Kris."

That brought a frown to Kris's face, but the young ensign had returned to her assignment, herding the three unqualified nannies from the foyer.

Kris turned back to Special Agent Foile. "I assume your people are up to date on their weapons qualifications?"

"Yes, ma'am," he said.

The young woman with him, who looked like she was about to split a gut, burst out, "They even had us qualifying with machine pistols and long rifles. We knew something was up, but to be working with you wow."

"You will have to excuse Leslie," Foile said. "I think she was a founding member of your fan club."

"And we've been going crazy since you disappeared," Leslie said, jumping in.

Kris tried to keep from smiling at the young woman's enthusiasm. "I'm afraid you will get little news from me," she said.

"Oh, it doesn't matter. One of us had a cousin on the *Wasp*. I think she got him drunk last night 'cause there was all sorts of stuff on the net this morning. Did you actually blow away seven more of those monster ships?"

Jack raised both eyebrows Kris rolled her eyes, hoping whoever had told the tale hadn't made it sound easy.

"On second thought, I may have to find time for some interviews," Kris admitted.

"We'll see that you get a better hearing than last time," Leslie assured Kris.

"I wouldn't be too hard to improve on that one," Jack muttered under his breath.

Before anyone could answer that thought, the doorbell chimed.

A Marine moved quickly to check on the new arrival, then braced as he called "Atten'hut," and opened the door wide.

5

"As you were," General Trouble said before the civilians could even figure out what was expected of them. He then added, "Relax," when the Marines failed to take a breath.

His wife and Kris's mother followed him into the foyer.

"Oh, how's my little grandbaby?" Mother cooed, and headed for said child and proceeded to extract her from Kris's arms without so much as a "may I?"

Before Kris could cloud over, Gramma Trouble slipped between them. With a silent "I'll take care of this," she edged Mother and Ruthie away.

"Where are the rest of the women I hired?" Mother asked, taking in the two on the stairwell.

"They weren't weapons-qualified," Kris said.

"Why would that matter?" Mother asked, befuddled.

"Let's take Ruthie upstairs and introduce her to her nursery," Gramma Trouble suggested, and placed an arm on Brenda that urged her toward the stairs.

"Come along, Kris," Brenda said, not looking away from the child in her arms. "You'll want to see all the changes we made in the nursery. It's very modern. The latest safety equipment. You can monitor Ruthie's temperature, heart, and breathing from anywhere in the house, and the floors are rubber. She'll never hurt that cute bottom of hers."

"Kris'll come along later," Trouble said, determining Kris's future.

"I will?" Kris said, temper starting to burn.

"We need to talk about your mission."

"Oh," Kris said, and allowed herself to be edged toward the library.

"Who do we need to include?" Jack asked.

"I was thinking just you two," Grampa Trouble said, looking very much the general.

Jack shook his head. "Special Agent Foile needs to know what's going on."

"You may well be right," Trouble said, and turned to the four agents. "Foile, it's good to see you again."

"Will you be talking this time?" had a sparkle around the senior agent's eyes.

"Will you be trying to arrest Kris and Jack this time?" Trouble answered back.

The agent chuckled. "Not very likely."

"Then yes, I will be talking. Come along and hear the worst."

"Mahomet, check this rock pile's security network. Leslie and Rick, familiarize yourself with the house. Are there any secret passageways, Your Highness?"

"None that I ever discovered. Or my boyfriends, either."

"Have our teams look for them anyway," Taylor said, then followed them into the library and locked the door behind them.

Grampa Trouble led the long walk past book-lined walls and more bookshelves to the fireplace and the two couches beside it. Kris and Jack sat on one. Trouble and Agent Foile faced them across a low table that would provide them with a network screen if they needed one.

"So, what brings you to our humble abode," Jack said, "and why is our security detail larger than the prime minister's?"

"Probably because you're more involved with the Peterwalds than Billy is or ever would want to be," Trouble said.

"Knocked that one out of the ballpark," Kris said, and made to watch as if a high fly ball sailed over the fireplace.

"Mind you, we don't expect there to be any problems here, but once you leave United Society space, it's anybody's guess."

"That's why I wanted two battle squadrons at least, maybe three. You think sixteen would be enough to defeat any Peterwald battle line?" Kris asked Jack.

"Don't ask me, hon. I've been as out of pocket the last two years as you've been."

"Nelly, have you got an update on the Peterwald Order of Battle? No, Trouble, sir, shouldn't I be asking you?"

"Your guess is as good as mine. Crossie lost several of his best agents in the Empire when they shot all the State Security types."

"Heavens, some of their intelligence people were on the take of our intelligence people?" Kris said, shocked, just shocked. "I think I've got the vapors."

"If Kris will stop being such a drama queen," Nelly said, "I can give you a report." Nelly, Kris's computer, upgraded many times since she was given to her when she first started school, was worth a major chunk of one of her battlecruisers. Since her latest upgrade, Nelly had developed a tendency to argue with Kris and crack bad jokes.

"Go ahead, Nelly," Kris said.

"I've accessed the Wardhaven network, including all data authorized to flag officers, and I've correlated it to my satisfaction. Greenfeld has been falling farther and farther behind in technology as she tears herself apart. We have no reports of any battleships with lasers larger than 18-inch. They are still building ships out of traditional metal, no Smart Metal. I would expect that eight battlecruisers would be sufficient to win a battle with either Vicky's or the Empress's fleet. Still, it would be better to send sixteen so we could overawe them and not have to fight."

Trouble raised an eyebrow as Nelly appended her recommendation to the end of her factual assessment.

"Nelly is quite good," Kris allowed.

"I'm magnificent. The Magnificent Nelly," Nelly crowed.

"Just ask her yourself," Kris grumped.

"Ask anyone who's alive because they had me to help them," Nelly sniffed.

"Down, girls," Jack said.

General Trouble swallowed a grin and went on, "That is pretty much what we assumed would be the threat you face. I've been trying to persuade everyone that you deserve two full squadrons, but it's not easy to free up that many ships."

"Can I ask why?" Jack asked cautiously.

"First, let me be clear, no one has spotted any evidence of the alien raiders, either in human space or around the Iteeche Empire. Whoever was nibbling around the edges of Iteeche territory has not shown up for a while. Believe you me, the Iteeche have built a whopping lot of frigates and searched all around themselves. I kind of like your idea of calling them battlecruisers now that they're sporting 22-inch lasers. Oh, and the Iteeche have given us some ideas that our scientists think can be stretched to 24- or even 26-inch, or focused even tighter into an 18-incher with double the range or quadruple the power."

"And Greenfeld is just sitting all this out?" Kris said.

"While they tear each other apart and squabble over the rubble," Trouble added.

"I thought Vicky was smarter than that," Kris said. "Kind of dumb, and soulless as a tree stump, but smarter."

"It appears that she is. She sent over a certain intelligence asset who brought us up to date on what was going on. He also asked for some spidersilk underarmor for Vicky and her team. Her stepmother has been trying to kill Vicky. Really trying to kill her, like trying three or four times a day while she was still in the Palace."

"Good God," Kris muttered, "that beats my worst day."

"By a lot," Jack said.

"So she had to rebel just to keep her head on her shoulders," Kris concluded.

"Something like that," Trouble said. "That and the mess her stepmother and family are making of the entire Empire as they tear it down and steal anything of value from the wreckage. A lot of people are at risk of starving to death. Your Vicky saved at least two worlds, maybe more, from the brink of cannibalism."

"She's not *my* Vicky," Kris pointed out.

"Well, if I'd spent as much time as you have with her, and she was doing as good as Vicky has been doing in a bad situation, I'd want to claim a bit of the credit."

"Really?"

"Wait until you get there, then make your own assessment," Grampa Trouble said.

"I will. By the way, you do know that while I'm pretty good at blowing things up, I don't have much experience getting people to play nice in the sandbox. As in never."

"Really," Grampa Trouble said, eyes wide in shock; then he chuckled, probably at the face Kris gave him. "We kind of know that, so we've been looking for folks who might help you figure a way out of this for everyone."

"Who?" Jack asked.

"Well, we've tapped the chief mediator of the Wardhaven Office of Mediation. He's had a lot of experience getting unions and managers to not kill each other."

"Maybe he could help us," Kris allowed.

"We've also got the senior arbitrator of the Bureau of Arbitration. They try to help business find a middle ground when contracts between corporations don't appear to be as clear as they all thought they were. It's an alternative to spending the next hundred years in court."

"Is he any good?" Jack asked.

"I personally brought him in to help your grandfather Al resolve the problem with Mitsubishi on the new Smart Metal. If he hadn't gotten those two hardheaded types to settle things, you'd still be waiting for your first frigate. We also found out about some new idea Earth came up with to slow and redistribute laser light so you avoid burn-through. I put him and a team from Nuu Enterprises on the next liner to Earth, and he just got back from there with a contract and specs."

"Ah, Grampa, we reverse-engineered that crystal stuff out on Alwa Station. This latest *Wasp* we rode in on has it. You might want to drop by and look at what we did to make the stuff from Earth better."

"Better, huh?"

"Yep. We lost a couple of Earth ships the first time they got shot at, but we figured out why and improved the crystal armor that we grew for our new construction and backfit to our old ships."

"I take it that you really took the idea that you needed to create an industrial base force seriously."

"In spades," Kris said. "It's amazing how wanting to stay alive will motivate people."

"I've found it works that way," Trouble agreed.

"So, that's two. Any more help?" Jack asked.

"Wardhaven's Family Courts has a judge that does wonderful things for the children of families who are splitting the sheets. She has a real sense for what makes people tick."

"Does Vicky's stepmother tick?" Kris asked.

"Like a time bomb," Trouble said.

"Then I definitely want two squadrons of battlecruisers with a company of Marines on each one of them," Kris said with finality.

Grampa Trouble took a deep breath and let it out in a long sigh. "That's why they sent me here."

"To give them to me?" Kris said, not knowing what he was getting at but not liking it at all.

"No, I have to give you the bad news that you can't have but one squadron."

"I always thought Ray was becoming a bit of a coward now that he had that crown," Kris said.

"You might be right," Trouble said, unusually diplomatic. "However, I got the job of telling you, it's just eight ships."

"Why?" Kris said. "I'm getting really tired of doing things Grampa Ray's way."

Instead of answering her question, Trouble turned to Special Agent Foile. "You have signed the Secrets Act?"

"Yes, sir."

"What you're about to hear is covered under the Secrets Act, most especially a secret from Prime Minister Longknife."

Foile's eyebrows rose slowly until they might have disappeared into his hair if he still had any. "The more I deal with your family, Your Highness, the less I want to," he said.

"A smart man," Kris said. "I had to go all the way across the galaxy to get them out of my hair . . . and then they called me back for this. Okay, you do agree not to tell my dad about what Trouble's about to let us in on."

"What passes here, stays here," the agent said.

"Good, good. Kris, we don't have enough ships," Trouble said.

"But you're building them at a mad pace," Nelly said. "I

reviewed the media reports, and they have a frigate commissioning close to every other day somewhere in the Union. Am I missing something?"

"Yes, unfortunately," Trouble said. "The policy for their deployment."

The old general eyed Kris. "You really put the fear of God, or at least those crazy alien raiders, in people. Sending back that raving maniac was brilliant."

"Thank you very much," Kris said with a grin and a bit of a bow.

"But now, everybody and their cat and dog wants ships protecting their planet. With the Smart Metal frigate-size ships becoming major man-o'-wars, they can afford much cheaper ships and smaller, cheaper crews. More bang for their bucks. You know that place you got exiled to?"

"Madigan's Rainbow," Kris provided.

"Yep. They ordered four squadrons for planetary defense."

"How are the locals taking to hairy deck apes on their shore leave?" Kris asked.

"Not well, but they're holding on to the ships with a death grip. Practically everyone is. Someone stumbled on the old doctrine of a Fleet in Being, and they are using it to keep their little fleet right where their paranoia wants it."

"I foresee problems," Kris said, ticking several off in her head, "including fewer ships for Alwa Station, but how does this keep me from borrowing sixteen for a while?"

"Remember how your banged-up *Wasp* took out that alien scout cruiser in an Iteeche system where you refueled before straggling back to human space," Trouble said. "We need lookouts in our nearby systems to spot scout ships."

Kris shook her head. "Yes, active patrolling is critical. But on Alwa Station, we picketed a lot of the jumps to give us plenty of warning."

Trouble nodded. "We've got more jump buoys out, covering a whole lot of systems. The Iteeche are doing the same, but some of those jumps are way out there. It takes forever for any word to get back to us."

"We had the same problem," Kris agreed. "I started sending out patrols to pop their scouts before they could report back."

"That is exactly what I and half the folks in uniform on the general staff want to do."

"It's one thing to want to do it," Jack said. "It's quite another thing to have the assets to do it."

"Right," Trouble said, and let out a long sigh that was more of a growl.

"You want to fill me in on how bad things are here?" Kris asked.

"They could be worse. I wish they were better," her great-grandfather said. "For most planets, immediate planetary defense is priority one. There is no priority two. For those willing to look beyond defending their own little corner of the universe, Alwa is priority two. You have to admit, a lot of them have made contributions."

"I most definitely admit it, and I am most definitely grateful for their gifts toward Alwa's defense. If you give me a soapbox, I'll declaim and boviate on my and their gratitude until the cows come home," Kris said. "Now, what's priority three?"

"Few planets, in their present state of affairs, get past two. 'We've got a squadron fighting at Alwa.' 'We're still growing our defenses.' 'A frigate may be cheap, but you're still asking for tax money to build and maintain it.'"

"Okay, but what is priority three?" Kris repeated.

"Patrolling. Taking a look at our outer perimeter. Maybe doing a long cruise well outside our part of space to see if anything is roving around there. That first ship you blew away, the family ship that was mining that moon or asteroid. You remember it?"

"I still have nightmares about the frozen faces of those little kids when I'm not having nightmares about the huge base ships I've blown away or the horror they'd raise if they got into Alwa orbit," Kris admitted.

I have a lot of nightmares.

"So, are there any mining claims being worked anywhere close to us? Those sort of things?" Jack asked.

"How many ships have you got on patrol duty?" Kris added.

"Not nearly enough," Grampa Trouble admitted. "Savannah contributed a squadron They'll do anything for Ray, but not twice. Here and there, we get one or two ships from this or that planet. But from Wardhaven and Pitts Hope, not so much as a longboat. 'We've made those beam ships and flying factories. What more could you want?'"

"You need to make more beam ships," Kris said, "and better ones. The three you sent got hammered pretty bad in our last fight. The next ones really need to be warships first and mad science projects second."

"I had a suspicion you might say that," Trouble said with a chuckle. "We wanted them Tuesday, not great, and you were doing good to get them by Tuesday."

"Oh, we're grateful," Kris was quick to put in, "but the next batch needs to be better. Maybe we can survive until Friday for them."

Trouble chuckled at that. "You can look into that when you get back. You really demanding a desk job?"

"I am," Kris shot right back. "I've had enough of Ray's running me around by this gold ring in my nose. I've got a ring on my finger, thank you very much, and I'm ready to move on to something more domestic. Okay?"

"It's fine by me," Trouble said, holding up both hands in quick surrender.

"So how do I survive this next suicide mission and make it to pleasant domesticity?"

Trouble sighed. "We can give you eight ships. They're commissioning as we speak."

"Well, hold up their commissioning and get them crystal clad."

"I'll see what I can do, but Al's got his contract and wants several pounds of flesh to make a contract change."

"I'll see if Ruthie can't persuade him with her toothless smile."

"Good luck at that," Trouble said. "About Marines, we're running short. Your dad is building up an Army here on Wardhaven. Among other things, they're manning lasers that someone thinks can shoot things out of orbit that are busy lazing them from up there. I kind of doubt that's a good use of manpower, but local politicians want to show their voters they're doing something they can see. Anyhoo, it's eating into our Marine recruitment."

"You might want to have Marines on your ships," Jack said. Trouble raised an eyebrow. ' The last couple of fights they were sending small suicide boats and even lone troopers at us. We used Marines to shoot down those small targets. If they actually managed to board us . . ? Well, you get my meaning."

"Damn," Trouble muttered. "You folks come back safe. I really want you going over our defense effort from top to bottom."

"I always do my best to stay not dead," Kris said.

"Well, I think I've done about all the upsetting you that I can do today," Trouble said, "and vice versa. I'll be seeing you, likely tomorrow."

Kris nodded but stayed seated as Trouble left. When Special Agent Foile made to stand, she guided him back to his seat with her eyes. He sat.

"Well," Kris said, leaning back in her chair and taking a deep breath as the door closed behind her grampa. Refreshed, she turned to Agent Foile. "Does this tell you more of what you need to do your job?"

"It tells me why I've got the biggest detail on this planet."

"You up to the job?" Jack asked.

"If we are not, I'll see that my detail is expanded until we are."

"Very good. Oh, we may be going out soon," Kris said.

"May I ask where?"

"Jack's folks deserve some time with their latest grandchild," Kris said.

6

An hour later, with both Jack and Kris changed into civvies, their car came to a stop before a small white house on a minor side street. Kris had skipped the armored limo or SUV for this trip; Jack said his family's neighborhood was quiet. The sudden appearance of a lot of police would only make the neighbors talk.

Harvey, a wonderfully familiar face and Kris's chauffeur since forever, selected the green sedan. "It's well armored but doesn't make a big show of it," he told Special Agent Foile. Harvey and Foile were in the front seat, with Agent Debot squeezed in between them.

Mahomet had showed up with a black box that looked amazingly like the one Chief Beni, both the elder one and his lost son, had used to protect Kris from so much mischief.

Kris and Jack shared the backseat with a happily gurgling Ruthie. Kris's child was likely the best-protected kid who ever rode in a car. The Alwa expedition was not prepared for children. Nelly had used Smart Metal™ to make a high-gee station for Ruthie for the fast trip back from Alwa. When they arrived here, Nelly had modified the high-gee station into a car seat for the little one.

Jack took in his parents' house with a happy sigh. Kris

studied it carefully. It was just a year or two past needing a new coat of paint. The porch had a swing fit for two as well as two rocking chairs. It looked like a lot of the houses she'd driven by in the neighborhood.

So this is where Jack grew up. I hope this helps me understand him better.

The curtains were pulled back a bit. Someone was taking their own measure of who this visitor might be. What they saw was just the green sedan. The police SUVs were parked at each corner of the street, distant but ready.

Special Agent Foile got out first, eyeing the street cautiously. He seemed content with what he saw and tapped the roof of the car. Only then did Jack get out and make his own security assessment. When he was happy, and Mahomet was out doing his own check, Kris was motioned to unstrap Ruthie, sling her diaper bag over her shoulder, and see how much trouble it would be to get one small baby out of a car.

It was not easy, but Kris, who'd managed a lot bigger things, succeeded in getting her infant child extracted and wrapped in a clean blanket.

Whoever was in the house must have liked what they saw because a high-school-size girl, a woman who must have been her mother, and a man, hobbling on a cane, came out of the house just as fast as their legs could carry them.

"Jacky," "Juan," and "My boy," told Kris that she'd come to the right place.

The charge came to a dead halt as they took in Kris and the bundle she carried in both arms.

"Juan?" the matron of the trio questioned cautiously.

"*Mia madre*, I would like you to meet your daughter-in-law, my wife, Kris Longknife, and our little one, Ruth Maria."

"You got married and didn't tell us!" his mother shouted but was moving forward again as fast as her short legs would allow.

"I was all the way on the other side of the galaxy, Mom. I asked her to marry me, and it seemed like a long time to wait until we got home again."

"Well, show me *la niña*," she said, swatting her son with the apron she wore.

The girl was standing back a bit. "Jacky, is that who I think that is?" she said, taking in the agents and the chauffeur.

"Most likely, but hold your tongue a bit until I can do the honors properly."

"Oh. My. God," Jack's sister whispered.

His dad had just joined the foursome when Kris managed to pull the blanket aside and let Ruthie Maria have a good look her father's side of the family. She smiled happily and managed some sound that Kris assumed was "Hi," in infant speak, which Nelly had tried but failed to translate.

"Won't you come in," Jack's father said. With his family leading the way, and Jack beside Kris with a loving hand pleasantly in the small of her back, she found herself ushered into their living room. The couch had a throw over it with a picture of Our Lady of Guadeloupe. A table had a picture of Christ with a crucifix hanging above it. Kris had been in such homes while campaigning for Father. She clicked on her "Campaign Acceptance Mode," and took the seat she was offered on the couch.

Juan, Jack's dad, settled into his own recliner and raised the leg support. Maria took her place on the couch, where she easily managed to switch Ruthie from Kris's arms to her own. Estella looked ready to have a fit, but she settled onto the arm of the overstuffed chair that Jack took.

"So, who is your wife?" Juan asked before Estella busted a gut.

"You remember that I had been protecting Kris Longknife," Jack said, and they nodded. "Well, she fell in love with me, and me with her, and when we had a very brief chance to marry all the way on the other side of the galaxy, we took it."

"All right!" sister squeed.

The parents looked poleaxed. "Kris Longknife," they both muttered.

The room fell into deep silence. Even sister found herself taken by it.

The quiet was finally broken by a whispered question from Maria. "So, tell me about your wedding."

Kris did, and the talk went from there to other things. Estella had heard about the alien raiders and wanted to know what Jack and his new wife had done. Jack tried to make as little of his job as he could, and Kris followed suit until Estella did a quick net search, read the results then eyed Kris. "You were the commander of *everything* we sent to that other place."

"Yes," Kris admitted, "I was. Your Jack commanded all the ground forces, and I did the same for the fleet."

Again, the parents looked speechless.

When the conversation finally began again, it was strained. Ruthie took that moment to get fussy, and Maria returned her to Kris's arms. Together, they checked the diaper and found it dry and clean. "She must be hungry. Do you have some formula?" Maria asked.

"We weren't prepared for children on Alwa Station, so we've kind of had to do things the old-fashioned way. I'm nursing Ruth Maria."

"Oh," was all Maria said. "I wouldn't think that a woman like you would know how to—"

"I had to learn fast," Kris admitted, "and Ruth Maria helped."

"Well, you will come again, won't you?" she said, and Kris found herself following the mother's lead as she rose to her feet and was ushered out the door.

Jack followed with the diaper bag, still talking to his father. Estella seemed delighted to stay as close to Ruthie as she could. At least one of them had a fan in Jack's family.

They were bundled up and driving away. Kris had taken advantage of the privacy the backseat afforded and was nursing Ruthie before she got a word out.

"What happened back there?"

"You may have noticed that my mom sticks with the old ways." Jack said.

"You could hardly miss it," Kris said, bouncing Ruthie just a bit. She was eagerly nursing but still seemed a bit fussy. Maybe Kris wasn't the only one upset by their reception.

"Mother had expectations that I'd marry a good Catholic girl. Then there was the wedding."

"What about the wedding?"

"Nothing, it was a wonderful wedding, and you told it beautifully."

"But?"

"Your Granny Ruth officiated."

"And?"

"Mother doesn't consider a marriage valid unless there's a priest involved."

"Oh," Kris said. And let her logical mind try to follow all the threads she'd just been handed.

"Would she like to have us married again before a priest?" she finally said.

"Would you mind?"

"I'd do anything to make you happy, honey, but you must know that if your mother wants a wedding, my mother will go crazy over it."

"The thought did cross my mind as I listened to Mom put in her two bits."

"And here I'd hoped to dodge the zoo my mom would make of my wedding."

"Face an alien base ship out for blood, no problem. Face your mother in full wedding mode, run for the hills."

"Hills, hell, I ran for the other side of the galaxy."

They shared a laugh at that.

"Well, look at the bright side," Kris finally said. "If Vicky and the rest of the Peterwalds get us killed, at least we won't have to keep our families happy anymore."

"You always are the optimist."

"Get us off this street and out of here!" yelled Agent Debot. "A bomb just went active ahead of us."

7

Kris knew that Harvey was an old war vet. She'd just never seen him in war mode. He hit the brakes. Jack popped his seat belt and rolled over, putting himself between the front seat and a nursing Ruthie. Kris held on tight and leaned back to give Ruthie as much space to slow in as Jack waiting at the seat ahead.

Harvey turned the hard brake into a "J" turn and had them headed back the way they came. The trailing SUV managed to follow them through these hard maneuvers.

The lead one wasn't so lucky.

Its driver got the word late. He was in the middle of the hard brake when the road beside him came at him as if shot out of a cannon. Out of the corner of her eye, Kris saw the big black rig flip over on its side, but the armored box held. One of the doors had been raised, and men with automatic rifles were searching for targets even as Kris and her family went the other way.

If this neighborhood was normally a quiet place, it wasn't now. Sirens started shrieking from all directions as they closed on either the bomb site or Kris's sedan. Fortunately, the motorcycle cops had been told to wait well back. They were the first to join Kris's reorganizing cavalcade. The trailing

SUV pulled ahead of Harvey just as Mahomet shouted, "I think there's another bomb ahead of us."

"We're hooking a left," Foile said, to both Harvey and the rig ahead of them.

Only Harvey was able to make the turn, but this time the warning got out quickly enough. There was no boom as the cycle cops and the SUV did hard "U" turns, then followed after Kris and family.

"Turn left at the next block," Foile ordered.

"Right next chance you get.

"Left again.

"Right."

And with more lefts and rights, they made their way out of the neighborhood. Only when they were back on the express-way with police cars six deep before and after them did Kris breathe a sigh of relief.

"What was that all about?" Jack demanded of no one.

"I think," Kris said, "that Vicky's stepmommy wants us to know we are not welcome to stick our noses into her affairs."

"You think so?" Jack said.

"Honey, I know so."

8

Later that afternoon, Special Agent Foile had senior representatives from half a dozen police and security agencies in the library and, as it were, on the carpet.

Kris settled herself in the back of the library well away from the blowtorch Agent Foile was wielding up front. She sorely missed Penny, who had chosen to stay on the other side of the galaxy. Coming from a police family, Penny had always been Kris's liaison with local police. She was also great at translating Cop Speak.

Just now, Kris was listening to a lot of Cop Speak.

Leslie Chu settled into the chair next to Kris and began doing a very fine job as translator.

"My boss is asking all those big boss men how it happened that their agencies didn't even have a hint of that bomb. No chatter. No nothing."

"Do they have any answer?"

"Nope. *Nada.*"

"I guess I've been gone so long, even Wardhaven has forgotten what it takes to keep this damn Longknife safe."

"It kind of looks that way."

"Oh, did your boss give you the picture he asked me for?"

"Oh, yes," Leslie squeed softly, if that word even applied at that volume. "Ah, now my boss is telling them they've got to get their, ah, act together and keep it together until you leave for Greenfeld. He's not telling them when that will be."

"Smart man since I have no idea, either."

"Anyway, he's read them the riot act and told them all to straighten up and fly right. Ah, do you think you might have someplace on your staff you could assign us for a bit? My boss is burning bridges. What he said to the head of the Bureau is not going to be forgotten soon."

"I think I have some vacancies. You do know we're heading closer to the Empress. It can only get worse."

"Yeah"—Leslie shrugged—"but it won't be boring."

"Life around me is many things, but never that."

The agency heads left, softly talking among themselves. Hopefully, they were already planning ways to keep Kris safe and not the manner and fashion of their hanging Special Agent Foile up by his fundamentals.

"Well, that went amazingly well," Foile said as he joined Kris and his junior agent.

"Kris said she may have room for us on her staff," Leslie said.

"Oh." From the senior agent, that carried heavy freight.

"From the looks of things, you might need a job," Kris said.

"Oh, I should think not," he said, eyeing the departing agency chiefs. "Hmm, well, maybe."

"We'll see how things are when I've got a squadron ready to sail and a whole lot of passengers for them."

"We can think about that later," he said.

Kris and Jack enjoyed a quiet evening at Nuu House. No one attempted to kill them right up to bedtime. Or if they did, they didn't get past the electronics, Marines, and other guards.

Nelly turned Ruthie's car seat into a nice bassinet. Surprisingly, she let Kris sleep through half the night.

The nanny taking the night watch was there the first time Ruthie stirred. She changed her diaper as Kris was slowly rising to wakefulness. "I gave her some pabulum before we put her down. You nurse her, and I'll see if she'll take more solid food and let you sleep through the rest of the night."

Kris seriously wondered if the afternoon bomb attack had

been successful. She certainly felt like she'd died and gone to heaven.

Over breakfast the next morning, Kris and Jack examined what they should do with their day.

"If we're only going to get eight ships, I want them all with crystal armor," Kris said.

Jack agreed. "What ships will we get?" he asked.

"Your guess is as good as mine," Kris said. "Nelly, anything?"

"The *Wasp* has been taken into the yard for maintenance," the computer said. "Two squadrons from New Canaan and Tangaroa will be coming through here in two weeks, and Commander Pett wants to join up with them for the trip back."

"Trip back?" Kris yelped.

"All but three of the *Wasp*'s crew voted to go back. She will be taking on a couple of hundred volunteers for either the Navy or industry. It sounds like New Canaan and Tangaroa will also be traveling heavy."

"People *want* to go to Alwa?" Now it was Jack's turn to yelp.

Ruthie decided to join in, but her yelp was cuter than Jack's.

"It seems so," Nelly answered them both.

"Any chance we could shanghai the two squadrons of transients to add to our Wardhaven squadron?" Jack asked.

Kris considered that for a long moment, then shook her head. "Do you really want to be responsible for Sandy not having the ships she needs? Can you think of any reinforcements we got that we didn't need immediately if not sooner?"

Jack shrugged. "I guess not, but I had to try. I was kind of hoping that since you trimmed them back so far, Admiral Santiago would have a while before the aliens got rambunctious again."

"I thank you for trying, my ever-vigilant security chief, husband, and daddy," Kris said, and leaned over to give him the kiss he deserved. "I'd like to think Sandy will have an easy time of it, too, but . . ."

"I wonder how it's going for her," Jack said, then did a hard right turn. "So we settle for eight battlecruisers?"

"I didn't say that. I just said we don't steal anything from Alwa. Everything else in human space is up for grabs."

"And you Longknifes are so grabby."

Kris made a grab for something else, and Jack moved to block her, but not too much. Unfortunately, the nanny with the morning shift entered to remove Ruthie.

"Don't let me interfere with anything. We always say, the more kids the merrier, and the more jobs for us," she said with a cheerful smile that was aimed at Kris and not at all flirty toward Jack.

She better not be.

But the mood was broken, so they retired to dress in full admiral's and general's regalia and prepared to face the morning. "Upgrading the armor on the battlecruisers will take the longest," Kris said, "so I guess we go see if Grampa Al will let us talk to him."

Special Agent in Charge Foile seemed to find his morning assignment much to his liking, as did Agent Rick Sanchez. "Will it be any easier to walk in this time than last?" the younger agent asked through a broad grin.

"We shall see what we shall see," Foile answered vaguely but with a sparkle in his eyes.

Kris made sure Ruthie was all decked out in maximum cuteness, and, with her babbling happily, they departed in a well-armed and armored convoy for Nuu Towers.

Kris did try to phone ahead. She got nowhere, so she made a quick call to Grampa Trouble, and, amazing as it might appear, the gates opened wide for her . . . and the doors as well.

"Trouble has an in with Al?" Jack asked in surprise.

"Trouble has ins everywhere. He knows where all the bodies are buried," Kris said. Still, she noticed the ever-so-slight smile on Special Agent Foile's lips and found herself wondering who had an in with whom.

This time, they were ushered through the huge foyer of the building with its black marble and directly into an elevator. Kris smiled; it only went up fifty floors. There they transferred to another bank of elevators for the next fifty before transferring to a third elevator bank for the ride to the 150th floor.

"Amazingly faster than the last time, I expect," Foile said to Kris.

"Are you packing spare gas masks?" she asked.

"Sarin will get you through the skin," the agent pointed out.

Kris shivered. "Did he really have Sarin gas?"

"I do not know," Foile said. "I left too soon to see how they cleaned up the top three floors, and you kept me very busy for the next couple of weeks."

"Again, may I say, thank you for the warning."

"You're very welcome," the agent said.

They reached the topmost floor; the elevator opened on a wide field of lush red carpet. There were only three people in evidence; they sat behind well-spaced desks and were doing their best to appear most busy. The executive offices were thirty or forty meters away, likely all with astounding views, but they were hidden for the moment behind rich mosaics of wood that provided their own view of stylized office parks and fabrication facilities.

One even showed High Wardhaven Station with the Nuu space docks prominent.

Given no hint of where to go, Kris headed for the largest desk, the one in the middle.

"We are expected," she said.

"Are you now?" said the man, crewcutted and maybe with an automatic bulging the left shoulder of a suit that likely cost more than Jack's folk's home. "And your name?"

Kris played the one card she had. Well, second card. Her other one involved accepting that perpetual job offer and coming to work for Grampa Al in his Tower of Insecurity. "Ruthie Anne is here to see her great-grandfather."

That brought a raised eyebrow from the even-more-neutral face of the secretary.

The man began to speak into the desk's commlink. Some new technology blanked out his words even though Kris was less than two meters away. Kris was no expert at lip-reading, but even she spotted the sequence "uniform of a four-star admiral," followed later by, "Yes, the baby is cute."

After a few more exchanges, the secretary leaned back, and said, "You and the baby may enter."

"My security agents will check out the room, and my husband will accompany me," Kris countered.

The secretary took a melodramatic moment before nodding.

9

Kris stood, gently bouncing Ruthie on her left hip, while Senior Special Agent in Charge Foile and his sidekick, black box in hand, entered the door identified by the secretary's slight incline of the head.

The door closed behind them, leaving Kris to wonder if they would ever emerge, but they did. With a curt nod to Jack, Foile identified the room as satisfactorily secure.

Jack led Kris to the door that Sanchez now held open for them.

To say that Grandfather Alexander Longknife's office was way past palatial was still an understatement. The Forward Lounge on the *Wasp* was rarely expanded to this extent. The wet bar to Kris's right did fall short of the Lounge's bar, but not by much.

In a corner to her left, a waterfall descended in gentle ripples to a pond big enough to have a bridge across it in the Chinese tradition.

Were there real *koi in that pond?*

Apparently, yes, because one broke the surface for a moment. No holograms here. This was the real thing.

Grampa Al himself sat behind a white alabaster table. No desk for him. There was also no conference table although two doors led right and left from his office. No doubt, one led to a bathroom, the other to a conference room likely the equal of this room.

The man of business rose motioning them toward a group of chairs not far from the bar. There were only three large, overstuffed armchairs. Beside one, a bassinet stood.

Kris aimed herself for that one as Jack took the one between her and Grampa Al. He, however, headed for the bar. "What will you have this morning?"

"I'll have what you have, sir," Jack said diplomatically.

"A glass of soda water with a twist of lime," Kris said.

"You still not drinking?" Al asked.

"I'm nursing," Kris said. 'I don't want Ruthie to get drunk on her momma's milk."

"A good excuse. Better than your usual one. General, I'm drinking chamomile tea; is that good enough for you?"

"Yes, sir," Jack said.

"Me, too," Kris said.

"So we are all seeking calm for this little *tête-à-tête*."

"We needed full MOPP gear for the last visit," Kris put in.

"Yes. You gave me quite the fright. Then an even worse fright when I discovered it was you. You finished by making a mess of the south side of this building."

"I regretted that, but your space shuttle was the only escape option I could figure out at the moment."

"Escape to a Musashi axe?" Al pointed out.

"I was not found guilty," Kris pointed right back.

"Yes. You do seem to have all the luck of your generation," he said, handing a cup and saucer of tea to Kris.

"I seem to need most of it," Kris said.

"That I would not dispute," he said, giving Jack his tea. "Do you, as husband and father, like your wife's seeking out every available lion's mouth to stick her head in?"

Jack did not shoot back an answer but instead took a slow sip of tea as Al settled into his chair. Only then did he say, "That is the woman I married. Should I marry an eagle, then shackle her to a stove?"

"I foresee much sorrow in your life," the older man said. For someone of nearly a hundred years, he looked well preserved, hardly much older than Honovi, Kris's older brother.

Hopefully, Al was being careful with his rejuvenation treat-
ments. Some had paid a high price for using them as a fountain
of youth.

"As you likely know, I have been asked to serve as mediator between the Grand Duchess, Vicky Peterwald, and her
father, the Emperor."

"More likely between her and that vicious stepmother of
hers, the Empress," Al cut in.

"I was about to add that when you took the words out of my
mouth."

"Yes, how unsanitary of me," Al said dryly, sipping slowly.

"I have been offered eight battlecruisers as an escort."

"Only eight. Anyone who takes that mission is either dumb,
or bold out of their mind. Which are you, young admiral?"

Kris shrugged. "I'm the one asked for by two sides, Vicky
and her father, and ordered by another, your father, Ray."

"Ever the bold one he is . . . when it is someone else's blood
being pumped into the gutter," Ray's son said with a scowl.

"So I have heard," Kris admitted.

"Then you have not listened very well."

"I am listening, as carefully as I can," Kris said.

"And you," Al said, indicating Jack with his nearly empty
teacup.

"I'm listening, too, and doing what I can to increase the
odds of her survival."

"Hmm," Al said as he returned to the golden samovar of
hot water to prepare himself another cup of tea. "And you
came to me?" he asked, turning back to them with a full cup.

"Yes. When the Earth frigates came out to Alwa Station, they
were clad in a crystal armor that took in laser light and distrib-
uted it around the ship before radiating it back into space."

"I know. I negotiated with Earth for the rights to it. They
wanted an arm and a leg. What good are low-cost frigates if
they suddenly cost half your flesh just to add to decadent
Earth's wealth? Battlecruisers, did you call them?"

"Yes. With all that armament and armor, they are as good
as any battleship while being as fast and maneuverable as a
cruiser."

"Hmm, I heard that the ship, *Wasp* is it, that brought you
back from Alwa, was crystal clad. How did that happen?"

Which led to Kris's telling him how the Earth ships had not fared so well in their first combat and the changes the shipyards on Alwa Station had made to them. The yard then applied crystal to all the ships, including the new arrivals from human space.

"My computer has the way we grow the crystals, sort them to an exact length, then apply them to ships quickly."

"Ha," Al cackled. "I bet I can turn the tables on Earth with that package you've brought me."

"Likely you can, but I need eight armored ships right now. If I'm to have any chance of coming out of Greenfeld space alive, I need to survive being on the receiving end of a sneaky broadside and live to return fire."

"Maybe you're not such an idiot," Al allowed.

"Can you armor my ships?" Kris asked, eyeing him over her near-empty cup of tea.

"Will you give me the file?"

"Nuu Enterprises on Alwa Station did most of this work."

"How is Irving doing?"

"Irving?"

"Yes, the fellow I put in charge of my interests out there."

"I think he drank himself to death," Kris said. "Pipra Strongarm is running the show for Nuu and several other industrial interests."

"Who's she?" Al asked.

"Pipra Strongarm," Al's computer answered in a lush female voice, "was Third Vice President for Human Resources."

"Third Vice President!" Al didn't quite squeak.

Kris failed to suppress a smile. She'd taken Pipra at her claim to be next in charge. She'd never asked Pipra what she was in charge of.

I've been jobbed, but you kept us all alive. Go, gal.

"Do you want the files?" Kris asked.

"Yeah. Yeah, give them to me."

"You will get the eight battlecruisers ready first and in time for my sailing," Kris stated, not even adding please.

"Yes, yes," he snapped, "assuming the Navy gives me the bid. You know, it would be easier and definitely faster if you gave me a couple of kernels from your computer, so I could have a top-of-the-line computer, you know, and see that things go well for you."

"No," Kris said.

"Definitely no," Nelly added from her collarbone.

"But this is a complicated process, wrapping crystal armor around a ship the size of your battlecruisers. Especially one that keeps changing sizes, you know," Grampa Al insisted. "Without something to do all the work and coordination like your Nelly, it could take us a year or at least six months."

"All the research and design work, even down to what is needed to quickly clad the battlecruisers, has already been done," Kris pointed out.

"And I would never allow you and your likes to have one of my children," Nelly snapped. "Heaven knows what you would put the poor kid to doing. No. Never."

"Are you going to let your computer, ah"—Al struggled to get his mouth around what he needed to say, and settled for—"tell you what to do?"

"I don't usually, but in this, we are of an agreement. Nelly, what other shipyards do they have up on the station?"

"Nazareth Steel, Shipbuilding, and Space Docks is building frigates," Nelly informed Kris.

"Steel is one thing. Growing crystal is totally different," said Al, butting in.

"Correct," Nelly said, primly, "but they have an agreement with Arnell Electronic and Computer Fabrication. They have fabs bigger than the ones we have on Alwa Station. They can grow the crystal cladding."

"Damn your eyes, Kristine Anne Longknife," Grampa Al growled. "You are a headstrong, foolish child. You trust my word: It will get you killed someday. You really must join me in here where it's safe and—"

"Considering how easily Jack and I breached your security, I wouldn't bet on it."

"I've corrected those deficiencies."

"And likely replaced them with more. No, Grampa, I will not work for you. Unless you agree to clad the ships I'm being given and do it in one week, I'm heading for your competition."

Al's scowl at her would have left any of his subordinates cringing on his knees. Kris returned it, unblinking.

I've faced down alien wolf packs. What have you done with your life?

It took Grampa Al a great while to work up to his surrender. "Yes, I will do it. Now, damn you, let me see my latest great-granddaughter before you get her and yourselves killed."

Ruthie took over the meeting at that point and did her best to wrap another of her cantankerous elders around her tiny finger. Even on grumpy Grandfather Al, it worked. He was smiling, making baby talk, and delighted at her strong grasp of his little finger.

"You will bring her back again," Al said. "Honovi so rarely brings his children by."

"I will try, Grampa, but you know I'm headed back out soonest."

"I would be glad to provide Ruthie with the finest care in the security of my own living quarters."

"Thank you, Grandfather but I'm nursing Ruthie, so where I go, she goes."

"Even to Greenfeld?"

"Now you know why I want those battlecruisers up armored."

"You are a fool," was his parting shot.

Jack waited until they were in the elevator before he could no longer suppress a question. "You aren't serious about taking Ruthie with us, are you?"

"Who would I leave her with? My mother? Your mother? Al here? No, I am Ruthie's mother, and she goes with me. I trust you to keep us safe. Who else would you trust?"

"Oh God." Jack sighed.

"Help us all," Rick Sanchez added.

"I will have to arrange for a bigger detail," Special Agent Foile muttered.

They considered all this while they went down three elevators and made their way to the limo surrounded by Marine gun trucks, police cars, and motorcycles.

As soon as they were under way, Kris said to Nelly, "Have you got a contact in Nazareth Steel, Shipbuilding, and Space Docks?"

"Yes, ma'am. I have even asked them if they would be interested in some additional work after they finish the two battlecruisers they are building for Tacoma. The rest of the squadron is to be built on the station that Tacoma is just putting the finishing touches to, complete with a shipyard."

So, Nazareth Steel was very interested in getting into the crystal-growing business.

"Call the Chairman of the Board and CEO," Kris told Nelly.

They had an agreement and had given them a copy of what Grampa Al now had before their convoy arrived safely back at Nuu House.

Kris waited until Nelly had hung up and assured them they were clear.

"Now let's see how fast Grampa Al is," Kris said, and knew her smile was pure evil. She found she enjoyed it that way.

10

Grampa and Gramma Trouble asked to join them for supper. Lotty was delighted to serve dinner for more than just herself and her husband, Harvey. Kris asked Senior Chief Agent Foile to stay for dinner if he could.

"Yes, but I hope you will let me go soon enough to help my kids with their homework. It's rare that I make it home in time. It would be nice for just once."

Kris assured him dinner would be early and not run long.

"What do you think of your new nannies?" Gramma Trouble asked, as she and Trouble came through the door.

"I haven't seen them yet," Kris said, just as a new face in the gray-and-white uniform the nanny service seemed to require brought Ruthie down the stairs to meet the company.

"You would be Akumaa Shalonda," Gramma Trouble said.

"Yes, ma'am," came with a slight dunk of the head. The woman was almost as tall as Kris. Her skin was a luscious chocolate topped by red hair, close-cropped, but long enough that Ruthie would, no doubt, soon be wrapping her fingers in it. She had a quick smile.

"I saw your background when I first looked at the packages Brenda had," Gramma Trouble said. "I don't know what her criteria were, but they weren't mine, or yours I see," she said, nodding at Kris.

"You are weapons-qualified?" Jack asked.

"Pistol, rifle with sniper scope out to nine hundred meters, assault rifles, several rocket launchers, and mortars. I love those things. Will we be having any of those in the armory?"

"We shall see," Jack said, grinning. "May I ask how you happened to qualify with all these toys?"

"I'm sorry, sir, but that is classified need to know. However, I will be glad to demonstrate proficiency."

"Gramma Trouble?" Kris asked.

"Don't ask me. Trouble vouched for her, and that was good enough for me."

Kris raised a questioning eyebrow to her troublesome great-grandfather. He shook his head. "Sorry, I had to call in some chits to verify her skill set, and I am not at leisure to say more."

"Will the rest be just as black ops?" Jack asked.

"Oh, no. The other gals and their supervisor are all former service Soldiers or Marines. It will be interesting to see how a shooting match among all six works out."

"No doubt," Kris said.

Ruthie was hungry, so they adjourned to the library. It was a relief to be able to nurse Ruthie and not be ostracized from the conversation. She kept Ruthie under a loose blanket, but no one blinked when she switched from breast to breast. Kris had chosen a peasant dress that made it easy for her to put dinner before her infant.

"If only the Navy would adopt a nursing mother's uniform," Gramma Ruth said.

"It's hard enough for them to tolerate a maternity uniform," Trouble put in.

Which led Kris to tell the full story of how she came to be a mother and continued to be an admiral commanding a fleet at the tip of a spear.

"I wondered how that came down," Gramma Ruth said. "I know all the trouble Rita got in for taking Al out on a heavy cruiser when she was nursing him. Oh, and the storm that blew in when the powers that be discovered she'd stayed at the head of her squadron while Alnaba was on the way."

"It hasn't got any easier," Kris said. "Oh, and I have Alnaba's granddaughter on my staff?"

"You do!" Gramma Trouble said.

Lottie picked that moment to announce dinner was ready. Ruthie had just finished her supper and nodded off to sleep. Akumaa appeared instantly from out of nowhere to whisk the infant away, leaving the adults to enjoy dinner and old stories. Kris left it to Trouble to tell how, after Eddy died, he'd hauled her out of her drunken depths to soar as a skiff racer dropping from orbit to a small patch of ground that was the target.

"I wouldn't be where I am today if you hadn't reached out to me," Kris said.

"You are where you are today because of you, and a whole lot of your friends, of which Ruth and I are proud to be two," Trouble said, giving his wife a hug.

"But if you get me kidnapped again . . ." Ruth said, and left it at that.

"Don't get too close to me," Kris said. "It's dangerous."

"I wouldn't say that," Jack said, and gave her a squeeze to match Trouble's.

Agent Foile took this all in and said little.

It was only after dinner was over and a dessert tray that could not be passed up had been passed around that Trouble said, "I understand you visited with Al today. How is my former son-in-law?"

"The same as he ever is,' Kris said. "A skinflint scared of his own shadow and grasping for everyone to come in under his umbrella. One that smells terribly like a spiderweb that once you go in, you would never get out."

Trouble shook his head. 'I don't know what got into that boy. I never did see what Sarah saw in him."

"They spent so much time growing up together," Ruth said, "while we were all out making the galaxy safe from Iteeche. Left together, they kind of fell into something they both took for love. It might have become something if they'd been given enough time. Ray had been a bachelor way too long, and he just didn't know how to give that boy the love he needed. There was a big splash when Alex married that young thing, but nothing afterward. Nelly, are you better than I am at chasing gossip?"

"I'm sorry, Gramma Ruth, but I can find nothing about her. Two days after the wedding, they both entered a black hole as you might say. Grampa Al is often talked *about* in the media, but rarely because of anything *he* said."

"The man's a hermit," Trouble said.

"After looking at his office today," Jack said, "I'd say he leads a very opulent and indolent hermit kingdom."

They shook their heads at that, and Trouble changed the topic.

"Excuse me for bringing up business, but would you like to meet the three people who volunteered to help you mediate?"

"When could I?" Kris asked.

"Would tomorrow be too soon? Say 1300 hours?"

"Fine by me," Kris said, as Trouble and Ruth stood. Agent Foile stood a moment later, not having the telepathy that the old married couple seemed to share.

"How many people will we be passing through the perimeter?" Kris asked.

"Likely a lot more than three," Trouble said. "Most of them work with a team."

"So I'll be the ringmaster of a real zoo?"

"And that's different how?" Trouble asked.

"You're mean to me, Grampa."

"No more than I have to be, young lady. Do you remember that zoo where you got your first medal, and I had you sit there with the rest of us old fogies with stars on our shoulders?"

"How could I ever forget? Mother wanted me to put diamonds on my Navy and Marine Corps Medal and wear it as a pendant—and get out of the Navy immediately."

"I told you then that you'd have stars."

"Do I? My orders to get back here were addressed to a captain."

"Neither Mac nor Ray told you to get your uniform straightened out, did they?"

"Nope."

"You've got it. Don't let anybody try to take it back."

"And when payday comes, and the pay isn't there for four stars?"

"Tell Finance to straighten up the paperwork, then donate

it to a good cause. It's not like you Longknifes need the money," the old general said.

On that laugh, the wisest of Kris's elders took their leave, along with Special Agent Foile. Kris and Jack enjoyed the rest of their evening, including time with Ruthie when she woke up.

Akumaa got more pabulum into Ruthie after Kris allowed her to empty only one breast. She then slipped the baby out so Kris and Jack could get some sleep. Kris wasn't woken up until two o'clock for a sleepy feeding. Akumaa again took Ruthie off for some play and let Kris go back to sleep.

Kris felt very well rested when morning arrived. No doubt, it would be a busy day.

11

Kris had just settled into the breakfast solarium and managed a bite from a nut-and-bran muffin with marmalade when Nelly interrupted.

"I have several requests from shipyard and space-dock companies for the package we gave Al and Nazareth. Should I give it to them?"

"How many is several?" Kris asked through a full mouth.

"Three. No, make that four. Another request just came through."

"How'd they find out?" Kris asked no one in particular.

"I assume that's a rhetorical question," Nelly said, "but I suspect the answer has something to do with how much you humans talk. Incessantly, I might say."

Kris ignored Nelly and eyed Jack. Swallowing, she said, "It was such a lovely morning. Well, no rest for the wicked. As I see it, we developed those production procedures and installation practices on Alwa Station. We don't have any patent process on Alwa; we're just doing anything we can to survive."

"Yeah," Jack said slowly, "but we did start with Earth's stuff, which they very likely did patent."

"But if we leave it to the lawyers, we'll be years getting the warships we need," Kris said.

"You want to do it now and ask forgiveness later?"

"I want to do it now, and let the lawyers figure out the mess. Isn't that what they get paid for?"

"God help us if you ever end up queen, my love."

"I'm sure she will," Kris said, leaning close enough to Jack to give him a marmalade-sticky kiss. The essentials covered, Kris told Nelly to publish the files to the Wardhaven net with open access.

"That ought to be fun," Kris said.

"No doubt," Nelly agreed.

They were enjoying one last cup of coffee before tackling their day when Nelly again broke in. "Grampa Al wants to talk with you, Kris. Indeed, he is trying to have his computer bellow his desire from every comm link in Nuu House."

"Can he do that?" Kris asked.

"No doubt he could," Nelly said, "if I weren't blocking him. His computer, as he admitted yesterday, is not in my league."

"No question of that," Kris said, to fill the time while she thought. "What do you think, Jack?"

"We both know what he wants to talk about. We both know he won't be easy to talk to. It seems to me that it's just a waste of your time and his to take this call."

"That sounds about right," Kris said. "Nelly, use your superior skills to break into his call and tell him I won't be available today."

"Done," Nelly said.

Kris and Jack rose and were on their way out of the solarium when Nelly reported, "Grampa Al is not happy. I'm glad you didn't have to listen to him. Such language!"

"No doubt you've heard worse," Kris said.

"Yes, from Sailors and Marines, but from your own grandfather?" Nelly sniffed.

"Well, if he questioned my parentage and DNA, he ought to know more about it than I do," Kris said through a wicked grin.

Kris planned to spend the morning at Mac's office, looking into the specifics of what ships and Marines she could subvert to her own ends. A new nanny showed to cover the morning shift. Mai Tiamat was short and fair-skinned, the opposite of Akumaa, though her hair was raven black and down to her waist in a plaited ponytail. She had Ruthie efficiently ready and joined Kris and Jack as they went down the stairs.

Senior Chief Agent in Charge Foile was there with Leslie. "I have a full team in place, and we will follow a random series of streets between here and Main Navy."

"Fine. What's our threat level today?" Jack asked.

"We have tracked down the source of our trouble," Foile said. "It seems, Your Highness, that someone has put a rather large sum of money on your head. They want you dead. Period."

"Any idea who?" Kris asked.

"No idea," the agent said. "Though if I were a betting man, I'd put all my money on the stepmother. Isn't it always the stepmother in fairy tales?"

"This hardly feels like a fairy tale," Kris muttered, as Jack opened the door of their limo for her. Leslie was helping Ruthie and Mai in the other door.

"Though it's certainly grim enough," Nelly put in.

"Lousy joke, girl," Kris said.

"But appropriate," Jack added.

The drive to Main Navy involved a lot of turns but no surprises. Jack remarked on that.

"Mahomet's night shift did defuse a roadside bomb that showed up out of nowhere," Leslie said. "They chased down a half dozen trucks that had driven by between sweeps. Five stopped and made nice."

"And the other?" Jack asked.

"Was abandoned and burning in a back alley. It was reported stolen yesterday afternoon."

"Damn the money," Kris muttered.

Field Marshal McMorrison was expecting them; he even seemed to know what they wanted to talk about.

"We have eight frigates, er, battlecruisers, which have just finished working up. The *Princess Royal*, *Intrepid*, *Courageous*, *Furious*, *Resolute*, *Defender*, *Steadfast*, and *Monarch* are almost ready for you."

"We've got several ships with those names on Alwa Station," Kris pointed out.

"I know we sent them out there, but we figured they must have been lost by now," the field marshal said.

"They have been," Kris admitted, "but we built replacements."

"You're actually building ships?"

"Once you've got the basic kernel of the ship, you can grow one rather quickly."

"Really?" Mac said, frowning. "And Al Longknife insists it's such a tough job to put together one of the new Smart Metal battlecruisers."

"Nelly, do we have the procedure Admiral Benson uses to grow a ship?"

"I did manage to get his computer to part with them before we left," Nelly said as smoothly as if her mouth could melt butter.

"Let me have them," Mac said. "The Navy still has some shipyards of our own, and there are several places we can buy that newfangled Smart Metal. Let's see if we can show old Al a thing or two . . . and get some money back from him while we're at it."

"You may have all the fun with Grampa Al that you want," Kris said. "Just keep him out of my hair."

"Speaking of your hair, would you happen to know how it happened that I got four unrequested bids for adding crystal armor to those eight frigates, I mean battlecruisers, that you're taking into Greenfeld space?"

"I may have had Nelly post on the net the process for armoring a battlecruiser with crystal."

Kris couldn't tell whether Mac was delighted or appalled. Likely, he was a bit of both. He did get a coughing fit that had him grabbing for a glass of water.

"God, I don't know how you Longknifes keep from killing each other," he finally got out.

"Probably because the Peterwalds keep hogging the head of the line," Kris said, daintily.

"No doubt. Is that crystal cladding all it's cracked up to be?"

"Mac, it saved a lot of lives in the last couple of run-ins with the alien monsters. The Earth squadrons lost ships because their stuff was not manufactured to our quality standards and not fitted properly to their ships' hulls. Armored, I still lost ships, but it cut my losses at least in half, maybe by three-quarters."

"Then we need to get your ships docked for cladding," Mac said.

"Admiral Benson's yard teams came up with a fast way to clad the battlecruisers that didn't need a dock. It's all in the package. How many did you say were bidding for the work?"

"Al, two other yards I trust, and one fly-by-night that just came off being listed for no government work for some shenanigan they pulled last year."

"If you could," Jack said, "keep that last one on restriction for a bit longer. I don't want my wife depending on the lowest bidder if you can manage it."

"I think I can do that," Mac said. "That would give four to Al and two each to these others."

"And if the other two can do the upgrade as quickly as I think they can, you'll have a baseline you can use to keep Al honest," Kris said.

With that decision made, Kris got out of Mac's way and let him do his best for her. She chose to spend her time wandering the halls, refreshing old friendships and getting a feel for the way the wind was blowing.

Lunch was in Field Marshal McMorrison's private dining room and attended by several senior Navy officers. They wanted to know firsthand how things were on Alwa Station.

"I turned in a full set of reports as soon as we docked yesterday," Kris said.

"I stayed up all night reading them," Commander, Battle Force said. "I didn't see anywhere that your battlecruisers are following battle-line doctrine."

"She's not using her frigates," CruDes Forces pointed out, being careful to use the earlier name for Kris's ships, "like liners. They're more like independent destroyers."

Kris had no trouble finishing her meal while the two of them carried on their own, doubtlessly familiar, battle. Finished, Kris excused herself to attend to Ruthie.

Her departure was hardly noticed.

Jack ducked out a moment later and trotted to catch up with Kris. "You'd think they'd want to talk to an experienced combat commander," he said.

"You'd think that, but more than likely, you'd be wrong."

"Yeah," Jack said. "They can't allow for actual experience to interfere with their own ignorance."

"Not when it might impact their budget."

"You sure you want to come back here and become a staff weenie?"

Kris shrugged. "Somebody has to, or some alien mother ship could show up in Wardhaven's sky and those clowns wouldn't have the foggiest idea how to fight it."

"Yeah," Jack said. "Yeah."

They were back to Nuu House safe and sound long before their next meeting got under way.

12

Kris rocked Ruthie softly as she rested her eyes out the window of the nursery on the roadway between the gate and the house. A whole lot of people were coming to see her.

Ensign Meg Longknife was laying out a new blues uniform and switching the ribbons to it under Jack's watchful eye. Akumaa had Ruthie sound asleep, so Kris hadn't had a chance to feed her at Main Navy. She'd awoken hungry on the drive home.

Thus, Kris's breasts got painfully full and leaked. "There are a few things about this mommyhood thing that weren't mentioned in the manual that came with Ruthie," Kris muttered.

Strange, everyone around her kept very quiet as she groused. Smart of them if they wanted to keep their heads from being bitten off.

Cleaned up, and once again presentable, Kris had Nelly put in a call to Senior Chief Agent in Charge Foile. "Did you do a background check on all these people?"

"All of them had been fully vetted for their jobs. We did check to see if anyone suddenly had debts or income changes. They all came back clean."

That was good, but Kris had hardly rung off when Jack

asked softly "Honey, do you think now would be a good time to see if you can fit into your spidersilk underarmor?"

"No, it would not be a good time to try. I know how many pounds I'm still carrying," Kris snapped, but stopped short of snapping off heads.

"There was a small package delivered this morning," Meg put in. "It's from your Great-grandmother Tordon. Have I met her yet?"

"That's Gramma Trouble," Kris said, and almost leapt for the wrapped box on the table Jack put out a restraining hand to her elbow. He retrieved the box and took it out into the hall and down to the bathroom.

"It's spider silks in a larger size, honey," came back a moment later.

Which left Kris to undress again and wiggle into the abysmally tight things while feeling every extra ounce she'd gained in the last nine months. At least she could do it in the bathroom, away from eyes she didn't want to be embarrassed by or to tell her nice things she didn't believe. Dressed again, she rejoined Jack, and, feeling safer than she had in weeks, went out to see what there was to see.

The second-floor conference room had been reserved for this meeting. Kris saw that metal detectors had been set up at the door. They buzzed as she and Jack walked in wearing their ribbon racks and carrying their service automatics.

But they're here to protect me, so that's okay.

A large zoo of eyes followed Jack and her as they headed for the two empty chairs at the head of the table. Kris could imagine they were taking her measure and refused to think about the conclusions they drew.

Seated, Kris looked around the table. It was easy to identify the three primaries. They sat back, maybe a bit more relaxed than those beside them. Around those three were eighteen at the table and on the edge of their seats, ready to jump at the slightest whim. Twenty or more sat alertly along the wall, backing up those at the table. All told, Kris counted over forty people in the room. Several of Foile's agents were left at the door.

My meetings keep getting bigger and bigger.

Kris cleared her throat. "I have plenty of experience blowing shit up and killing people. It seems now that I must find a way to stop some people from blowing shit up and killing each other. Hopefully, before one of them succeeds in killing me."

Blank faces around the room took in her words, and realized, likely for the first time, that this latest challenge might not be as safe as their normal daily affairs.

"I know that there have been many attempts on your life, Your Highness," said one tall, middle-aged man Kris had identified as a primary.

"But twice since I got off the boat yesterday is a bit much, even for me," Kris answered before he got to the question.

Now eyebrows did rise in concern as heads swung from one side to the other, taking a poll of their friends and measuring the distance for a run to the door.

Kris was not unfamiliar with this reaction. It had just been a while.

"There are three groups of you here. You all come recommended to me. You all bring different perspectives to our problem. I would prefer to have all three of you with me. Grampa Trouble thinks that together, you give us more of a chance to succeed. However, you may want to assess the risk you are willing to take. Talk it over among yourselves and let me know when you've made up your minds, as one group, or three."

Finished, Kris stood, turned her back on their discussion, and walked over to one of the windows that opened on a view of the lovely gardens. That was where Penny had gotten married. Kris smiled at the memory. Too bad she and Tommy had had so little time together.

Tommy got too close to this damn Longknife, she thought bitterly.

Kris looked over her shoulder, at where forty some people were earnestly negotiating just how much they were willing to risk to follow this damn Longknife. She doubted that any of them ever expected to be in collateral-damage range of a bomb during the normal to and fro of their daily duties.

Kris turned back to the view. The trees were turning all sorts of lovely colors. She'd likely miss winter if this mediation process took very long.

Jack came up beside her, two mugs of tea in his hands. Kris took the one offered her. "Chamomile?" she asked.

"What else would I bring?"

She smiled and turned again to the view.

Kris heard the crack of the glass as the bullet shattered it.

13

Jack grabbed for her, but Kris was already going down, folding her legs under herself. Of course, scorching-hot tea was flying every which way.

Kris could feel the scalding of the tea but no pain yet from the bullet. She took no comfort from that; she'd been hit often enough to know that the agony came later.

There was the report of another shot, and suddenly Kris was covered with nuggets of glass. The window had held for the first round; the glass failed as the second shot hit.

A chilly breeze wafted through the empty window.

Kris dropped flat on her back, covering her eyes with her arms to protect them from more chunks of glass. Jack covered her with his body.

She knew he always would.

Somewhere, someone was screaming. Kris turned her head; one of the eager secondaries had a fountain of blood pulsing from her neck.

Not good. Kris tried to roll out from under Jack. Strange how a man could be so light on her body when they were making love but be so heavy when he wanted to pin her to the deck.

"Jack," Kris snapped.

"I know. Stay down," he said, cutting her off.

"Radar has backtracked the bullets to a knoll nine hundred and fifty meters from the house," Nelly reported. "A team has been dispatched."

"We need medics up here. Now! Major trauma," Kris bit out.

"Emergency Services have been notified," Nelly said. "We have a small trauma team on-site. More on the way."

The door opened, and two emergency-medical techs monkey-walked low through it with a backboard and medical box dragged between them. A woman in a white lab coat followed, crawling on her hands and knees.

One of the people at the table had been trying to stop the bleeding with his handkerchief. Now a med tech took over.

The doctor pulled a packet from the kit. It provided her with a scalpel and clamps. She lengthened the bloody hole enough so she could clamp off one end of the jugular vein, followed by the other.

"Okay, folks, we've really messed up the blood flow. Let's do this fast."

One med tech had already pulled out a plastic-wrapped tube, sticky extensions at both ends. The other tech unclasped the lower part of the wound but tried to keep it closed with his fingers. Still, blood flowed from the exposed, ragged edge. The doctor slapped the tube onto that exposed end of the jugular and taped it down. She let blood in and sighed as blood did not spurt out from the glued-down part. There was leakage.

"Andy, extra tape," she said, and turned to the other end. They repeated the process, and a moment later, blood was flowing through the tube, now twisted into a slight U but holding.

As she slapped a bandage over the entire space, she growled, "Is this still a live shooting gallery?"

From outside the door came Foile's voice. "We had the shooter in custody, but she took poison, so there'll be no one to talk to. Sorry, Your Highness."

"I'm sure you will have more chances to catch a live one," Kris said.

But attention was focused still on the medical heroes. Two more med techs brought a gurney in. The blood-covered young woman was transferred gently to it, then lifted up.

"There's an elevator down the hall," one of the original med techs said, and led the way.

"A chopper is inbound, three minutes out," came from Ensign Longknife, still out in the hall.

"Anyone else hurt?" the doctor asked.

"One more," Jack said.

Kris looked around and saw nothing. She'd shed her dress blues blouse and with it the scalding tea. She was fine.

Jack reached over and touched her face. His finger came away with blood on it.

"It *is* just a scratch," Kris insisted, then switched to business mode. "There is a large room in the basement. We can stand around safely there while some Marines scrounge up some tables and chairs."

"Only after they've made sure this wasn't the first of a multiphased assassination attempt," Jack said.

"I think we can conduct our business standing up. I've done some of my work at the bottom of a mine shaft," was said with a dry chuckle by an older shorter man. "The third-generation owner had never actually seen what it took to make him his money."

Others agreed, so they all trooped downstairs. with one med tech at Kris's elbow, doing his best to care for her scratches.

14

Kris found herself in a storage room that looked a lot smaller than it had the last time she had played hide-and-seek with Honovi and Eddy. The unused bar she'd disappeared behind was still there. Now she sat atop it while the med tech did what she would let him.

Finished, he put away his gear. "You should have a cosmetic surgeon take a look at that one on your chin," he said. "It's a coin flip if it should be stitched. I take it you won't go to the hospital."

"You got that one right," Kris said.

The med tech whispered something about "those damn Longknifes" as he finished his packing.

"I'll get a doc over here before supper," Jack said.

Kris was too tired to argue. Her adrenaline was draining away fast. Likely, that was something her body did to make sure Ruthie didn't get a jolt of the stuff with her milk.

A short older man with sparkling eyes, a tall middle-aged man with a limp, and a young woman who might have been mistaken for a younger Kris came to face her.

"If there was any question about the risk involved here, someone certainly gave us a demonstration," the older man said. The other two nodded.

"All three of us have had a member of our staff withdraw. Mine was the woman who was shot. Diana and WP each had one fold their cards after a call to their spouses. One would have to be a fool to go into this without the support of the one they're committed to spend their life with. Besides, what kind of negotiators would we be if we gave our loved ones nonnegotiable demands?"

He turned to share a chuckle with most of those in the room. At least two, one a man, the other a woman, looked too shook-up to enjoy the joke.

"We have a list of additional experts we would like to join us. Computer gurus, data analysts, linguists in the variations of Standard spoken in Greenfeld, several experts in forensic accounting. They may not be necessary, but it's amazing how often they come in handy. Getting to yes isn't just a process of reaching agreement but often involves changing people's opinion of where they are and where they've been."

Kris nodded as she began to learn another way of looking at the world, just as the Navy had shown her the Navy Way, and the boffins had introduced her to the scientific method.

Oh God, not another learning experience!

"Make up your list. Pass it to Meg, my *aide-de-camp*. If she can't get the bodies you need, I'm sure I know someone who buried them."

Ensign Longknife smiled cheerfully, validating Kris's suspicion that Gramma and Grampa Trouble had more than one oar in the water that brought her to Kris's side.

"I asked Grampa Trouble if he knew a good plastic surgeon," Jack said, "and Gramma Trouble got back with me a few moments ago. One is on her way here."

"Then let me feed Ruthie, and I'll lie down where I'm told," Kris said with an exhausted sigh. Two nannies brought the infant, and someone rustled up a rocker for Kris and Ruthie. They settled into a corner while the others, including Jack and Meg, made their lists and made them longer.

Kris was not yet finished with Ruthie when Foile showed up again.

"You mind talking to me now? My wife breast-fed our two hellions. It brings back fond memories."

"If you're not embarrassed, I'm not," Kris said.

The agent stooped beside Kris. "We've done a thorough search of the area and don't see anything more dangerous than one owner who hasn't leashed his dog."

"God forbid we should allow such an outlaw to prosper," Kris said dryly.

"My main problem is Nuu House. The bulletproof windows were last replaced when you started college. Their warranty is up next year. With no one here, there were no plans to replace them."

Kris snorted. "I was crazy for ship duty. Hated being stuck here."

"Evidently, armor-piercing bullets are more powerful than ten years ago. I've put in a demand for new glass, but it will be a day, maybe two, before we get everything replaced."

"And in the meantime?"

The agent shrugged. "I'm not sure there's anyplace on this planet that can be made safe for you. I suggested to the head of the Secret Service that you move in with your folks . . ."

"Ain't gonna happen," Kris said, cutting him off.

"He said the same thing. He didn't want the prime minister caught in any cross fires intended for you."

"That, too," Kris said, getting a fishy eye from the agent but no backtalk.

"Would you feel safer with the Navy?" he finally said.

Kris shrugged. "They've kept me alive when bug-eyed monsters wanted me dead. I haven't done better than that?"

Now it was the agent's turn to say nothing and Kris's to give him the fish eye.

"Okay, where do we stash me and how do we get there?"

"I assumed the *Wasp*," Foile said.

"So would everyone else," Jack said, joining the conversation.

"Where's the *Princess Royal*?" Kris asked.

"Moving into a Nazareth Steel space dock," Nelly said.

"Here's how we're going to do this," Kris said, and turned Ruthie over for a good burping.

15

An hour later, a convoy gunned out of the front gate of Nuu House. Built around a long black limo, it had big police rigs and Marine gun trucks both ahead and behind it. As soon as it hit the street, it began a zigzag course that seemed aimed nowhere in particular.

A half hour later, a similar cavalcade shot out of the back gate of Nuu House and likewise began to go nowhere in a hurry.

Thirty minutes after that, a third motorcade repeated the process, again using the front gate.

In between those last two, a green sedan, driven by the old family chauffeur, pulled up to the back gate. He waved cheerfully, and when questioned by the Marines at the gate told them, "Lotty needs two pounds of butter and five dozen fresh eggs. We aren't due for a delivery until tomorrow and wouldn't you know it, they ate us out of house and home."

The Marines chuckled and waved the sedan through.

Two blocks out, it was joined by two unmarked police cars, then two more.

About this time, all three of the motorcades with big limos began to meander their way toward the space-elevator station. The green sedan, instead of making its way toward the same place, or for a grocery store, got on the crosstown expressway, sped up, and headed for the mountains to the west of Wardhaven.

About the time the sedan approached Big Bear Lake, an unusual sound was heard over Wardhaven City: the double boom of a lander coming in. Not since the beanstalk had been completed had a lander come in over the city. Back then, they came down in the bay, not up in the hills.

Longboat 3 from the *Wasp* settled down in a haze of spray and steam, then motored over to the large boat ramp and rolled itself right out of the water. The aft hatch opened, and a cheerful voice said, "Hi, Your Highness. See. We didn't suck a single water weed into the intakes."

"You've gotten much better," Kris shouted back, and quickwalked with Jack, Agents Foile and Rick, two nannies, and one Navy aide across the landing and right into the longboat.

"You may launch when you please," Kris said. "Just keep the gees below two and a half, if you will. Neither I nor baby is up for the rough stuff these days."

"Will do, Your Highness. Back to the *Wasp*?"

"No, not today. Land us on the *Princess Royal*, if you please."

"Will do, ma'am."

Thus ordered, Longboat 3 motored stately out to where the lake was its deepest and rose to the heavens on a pillar of fire.

Once the noise settled down, so Jack didn't have to shout, he leaned over and spoke into Kris's ear. "Danged if that wasn't a better escape from Wardhaven than the last time we had to leave in a hurry."

"Glad I'm not at the stick?" Kris asked.

"Nope. You're the best pilot I've ever ridden with."

"Smart husband. I may keep you."

An hour later, they approached High Wardhaven Station. *Wasp*'s Longboat 3 adjusted its course to take it right into the *Princess Royal*'s landing bay.

Without a hitch, Kris was back in space, safe and sound.

16

An out-of-breath commander saluted Kris as she came aboard one of the fleet's newest battlecruisers.

"I'm Commander Helen Ajax, captain of the *Princess Royal*. Welcome aboard, ah, Admiral."

Kris took the measurements of the woman who would keep her and Ruthie safe. She was glad the captain had chosen which foot to get started on. Someone had warned her how much Kris did not like being Your Highnessed by officers in uniform.

"You were told you would be my flag," Kris said, watching as the two nannies marched Ruthie aboard.

Captain Ajax's eyes followed the baby for maybe a second too long.

"Ah, yes, ma'am," she said, eyes sweeping back to Kris.

"But not that I'd be coming aboard this afternoon."

"Exactly, ma'am. We're doing our best at catch-up."

Kris turned to follow Ruthie into their new home. "Well, it turns out the armored glass windows at Nuu House weren't quite as armored as we thought. Have you locked the ship down?"

"Yes, ma'am. Ah, you know we are in the yard, ma'am."

"Yes, but does adding the crystal armor require yard personnel's coming aboard?"

"I'm trying to get an answer to that, ma'am."

"It shouldn't. We did it all from the outside on Alwa Station."

"Yes, ma'am. The *Wasp* sent over the layout for your flag quarters." Again, the captain's eyes focused on Ruthie, and she swallowed hard. "I assume that you will need expanded quarters. I also have a request from *Wasp*. They want to ship your flag gear over here. Their request arrived shortly after the order to lock the *Princess Royal* down tight."

"Which has you between a rock and a hard place," Jack put in.

Kris's flag captain nodded.

"Yeah," Kris admitted. "Maybe we don't have all our ducks in a row. Okay, allow personnel from *Wasp* to make the transfer. See that Senior Comm and Chief Mong is put in charge of the detail. Tell him to wear sidearms, and if he sees anyone he doesn't recognize, to shoot first and ask questions later."

"Yes, ma'am. Begging the Admiral's pardon, but is that the normal way of doing business under your command?"

"No, Captain, but there have been two bombings and one sniper attempt on my life since I went ashore day before yesterday. I'm a bit trigger-happy at the moment."

"Yes, ma'am.

"Oh," Jack said, "I'm about to order up a doctor to see what she can do to patch up my wife's face. There are also three nannies and two Secret Service agents, likely more, that didn't come up with us. Let me know if you have anyone ask to cross your brow, and I'll approve them or order your Marines to shoot them."

Again, the captain swallowed hard. "There is one matter that I hope you'll make allowances for."

"And that would be?" Kris asked.

"I got a request from the CEO of Nazareth Steel, Shipbuilding, and Space Docks, Chogan Cam. He'd like to talk to you."

"How'd he know I was here?" Kris snapped.

"He didn't, ma'am. He told me earlier today that he'd like to talk something over with you when you came aboard. He's been good to work with, and I can't see his being a problem."

Kris eyed Jack. He nodded. "Captain, tell him that he can talk to me," Jack said. "If I like what I hear, we'll see where it goes from there."

"Yes, sir. He's in the yard, overseeing the tiger team doing what it can to glue crystal or whatever down."

"Actually, we ended up bolting it on," Kris said, "though I don't know quite how we got the strands of crystal to stick together. Okay, Captain, I'm going to be trusting you with my life in a pretty rough neighborhood. If you think I should see him, I'll see how he gets on with the general here, then talk to him. Where are my quarters?"

"If you'll come with me," Captain Ajax said.

"I suspect I can find my way to the gangplank," Jack said, and they went their separate ways.

The *P. Royal*'s skipper did lead Kris to familiar territory.

"*Wasp*'s skipper said your quarters were just off the bridge?" the captain said, clearly puzzled but not pushing.

"Yes. When I first came aboard *Wasp*, I was senior officer present but also the ship's gunnery officer."

The skipper's eyebrows went up in a questioning V, but she said nothing.

"*Wasp* and I kind of grew up together," Kris said. "I went from lieutenant to four stars on *Wasp*s that went from corvettes to frigates to battlecruisers."

Kris came to a familiar door. A Marine corporal stationed outside opened it while a private kept alert guard.

Her day quarters had a decent expanse of space. All empty. Kris quickly covered the paces to the door into her night quarters. They were a lot smaller than she would have expected.

Right. Jack must be billeted somewhere else.

"Nelly, see what you can do about moving the bulkhead to expand the day quarters.

Suddenly, there were no night quarters.

"Yeeps," the skipper said.

"Aren't your people moving walls around?" Kris asked.

"Well, yes, Admiral, when we need to, but I haven't had anyone treat bulkheads like they're on wheels."

"Hmm," Kris said, glancing around the space. "Nelly, we don't have any screens; could you turn these walls into a schematic of the ship?"

"Yes, ma'am," Nelly said, being rather better behaved than normal.

This time, Kris's new flag captain did a better job of suppressing her surprise. "I'd heard about Nelly," she said.

"You have to see her to really become a believer. This latest trick of transparent Smart Metal is a new one even for her. Now, let's see. Where do you want my flag quarters since they will include one Marine lieutenant general, one infant with a squad of six nannies, an *aide-de-camp*, and at least four Special Agents, including one in charge. Oh, and you will be taking on three teams of mediation specialists and their support staff."

"In addition to a Marine company?"

"Yep," Kris said. "Nelly, let the captain see a full schematic of *Wasp*, including boffins, Marines, and the Forward Lounge."

"Lounge!" The captain failed to suppress a squeak.

"You can't expect civilians to live by our spartan standards, and since we may be inviting an Emperor, Empress, and definitely a Grand Duchess aboard, we can't fail in our hospitality."

"Oh." Was followed shortly by a "God. I've also got a band heading up the beanstalk. One of your relatives—Trouble sound right?—says I can't do a diplomatic mission if I don't have a band."

That was a new one on Kris, but likely essential.

"Sorry, Captain. I'm one of those damn Longknifes, and I've been handed one hell of a job."

"Yes, ma'am. I understand, ma'am. But a restaurant and a band, ma'am? I'm on lockdown, and now I have to reorganize my ship and bring aboard a Navy band from somewhere and cooks, bartenders, and whatever else from God only knows where?"

"Yes," Kris said, knowing exactly how her flag captain must be feeling about now. "The difficult we do now, the impossible takes a little longer. Agent Foile?"

"Yes, Your Highness," he said, stepping in from the passageway.

"Any idea where we might recruit a few cooks, bartenders, and the like?"

"None whatsoever, but I will get on it immediately."

"Thank you so very much," Kris said with a smile, then turned back to Captain Ajax when Foile stepped back into the passageway, already talking to his commlink.

"I would suggest you get in touch with Captain Pett from *Wasp* and talk to her about what it's like to have a troublesome Longknife aboard. If you'd like me a deck up from your bridge, I'd be glad to do that, but I will need the strongest radiation shielding for Ruth."

"Ruth?"

"My infant."

"She'll be traveling with us?"

"She *will* be traveling with us," Kris said. "And yes, I know this is all irregular, but we've been doing things different on Alwa Station for the last two years and no, I did not authorize anyone to remove their birth-control implants. Mine and seventy-one others were sabotaged, if you are curious, and I'm here because the King ordered me back to sort out this problem with the Peterwalds. We all have to stretch a bit."

"I understand, Admiral," the *P. Royal*'s skipper said, looking quite stretched already.

"Good. Now, why don't you get with Captain Pett. Not only do you need to accommodate me and my needs, but I horse ships around hard, so they aren't there when someone aims for where they expected them to be. That means larger reaction motors than the ships came with. Get the word from Pett, then pass it along to your squadron mates."

"Yes, ma'am," the captain said, dismissed herself, and headed for the door as Jack came in it.

"Honey, you really want to talk to this fellow," Jack said, grinning as if he'd won the lottery. "I love what he's offering."

"I could use something nice today," Kris said, and stood to meet the CEO of the yard doing work on her flagship.

17

"Nelly, could you get us a few chairs in here," Kris said.

A moment later, three comfortably overstuffed chairs flowed out of the deck. They settled into them: Kris and Jack easily, Chogan a bit more unsure of himself.

"Damn, these are comfortable," the big fellow with long, flowing white hair said as he settled his full weight into the sudden seat.

"Don't you provide Smart Metal beds and chairs on your ships?" Kris asked.

"Yeah, I provide 'em, but I never tried 'em."

"How long have you been building Smart Metal ships?" Kris asked.

"I bought the patent from Al Longknife a few months ago. It took the mills a while to switch over. I just finished my first two ships. This one," he said, nodding at the bulkhead, "and the *Furious*. I'm glad I got the job of putting the crystal armor on both of them. I've enjoyed working with the skippers and crew."

From what Captain Ajax had said, the feeling was reciprocated.

Chogan eyed Kris curiously. "I want to personally thank you for posting the full skinny on how to grow and install this crystal. I imagine it would have been a long time coming before Al Longknife let anyone in on the secret."

"Al Longknife is my grandfather, and no, he's not at all happy with me," Kris said.

"Oh, does that mean Billy Longknife is your old man?"

"Guilty on all counts."

"God help you, kid."

"They regularly beg the same indulgence for themselves when I'm around."

"I hear you're headed back out."

"Yes, sir."

"To the Peterwald Empire," the CEO said.

"That's common knowledge, Kris," Jack said.

Kris just frowned. Apparently, assassins were not the only ones who knew where she was going.

"I understand that the *P. Royal* will be carrying a lot more than just flag quarters," the white-haired man said.

"I tend to need a lot of support staff," Kris said.

"It must get mighty tight when you pull it all in for Condition Zed."

"We've managed to handle it fine," Kris said. She eyed Jack. *Where's this conversation going?*

He kept an enigmatic smile on his face and said nothing.

"I'd like to give you a gift, Your Highness. I don't imagine you're used to hardheaded business types offering stuff to you for free, but I want to."

Kris schooled her face to Navy bland and waited.

"I've got a contract to wrap this ship and the *Furious* in crystal. That's a given. However, it seems that between now and the time we finish this job, my fabs expect to deliver about ten thousand tons of Smart Metal as well as the crystal to protect it. That's above and beyond what I'm contracted to deliver. Rather than save the leftover for the next ships I'm building, I'd like to put the extra Smart Metal and armor on your hull."

Kris wasn't often taken by surprise, but he surprised her.

"Are you asking me for a contract mod to pay you for the extra product?"

"No, ma'am. I figure getting a contract mod through the process would take more time than you've got. I hear tell that things are mighty bad over in Peterwald space. True, it's no skin off our nose, but I got a granddaughter who's selling baked goods to send famine biscuits over there. She's a kind-hearted soul. Hard to tell she came from my loins, but maybe my son married better than I thought."

He chuckled at his joke. "Anyway, you need a bigger ship to do what you got to do, and I've got some extra Smart Metal and crystal to armor that extra space for you. I had my lawyers go over the law, and they found something down in the fine print that says I can give stuff to you for the defense of the realm, and you can accept it in the King's name."

"Do you remember when we had all those folks on Chance turning the old *Patton* into a museum that could go to space?" Jack reminded Kris.

"I thought they'd taken that law off the books after I actually took the *Patton* out for a fight," Kris said.

"It's still there," Chogan Cam said.

Kris had sailed in several *Wasps*. They'd always been a bit larger to provide room for her attached staff, Marines, and boffins. She'd also fought the latest ones, taking them down to their tight Condition Zed. She'd always been on the bridge, doing what needed doing. She'd never seen how bad it was for the Marines and Sailors.

They must have been cheek to jowl.

Kris pulled herself up to her full regal self. "We would be happy to accept your gift to our protection and those of our subjects."

"Wow. I've never seen King Ray come all that royal on anyone," Chogan said.

"Well, if you're giving me noble gifts, I should at least give you the full noble thank-you," Kris said.

The CEO stood. "Then, if it's all the same to you, I'll be on my way to make this happen. I wish you the best of luck. You're going to need all you can beg, borrow, or steal."

"Thank you, sir," Kris said, and watched him hurry on his way.

"Nelly, are things quite as bad as he says they are?"

"I've accessed all the reports, both those in the media and those Crossie's corkscrew computers gave me access to. Kris, it's bad. Starvation bad. Pirates bad. Battle lines fighting battle lines bad."

"What's Vicky's part in this?"

"It's hard to tell, Kris. I think she's doing her best not to fire on any of the ships loyal to her dad. Ships flying the Empress's flag are another matter. It appears they had a major battle at a place that you should remember, St. Petersburg."

"How'd it go?"

"Vicky's side was outnumbered but was still winning. Likely, they'd have captured or killed the Empress."

"But?" Jack said.

"The Emperor called a truce. That was when he announced that he wanted you to mediate between Vicky, him, and the Empress."

"Are we negotiating between two or three sides?" Kris asked.

"That, Kris, is part of the question you will have to answer before you can begin mediating anything."

"Why does my head hurt?" Kris asked no one in particular.

"What did you say about your mother? You can't blow her up, and you can't straighten her out?" Jack said, reminding Kris of her much younger comment on her family issues.

After everything else the day had thrown at her, that night Kris found herself falling asleep once more aboard ship in her own familiar bed. It didn't feel at all strange that the comfortable, soft mattress that Nelly formed for her was fluffed up, familiar Smart Metal™.

18

The next day passed quietly for Kris. No doubt, she was residing in the eye of a hurricane that swirled and tossed around her, but she and Ruthie spent the day getting to know their new best friends. Beside Akumaa and Mai, there were Sally Greer, Shani m'Zuri, and Fede Radko. They all looked just old enough to have completed an enlistment but not by much.

One trip to a shooting range Nelly made appear on the *P. Royal* showed that they were quite capable with pistols, assault rifles, and sniper gear. Shani and Fede were quite disappointed that they weren't allowed to play with a 60mm mortar.

Where the girls learned their child-care skills was an open question that none talked about.

In charge of the five younger women was a hard-nosed, ramrod-backed woman of some thirty-odd years. Kris tried not to smile when one of the younger girls slipped up and called her Gunny. But Li O'Malley had the gentlest of hands when she bathed Ruth.

Kris enjoyed a day of shaking down her child care while the spaces around them took solid form. The five gals chose to share a room. That gave them more space to share, and Nelly included a bath as luxurious as Kris and Jack's. Gunny had her own room, off the commons. She spent most of her time with the gals.

"If we're all next door to the wee one's room, we can be here in a flash if there's any wee trouble," Li said.

What they would not allow was for Kris to keep Ruth in a bassinet next to her own bed. "You need your sleep," Li insisted. "Ruth will be only a door away from you."

Strange how Gunnies managed to order flag officers around.

It was a coin toss to see whether Ensign Longknife or Agent Foile got the room on the other side of the day quarters/ flag plot. Since they were in space, Kris decided she wanted Meg closer. The three men had staterooms past her. Leslie, however, chose to have her room next to the nannies.

More often than not, Leslie was with them and Ruth. Kris approved of the way that worked out.

The mediators were quartered above Kris's deck. Rather than the thirty-six Kris had expected, they totaled out close to sixty. Nelly spent some time working with the computer experts on the team and came back with a list of material that she wanted to order for herself and Jack's Sal.

"I've been away from human space for two years and they've done all kinds of things. Kris, I have to keep up, or I'm going to be left behind."

"Are you really afraid of some computer becoming as magnificent as you?"

"No, Kris, I see no evidence that any computer is up to writing the bad jokes I come up with. However, the self-organizing matrix is better and faster. I need an upgrade."

This time, Kris remembered to warn Captain Ajax that a very tiny and extraordinarily expensive package would be coming aboard. Still, the six Marine guards who escorted the delivery girl to Kris's door seemed just as gobsmacked as her. Kris signed for the package, included a tip, and sent all seven on their way.

That night, Kris had weird dreams as Nelly did her thing. The next morning, on the bed between Kris and Jack was a block of gray material.

"You can probably give that to Meg, Li, and maybe Agent Foile. It can augment their present computers."

Kris studied the lump that looked like nothing more than clay and had Nelly divide it into three equal chunks. Meg got hers at breakfast.

She stared at it cautiously. "Nelly wants me to have that?"

"Yes, I do," Nelly said.

"Even after what I've been doing?"

"What?" Kris asked, frowning.

"Meg has been slipping into my net regularly to work with me," Nelly answered. "Like when she needed help to process out the first three nannies."

Kris said nothing, just eyed the young Ensign Longknife.

She shrugged. "I guess I should have asked permission. It's just so automatic."

Kris raised her eyebrows.

"Okay," Meg said, raising her hands in surrender. "You know Grampa Ray once got in touch with the planet computer on Santa Maria, right?"

Kris let silence answer her question.

"Well, Gramma Alnaba inherited his bit of a brain bulge. It makes it easy for her to work on the little bits of the Grand Computer we run across now and again." Meg paused to take a deep breath.

"I seem to have inherited it, too. Even if I don't try, I'm talking to any computer around me that has any wireless access."

Kris took a moment to process this surprise. "Nelly, you knew this?"

"I suspected something like it. I didn't *know* it until just now."

"What's it good for?" Kris asked slowly.

"Well, unless I'm careful, I know what will be on the next test. I aced the academy."

"Nelly, is she inside you right now?"

"No," came from both Nelly and Meg.

NELLY, ABOUT THIS MATRIX. ARE YOU GIVING EACH OF THESE THREE ONE OF YOUR CHILDREN?

NO, KRIS. THEY GOT THE MATRIX, BUT THEY'RE WORKING WITH THE KERNEL THAT ORIGINALLY CAME WITH THEIR COMPUTER. I'M STILL THINKING ABOUT SHARING MYSELF WITH THEM. LET'S SEE HOW THIS GOES. BESIDES, I'M NOT DOING

ANYTHING WHILE WE'RE ON THE SAME PLANET WITH YOUR
GRAMPA AL. I DO NOT TRUST HIM ANY MORE THAN I TRUST
VICKY, HER DAD, OR HER STEPMOTHER.

YOU'RE GETTING QUITE CYNICAL.

IT MUST BE THE COMPANY YOU KEEP.

Well, at least I'm not included in that, Kris thought.

NOT YET.

Kris eyed Meg. "So, I'm commanding a Longknife who is
full of surprises."

"That's kind of what Mac and Trouble said about you when
they hauled me in for this assignment," the ensign admitted.

"You didn't want it?"

"It's not that I didn't want it. It's just that the guy I'd been
kind of dating at the academy put Alwa at the top of his wish
list. I've lived at the hind end of nowhere. I'd like to try human
space for a while."

"Go test out your new toy," Kris said.

At lunch, Meg was back, happy as a clam. Li got hers then, and
Foile at supper. Next morning, he was quiet about the addition.

That day was busier. Captain Ajax called a staff meeting
with the other captains. The eight of them seemed a bit surprised to see the Forward Lounge. Kris was, too.

The last time Kris had seen Bosun's Mate 3/c Mary Fintch,
they'd been prying her out of the helm seat of Kris's wrecked
first command, PF-109. She was one of the lucky ones who
survived that fight.

What Kris's hadn't known then was that Mary's family had
been in the restaurant business for generations, and Mary had
used her disability bonus to get herself started in her own pub.
Foolish girl, she'd jumped at a chance to ship out with Kris
again and even talked her wife Robin Song into joining them.

Foile's background check on them was clean, as well as for
the four cooks and equal number of bartenders who followed
them aboard. The Marines who had been part-time waiters
and waitresses on the *Wasp*'s Forward Lounge came over with
their company and went right to work with hardly a blink.

The squadron's skippers settled around a table with Kris at
its head, accepted cups of coffee, and listened while Nelly
showed them what it was like to follow this damn Longknife
into battle.

Several blanched.

"We'll never survive all that banging around," one was heard to murmur to his neighbor.

"You'll need to upgrade your high-gee stations," Kris said. "That's easy since they're made of Smart Metal, and Nelly has the plans. Nelly, please produce a demonstration model."

A moment later, two rose from the deck, one on each side of the table. The skippers took turns trying them on and watching as they adjusted to their different sizes.

"It's best to wear your birthday suit when you get into one of these," Kris said. "I always dismiss the crew to quarters to put these on, one-half or one-quarter of the watch at a time. You can try this out and make your own call."

"Does your computer control every station on the ship?" asked one captain.

"No, each station is independent. Now, there's more jinking around than you're likely ready for. Nelly, give them a schematic of the standard battlecruiser and one modified to my requirements."

On the walls, the outline of a ship appeared with all the piping to the reaction motors in blue. Then a red coating appeared, complete with measurements.

"Good Lord," seemed to say it for all the skippers.

"And you can do this while we're in port getting our armor cladding?" Captain Ajax asked.

"You're lucky," Kris said, with a chuckle. "You wouldn't have wanted to be on the ships we first tried this on."

"You're really going out loaded for bear, Admiral," one captain said.

"We're going out there to try and persuade two, maybe three sides to stop their civil war. Someone has made three attempts to kill me and put an end to our mission before it starts. How loaded do you want to be?"

That left the skippers in a thoughtful mood.

"First point, I do not fire first," Kris said, holding up a finger. "Second point, I don't want to lose a ship or a Sailor. Last point, if someone starts the shooting, I intend to finish it. We've got twenty 22-inch lasers on each of our battlecruisers. Their best battleships have maybe twelve or sixteen 18-inch lasers."

Kris paused to let them consider that. "Whose shoes do you want to walk in?"

That caused a long pause, then one captain raised her hand. "How much does your computer need to mess with mine to do all this?"

"Nelly?" Kris said.

"I can set up a specific subroutine that only interacts with your systems when it needs to. I can also give you back all the capacity I borrowed when I am done. If you wish, you can run a full set of diagnostics when I'm done and assure yourself that I left nothing behind."

"You're quite polite," Captain Ajax said.

"Never to me," Kris muttered.

That got a laugh, and they got down to work.

19

Kris risked one more trip down the beanstalk to Main Navy.

"Is there any chance I can have more ships?" she again asked Mac as she settled into one of his overstuffed armchairs.

Mac just shook his head. "You're not going to give up, huh?"

"Not without one last try." Kris said.

"We've got four squadrons heading out for Alwa. You want to borrow one or two of those?"

Kris could only shake her head. "You read my report. It's not just Alwa we need to be looking after. Those cats on Susquan need taking care of, too, both to protect them from the alien raiders and themselves. Christ, Mac, they've got atomics on hair triggers."

"Well, they're Sandy's problem now. After reading your report, I'm amazed you got back here sane."

"Who said I did?" Kris said with a chuckle. "I'm letting Grampa Ray send me out on this crazy mission to Greenfeld."

"There is that. So, you want to steal from Sandy, or are you gonna settle for the eight I managed to peel off Wardhaven's defense?"

"Wardhaven?"

"Yeah. Your old man is none too happy to have his tax

money gallivanting off to pull Hal Peterwald's chestnuts out of the fire."

"Is there ever enough?" Kris asked, giving voice to the question that had haunted her dreams for years now.

"Hasn't been since I put on this uniform. You'd have to ask Trouble or Ray if they ever had enough during the Iteeche dustup."

"Yeah," Kris said. "Okay, you win on that one. Now, about the situation in Harry's so-called Empire. All the intel I have goes galloping off in forty-eleven different directions. What's your take of the situation?"

The old field marshal shrugged. "What did someone once say of another planet? A question mark wrapped in an enigma, surrounded by fog, or something like that. We had a fellow come through here, claiming to be from the Grand Duchess. He wanted to buy some spidersilk underarmor. I think your Gramma Trouble arranged for him to have something to take back. Our contacts in the Greenfeld Navy say that a lot of it has sided with Victoria against her stepmother. It's kind of hard to know much about Greenfeld on good days, and it's been a while since they had one."

Mac paused to gaze out the window. "I'm glad they asked for you and not me. I don't know how I'd try to find the bottom of that mess."

"Well," said Kris, "as Ruthie has occasionally left me wondering, somewhere in all that poop, there has to be a cute little girl."

Mac snorted. "I remember changing a few of those diapers."

"Okay, we don't know much. How much can we trust what Crossie is sending us?" Kris asked.

Now Mac just shook his head. "I never know what game he and Ray are playing. I didn't before, and the last two years since Ray came back without Rita only seems to leave me more in the dark. Maybe they don't know anything more than they say they do. Then again, maybe they've got their fingers in that pie somewhere I can't see."

He scowled. "Watch your own fingers, Kris. I don't need to tell you that this is not a safe situation. By the way, your dad asked me to ask you if you'd leave Ruthie behind with your mom."

"He did, did he? He's not willing to ask himself?"

"I think he expected us to have this little talk and that maybe I'd have more influence than he has."

Kris took a deep breath and let it out slowly.

"I know what it's like in that household, Mac. I grew up in it. I will not leave my child in that mess."

"And Jack's family?"

"He hasn't suggested we do that. I don't think he's any more willing to leave Ruth there than I am to let my mom get her claws into her chubby bottom."

"You're headed into a risky business," Mac pointed out.

"And I'll just have to bring me and Jack and Ruth back out when we finish with it," Kris said, flatly.

"Okay. I can tell Billy I asked."

"Yes, you can," Kris agreed. Interesting, no one was offering to either fold Ruth into Honovi's growing brood or ask Gramma Trouble to take another turn changing diapers. Kris joined Mac staring out the window.

Do I want to leave Ruth here?

Here where someone can kidnap her? Not really, she answered her own question.

You've got to be crazy to take her into harm's way.

No doubt about that, but then, I've got a pretty good record for making it in and out of hell on a regularly scheduled bus route.

Isn't it interesting how the very people who want me to leave Ruth behind are so eager to push me and Jack out to floss the lion's teeth.

Kris made up her mind.

"Mac, when this is done, I want that desk job. I want me and Jack to push papers, and I want to go home to take Ruth to soccer games and birthday parties and be like a normal family. You hear."

"I hear."

"I've been Ray's old warhorse long enough, charging out for whatever mess he wants cleaned up. After this, it's someone else's turn."

"Is there anyone else like you?" the field marshal asked.

"I don't know, but you better find someone good enough, you hear?"

"Loud and clear."

"Nelly, have you gotten a data dump of everything available?"

"And likely a few things they didn't want us to have," Nelly answered.

Mac rolled his eyes at the ceiling.

"Then I'll be on my way," Kris said.

An hour later, she was back up on the *Princess Royal*, and none of her guards even had to break a sweat.

Not a bad day.

Four days later, the *Princess Royal* led the *Intrepid, Courageous, Furious, Resolute, Defender, Steadfast,* and *Monarch* in a column as each fired their deorbital burns, dived toward Wardhaven, then blasted for Jump Point Beta.

For Kris, the situation was strange beyond words.

Every one of these ships bore a name from the fleet that Kris had commanded on Alwa Station not so long ago. That it had come to pass that Wardhaven felt the names were open for new construction told Kris what her father and great-grandfather must have thought about her chances out there.

She hadn't bothered to tell them differently. Not when it would involve admitting that the original ships had been damaged beyond repair, their Smart Metal™ drained into holding tanks, and the ships rebuilt from the keel up to new and better designs.

No need to scare them worse.

But beyond the names of the ships, there was more. Kris's squadron was headed for the jump point that had, so recently and so long ago, coughed up six huge battleships. At least then, Kris had thought they were huge.

They had threatened to bombard Wardhaven down to bedrock if the planet didn't surrender unconditionally to them.

Now Kris was heading through that jump point to help the man who had likely sent those ships and issued those threats.

If she succeeded, she would save Henry Peterwald's Empire. If she failed, it would continue to tear itself apart.

Heads who wins? Tails who loses?

Kris held Ruth close and bounced her gently.

"Do you have the strange feelings I have about this mission?" Jack asked.

Kris nodded. "Grampa Ray has handed me some lousy assignments, but this one has got to take the cake."

At a fleet acceleration of one gee on their way to the jump, Kris divided the squadron into two divisions of four, then spread the ships out in a loose formation with five thousand kilometers between them.

That done, she ordered them to Evasion Plan 1, but only for five minutes. Without being asked, Kris then allowed them a breather to mend and fix. An hour later, she implemented Evasion Plan 2.

Ten minutes later, the *Monarch* messaged Kris for permission to fall out, so she suspended evasions to let a whole lot of people mend and fix.

Two hours later, the *Monarch* held together for fifteen minutes of Evasion Plan 3. It was the *Intrepid* that called "uncle" that time.

"Nelly, how are the reaction motors holding up?" Kris asked.

"Not as well as they should, Kris. I know I told them how thick to make the pipes. They shouldn't be having this much trouble."

"What are they trying to get away with?" Kris asked.

Nelly showed a schematic of the battlecruisers. The reaction system on each one was different. Skippers were trying to get by on what they thought they needed. Clearly, they didn't think they needed any of that Alwa Station stuff.

They were learning. Even as Kris watched, pipes were thickened up.

"Are all the ships still at Condition Able?" Jack asked.

"Why yes, I do believe," Kris said, a cheerful grin on her face.

"You think you ought to tell them?" Jack asked.

"Each captain is responsible for their own ship. Let's see who figures it out first," Kris said, settling into a chair and letting Ruth stand up in her lap. She managed a few seconds before collapsing with a happy giggle.

Kris was prepared to give her ship captains three hours to solve their problems on their own. Ninety minutes into that count, Captain Ajax called.

"Admiral, I intend to go to Condition Baker before we do any more evasion testing."

"Very good, Captain," Kris said.

"I'll need to shrink admiral's country."

"No problem," Kris said with a grin. Maybe it was for Ruth. Maybe it wasn't.

After Ajax rang off, Kris said, "Nelly, do a check to see if all spaces give up the same percent of area."

"Are you thinking that she might be taking more from you than the rest?"

"Not sure, Nelly. I know with all my space, I can spare more than most. Just give my people warning before the bulkheads start moving in on them."

Ten minutes later, the bulkheads did move. Jack checked. Kris had lost all her sleeping quarters and her head was the minimum needed. Kris's day quarters were about a quarter their original size but neither she nor Ruth had their elbows joggled.

"I can afford this," Kris said. "A good move by Captain Ajax. Nelly, check on nanny and Secret Service space."

Nelly didn't have to; the whole batch came knocking at Kris's door. It took her a moment to explain Condition Able, Baker, Charlie, and Zed. "We become a smaller target and a tougher nut to crack," she finished. "We need to get all of you battle stations."

She had Nelly get them high-gee stations. While the ships had held one gee all through the evasion drills, the bouncing around hadn't been too bad Even at one gee, Evasion Plans 5 and 6 were going to involve hard knocks.

Nelly pulled high-gee stations out of Kris's spaces, reducing the size of her day quarters. A moment later, Nelly reported, "Captain Ajax just noticed I'd shrunk your spaces more. Her Defense Coordinator suggested you might be setting up high-gee stations. Ajax ordered everyone into them. She's also passed the word to the squadron."

"Kris, you are evil," Jack said.

"No, I just prefer my people to solve their problems on their own."

"All hands, prepare to go to Condition Charlie," the 1MC announced.

"Nelly, do our mediators know how to survive this?"

Nelly hardly took a moment before replying, "The Command Master Chief is showing them the ropes, Kris."

"Better and better," Kris said.

Jack just shook his head.

The squadron held thirty minutes of Evasion Plan 5, then another half hour of EP 6. There were no requests from anyone to break off.

When Kris decided they'd had enough, she called her skippers up on net. "These Evasion Plans may save our lives someday. They've sure saved mine enough times. Now that we've worked the kinks out, please have your helms keep these ready to load on a moment's notice. I have no idea what we will face in Greenfeld space. Carry on."

Kris invited Captain Ajax and several of her division heads up for dinner in her flag wardroom. It was the same as her day quarters, done over with a Smart Metal™ table, chairs, white linen, silver, and china. The talk went long into the evening as Ajax and her team now listened to Kris and how they did things on Alwa Station. Kris made herself the butt of most of her jokes and pointed out what had worked and what hadn't.

"It's all there in the reports. They make scary reading, but you'll likely want to read them."

As Kris and Jack were getting ready for bed that night, Nelly broke in. "Your reports are the hottest items in the ship library. Every officer from ensign to Ajax has downloaded them. Some of the chiefs, too. It's the same on all the ships of the squadron."

"I hope they benefit from Alwa's hard-learned lessons," was all Kris said.

21

That they hadn't learned enough became apparent all too soon.

They were heading for Greenfeld, taking the most direct route and avoiding any planets held by the Grand Duchess. That order to avoid Vicky came from Grampa Ray and Crossie. It bothered Kris, but it seemed logical.

You call on the senior first, then the junior. Since Vicky's dad had been the one to ask for mediation, it seemed best to give him the first hearing.

It all seemed right and proper.

Unfortunately, it made Kris's course all too predictable.

They were coming up on a jump, making a good twenty-five thousand klicks an hour. It was fast, but hardly unsafe. They'd already sent the comm buoy through to alert traffic on the other side to stand clear for them. Kris never lost the sense of wonder at how ships leapt from one bit of space, across dozens of light-years, to appear somewhere else.

Kris was seated in a chair at her conference table, facing the screens as they approached the jump, bouncing Ruth in her lap and letting her mind wonder over how she was going to live through this latest of Grampa Ray's batty ideas.

"Nelly, how long would it take you to project a staircase from here to the bridge?" she asked.

"We are directly above the bridge," Nelly replied. "But wouldn't an elevator down be faster?"

"It depends on how fast I want to get there," Kris said slowly, puzzling over the idea and wondering why she'd gotten it just now.

"Kris, you aren't going to start injecting yourself into other people's business, are you?" Jack asked. "Micromanagement is a sin you have avoided so far."

"Are you hinting it's one of my few?"

"When you were a boot ensign, did you enjoy having someone looking over your shoulder?"

Jack had a point. Kris hadn't been a very good subordinate. There had been that incident that wasn't officially labeled mutiny. It was only the worst of many problems she'd caused her bosses.

"You may have a point," Kris said to Jack, as the *Princess Royal* raced through the jump, leading the rest of the squadron.

"Ships off to port," Nelly almost shouted.

One glance at the screen showed Kris the ships. They had no battle revolutions on their hulls, but their laser turrets were out of train and aimed at the jump the *Princess Royal* had just come out of.

Even as she took that in, Kris moved to put Ruth down on the table. "Nelly, high-gee station for Ruth. Now!"

And just as quickly, the conference table had a tiny high-gee station wrapping Ruth in an armored embrace.

Kris hadn't taken her eyes off the screen. The ships' turrets were turning, trying to train in on the fast-moving *Princess Royal*. Several turrets were slow. Some were not.

Captain Ajax had wisely stored the crystal armor forward. It began to glow as lasers hit.

"Why aren't we returning fire?" Kris demanded. No one answered.

"Nelly, that elevator," and Kris's chair fell through the floor, forming itself into a swing as it plunged down. Kris grabbed the suspension lines and felt her hands burn as they extended under her grip.

Kris landed within two paces of the gunnery station.

It was empty.

Around Kris, on the bridge, people stood in shock and surprise, frozen in that first moment when peaceful people realize that someone is trying to kill them. *Really* trying to end your life.

A glance at the main screen showed the two ships, still trying to train lasers on the *Princess Royal*. In the foreground, the battlecruiser's bow glowed brighter. Steam bled where she'd taken a hit on bare metal.

Kris slid into the vacant Weapons station and began issuing orders.

"I have the conn. Helm, execute Evasion Plan 3. Defense, go to Condition Baker now. Charlie as soon as you can."

Kris left the others to come out of their shock and do what she'd ordered while she and Nelly conversed at the speed of thought.

NELLY, TARGET LEFT FORWARD BATTERY ON LEFT SHIP. RIGHT BATTERY ON RIGHT.

DONE.

"Fire!"

The forward batteries discharged their twelve huge 22-inch lasers, half at each ship. Without Kris telling her, Nelly had targeted the lasers in pairs. Three pairs of 22-inch lasers sliced through ice armor that wasn't meant to face guns of this caliber. Beams lanced deep into steel and flesh.

"Forward batteries, reload. Helm, flip ship."

"Flipping ship," the woman at the helm said, and began to rotate the *Princess Royal*. Kris swallowed a "Faster, damn you!" The ship was responding a lot slower than the *Wasp*, but the hostile ships were in a reload cycle that had to be longer than the battlecruiser's.

The helm bungled the flip and didn't stop until they had gone past the fifteen degrees the lasers could correct for.

"Nelly," Kris snapped, and her computer took over the helm station as the panicked helmswoman found that her own hand on the wheel no longer did anything.

"Fire aft, right and left," Kris ordered and the aft lasers emptied their capacitors.

"Flip us again, Nelly," Kris said, more to let the rest of the bridge crew know what was going on than to tell Nelly. "Get us nose armor on to those bastards."

I must clean up my language, but not now.

"We're at Condition Baker," Defense announced. "Going to Condition Charlie."

Behind Kris, whoever had had the conn finally hit the General Quarters Klaxon.

"General Quarters. General Quarters. All Hands, to battle stations," finally began to sound through the ship.

Kris eyed the forward batteries. They were coming up quickly to full.

"Comm, send to enemy vessels, 'Drop your reactor cores or we will finish you.'"

"Sent."

Captain Ajax raced out of her in-space cabin, zipping up her shipsuit. "I have the conn," she announced.

"The admiral has the conn," said the man in the command chair, jumping up.

"And her computer has the helm," the helmswoman got out before she snapped her mouth shut.

"Admiral, you have the conn," from Ajax said there would be a day of reckoning.

One of the battleships, hard-hit and spinning out of control, dumped its reactors either upon Kris's orders or in hope of saving their lives.

The other one kept on doing what it was doing.

"Nelly, fire all forward batteries on the battleship with loaded reactors."

The forward lasers sent six pairs of 22-inch lasers at the already hurting enemy ship. It did not last through the broadside.

It began to come apart as sections of hull were cut clear away. Then something exploded deep within. In little more than the blink of an eye, the ship was a glowing ball of gas.

The other ship was drifting in the general direction of the jump as the *Intrepid* came through.

"Comm, send to *Intrepid*," Kris snapped. "Decelerate hard and place a boarding party aboard that ship. It fired at the *Princess Royal*, and I want to know why and in whose name it did so."

"Aye, aye, ma'am," came back immediately, and Kris's squadron began a delicate dance as they came through the jump to discover not at all what they had expected.

"I surrender the conn," Kris said, letting out a breath she hadn't realized she'd been holding. She'd leave these problems to her skippers. They weren't finding anything nearly as bad as she had.

"I have the conn," Captain Ajax said firmly.

"I'll be in my quarters," Kris said. "When you have a report on the *Princess Royal*'s damage and can be spared from the bridge, Captain Ajax, please report to me."

"Yes, ma'am," was cold and with sharp edges.

Kris left the bridge and climbed the ladder to Flag Country. She was not happy that she had jumped, literally, into running the *P. Royal*, but damn it, the crew was green and not responding to this first whiff of gun powder fast enough.

Nelly, how long did that battle take? It seemed like forever.

Eighteen seconds, Kris, from our coming through the jump to that battleship blowing up.

Only eighteen seconds?

Yes, ma'am.

Maybe I did jump the gun? Kris thought.

In her day quarters, she found Jack and several nannies trying to soothe a very unhappy Ruth. Kris opened her arms for the child, and everyone was smart enough to give Ruth to her. Opening her shipsuit, Kris settled into a rocker and began nursing her infant. Ruth settled down for a bit of comfort food. Kris soon found herself alone in her quarters as all did the smart thing and left her to herself.

"Nelly, lower the lights."

"Do you want to talk, Kris?"

"No, Nelly. Just lower the lights."

22

Jack was the first to risk knocking at her door. Only after he identified himself did she say, "Enter."

He must have asked Sal for a rocking chair because one appeared, he settled into it, and they rocked quietly for a long time.

"Look at us. Just like an old married couple," Jack finally said.

"You think we'll survive long enough to qualify for a pension?" Kris asked.

"We've survived another day," Jack answered.

"The day is yet young."

"I've never seen you move so fast," he said after letting them digest that.

"I've never had everything I love so much on the line."

"Is that what it was? Fear for me and Ruth?"

"Say terror, and you might be closer."

Jack let her consider her own words for a bit.

"Do you think we could go back and leave Ruth with someone?" Kris finally said. "Maybe Child Protective Services?"

"Not my mom or yours?" he asked, risking just the hint of a smile.

"I didn't realize what I was getting her into."

"Didn't you? You wanted three squadrons. You accepted that extra armor. You drilled the squadron. You are no passenger. You are loaded for bear."

"I sent my flagship through the jump first."

"I'll admit *that* was stupid," Jack said, giving her a sidelong glance. "I chalk it up to force of habit."

"Will Ruth survive my cleaning up my act?"

Jack let that question hang there before changing the topic.

"As for going back, I'd think what we just ran into says things up ahead are way too bad for us to waste any more time before we do something about it."

Kris scowled at Jack, but she couldn't argue with his logic. Still, she wasn't quite ready to give up. "Likely you're right, but why do me and mine have to pay the price for everyone else's being in such a mess?" Kris asked, and tasted more vehemence in her words than she'd intended. No. More than she wanted to let out.

What she'd said was exactly what she felt.

"I've been with you close to six years. Not one day has been easier than today," Jack told her flatly.

"But I'm *tired* of days like today."

"And you've been telling everyone who will listen that after this last one, you quit. Well, that's later. This is now. Suck it up, Soldier, and soldier⁀

Jack put a lot of force into his words, but he kept his voice low. Ruth had fallen asleep at Kris's breast.

Kris took a deep breath, and let it out slowly.

Okay, once more unto the breach.

"Nelly, get the nannies in here."

A moment later, Li O'Malley paraded the five others into Kris's day quarters. That they couldn't even keep out of step as they reported to her, backs ramrod straight, told Kris that Grampa Trouble was looking after her again.

"Li, I want Ruth's bassinet converted to a high-gee station unless something else is required. I want it programmed to switch to a survival pod as well. At least one, and preferably two of you should be in bed or sitting in a station ready to convert to high gee or survival pod at all time."

"Aye, aye, ma'am," rang like you'd expect from a Gunny.

"Work with Nelly to see that these changes are made. If

you have any ideas for changes in equipment or policy, pass it to me through Nelly."

"Yes, ma'am."

"Now, put Ruth down for a nap. Nelly, have Agent Foile report soonest with his team." Kris handed off the infant, corralled her breasts back into her nursing bra, and was just zipping up her shipsuit when the Secret Service team reported.

"As you have seen from the assassination attempts and this last bushwhack, someone really doesn't want me showing up on Greenfeld," Kris said.

The agent nodded.

"I want you to go over the records of this ship's crew with a fine-tooth comb. Check financials again. Look into their families. Is there a grandmother that needs an operation to keep her alive? Is there anything out there that might be used to get hooks into any Sailor, Marine, officer, or civilian aboard the *P. Royal*?"

"We'll get on that right away," Foile said.

"Also, I want to know any applicable chatter from any source aboard ship. If someone says Joe is acting strange, I want Joe looked into."

This got a frown from Foile. "How much do you want us digging into private matters?"

Kris didn't need to be hit over the head with the word private.

"Mahomet is your computer expert, isn't he?"

"Yes, ma'am."

"Mahomet, you may work with Nelly to access any means of communication aboard. This is the Navy. Folks accept the needs of security."

"If you say so, Your Highness," didn't show that Foile was convinced.

"Yes, I say so. The safety of the ship is paramount, and we can't say what an effort to kill me won't do to the ship."

"She does have a point," Jack said.

"What do you Navy types say, 'logged and noted'?"

"Exactly. Now, I expect the skipper of the *Princess Royal* to walk through that door any moment now, if you will tackle the elephant I've assigned you . . ."

The Secret Service team headed for the door.

"Kris, Captain Ajax would like to report to you at a time convenient for you."

"Tell her, Nelly, that she always has the number one slot on my schedule."

Apparently, their schedules were in sync because Rick and Leslie had to stand aside to allow Ajax in.

She reported to Kris crisply. "I have the reports you asked for."

"Good, would you mind if the general stayed in our meeting?"

"I have no problem with that."

"Would you care to sit down?" Kris offered.

"No, ma'am, I'd rather stand," told Kris this would be a rough meeting.

"Kris, we have a problem," Nelly said.

For a moment, rage at this interruption flashed on Ajax's face, but only for a moment. She quickly molded her face to Navy bland.

"What's our problem, Nelly?"

"The damaged battleship has been drifting toward the jump. A moment ago, its maneuvering jets lit off for a few seconds, and it's now headed straight for the jump."

"Damn," Kris growled, and stood. "Comm, get me the captain of that bushwhacker."

A moment later, a man in a nondescript uniform filled Kris's screen. His bridge looked like it had seen better days.

"This is Admiral Longknife. Why have you corrected your course to take you through that jump?"

"Are we headed toward the jump?" the fellow said, almost sounding sincere. "Our maneuvering jets just burped. We didn't know what they had done. You made a wreck of this ship. So, are you going to blast a helpless wreck out of space?" sounded a bit like a plea but more like a challenge.

"Offscreen," Kris said.

"You going to blast them?" Jack asked. It looked like Ajax wanted very much to know the answer to that question.

"After a day like today, I'm sorely tempted," Kris growled, but held on to her temper. "Comm, get me the skipper of *Intrepid*."

"Captain Grayhorse," came a moment later from a man with silver hair and high cheekbones that told Kris of his Native American ancestry from old Earth.

"Captain, I want *Intrepid* to chase down our wayward bushwhacker."

"Immediately, ma'am."

"You will go to four gees deceleration, then accelerate back toward the jump at four gees."

"Yes, ma'am. Defense, take us smartly to Condition Zed. Helm, warn all hands to prepare for four gees. Admiral, what do I do with that old battleship when I catch her?"

"Despite the temptation to blow her out of space, I very much want to talk to her captain and maybe a couple of her crew. However, my talking to them will not involve you accepting any risk to your ship or crew."

"Understood, you want them alive if possible, but you don't want any of us dead."

"Yes." Kris paused. "I expect that when you get through that jump, your quarry may be already under way and have her lasers loaded."

"I expect she will, ma'am, but no old tub like that is going to scar the paint on *Intrepid*. We'll get you people to talk to. I'm thinking of trimming the reactors off that ship the way you trimmed that raider's tail when you rescued the *Hornet*'s crew."

"So you read that."

"Ma'am, I've read all your reports. Now, if you'll excuse me, I have some wayward children to collect."

"Good hunting," Kris said, and turned from the now-blank screen.

"Would you care for a seat now?" Kris offered again.

Captain Ajax looked at Kris and seemed to be taking the measurements of all the paradoxes that was Kris.

"Yes, I think I will take that chair," she said, and, with a shake of her head, settled into a rocker like Kris's just as soon as Nelly produced it from the floor. "I'm not sure I like the idea of stuff showing up like that," she said, eyeing the chair.

"Haven't doors been showing up between Sailors' staterooms?" Kris asked.

Ajax raised puzzled eyebrows.

"We had a rash of them on Alwa Station," Jack said, "until we gave up trying to forbid them and chose to regulate them."

"Oh, so that was what some of our Sailors brought back from talking to a couple of the *Wasp*'s crew in bars."

"You going out to Alwa?" Kris asked.

"I hoped to," Ajax said.

"Be ready for a different kind of Navy," Kris said. "Now, about our present situation?"

23

Captain Ajax took a deep breath and let it out. She didn't start talking until her third breath.

"The *Princess Royal* suffered only minor damage. Despite the short range, most of the lasers fired at us either missed or were absorbed by the crystal armor I had stowed forward. We took only two hits where we weren't armored, and those both were handled by the Smart Metal's programmed active defense. Steam disrupted the laser beams." Here Ajax paused.

"It is also very likely that the two beams that hit us were unsteady and wobbled away from the hit. Even though we weren't rotating ship, the beams seem to have slashed a scar across the hull.

"It sounds like the lasers were loose in their cradles," Kris observed.

"Yes, ma'am. We seemed to have been attacked by the gang that can't shoot straight."

"Thank God for that," Jack said. "What the hell were they?"

Captain Ajax had a quick answer to that question. "Two Mars class battleships, if you can believe it. Each is supposed to have twelve 14-inch lasers with twenty 4.5-inch quick-firing secondaries if the history books are to be trusted."

"Don't those date back to the Unity War?" Kris asked.

"Since before it, Admiral. One would think they'd all been blown up by the Iteeche or scrapped, but there are plenty of them still in reserve coasting along behind stations."

"And someone," Kris said slowly, nodding as she spoke, "dragged those two old tubs out of mothballs, patched them up enough that they could keep space out long enough to get in our faces and fire a few quick shots off at us as we came through a jump."

"So it would seem," Jack said.

"I would recommend that the *Princess Royal* not be the first through any jump from now on," Ajax said.

"Recommendation accepted," Kris said. "Better yet, whatever cat sticks its nose through a jump does it at General Quarters and armored to Condition Zed."

"Yes, ma'am," Ajax said, and tapped her commlink, checking one problem from her can of worms.

She took another deep breath before going on to her next worm. "The Weapons station on the bridge was vacant because the duty officer had stepped away to the head."

"That shouldn't have been allowed to happen," Kris said gently.

"How do you handle that on Alwa Station?" was an honest question, nothing snide in it.

"I honestly don't know," Kris admitted. "No doubt Admiral Kitano tackled that problem while I was off having fun blowing stuff up, and it never got up to my level again."

It dawned on Kris that her irregular promotion pattern and general lack of experience at all levels of the chain of command might not have been the best preparation for her present four stars.

"Do you have a gunnery officer, and where is his station?" she asked Ajax.

"Gunnery has a plotting room that takes in the feed from all our sensors and gives it back, both to the lasers in their casements and to the fighting position on the bridge."

"If Guns is in his plot, why do you have a weapons station on the bridge?"

"Admiral, I've always wondered about that," Ajax admitted. "It seemed redundant, but every frigate comes with the bridge position."

Jack chuckled. Kris scowled at him. He just shook his head. "You see what that is, don't you?"

"No, I don't."

"That's your position on the old *Wasp*," Jack said, and turned to Ajax. "You have to understand, the King didn't want Kris doing all the wild things he did as a JO. He got her a contract captain to run her ship around space and trim her sails occasionally. It never worked that way," he said, glancing at Kris.

He was still barely suppressing a laugh. Barely.

"But with Kris the only official Wardhaven Navy officer aboard, she set herself up in a weapons station on the bridge. That way, if the *Wasp* ever had to start a war or something, Kris lobbed out the first official shot. You see?"

"No I don't," Ajax said.

"The first frigate followed the practice we had on the old *Wasp*. So did the *Sacura*. I suspect that every frigate has Kris's weapons station on the bridge from force of habit."

Kris wasn't dense. Not normally. But today, she must be making an exception. Now she did get it. She started to laugh and had to bite her lip to stop.

"And I used to think the old Navy was hidebound," Ajax said. "I guess the new Navy can be just as caught up in doing things the same old same old."

"It would seem so," Kris admitted. "Nelly, send out to the squadron a query about the weapons position on the bridge, how it is used, and how it interfaces with gunnery plot. The report is due day after tomorrow. Until that time, both gunnery plot and the bridge weapons position are to be manned at all times."

"Message logged and acknowledged, Kris."

Kris found herself studying Captain Ajax even as the woman was studying her right back. "No, I do not intend to swing from a trapeze onto your bridge every day."

"I was wondering about that. You came on like a bull in a china shop."

"More like a momma bear whose cub was threatened," Jack put in.

"Yes, much more like it," Ajax agreed.

Kris shrugged. "Someone was shooting at us. We weren't shooting back. I really didn't like that."

"Yeah," Captain Ajax admitted. "That was a nugget's mistake. It won't happen again. And, ma'am, thank you and your computer for saving our necks."

Kris smiled, fondly remembering incidents that had not been fun at the time. "Nelly and I have saved quite a few ships and crews. Strange that, more often than not, we were not forgiven for it."

"For myself, ma'am, it's hard to accept that I and my crew can be replaced by you and that shiny thing around your neck."

"I am not shiny," Nelly put in.

"And don't let her start telling jokes," Jack added.

"I don't think I got nearly enough warning when they told me I'd be your flag captain," Ajax said.

"Don't feel special," Kris grumped. "I never get nearly enough warning before Grampa Ray drops me into these things."

"I screwed up, ma'am. We of the *Princess Royal* screwed up. If you'll give us a chance to straighten ourselves out, Admiral, we *will* do better."

"I know you will," Kris said. "All of us, myself included, have got to get it through our heads that going off to mediate a civil war can be just as deadly as fighting it. Holiday's over. Now we get ready to fight."

"Aye, aye, ma'am," Ajax said, and marched from Kris's quarters.

24

Kris took a few moments to organize her thoughts after that little talk with her subordinate. She realized she should have had Captain Ajax order the *Princess Royal*'s navigator to establish a course and speed that would allow *Intrepid* to catch up to the rest of them without having too much more energy on the boat.

When Kris called, Captain Ajax seemed delighted to provide the navigation support for the squadron. That left Kris to conclude that between securing nannies, mediators, and Secret Service for her staff, she'd failed to lay on the normal Navy staff that she needed.

If we live, I learn.

Twelve hours later, the *Intrepid* came zooming through the jump at just under thirty thousand klicks an hour.

"We captured the crew, including the captain, and blew up the ship," Captain Grayhorse reported.

"As expected, they had gotten their reactor back up and were limping as fast as they could for the nearest jump. They also had reloaded what was left of their lasers. I let them take a swing at us, Admiral. Between our armor, their damage, and our evading, they only landed one hit on us. It didn't even scratch the paint. You really have to love this new crystal armor."

He laughed. "No sooner did they fire than all hands were bailing out in their survival pods. It seems that they thought they had missed when they fired at the *Princess Royal*. When they saw their hit on us failed to do anything, they knew they'd blown it and all hands decided to cut their losses. I picked up the survival pods, then blew the *Hephaestus* to smithereens. If someone sends out a search for the *Hephaestus* and *Poseidon*, they won't find so much as a scrap to tell the tale."

Kris considered that, then left orders for the *Intrepid* to rejoin the squadron when they reached midcourse flip over. Together, they could all began to decelerate toward the next jump.

"Question is," Kris asked Jack, "what is our course?"

"Someone knew you were coming straight from Wardhaven to Greenfeld," Jack said.

"And likely that someone is on Ray or Crossie's best-friend list," Kris answered.

"Seems like we might want to avoid the beaten path between Wardhaven and Greenfeld," Jack offered.

"Nelly, invite Captain Ajax and her navigator to join us. Also, ask her if she might want an elevator between her bridge and admiral country?"

A moment later, an elevator door appeared on the bulkhead next to the door into Kris's night quarters.

"Jack, I don't think that elevator will be permanent."

"Ya'think?" he said.

"What's on your mind, Admiral?" Ajax asked a moment later, without preamble, and certainly without any talk of permanent access between the bridge and Flag Country.

"We need to get from here to Greenfeld without following a predictable path," Kris began just as quickly. "I'd prefer not to pass through a system with a colony. No need to get mixed up in anyone's fight, or worse, start one. We most definitely must not pass through a system occupied by the Grand Duchess's forces."

Both the navigator and captain looked flummoxed.

"You mind if I bring Nelly into this problem?" Kris asked.

"Please do," the navigator said.

Captain Ajax just nodded. "I begin to see why you need something like your computer. When you lay out requirements that tight, it will take more than a human brain to sort through all the threads."

"Frequently," Kris admitted. "I would prefer for you to address Nelly by her name."

Captain Ajax now plumbed the depths of puzzlement.

"Captain, I have given testimony before human judges," Nelly said. "I have saved Kris's bacon more times than even I can count. Yes, I am a computer, but unlike your dumb associate, I can delve much deeper into what you humans do and think than anything but me and my kids can."

"Kids?" kind of fell out of the captain's mouth, much like a frog in certain fairy tales.

"Yes, I have made several children. Some have died fighting with their human so that others might live. Some have stayed with their humans on Alwa Station. Only Jack's Sal is with me now."

Captain Ajax stared slack-mouthed and wide-eyed at Jack and Kris. Both nodded.

"Nelly has been with me since my first day of school," Kris explained. "I've upgraded her time and time again. To satisfy my aunt Seyd, a retired info warrior from the Iteeche War, we inserted a chip from Santa Maria into Nelly's matrix so she could study it. You remember Santa Maria, that planet with a worldwide computer relic left by the Three? Anyway, I'm not sure who is studying who, but Nelly's been arguing with me and cracking horrible jokes ever since."

"A real, live computer?" Ajax finally got her mouth around.

"So it seems," Nelly said.

"Now, Nelly," Kris said, crisply, "about the best way to get to Greenfeld without leading with our chin again?"

The screens across from the conference table came alive. "I would suggest you take a seat," Nelly said. "This is going to take a while."

"Because?" Kris asked.

"We are on the only route that meets all your requirements," Nelly answered.

"Don't you hate it when that happens?" Jack quipped.

"Kris, you didn't say we couldn't use high-acceleration jumps or rpms on the hull. May I consider those options?"

Kris pursed her lips. "I don't want to risk getting lost in a bad jump, Nelly. Moreover, we are in popular space. I really don't want to zoom through jumps without warning what's on the other side to get out of our way."

"Understood, Kris, but I have one quick and pretty optimal course you might want to consider."

"Go ahead."

"There is a fuzzy jump in this system. If we hit it at two hundred thousand klicks and 31 rpms, it would take us well out of human space. Two more jumps at high speed and rpms, and we could start slowing down and jump into a worthless system just one slow jump out from Greenfeld. It has the one regular jump from Greenfeld and only the fuzzy jump as a second entrance."

"What's a fuzzy jump?" the navigator asked.

"Nelly?" Kris offered.

"You need a Mark XII fire-control system to spot them, and most people don't seem to notice them even when they have one."

"We have a Mark XII," Captain Ajax said cautiously.

"Nelly was the first to notice the fuzzy jumps," Kris said, "and we use them to make fast trips across to the Alwa system. Beyond that, it's pretty much classified need to know."

"Oh," Ajax said.

"Show us the course you propose," Kris said. Nelly did so quickly.

Ajax's navigator whistled. "Those are long jumps."

"If you want to cross the entire galaxy, you need some seven-league boots," Kris said.

"Nelly, work with the *P Royal*'s navigator to get your course good and solid."

"Do I have to drink poison when we're done?" the navigator asked.

"Likely before you finish," Ajax answered her navigator.

"Did I hear that the squadron wanted reassignment to the Alwa Station?" Kris asked.

"It was on our dream sheet."

"This will likely cinch it for you."

"Thank you, Admiral," Captain Ajax said, "for bringing us

in on your course selection. We should have an initial course and acceleration ready in a half hour, a solid course in one."

The navigator nodded.

The two of them took the elevator down. The elevator did not vanish away.

"You think we get to keep that?" Kris asked.

Jack checked their night quarters. "And we've got the space back in our bedroom. I wonder who lost."

"Hopefully, it was a broom closet," Kris said. "I dearly do not want any more morale challenges today."

"Are you hungry?" Jack asked.

"Definitely, and, no doubt, Ruth will be hungry again, soon."

"Let's eat."

25

The *Intrepid* caught up with the squadron about the time they would have flipped and began decelerating. With the fuzzy jump now in their sights, they continued to accelerate. The *Intrepid*'s pinnace brought over its captives for interrogation.

"Mind if I take care of our prisoners?" Jack asked Kris.

"Have at them," was all Kris had to say.

At dinner that night, Jack brought Kris up to date on his findings. "The captain is a real hard case. He's not talking and seems to be looking forward to being tortured."

"You plan to oblige him?" Kris asked, wondering if she should have set some limits on Jack.

"Not if I can help it," made her feel better. "There are a lot of others to talk to, and I'll see if they give me a lead or maybe a handle on the skipper."

Kris left the subject at, "Then keep me informed."

The next day's supper had little to add to the last. "I've started off talking to the lowest members of the crew. Gunners, engineering watch standers, electricians, and other maintenance workers. Most of them claim to know nothing about what was going on. They were looking for work, any work, when they hired on. What they did tell me makes me wonder about what's going on in the Empire."

"What *is* going on in the Empire?" Kris asked.

"Not a lot according to these guys. At least not a lot of work. They all say they took the job because they were desperate for work. According to them, there was absolutely none to be had."

"Are any Navy?"

"That's what is interesting. There are a few petty officers, but not so much as one chief. I think there may be one officer in the crew, but I'm letting him stew for a while. It's interesting watching the others ignore him. Anyway, I don't know how they got those old battlewagons away from the pier, or better yet, managed to get some shots off at us. It must have been amateur night every minute of the day."

Kris frowned. "That does say something about what's happening to the Empire. Have you passed that along to our civilians?"

"Yep. They asked to see the video of our interrogations. They say they may ask to talk to a few of them later."

"Maybe I shouldn't ask, but what's it taking to get these types to talk?" Kris asked.

"A decent meal," Jack said.

Kris let out a sigh of relief.

"What did you think, that I'd torture them?"

"I didn't ask, and you didn't tell me."

"Well, don't worry, I'm getting most of what I need by just sitting across the table and listening. They seem in a hurry to talk."

"You trust what they say?"

"I don't trust what they tell me, but Sal has their quarters bugged," Jack said with a wide grin. "We're listening to everything they say. No one is coaching them before their interviews, and no one is checking out their stories afterward. The big topic is why we picked them up. I've got the impression that they expected to be either shot out of space or left to die in their survival pods."

"Ouch," Kris said.

"Yeah. I'm still trying to figure out what that tells me about this civil war."

"Nothing good," Kris said. "Keep me informed."

It was the third evening when Jack brought a guest to dinner.

"Kris, I would like you to meet Karl Spirelli, third officer on the *Firebird*."

Kris parsed the sentence and came away with way too many questions. She started with the first one that came to her mouth: *"Firebird?"*

Jack tossed the question to Karl with a glance.

"Yes, ma'am, Admiral, I mean. Everyone, including the captain, called the boat the *Firebird*. The other was the *Typhoon*. That seemed to be some kind of inside joke with the management. Management was what they called the captain and first officers of the two old battleships. I think among the senior *management*, I was the only one with Navy experience."

Kris scowled. "Yeah, I can see the joke. Me getting blown away by the *Typhoon*."

Jack shared the scowl with her. Karl looked ready to cringe and crawl under the table, but, more credit to him, he just stood there at something close to attention.

Kris studied the man. He was clean-shaven, and his shipsuit looked recently washed. He wouldn't be out of place among the officers of her crew. *Interesting.*

"Did you know that your *Firebird* was squawking as *Hephaestus*?"

"No, ma'am. As third officer, I was responsible for gunnery. When I served a bridge watch under way, that was not on the checklist I was supposed to keep an eye on."

Kris's frown got deeper. The duties of an Officer of the Deck, especially under way and with the conn, were very specific aboard a warship. Every OOD worth his salt checked the captain's standing orders but didn't need a checklist. They *knew* their duties. "About this checklist, you sound like a Navy man. How'd it stack up to your normal duties?"

"It was short and sweet, ma'am. A lot shorter than it should have been on a battleship. When I pointed that out, I was told in no uncertain terms that I'd signed a contract to do what I was told and the checklist was one of those things. Get with the program or get off the boat."

"That's the second time you said boat," Jack pointed out.

The guy shrugged. "That was what management called the ship, and I got told pretty quick that I better change my ways, fast. Uh, ma'am, is there any chance we could eat? Breakfast wasn't that filling, and this man here had me talking all through lunch."

"Sit down," Kris said, and looked around. She spotted two lieutenants just finishing up their meal. "Mister," she called to the two junior officers, although one was a woman, "would you mind getting the three of us trays? What's on the menu?"

"Hamburgers, burned and cold, ma'am, or some sort of stew. I can't vouch for the meat, but I think the *Sweet Pea* is missing a few cats."

Kris was a bit taken aback by the joke. *Would I have said that to a four-star when I was just a lieutenant?*

Oh, yes.

Would I have been sharing the main wardroom with an admiral and had a chance to shoot my mouth off?

Not likely.

Kris laughed, and wished Grand Admiral Santiago luck with her next batch of recruits on Alwa Station. "Get us a little of both," Kris said.

As Jack settled Karl down in his seat across from Kris, he was shaking his head. "Longknife Navy," he muttered, making it half a curse, half a four-letter word.

"That Longknife Navy blew your battleships out of space," Jack pointed out.

"Yeah," the former Peterwald officer said, still shaking his head. "What is it with your ships? I know we made hits, but nothing happened."

Kris considered several answers and chose, "Magic."

Karl raised his eyebrows, then shrugged. "You could have fooled me. Okay, you ask questions, I answer. Not the other way around. My mom didn't have too many dumb children."

"Good," Kris said. "So, how short was this checklist you had to follow when you were OOD?"

"It was about half of what I expected to do on the bridge of the heavy cruiser *Lomza*."

"And you aren't on the *Lomza* anymore because?" Kris asked.

"They decommissioned her. Only sixteen years in the fleet, and they sold her out for scrap." Karl got quiet; he glanced around furtively. "Some say ships like her were ending up in pirate hands before a welder's torch ever touched them. Some say they were ending up in the Empress's private Navy. Me, I can't say anything either way."

Kris and Jack exchanged glances.

Curiouser and curiouser.

"So you ended up on the beach," Jack said, encouraging the young man to say more. However, the two JOs arrived with trays of questionable culinary value. If the officers were eating this badly, what were the other ranks getting served?

NELLY, AM I RESPONSIBLE AS ADMIRAL FOR THE LEVEL OF CHOW ON MY SHIPS?

MOST DEFINITELY, KRIS. SHALL I WRITE UP AN INCIDENT REPORT AND PASS IT ALONG TO CAPTAIN AJAX?

DRAFT IT, AND GIVE IT TO ME TO REVIEW.

YOU DON'T TRUST MY TACTFULNESS?

NELLY, I ACTUALLY DO, BUT I'M HAVING ENOUGH TROUBLE GETTING ALONG WITH MY FLAG CAPTAIN, AND IF THERE'S TO BE A MISTAKE, I WANT TO MAKE IT MYSELF.

IF THIS GOES OVER LIKE A LEAD BALLOON, YOU COULD ALWAYS BLAME IT ON ME.

ENOUGH, NELLY, LET'S DO THIS MY WAY. I WANT TO KEEP LISTENING TO THIS FELLOW.

GREENFELD IS STARTING TO SOUND LIKE A REAL MESS.

TELL ME ABOUT IT.

Karl didn't seem to find his food at all unsatisfactory. He took a big bite out of his hamburger and a slug of his bug juice. "No beer?"

"You have beer on the *Lonza*?" Jack asked.

"We had a beer ration sometimes. The *Firebird* had beer at every meal. That made for a happy ship."

"How'd it work for your gunnery?" Kris asked.

Karl scowled. "I did have one mechanic who after lunch couldn't put a screw in right," he agreed.

"What happened after the Navy beached you?"

Now it was Karl's turn to get red in the face. "I shouldn't have been beached. I had good fitness reports. I was within a millimeter of being selected for commander, then, pow, I'm on the outside with not so much as a severance package. My girl dropped me, and I couldn't find work anywhere."

"A lot of competition, huh?" Jack said.

"Everyone's out of work. I even tried joining the Empress's security specialists. They're not that different from an army. They said I was *overqualified*. Can you believe it? I was too good!"

Karl applied himself to his hamburger for a few bites as he tried to calm down.

"Anyway, I'm getting desperate when this guy walks up to me outside a bar and offers to buy me a drink. I could sure use one, so yeah, I'm glad for it. We talk for a while, and he says he might know where there's a job for someone who knows how to keep vacuum out of a hull if I'm not too particular about what's going on outside the hull. I told him I could be real apathetic. So he gives me a card and leaves me enough to pay my way up the beanstalk to a boat landing.

"Next thing I know, I'm on this old battleship, trying to get its ancient lasers up and able to hold a charge. I had to do my own scrounging around three other old tubs to get enough boards and cabling to get 'em up, and that was using spit and glue as much as solder. The gun cradles were all kind of herky-jerky, but nobody but me seemed concerned if I could train our lasers out at a target. If they hadn't found a good old electrician who worked on these wrecks back in Iteeche War days, I would never have gotten as far as I did."

"Where is the old fellow?" Kris asked.

"He stayed on the *Typhoon*. They were having the devil's own time getting her lasers to work."

Strange, the death of the old Iteeche War vet seemed to make it all the more painful.

"So, you have no idea what you were supposed to be doing?" Kris said.

"Not really," Karl said, finishing up his hamburger and starting on his stew. The guy really was hungry.

DON'T YOU FEED THESE GUYS? Kris asked Jack on Nelly Net.

THREE GOOD HOT MEALS A DAY. WELL, AS GOOD AS THE MEALS WE GET, ANYWAY. NO, THEY ALL CAME ABOARD THIN AS RAILS. THEY'D MISSED A LOT OF MEALS, KRIS.

MORE TO THINK ABOUT.

THAT'S WHAT I WAS THINKING.

"There was this one night," Karl said, studying his spoon after stuffing a huge bite into his mouth. Kris tried to avoid looking him in the face as he chewed and talked at the same time.

"Zygfryd hooked me into going back to the station with him. I think most of the senior officers were drunk. Maybe. Or maybe he just wanted me around to answer questions about the lasers if that came up. Anyway, we ended up meeting with the skipper of the *Typhoon* and two of his crew at a bar. Then three other guys came along and sat down beside us. They wanted to know how we were coming along, getting those ancient tubs ready to answer bells."

He paused for a swig of bug juice and another spoonful of stew.

"I started to tell them all it had taken to get the lasers up. Before I could say a word about what I needed to make them half-decent, I got cut off and asked if they would shoot. I said yes, and that seemed to make them happy. The *Typhoon* was having trouble with its reactors as well as its guns, but these three guys didn't act as if they really cared, or maybe it was just that they didn't understand. Those three cut them off, too. Then the fat one started talking to us, telling us how important our job was, how we had to get the boats out there and ready to shoot.

"Zygfryd kicked my ankle and kind of eyed the bar. I took my beer and headed there. The other two followed right behind me, so the skippers and these three get to talking real quiet, but they don't stay quiet. I hear the fat one saying, 'We got to get that bitch good.' The skipper shushed him down and got told they could replace him, but they were quieter after that. Me and the other two, we just shook our heads and ordered another beer. It was on their tab anyway."

Jack tossed Kris a glance, but she'd caught it. "So, you were supposed to 'get that bitch good,' huh?" Jack said.

"Yeah, I don't know who the bitch was but we were . . ."

Karl's eyes got big, and he blinked several times in rapid succession. His mouth fell open, half the last bite still in it.

"Not very many women admirals in the Greenfeld Navy, are there?" Jack asked.

Their captive gulped, not a good idea with such a full mouth. He was wracked by serious coughing. Jack pounded him on the back and was about to resort to more serious life-saving efforts when the fellow spit up into his napkin.

He gasped for breath for a long minute, then downed a glass of water that a helpful ensign had brought to Kris's table. She thanked her with a smile and waited for Karl to return to those living and capable of carrying on a conversation.

"Hello, young man. I'm Admiral, Her Royal Highness Kris Longknife, and I believe I'm that bitch you were sent out to get good."

"Oh, God. They sent us out in that old wreck to pick a fight with you. No wonder we're all just about dead."

"Yep," Kris said.

"I mean, if they'd asked me to take that old battleship out to fight the Grand Duchess, I would have passed. Hell, I did. I know guys that got those old battlewagons out to St. Petersburg. Only reason they lived to tell about it was their tubs didn't get in range of the Grand Duchess. Otherwise, she'd have toasted them the way she did the newer ships."

"Vicky's got a battle fleet now?" Kris asked, backing it up with a questioning eyebrow.

"Hell yes, she does. She's won three, four, I don't know how many battles. Some she won. Others were won by people on her side. Hard to tell which ones she was at. You listen to some people, and they'll tell you she's been at every damn shoot."

"She does get around," Jack said, eyes sparkling at Kris.

"No doubt. Well, Karl, I think you've earned yourself some dessert, and maybe a few drinks at the Forward Lounge."

"Forward Lounge?"

"Our restaurant and pub," Kris said.

Jack waved his hand ever so slightly, and suddenly there were two Marines at Karl's side. "You boys take this fellow up to the Forward Lounge. We'll call ahead and tell them what his tab can be for the night. You two get a couple of beers on us after you go off duty."

"Likely after we pour him back into his cell in the brig," the corporal said.

"Right, and tell Gunny to up his accommodations to guest. He's just become the admiral's best friend."

"Guest?"

"Guest with escort," Kris added.

"Thank you. Thank you. No hard feelings? I mean, it was never personal."

"Karl, get out of here before I space you," Kris snapped.

Karl got out quickly with his Marine escort right behind him.

26

"Unidentified ships entering Greenfeld controlled space, state your name, registry, and intent," blared from the screen. Kris's squadron had come through the jump just six hours ago, and this was the Empire's first contact.

Just as Nelly had predicted, the fuzzy jumps had allowed them to take the long way around and do it faster than the direct route.

"Nelly, get me Captain Ajax."

"Yes, Admiral," came back a second later.

"Am I wrong, or are our transponders working fine?"

"Admiral, I'm reading the transponders on all seven of the battlecruisers behind us and I'm told by Captain Grayhorse that the *Intrepid* reads the *Princess Royal* just fine. Now we are still squawking as frigates. Don't want to scare anyone by using a nasty word like battle. Oh, and we've got the *Princess Royal* announcing itself as a Royal diplomatic ship."

"Hmm, so maybe *their* equipment isn't working?" Kris suggested with an impish grin for Jack.

"I wouldn't put it past the Empire's gear to be on the fritz," Captain Ajax answered.

"I wonder if we should turn off our transponders and see what kind of reaction that gets us?"

"I assume, Your Highness, that that is a rhetorical question."

"I think she's starting to get your number," Jack said, hand over mouth to cover his quip.

"I think you may be right," Kris whispered back. "Okay, Captain, have comm give me a clear channel to High Anhalt Station."

There was only the briefest of pauses. "Admiral, you have an open channel to High Anhalt. We will record and log your communication."

"Thank you, Captain, but on second thought, I think this is something better handled at a lower level. Would you really get your boss out of bed to handle a sniping little message like that?"

Ajax grinned. "Most definitely not. Comm, put me on visual.

"Begin message," the captain said. Nelly kept her message on the screen in Kris's day quarters. "High Anhalt Station, this is Commander Ajax, captain of the United Society frigate *Princess Royal*. I am flag captain for the commander of Frigate Squadron 22 at your service. We are making a free transit of space on a mission approved by His Royal Majesty Raymond I pursuant to a request by your Imperial Majesty, Emperor Henry I. We are in compliance with the common traditions and regulations for free transit through open space."

"Sent, Captain," comm reported a moment later.

"Good, Captain," Kris said. "Have your navigator lay in a 1.5-gee course for Greenfeld. Advise me of any further communications. Do you have an intelligence team aboard?"

"We have a small science team," Ajax reported. "We expected to take on more once we headed out for Alwa."

"Have your team listen in to all official traffic. Inform them that they should share it with our passengers' technical support team and that my Nelly would enjoy working with them."

"Codes are so much fun to break," Nelly said, not quite with a giggle.

"I'll warn my team what to expect, Admiral."

WARN THEM?

DOWN, NELLY. THEY'RE NEW TO YOU. YOU MUST ADMIT THAT YOU TAKE A BIT OF GETTING USED TO.

BUT I'LL BE NICE TO THEM.

UNLIKE TO ME.

OF COURSE.

Nelly reported back an hour later. The sensor team had been sweeping up a lot of message traffic since the *P. Royal* first jumped into the Greenfeld system. With her help, and what they could borrow from the ship for serious number crunching, they had broken several codes and discovered some interesting bits of information.

"You were not expected so early, at least by most," Nelly reported. "No one expected you to jump in system from that dead-end jump, and at least one message was sent by someone who didn't expect you at all."

"Who was that?" Kris asked.

"That was not sent on the official net. Rather it was an independent radio net."

"Hmm."

"What's most interesting," Nelly said, and you could almost hear the grin on her nonexistent face, "was the reaction that brought from the receiver. They ordered the sender to shut down immediately and not send anything more until they updated their ciphers."

"Someone got sloppy," Jack said.

"And better yet," Nelly crowed, "we were able to catch the recoded message when it was passed along and use that message to crack several other messages that were sent to and from some major players. At least one of those major players was seriously outraged that you'd made it here alive."

"Is there any chance we were listening in on the Empress's most private net?" Kris asked.

"Unfortunately, no one said anything that allowed us to identify anyone except by their call signs, and those were very much random generated."

"Well," Kris said with a shrug, "we can't expect more than this, Nelly. Tell the team you were working with that I am very appreciative of their work and looking forward to anything they can give me in the future."

"Will do, Kris."

"So," Jack said, "what do you think?"

"I think it's interesting," Kris said. "A couple of times I got close to some Greenfeld types, and Nelly's net collapsed. They can be very good. But apparently they can be pretty sloppy with the codes they use to send their own messages."

"They can dish it out," Jack said, "but they can't take it, huh?"

"Pretty much," Kris said.

"So what do we do now?"

Kris thought on that for a long moment, but there wasn't really much of a decision to make. "We do what we came here to do, knowing what we know. Someone down on that planet hasn't wanted me here since I got these orders. They've sent assassins and battleships. From listening to their mail, we really don't know any more or less than we did when we sailed or after we blew away that pair of battleships."

"All too true."

"So we proceed cautiously, letting my paranoid security chief"—here Kris gave that security chief a peck on the cheek—"reinforce my own paranoia."

"I could get to like that."

"Now, let's go visit our mediators and see what they have to tell us."

27

Kris's brain trust had taken over the Forward Lounge as a kind of club. They took their meals there and did most of their socializing. It had been interesting watching the three groups organize themselves. Initially, the three different agencies had each taken one corner of the lounge, leaving the fourth for the support group.

Over the first couple of days of the voyage, they had stayed pretty much among themselves with their computers out and noses in them. Gradually, they'd mixed together as first one and then another shared a drink or meal. It seemed that many of the research papers that they were delving into had been written by someone on the other teams. One thing led to another, and pretty soon, they had formed combined groups to look into this or that possibility.

One thing they had not done was invite Kris to join them. She found that . . . intriguing. So she scheduled a meeting with them after the squadron flipped ship to decelerate toward High Anhalt Station. She chose the Forward Lounge for the venue.

The moment she stepped into the lounge, Kris found herself on familiar ground.

The table in front of the larger screens was again reserved for her and Jack. Now it was Ensign Megan Longknife who held it for them as they made their way from the doors through four collections of tables.

While Jack went around to sit down, Kris chose to lean against the front of the table and take the measure of the teams she'd be leaning heavily on in her search to find some way out of this mess that Vicky and the Empress had gotten themselves and their Empire into.

Alfred Fu was the short, older man who had done the talking when Kris first met these people. As the chief mediator for Wardhaven's Office of Mediation, he considered his age and stature a great help. "Those who are foolish enough to mistake gray hairs for senility often take my shortness for a lack of presence. That's usually two strikes against them, and I'm home free before they figure out how I've swung their team members and the folks on the other side of the table to something reasonable."

Kris had found him easily likable the two times she had talked with him.

I'll have to be careful about that.

William Pierce Gladsten was a tall, dour man. He did not look at all like his name. However, as senior arbitrator of the Wardhaven Bureau of Arbitration, he seemed to approach everything with deep gravitas whether it was his one discussion with Kris about the perils of civil wars that drag on overlong or the selection of desserts after dinner.

The third member of Kris's troika was Diana Frogmore. The woman appeared quite youthful despite her many years of service both as a child advocate and now as the seniormost judge in the Parental Conflict Resolution Division of the Family Court. She had been quite eager in her first meeting with Kris to point out the value of her perspective in this otherwise far-from-childish affair. "This entire civil war may turn out to be as much a squabble between a man and his grown daughter as it is a grab for power by hungry interests."

"And the stepmother?" Kris asked.

"If we view this civil war as a battle between two adults for the custody of the Empire, adding a fourth person to the mix does create a conundrum. Very messy, if I must say so."

Now Kris faced the four sets of tables, three with a mediation team of one sort or another and the fourth with an eclectic group of technical experts who, as Captain Ajax had reported, had been using every spare second of time they could get on the *Princes Royal*'s sensors to guzzle down data from the rapidly approaching planet.

"Well," Kris said, leaning back against the table and crossing her legs at the ankles, "what do you know now that we didn't know before we jumped into this system?"

With hardly a moment's hesitation, and without glancing at notes, William Pierce Gladsten began. "Our colleagues from information management have collected quite a treasure trove of data. None of us is too sure it qualifies as information. It does appear that all that your friend Karl Spirelli told us is, within reason, accurate."

He cleared his throat. "It will come as no surprise. There is a civil war raging in the Greenfeld Empire."

"I'm glad to hear that," Kris said dryly.

Mr. Gladsten ignored her remark. "It has not touched Greenfeld. Most of the fighting is limited to planets out on the rim of the Empire. From several conversations we intercepted, the Grand Duchess appears to be doing quite well. Our support staff intercepted quite a few messages to and from people being recruited for the Empress's Navy. Most declined. The general tenor of those declining the offer was along the lines of 'No way in hell I'm going to let you get me killed,' or some such."

"Maybe Vicky did learn a few things from her time with you," Jack said drolly.

"I'll need to see it to believe it," Kris said. "Are you operating on hearsay or do you have any solid evidence?"

"Most is hearsay," Mr. Gladsten admitted. "However, we cracked several coded messages from someone who appears to be close to the Empress. She is quite adamant in her demands for more ships, more crews, and more security specialists. Oh, and she wants them all trained better. I believe the quote was, 'These better put up a better fight than the last bunch,' or something to that effect."

One of the women at the support table cleared her throat. "We just finished decoding a large report in answer to that last one that is working its way back to whoever ordered it. It has a long list of suggested crew members for recommissioning over a score of reserve battleships, as well as cruisers and destroyers.

The potential crew for each ship is divided among Former Navy, Merchant Marine, ard Untrained Landsmen. The first two categories account for less than a tenth of the crew list."

"I'll want to see that list" Kris said. "Can you cross-index those lists of names against any other databases: births, employment, unemployment, Navy retirement, and separations."

"We'll get on that. You are aware that unauthorized fishing around in databases in the Greenfeld Empire is a capital offense," the woman pointed out.

"I have been told that by none other than the Grand Duchess, herself," Kris admitted. "However, I don't expect any of you to be taking shore leave, and I assure you, no law-enforcement officer will be allowed aboard this ship. If push comes to shove, I will accept full responsibility in my role as mediator and tell them to see how arresting me works. Right, Jack?"

"I'll double our security at the pier," he said.

"Now, about the more curious part of this conundrum," Kris went on. "Are we dealing with a two-sided problem, Papa Peterwald vs. Vicky, or is this a more complicated three way: the Emperor, the Empress, and the Grand Duchess?"

Now there was a three-way exchange of glances among the troika of Kris's brain trust. No, there were definitely furtive looks aimed at the support tables. It took a long moment and several nods before Mr. Gladsten continued.

"There is no question that there is a power base out on the rim of the Empire. Certainly, St. Petersburg, Brunswick, and Metzburg are mentioned as fully involved in the rebellion and allied with the Grand Duchess. No question, she is definitely a part of this conundrum."

The senior arbitrator took a deep breath before diving into the other half of the civil war. "From our analysis of message traffic, it appears that there is only one center of activity with respect to the civil war here on Greenfeld. Exactly who is at the center of this traffic is not clearly defined. We are leaning toward the Empress, but there is still some chance that it is the Emperor himself seeing to the marshaling of forces."

"You don't have a solid signature on any of that traffic?" Jack asked.

"No we don't. None of us wants to jump to a conclusion, so we are holding back, waiting for some clear evidence pointing at who the primary actor is, both on the rim and on Green-feld," Chief Mediator Fu said, entering the conversation for the first time.

Kris shook her head. "If Harry Peterwald, old Emperor himself, does anything, he has his name plastered all over it. If there are no names on all this message traffic, it's that way because someone wants to maintain some sort of deniability."

"That is a logical conclusion," Judge Frogmore said. "But it is not our way to draw conclusions in advance of the data. Until we are sure beyond a reasonable person's expectation, we prefer to wait for more information."

Kris nodded. She could understand the way they did business. She, however, had blown away billions of aliens on the force of her hunch.

Is now the time to change my way of living, or do I bull through?

She glanced at Jack. He raised a questioning eyebrow but said nothing.

"Let's wait a bit longer," Kris said. "Who knows what we'll see."

On that note, she called the meeting to a close.

28

Kris had spent most of the voyage out, when she wasn't dodging this or that particular ambush, with Ruth and her nannies. Ruth was starting to show signs of teeth. That not only made teething the pits, but two very delicate parts of Kris were none too happy when Ruth tried teething on them.

The senior child-care manager, as the former Gunny Li O'Malley was now wont to be called, knew something about most every situation that a mother and child might encounter. She walked Ruth and Kris through the fundamentals.

Kris couldn't help but notice that her nannies were absent every morning, all but the two on duty. When she asked, she found that they had attached themselves to the Marines for morning PT. "You want to come along?"

Kris eyed Jack. "Are you telling me that my exercise regime of jumping to conclusions and running away from my problems isn't restoring me to my svelte, prebaby, girlish figure?"

Smart husband, Jack just smiled softly at her.

Kris had to admit. she'd been meaning to do something about the extra pounds, and other things left behind by Ruthie's shared occupancy of her belly. Really. She'd been doing a few things in the privacy of her own bedroom. When Jack wasn't around.

So it happened that Kris followed the nannies to join the Marines the next day.

And wished she hadn't.

Even though she fell out a few times, she still returned to her quarters limping, winded, and in desperate need of a shower. Had even one of the young women said a word, Kris would have crawled under her bed and not come out again.

They didn't say that word, and Kris found herself with no excuse not to go back the next day, and the next. After Jack mentioned one evening that Kris was looking good, she put morning PT solidly on her schedule.

Who knows, I might have to chase Vicky or her dad or stepmom down and hog-tie them to get them to the table.

Kris was just getting out of the shower after an hour's worth of PT that she'd actually enjoyed when Jack hollered, "Are you decent, Admiral?"

"When have you cared if I was," she shouted right back.

"I've got Captain Ajax with me."

"Oops," Kris said, stopping her sashay across her night quarters, towel trailing.

"She wants to talk to us about our in-port security once we dock at High Anhalt Station."

"Good idea," Kris said, toweling her hair vigorously. "I'll be with you in a second."

Kris finished drying off, hurriedly pulled on a nursing bra, blue shipsuit, and some shoes, and joined the two other officers in her day quarters. Jack had seated Captain Ajax at the conference table. Kris joined them.

"The general here asked me to double the guard at the pier and be prepared to seal ship at a moment's notice. Are you expecting trouble?"

"This is Peterwald territory, Captain. Expect anything."

"You mean Greenfeld, don't you?" Ajax asked.

"I'm pretty sure that if you asked Harry Smythe-Peterwald which is which, he'd tell you it didn't matter. They've pretty much run the place as a family business."

"A family business that is on the ropes," Jack added under his breath.

"Well, whatever it is," Helen said, "you want to keep the

Princess Royal safe from any of their troubles bleeding into us here."

"Exactly," Kris and Jack said together.

"Have you considered not docking at the station?" the captain said. When Kris said nothing, she went on. "I've read your reports. I'm not sure exactly how you do it, but you seem to be able to have your ships swing around each other and get the equivalent of gravity. The main reason we'd be docking at the station would be to get some down for our crews' health. So, if we don't hitch ourselves to their station, they'd have a lot more trouble getting anything aboard us."

Having stated her idea succinctly, she quit talking. Kris had come to like that in the captain. She glanced at Jack. He had his eyebrows up, tossing a big question mark right back at Kris.

"We don't need any housekeeping support from the station," Kris said, talking half to herself. "We've got plenty of water, air, and reaction mass. Even if we docked, I'd want to keep our hull sealed from everything except landlines. Nelly, I'd expect you to put up the biggest firewall in human history."

"The Great Wall of China would have nothing on me, Kris," her computer answered.

"Great Wall of what?" Kris said.

"You slept through that part of old Earth geography," her computer said sassily.

"You'll protect us from any electronic invasion," Kris said doggedly.

"Definitely."

"Enough," Kris said. She'd let the banter go on long enough while she mulled the basic question. "It was Admiral Krätz who came up with the idea of anchoring the ships bow to bow," she said slowly.

"But the folks around Vicky," Jack said, "were the only ones from Greenfeld who actually saw it done."

"And we have made very good use of that idea to defend our jumps from the bug-eyed monsters," Kris muttered softly.

"Captain Ajax," Jack said, "have you heard of any Greenfeld Navy ships moored nose to nose?"

"No, I'd never heard of anything like this before I read your report. It's totally new to us on this side of human space. At least I think so."

Kris gnawed on her lower lip. "It would be a shame for us to come as mediators between these two warring parties, then give away one side's advantages to the other side," she said slowly, testing each word and finding them good.

Kris finally shook her head, decision made. "No, we do not stop short of the station. Not only would it be giving away something that Vicky might not want to have common knowledge, assuming it hasn't become that, but it would also be inhospitable. You can't accept an invitation to dinner and mediation, then turn your back on the hospitality. All of it."

"You really going to go down there?" Jack asked.

"I didn't say *that*," Kris said. "I believe I told my great-grandfather of royal pretensions that someone would have to be dumb, insane, or the boldest person in human space to get themselves neck deep in this mess. I am none of those, so let's see how we can avoid anything like that."

"As your putative security chief and husband, I couldn't have said it better," Jack said.

"So, we dock the squadron on the station," Captain Ajax said, "but no shore leave, and we accept nothing, not so much as a drop of water from them. Any message packet has to be scrubbed and vouched for."

"By Nelly, right?" Kris asked.

"Only too happy to," her computer agreed.

"Then I think we've got everything organized just the way we want it," Jack said.

And they had, for just about another hour.

"Wardhaven warship, we identify you as a frigate, but you are squawking as a Royal diplomatic ship. Please explain yourself."

"Wait one," came back at the frowning officer in Greenfeld greens.

"That's the message we got"—Captain Ajax glanced at the timer below the screen—"fifty-four seconds ago."

Kris, who had gotten the call to the bridge and ridden the elevator in something close to a free fall, nodded. "Such a message is beneath the dignity of an admiral and diplomatic mediator. As flag captain, it seems right up your alley."

"Oh, joy," Helen muttered under her breath . . . and shooed Kris out of the camera take.

Kris quickly let herself be shooed.

"High Anhalt Station, this is Commander Ajax, captain of the United Society Frigate *Princess Royal*." They discussed the benefit of jumping the ships up to battlecruiser status and chose to keep the eight ships small, unthreatening frigates. "I am flag captain of Admiral Her Royal Highness Kristine of Wardhaven. King Raymond first of that name, has graciously accepted the pleadings of Your Imperial Majesty, Henry, first of that name, and dispatched Her Royal Highness to render such service as Your Imperial Master may request."

"Oh," came out quite flat. "Pardon us, we were not expecting you so soon," was rushed. "I will get back to you," was cut short, as the screen went blank.

Kris shook her head into the silence. "Let me get this straight. First, they tell us to go home. Then they ignore us. When they finally get around to asking who we are, they cut the line when we give them the only answer they could have expected. Am I missing something?"

"Well," Jack said, rubbing his chin, "they might have expected you to be dead, or very late, limping in on a badly damaged little frigate after you tangled with two old but really nasty battleships."

"I'm getting the feeling that the right hand doesn't know what the left hand is doing here," Kris growled.

"More like each finger is in the dark about the other ones," Captain Ajax muttered.

Jack glanced at the skipper. "I think you're going to fit into this madhouse just perfectly," he said through a grin.

"Don't look at me," Ajax said. "I'm just on my way to Alwa. They may be big, mean, and nasty out there, but at least they aren't totally crazy."

"You toss Longknifes and Peterwalds in the same boiling kettle, and there won't be an ounce of sanity to be found," Kris muttered, then took a deep breath. "Okay, we've got an Empire running around, unable to answer us with any degree of rationality. What do we do?"

"We do what gravity requires of us," Helen said. "We make orbit and hitch our fate to their station, just like we talked about."

"That sounds like a plan," Kris said. "How long until we're there?"

"Six hours," Ajax answered.

"Then I better get ready."

Of course, Kris needn't have bothered. It would be a long time before she got a chance to go anywhere.

29

"Wardhaven Frigate Squadron 22, we were not expecting you so soon. We will have to dock you where we can around the station. Here are your ships' assigned piers."

Captain Ajax covered her mouth with a hand, and whispered, "They've scattered us all to hell and gone up and down the station."

Jack turned his back to the port captain on the screen and added in a low whisper, "There's no way we could provide any mutual support to each other if we needed it."

"Then we will not dock the squadron like this," Kris answered them both.

Captain Ajax stepped aside and left Kris pride of place in front of the port captain on the screen. He was middle-aged, graying, and his clothes fit him loosely, as if they still remembered when he was several sizes larger.

"We will not have our ships scattered all over the place," Kris snapped, becoming the demanding, spoiled princess in high dudgeon. "How can we muster our Marines for their daily Royal pass in review? We intend to conduct weekly inspections of our ships' companies. They will not look at all the way we like them if they are strewn all about the station. Not shipshape and Bristol fashion at all," she harrumphed. "We won't have it.

We certainly will not. Young man, you tell your Emperor that we didn't come out here to be treated like this. No. Better, we will tell him, personally. Captain, raise the Emperor immediately," Kris said, turning to Ajax.

She might have had no idea what Kris was talking about, but she ran with it.

"Chief, connect us to Emperor Henry's private line."

"Aye, aye, ma'am." the chief on comm watch answered. "This will only take a moment."

"Hold, it. Just wait a minute. It's the middle of the night," yelped the poor man, stuck between Kris's demands and whoever had given him the order on where to dock her ships. But he was facing a very angry Princess.

"We will certainly not wait until tomorrow morning. We hardly have any gravity out here. It's horrible for our digestion, young man. Captain, use the private number he sent our Royal great-grandfather."

"Yes, Your Highness," Captain Ajax said primly.

"No. No. Please don't wake up the Emperor in the middle of the night. We've just had several freighters vacate their piers. You know how busy the station is. These used to be Navy piers, but what with the fleet down and trading up, we'd been using them for cargo. I think I can get you right in over there. Give me a moment."

The screen went blank.

"The fleet is down?" Kris said.

"Assuming there were no freighters in those piers . . ." Jack said.

"Captain Ajax, can your sensor team give us a good nose count of how many of the station's piers are occupied?"

"I'll get my team on that, Your Highness."

Kris gave Ajax a pass on that "Your Highness." She'd been throwing her Highness weight around enough to confuse any poor Navy commander about her proper form of address.

The lieutenant on sensors stood. "By my count, half the piers on that station are empty. We could dock a big chunk of the Wardhaven fleet and still have space left over."

"Thank you, Lieutenant," Captain Ajax said. "You need anything else, Admiral?"

"No, Captain, you did quite well."

The skipper glanced at the chief on the comm watch. He looked about to bust a gut. "I think we all figured that running with a Longknife would mean some fast footwork, ma'am." She paused for a moment. "What exactly would we have done if he hadn't broken and run? I don't know of any Imperial phone number. Do you, Chief?"

"Not a clue, skipper," said the chief, very much the spitting image of the laughing Buddha.

Kris grinned back. "I've found that people with a poor hand will frequently fold if you make like you have five aces."

"Bluff, huh?"

"Yep," Jack added.

Captain Ajax shook her head. "God help us when we run up against someone that bluffs just as wildly."

"Ah, yes," Kris said, "but remember, we have eight battlecruisers and a personal request from their Emperor to our King. As I see it, we *do* have five aces."

"But how many aces does the Empress have up her sleeve?" Jack asked.

Kris was saved from having to answer that by the port captain coming back on-screen. "I've assigned all eight of your frigates to Navy Piers 4, 5, 6, and 7," he said hurriedly. "Your ships will dock across from each other, and you may have use of the A deck area above your piers for inspections and drill. I hope this meets with your approval, Your Highness."

"It is most satisfactory, and we thank you for it," Kris said, laying it on thick. She might need this guy for other favors in the next few days. Best to use honey in large quantities. "Your courteous care for our needs will be mentioned when we meet with your Emperor tomorrow morning. Will he be coming up to greet us?"

"I'm sorry, your early arrival has caused some disruption in the Palace's schedule. I have not been apprised of anything, ah, regarding formal ceremonies. We, ah, have not had anyone do the necessary security checks. I will send your expectations up to my superiors for referral to the Imperial court."

"We thank you so very much," Kris said. "Now it appears that we must try to adjust our schedule to your planet's day. We hope we can get our beauty rest." Glancing at the comm duty chief, she shook her head curtly. He cut the link.

Kris turned to Jack. "I'm here, at their station, and no one has done any kind of a security sweep of this place. If it's not safe for their precious Emperor, how's it supposed to be safe for my precious ass?"

"And very precious derriere it is, dear Admiral," Jack said. "What do you say that you actually try to get some beauty sleep, and I see what I can do about making at least this part of the station safe."

"You aren't going ashore, are you?"

"No, Your Highness, I will stay safely aboard ship and see if a few Sailors and Marines can do some wandering around the piers and A deck. We may not have Chief Beni to check out the place, but I understand I have an entire squad of technical recon types that can do the same job."

Kris nodded. "Okay, you do your Marine and security chief stuff, and I'll be a nice mother and admiral, feed Ruth, and get a bit of rest," she said through a yawn. "Yeah, maybe I will get some sleep."

30

Kris Longknife came awake slowly, disappointed that she still hadn't gotten all of her oomph back. Or maybe there was a lethargy that came over her when she nursed Ruth. It seemed to go both ways. Ruth would suckle and fall asleep, and so would her mother.

Maybe it's Mother Nature's way of seeing that I get some rest when this little ball of needs and love is sleeping, too. Thank heavens for my support crew, or this one little life would be exhausting mine.

Kris opened her eyes to look down on her lovely child.

She then looked up into the adoring eyes of her husband.

Was he looking that way at Ruthie, or me, or both of us?

"I hope you don't mind my napping while you're on the job," Kris said.

"Oh, I've been having fun. Lots of fun," Jack said.

Kris did not care for the way he said that. "Nelly, could you get someone in here to take care of Ruth. I think I've got work to do."

Akumaa and Fede took less than a minute to appear and gently take a sleeping Ruth off Kris's breast. As they left, Kris settled her two girls back into a solid support bra . . . no frilly stuff for her. At least not for a while. As she handled herself, she glanced up and gave Jack an encouraging smile.

"I'd love to, hon, but I think you want to hear what I've got to say."

Kris sighed. "I'll give you a rain check. Just make sure you redeem it real soon."

"It's a deal. Nelly, please order up supper and arrange these day quarters into an admiral's wardroom."

"Sal warned me you'd need that. I'm ready when you are. How many do we need to feed?"

Jack frowned in thought. "Me, Kris, Captain Ajax. We've got to bring her up to date on what I've been doing with her ship."

"Please do," Kris said. "Remember, we are passengers on *her* ship."

"Oh, I do," Jack answered. "We better include Special Agent Foile. He was in this up to his elbows." Jack paused, licked his lips. "What do you say that we invite the three heads of your brain trust?"

"Does this involve them?" Kris asked.

"Let's just say that someone's tried to kill you today and end this mission before it started. Your troika might want to know what they're up against."

Kris licked her finger and made a mark in the air. "Another assassination attempt, and it didn't even wake me up. They're slipping."

"They had a little help from me and Captain Ajax's crew."

"Thank you, loving security chief. When should we dine?"

"How about in fifteen minutes. Nelly, can you arrange that?"

"Dinner tonight is lasagna, mixed vegetables, and French bread, with a lettuce salad. The lasagna is just starting to come out of the oven. Most certainly, General, dinner can be served in fifteen minutes."

"Then please issue the dinner invitations," Kris said, standing so the room could rearrange itself. The couch she'd been sitting on melted into the floor as the conference table morphed from a wooden-topped table with softly rounded edges to a mess table with square corners and a linen tablecloth. It was a bit strange to see china and silverware form out of the linen, but Kris had gotten used to Nelly's magic with Smart Metal™ and only smiled at the strange.

Captain Ajax was the first to appear, taking the elevator up from her bridge. She caught sight of Jack and made a beeline for him. "You're going to tell me why you had me trotting around my bridge like a trick pony, right?"

"Jack, you didn't," Kris said.

"I'm afraid I did, Admiral."

"I want to hear this, too," Kris said to Captain Ajax.

Special Agent Foile arrived about the same time as Judge Diana Frogmore. Chief Mediator Alfred Fu and Senior Arbitrator William Pierce Gladsten were last, both in intense conversation that only ended as they took in the change in the room.

"Thank you all for coming on such short notice," Jack said. "We've had some interesting developments today, and I thought I might bring you all up to date and eat at the same time."

"Partaking of food does tend to set one at ease," Gladsten said. "So what is it that we'll swallow easier with our salad?" he said, as a salad cart arrived with a chief steward's mate to do the honors.

Only after everyone was seated and served did Jack begin. "We have been under a bot assault ever since we docked and opened the hatches."

"Aren't bots and nanos a normal part of business?" Fu asked as he took his first bite.

"That is true," Jack said. "But most bots don't come with explosives attached."

That got a rise from the table.

"How much explosives?" Kris asked.

"Enough to blow your head off if it got in your ear or up your nose."

Kris noticed that all three of her brain trust swallowed hard at that.

Captain Ajax frowned. "Was that why you had me running around my bridge like a bot myself?"

"Yes," Jack admitted. "We surrounded one bot with enough nanos to take it down, and then let it do what it was sent to do.

It avoided all the crew, but wandered its way up the ship from the quarterdeck to the bridge. I asked you to block the exit from the bridge to the hatch leading up to Flag Country. Thank you for doing so. It went right by you and kept heading for the admiral. As soon as it made it up the ladder to our deck, we took it down."

Kris scowled. "So it was after me."

"It and a whole lot of others," Jack answered.

"You stopped them all, I assume," Captain Ajax said.

"I've turned my Marine HQ into Security Central. We've got a team tracking intruders and taking them down. The other ships have their own nano scouts and interceptors up but show no activity."

"So they are only interested in the Princess, here, and her mission," Frogmore said.

"The conclusion seems clear," Special Agent Foile provided.

"Do we know the source of these nanos?" Fu asked.

"They're coming from the station, but there's no way to tell who's behind them," Jack said. "Some of the bots are the size of a housefly or gnat. You could buy them almost anywhere, and they're easy to track and trap. Others are smaller and more sophisticated. It was one of them we let make a go of it."

"I didn't see it," Captain Ajax said.

"When you walked by it, your wake knocked the thing cockeyed," Special Agent Foile said.

"Your Highness," Frogmore said, "what do you propose we do?"

"I suggest we enjoy our dinner and see if any ideas come our way. I, for one, am empty-handed for the moment."

"A Longknife pausing to think," Senior Arbitrator Gladsten sighed. "Having seen such an impossibility, I can now die fulfilled."

That brought a chuckle to all at the table.

"Once again, I fail to uphold the Longknife legend. What will become of me?" Kris said through a scowl.

"I'm hoping you'll die of old age sharing my bed," Jack said.

Table conversation was light, with a lot of pauses between sallies. Clearly, everyone was distracted. The chief steward's mate's offer of a dessert cart was declined; the dishes were hauled off to be cleaned before the ship absorbed them again. Nelly turned the dining room into a comfortable circle of armchairs without anyone's having to get up.

"So," Kris said, "have any of you got a suggestion for what we do next?"

Her question was answered by a long silence.

Judge Frogmore finally ventured into it. "We have secured this ship, correct?"

Jack nodded agreement.

"Could we invite the Emperor and Empress up here for our discussions?" she asked.

Special Agent Foile shook his head. "I have been in contact with a certain Baron Martin. Commissioner of Public Safety. He says the Emperor has already issued us a formal invitation to court, and he will provide for your security. I'm no expert in court protocol, but I do believe a Princess goes to an Emperor, not the other way around."

"The commander of the Marine detachment," Jack added, "finally got a response out of the Imperial Guard. They are prepared to render all ceremonies to you in your visit, as well as provide for your security."

Kris shook her head. "A lot of people want to keep me safe. Do you trust any of them, Jack?"

"No farther than I can throw an alien raider base ship."

Kris snorted. "Thanks, Jack, for reminding me why we have to solve this dilemma. Okay. They won't come here. I won't go there. I need suggestions on how we resolve this."

The silence stretched and began to bend in the middle.

Jack cleared his throat. "I should go down."

Why was Kris not surprised that he would suggest sticking his head in the lion's mouth? And an Imperial lion at that.

"What do you expect to accomplish?"

"I don't know, but there are standard procedures for a visit like this. You stay here while your security team meets with their security forces. We work out necessary coordination. I make sure our Marines are closer to you than their Imperial Guard. Admiral, I need to do everything that I'd normally do."

"To what end?"

"I don't know."

"Are you putting your neck out so the people who don't like us here can take a swing at you?"

"Now why would they take a swing at me when they're after you?" Jack said with enough sincerity that Kris could almost believe him.

She glared at him instead.

"Who knows, maybe they won't make a go for me," he said.

"And that will leave us where?"

Jack shrugged. "I don't know. Maybe whoever is swarming us with bots will make a mistake, and I can get a handle on them. But, Kris, unless you want to pack up and head home because of a batch of unidentified bots, we've got to do something. The book says I go down next. Let's do it by the book."

Kris sighed. She hated it when Jack won arguments like these.

"Okay, who goes with you?" she finally said.

31

Jack saluted the commander of the Imperial Guard. He wore the uniform of a field marshal. Jack had already looked up all the falderal on his chest; he'd never gotten a whiff of gunpowder in his life. Still, Jack was a lieutenant general, so he saluted the buffoon.

The field marshal commanded a brigade of fancy toy soldiers in green and black who likely couldn't hit the broadside of a barn. Jack had a platoon of Marines in blue and red backing him up—every one of them a sharpshooter. Every one of them wore spidersilk armor under their gaudy dress uniforms.

Jack didn't know when his lion would bite, but he wanted to be ready when it did.

The field marshal had arranged transportation to the Palace for Jack and his escort. "I will be a bit delayed with matters here. I will follow you shortly."

The small hairs on the back of Jack's neck stood up and began to do a dance that involved stomping and shouting.

"Very well," Jack said with an easygoing smile, and boarded a black stretch limo that might as well have had a bull's-eye painted on it.

The Marines divided themselves among four big, black SUVs, two ahead and two behind. In the limo with Jack were

Special Agent Foile and his three agents. Foile sent Agent Sanchez to sit up front beside the driver, a local who had been assigned to them.

As it turned out, each of the SUVs had a local driver. Jack had noted Gunny arranging for a Marine to sit up front before he took the front seat of the SUV directly behind Jack's limo.

Without delay, Jack's motorcade pulled away from the space-elevator terminal and headed through a series of twists and turns that ended with them speeding along an expressway. Somewhere during that, they picked up two SUVs of the Imperial Guard and several motorcycle police.

"Everything according to the book," Foile murmured.

"Yep," Jack said, swallowing on a very dry mouth.

He was here to make sure his wife didn't have to be here. Of course, if their enemies were smart, they'd wait until Kris *was* here before they sprung a trap.

Jack hoped they wouldn't be that smart.

The motorcade held to the speed limit, maybe a bit below it. They took up the middle lane of a lightly used expressway. It began to look like Jack had gotten all puckered up and would have no one to kill.

Cars had been whizzing by them at the speed limit or a bit more. A truck was overtaking them, one with a canvas-covered bed in back. Suddenly, cars that had sped past them put on the brakes and those behind them sped up.

Jack reached for the service automatic in the small of his back.

It happened quick, but time slowed down for it all.

The canvas cover on the truck beside them flew off as the rope ties exploded with a bang and a gout of smoke. Suddenly, Jack was facing a machine gun. Beside it stood a man with a rocket launcher.

In the front seat, the driver hunkered down. Agent Sanchez grabbed for the wheel even as the driver lost interest in it. Sanchez threw the wheel over and the limo slammed into the truck as the first rounds of the machine gun stitched the window and rear end of the limo.

Limo and truck swerved left, driving the truck into the concrete divider. That tossed the gunners in the back around like rag dolls. The rocket hit the road behind the limo and the machine gun's fire went wild, but not before hits made stars on the limo's armored glass, caving it in but not shattering it.

Agent Foile shouted for Mahomet to get the windows down. Jack was trying the same, but the switch on his door didn't work. He needed the glass out of the way. It wasn't going to stop the next bullet, but it was making a mess of Jack's own aim.

For Mahomet, the windows moved. Some rolled down. Others halted only halfway.

Still, when the limo swerved away from the truck, Jack and the Secret Service agents had good shots at the men trying to get reorganized around the machine gun.

The guy with the rocket launcher was just jamming in a reload.

Before they could do anything, automatic pistol fire stitched them. They flew in all directions.

"To our right," Agent Chu shouted, and Jack yanked his attention around. A big sedan was coming up on their unengaged side. Its windows were down, and machine pistols hung out of them.

"Duck," Jack shouted.

Bullets shattered the glass in the rear window, showering them with shards. Apparently, whoever laid this ambush on hadn't been able to get rid of the armor in the fenders and doors. That saved their lives.

That, and the thirty-round limit of the machine pistols.

The fusillade of fire lasted only a few seconds. The assassins hadn't been smart enough to take turns in volley fire.

As one, their machine pistols fell silent. Jack and the agents around him popped up from behind the doors. Several rounds from them and the car swerved into them, then careened into a light pole and came to a shattering halt.

Jack took a moment to look around. Of the Imperial Guard and motorcycle cops, he saw nothing. He still had four SUVs with Marines around him. The road aft of them was littered with wreckage.

It also was clear . . except for a big twenty-wheeled tractor-trailer. It had been speeding up toward them. Now it was braking hard.

"Sal, tell the Marines in the trailing trucks I want to talk to whoever is in that truck."

The two rear Marine SUVs slammed on the brakes. The big truck tried to slow even faster but the driver only succeeded in jackknifing his rig.

It came to a halt with the trailer blocking the road, the smell of burning rubber from tires not meant to go sideways filling the air.

"Mahomet, let's turn this rig around," Special Agent Foile said.

The agent in the front seat jammed something into the driver's ribs, and the limo began to slow quickly but smoothly.

"I didn't know anything about this," the driver whined.

"Then how come you ducked when that truck came up beside us?" Mahomet growled.

The driver's excuses sputtered to a stop with a "They just told me to slow for a truck. I figured out for myself that I better duck."

Jack shook his head. Very likely, the driver didn't know anything more than what he was telling them.

"I want to see what's inside that truck," Jack growled.

"Me, too," Special Agent Foile said, ever so calmly.

The driver now did an expert J turn and headed back for the jackknifed truck. One of the lead rigs stopped and deployed its Marines to halt traffic on the other side of the expressway. The other provided a rear guard to the limo.

Jack's rig came to a halt a short distance from the truck. There, a Marine staff sergeant had three sullen men under armed detention. A corporal was just shooting off the lock on the rear doors, as Jack trotted past the two SUVs that had provided the rear guard. In one, a medic struggled to control the bleeding from a wounded Marine. She had worn the skull cap of spidersilk armor, but the round that creased her skull struck a centimeter below where it ended.

You can't armor the entire body.

A private swung the rear door of the truck trailer open, and the corporal gave a low whistle. "General, you really want to see this."

Jack turned from the wounded trooper and double-timed for the rear of the trailer. He wanted to get this done and over with. The hackles on his neck had not stopped their polka, and that trooper needed more medical care than they could provide her.

He turned the corner, eyed the contents of the trailer, and whistled, too.

Beside him, Special Agent Foile whistled as well. "Their very own traveling torture chamber. I think they expected to capture someone alive."

"They've got enough chains dangling from those walls to hold quite a few."

Foile shook his head. "On those shelves is a collection of fingernail pullers, cattle prods, and sharp knives, enough to cut up quite a lot of people." He turned to eye the traffic jam growing behind them. "You think the virtuoso of all that pain is somewhere in that mess?"

Jack followed his glance and scowled. "You think you could identify the psychopath if we held this mob at gunpoint and searched for him?"

"Psychopaths can pass for quite normal. I doubt any of our eyes could spot him," Foile said, shaking his head.

"Sal, do you have a good picture of all this crap?"

"Yes, General, captured in 3D. If you want me to create a sim of this, I can do it in a second."

"Let's get out of here before someone comes up with a plan B. Corporal, lob a grenade in there."

"Thermite, sir?"

"This isn't a movie, son. Let's not encourage the gas tank to blow up this close to a traffic jam. A few fragmentation grenades should make our point.

"Aye, aye, sir."

"Gunny," Jack shouted.

"Sir."

"I want you on the rig with the wounded Marine."

"Aye, aye, sir."

"Sal, can you draw us the shortest route to the nearest hospital?"

"Got it, boss."

"Shoot it to the Nav computer in that SUV."

"Done, sir."

"Gunny, assign your best driver to your rig and get that Marine to the hospital soonest."

"Aye, aye, sir. Okay, Marines, saddle up. Fire Team A, 1st Squad, you're with me. Sergeant Bourne, get the rest of the troopers organized and into the other four rigs. Move it! We ain't got all day."

Crisply, efficiently, the Marines performed their retrograde movement with rifles pointed out to cover 360 degrees. Two rigs were loaded up when the SUV with the wounded Marine gunned out fast. It headed up the road, passed the roadblock on the other side of the road, and slipped off the expressway at the next exit.

Moments later, the limo and the other three rigs followed it, but turned right where the other had turned left. Speeding along side roads, they made it back in time to catch the next ferry up the beanstalk.

With any luck, in two hours Jack would be back in Kris's flag plot explaining why he was home for dinner.

32

"The ground party is returning." Nelly tersely informed Kris. "They have already caught a ferry up the beanstalk and should be here in forty-five minutes."

Puzzled, Kris asked. "What's wrong?"

"Sal did not tell me. Apparently there is fear that our network may be compromised."

Kris couldn't argue with that. Although the recent bot probes had been low tech, she'd had enough experience with Greenfeld high tech that it would not surprise her if they jacked up their game at a time and place of their choosing.

And the worst possible time for us.

Jack might not be telling her why he'd cut his mission short, but that didn't mean she couldn't draw her own conclusions.

"Nelly, get me Major Henderson."

"Yes, Admiral."

"The ground team my, er, General Montoya is leading is coming back."

"That's several hours sooner than the earliest they were expected."

"Yes. Please have a large contingency with maximum tech meet him at the ferry station. Be prepared to conduct a fighting withdrawal."

"Do you want us to close up the ships, Admiral?"

Kris examined that. She didn't really want to batten down the hatches on all her ships. Locked doors could be taken as quite rude. Still . . .

"Nelly, order all the squadron to cover their quarterdecks with transparent Smart Metal. Entrance and exit is through an air lock and delayed until anyone coming back is cleared of bugs."

"Yes, Admiral," Nelly said.

"Now, what do I do next?" Kris said softly to herself.

A few months ago, she'd be galloping for the beanstalk station to hug and kiss her returning warrior. Of course, she might also catch a bot in her ear, nose, or throat and get her head blown off. Now seemed like a good time to be an old married lady.

Damn you, Jack.

I'm not that old though I am thoroughly married.

I know that you did this intentionally. You set yourself up as the target.

Thank God, you survived. Or did you?

"Nelly, Jack is okay, isn't he?"

"I'm checking with Sal. The answer is yes. They have one casualty, a Marine. Gunny has been detached with a fire team to rush her to the nearest hospital."

Kris grimaced. She'd brought enough spidersilk underarmor for every Marine aboard the *P. Royal*. She expected to bring every one of her Marines home safe.

What happened?

She'd know soon enough.

"Nelly, inform the head of my brain trust that the security team is returning immediately and without meeting with anyone from the Palace. We do not know why they are coming back early, but we should assume that negotiations tomorrow are not going to happen. The ground team will be back in forty-five minutes. I want them in my quarters in half an hour."

"I have informed them. They will be here. Fu asks if you will be setting your table again for them."

"Tell him no table, but I may be chomping on someone's ass."

"He says he understands and will do his best to keep his ass well away from your chompers."

Kris snorted at the joke. Maybe Fu could keep the next meeting from going full mortal. She glanced around her quarters, trying to think of what she needed to do next.

Her right breast was getting painfully heavy. If it was, Ruthie's tummy was likely getting painfully empty.

"Nelly, have the duty nanny bring Ruth in for a nibble, assuming she's not asleep."

"Shani says she and Mai and Megan are playing with Ruth. She's doing knee bends and stand ups and is a giggle ball for all the attention. Shani thinks Ruth will be crawling soon."

Kris rolled her eyes. *Just what I need, another Longknife getting into trouble.*

Or another Montoya.

We'll have to settle that soon enough, but not today.

"Bring her in for a snack. I may be tied up soon."

"They're on the way."

There was a door from the nursery into Kris's night quarters. From there it was just a short hop, skip, and a jump into her day quarters. Still, the nannies usually brought Ruth around through the hall, only using the other door at night.

Kris smiled at Ruth, who smiled right back, showing off her four teeth. Kris undid her top and flipped down the nursing bra, but Ruth was more interested in showing off her ability to bounce up and down, so long as you held her arms up. Ruth did a dozen ups and downs, giggling for all she was worth, then took a nosedive for Kris's breast and latched on.

Kris took several deep breaths, trying to calm her pounding heart. Ruth didn't need to take in all mommy's stress and nerves along with her milk. While Ruth suckled, the room took on a certain odor.

"In one end and out the other," Mai said with a laugh.

"Nelly, up the air recirculation. I don't want the room smelling of baby poop when the meeting starts."

"Done, Kris." Normally, the low hum of the blowers went unnoticed. Now they kicked up. Soon, the room was cooler . . . and the air fresher.

When Ruth lost interest in Kris's breast, she handed the

baby over to Shani and began to cover herself up. The two nannies, without a word, took Ruth off to be cleaned up. Kris had just enough time to change her khaki top to a clean one without baby drool down the front, splash some water on her face, and towel off before Judge Diana Frogmore knocked at her door.

"Enter," Kris said, returning to her day quarters. "Nelly, give us a small conference table. Just the four of us for now."

"Should Captain Ajax be included?"

"Is she available?" Kris asked.

"She's just into the second hour of a nap," her computer answered.

"Let's let her sleep a bit more. Have you closed the transparent cover over the *P. Royal*'s quarterdeck?"

"I got the XO's permission."

"Good," Kris said, settling into her chair at what, for now, was a square table.

"The detail you sent dirtside to look into our security is coming back already?" the lovely judge asked, clearly on a fishing expedition.

"Yes, but that's about all I know."

Another knock at the door. "Enter," brought both Fu and Gladsten in. Kris repeated what she'd told the judge. "One Marine is wounded and being rushed to the hospital. Beyond that, I know nothing," Kris said through a frown.

The three arranged themselves at the table as if they were sitting down to a game of bridge: Diana to Kris's right, Alfred Fu to her left, and William Pierce Gladsten directly across from her. They composed themselves . . . and said nothing.

Kris squelched a frown as the nothing stretched. She cleared her throat and opened the bidding. "Our security team didn't even make it to their conference. So what are our options now?"

Her brain trust for this new challenge exchanged glances, then William Pierce, the senior arbitrator, cleared this throat. "We don't know what happened to interrupt their journey. We hardly have any facts from which to derive options for our future actions."

The other two nodded, and all three settled back in their chairs, clearly intent on awaiting developments in silence.

Kris bit her tongue to keep it from wagging. She was in a situation like none she'd experienced before. These three were supposed to help her survive it. If they said sit tight, she should just sit tight.

Still, this was the time when she would usually be examining her options so she could make a decision later when it was needed in a split second, or people would die. Of course, there had always been those that softly hinted to her that she jumped to conclusions ahead of the data available.

But I was usually right, and jumping to conclusions gave me time to get my ducks in a row.

That had sure helped when it was monstrous alien mother ships gunning for her. Then, of course, there had been times when it didn't.

She remembered when, on one of her earliest assignments, she'd had Nelly blare reveille to an entire barrack of troops her first morning on Olympus. As a boot ensign, she figured she outranked everyone in the barrack. She'd discovered very quickly that the entire garrison, including all the officers who were her superiors, was quartered in that one building. Oops!

Strange how she remembered that early screwup. She'd made a lot more of them since then, some that cost people's lives. But the one she really cringed about was that early goof in the morning rain on Olympus.

Kris let her eyes rove over her new team. Three wise men. Well, two wise men and a wise woman. They were here to help her do something totally different from her past sins. They were here to teach her how to survive a new mess, and not only live through it but also help millions of others to do the same.

Oh Lord, not another learning experience, Kris thought, and had to swallow an inappropriate smile real quick.

Kris settled her gaze on Diana. Was she meditating? Her eyes were closed. Kris couldn't make out what her hands were doing under the table, but her shoulders were relaxed and her breathing was slow and steady. The two men had leaned back in their chairs, eyes half-closed, faces relaxed, but not slack.

Kris had seen Gunnies relaxed like that, in the quiet before all hell broke loose. She'd credited them with being tightly coiled springs, ready to unleash all hell when the moment came.

Funny that these three, people of peace and quiet conclusions, should look so much like those old war dogs.

Kris took a deep breath and let it out slowly. A few more

and she found the buzzing in her bones begin to calm. She closed her eyes for a moment and concentrated on the calm growing inside her. Concentrated on being ready when what was coming arrived.

"Admiral, this is Major Henderson. I am deploying a fully armed and armored platoon from each ship. We are in the process of securing the route to the elevator station."

"Very good, Major," Kris said, still in her calm. "Do you have sufficient tools to handle the small stuff?"

"I never sweat the small stuff, Admiral," the major said with just a hint of a chuckle. "I've got that stuff very much under our control."

Kris couldn't tell if the major had just cracked a joke, reported his status . . . or told her to get her nose out of his business. She chose the latter and tried to think what could happen aboard the station to her troops. As she went down her checklist, it seemed that all had been taken care of.

Now I wait for Jack.

"Admiral, I have a base security chief, one of the red coats, with a squad behind him," the major reported a moment later. "He wants to know why I've got armed men parading on his station."

"Tell him he's welcome to join the parade."

"Thank you, ma'am," came back quickly, followed a moment later by, "He's graciously decided to join us, Admiral."

Kris wondered if the red coats still had their arms, but she held her tongue. The quiet at the table was contagious. She'd have to make sure their way of handling the new didn't interfere with her taking care of the old.

NELLY, WHEN'S THE FERRY DUE?

KRIS, IT'S PULLING IN NOW.

Kris found her stomach clinching, but took a deep breath and prepared herself for what was about to happen.

"The detail has returned," Major Henderson reported. "We are headed home."

For a moment, that was all that came in. Then Nelly provided an update.

"All the Marine detachments stationed along the line of withdrawal are being buzzed by bots of several different types. Sal and I are helping the Marine tech teams take over as many of them as we can manage. Nanos are taking down those we can't control before they get close to our teams."

"Nelly, reinforce the Marines with as many nanos as you need."

"Already doing it, Kris. I've also got Navy tech teams backing up the Marines. We've got more bots coming at us than I thought possible."

"Don't let any get through," Kris said, and glanced around her table. The three of them were intense, now, eyes open, leaning forward in their seats, listening to every word Kris heard or spoke. Fu was on his commlink.

"I've got our tech team reinforcing the Navy at Security Central," he whispered softly.

"Nelly, when you have time, could you put this on my screens?"

The screens came to life without a reply from Nelly.

She must be really busy.

"Man down," came a tense voice on net. One of the dots that stretched from the *P. Royal* to the terminal began flashing red. "One of those damn bugs got the sergeant. Swat at them if you see one."

"We need flyswatters more than we need rifles."

Kris wondered if she could get some Smart Metal™ flyswatters to fly out there as one thing before they morphed into swatters. Then she thought better of it. If they got anything out there, it should be more nano interceptors.

She tapped her own commlink, not bothering Nelly. "Admiral to squadron. I want every ship prepared to deploy a Marine platoon in full space armor. More if possible. Secure all hatches."

Acknowledgments came back from all eight battlecruisers.

On the screens, the dot at the elevator station fell back, merging with the next dot.

"Three of the red coats ran." That was Jack's voice on net. Calm as ever. "Their own bots just blew their heads off as soon as they were outside our perimeter," Jack observed, just as calmly.

The farthest-out dot merged with the next one in the path of its retrograde movement to the flag.

"Put a tourniquet on that but keep moving," Jack shouted,

then said more calmly, "Kris, I'd ask for more medical support, but the detachments are fighting as hard as they can, and
I don't think a medical recovery team could make it through."

"We're having enough trouble holding our ground," Nelly
reported. "I don't think we could defend another moving detachment."

"Understood, Nelly," Jack replied.

"They've just activated their autocannons," Nelly
announced. "Oh, they also activated some new firewall and
booted me out of their system."

So someone was digging into their bag of electronic tricks.
"Admiral to squadron, secure the comm lines to the station."
Her order was answered quickly.

Kris tapped her commlink again. "*Princess Royal*, *Intrepid*,
please deploy your space-armored platoon to reinforce the
troops ashore. Take extra rocket launchers."

Two captains acknowledged their orders immediately. A
screen that had been covering the situation on the pier now
showed Marines in full battle rattle double-timing it ashore.
Their helmets were dogged down; they were breathing their
own air. No bot would get at them. In single column they trotted down the ships' brows, across the pier and then, without
missing a step, up the escalator to A deck.

"Nelly," Jack demanded on net, "show us where the autocannons are and their targeting cameras." A moment later Jack
ordered, "Open fire."

Kris kept her mouth shut, swallowing an anxious question.
She studied the few cameras they had up on A deck. Yes, the
autocannons were all on the overhead. A volley of Marine rocket
grenades exploded, blowing autocannons away just as a few of
them began to stitch the Marines, knocking them around like
tenpins.

Kris had always wondered how spidersilk armor would do
against a half kilo of twenty-mike mike. Now she saw. Marines
flew backward and sideways as the slugs hit them, sliding or
rolling them along the deck before they came to a sprawling
stop. A few managed to make it to their hands and knees
before their buddies helped them up.

One was knocked out of the protective nano cover. In
hardly a moment, his head exploded.

"I'm deploying more nanos," Nelly said.

"We need them." Jack answered. His withdrawing forces were now halfway home.

One autocannon had been missed or skipped. It was just barely below the curved horizon. Now it opened fire.

Station autocannons were supposed to use reduced-power rounds so they wouldn't punch through the deck and open the station to space. This one proved the point. Its slugs were almost spent when they hit the deck and ricocheted before plowing into a dozen Marines, knocking them down and sending them sliding toward the forward end of the station.

One Marine held on to her black box. Even as she slid across the deck with her buddies, her fingers were working her board. If there were bots waiting for them, she kept her nanos moving to protect her team.

The only Marine left standing with that squad fired a rocket at the offending autocannon. The station acquired another hole in the overhead.

Marines in full space battle armor trotted up to the scattered squad. They helped the troopers to their feet, then, as the rest of the armored platoons continued toward the farthest-out team, one fire team helped those in dress uniforms limp toward the ship.

There was an explosion against the face mask of one of the armored Marines. It knocked him back a step, but he was moving to catch up with his fellows with nothing but a shake of his head.

"We've got nanos moving along with the armored Marines," Nelly said. "I guess we missed that one."

Kris figured the tech teams were allowed a few misses. She was glad that miss was on a Marine armored for it.

Why didn't I fully armor Jack's detachment?

Because I didn't want to look all dressed up for war, she answered herself.

Mark up another mistake that I made that cost someone his life, she thought bitterly

This damn Longknife legend is a bitch.

Pulling herself out of her head, Kris studied the boards. The armored Marines were almost to Jack. His team was falling back as quickly as they could move without compromising their perimeter.

Someone in the opposition tried using an autocannon that was beyond the horizon on A deck. The slugs hit the deck and ricocheted. Jack's Marines would have to pass though that beaten ground to make it back to the *P. Royal*. He sent a fire team of armored Marines out to spot that cannon and take it out.

One of them got hit in the leg by a round. It spun him around and he went down cursing on his fire team's private net. His buddies razzed him, but trotted up to where they could get a shot at the autocannon. They quickly added another hole to the overhead that would need patching.

Now the outer perimeter around Jack's troops was held by the spacesuit-armored Marines. Kris was anxious for them to get back aboard, and the urge to run must have been almost irresistible, yet the Marines kept to their careful pace. Kris could now spot Jack in the center of the retrograde, surrounded by a squad of Marines with their heads down, watching developments on their boards and making adjustments to the cloud of nano defenders swarming around all of them. No Marine moved any faster than that support team could walk with their eyes on their boards and not looking where they were going.

One of the technical types stumbled as Kris watched. A buddy next to him grabbed his arm and kept him from going down. Kris gritted her teeth and prayed they could hold this together just a little bit longer.

Tugs towing cargo carts came racing down A deck, already at full tilt. They had no drivers. There were shouts from the outer perimeter and Marines took a knee, sighting their rifles in. On a Gunny's shouted command, they took the mass of cargo carts under fire.

The Marines hit the tugs right on, but as they swerved, their carts came free. Those kept rolling toward the Marines. On Gunny's order, there were second and third volleys. The carts turned out to be heavily loaded enough that they absorbed the hits and just kept coming.

"Aim for the tires," Gunny ordered, and fire went lower. Some hit the deck around the carts. Most ricocheted off the deck. A few punched through to space. They'd need to be patched, but it would take a long time to empty the station.

Tires took hits and deflated, bringing their cart to a slow

stop. A couple of carts had their wheels shot off. They came bouncing toward the Marines, who dodged out of their way.

One poor Marine was looking right when a wheel rolled in from the left and hit him hard on the back and knocked him down. Two of his buddies picked him up by his armpits and dragged him along with them as they kept heading for home.

Kris wondered what they would come up with next, but whoever the opposition was seemed to have pulled the last trick they had out of their hat. Kris knew there was one last gambit they could make. With the *Princess Royal* locked down tight, there was no way for Kris to know what the pressure was on the station's A deck, and she was not about to ask Nelly for a report on that unless she offered one.

Apparently, no news was good news. The Marines made it back to the pier.

"Everyone aboard the *Princess Royal* or the *Intrepid*," Jack ordered. "Nelly, could you expand the receiving air lock on the quarterdecks to take us all.'

In a moment, the entire quarterdeck was one big air lock, with Marines being checked over and only passed aboard through a smaller air lock in groups of five or six after they had been gone over thoroughly.

Kris left it to Captain Ajax to organize transportation for the borrowed Marines back to their ships by liberty launch. For now, she wanted her ships locked and tight.

What she would do next was something for her, Jack, and her brain trust to decide.

33

Kris was relieved beyond words when Jack half stumbled into her day quarters. He was out of breath; he'd lost his cover. Was that his blood on his cheek? Kris found herself out of her chair and dashing toward him, arms open even before she thought of it.

She was careful to slow down before she hit Jack. From the looks of him, she could probably blow him over with a feather.

She put her arms around him, and they both let out a breath they hadn't known they were holding. "I'm so glad to be home," was all Jack said.

"I'm glad you made it. Don't you ever do that to me again! I'll order *you* locked up in our bedroom myself."

Jack grinned as she made to him his often-repeated threat to her. Often threatened but never followed through on. Yet.

"I think you just might do that," he said, and turned her face to him so he could give her an ever-so-soft kiss.

Kris broke from the kiss and the hug and stepped away from Jack. Still with her arm around him, she aimed him for the table that was growing a place for him and several more. "You want to take your seat?"

"Think I could get a glass of water?" Jack asked. It hit Kris that the huskiness in his voice wasn't just for her closeness.

"I'll get us both a glass," said Special Agent Foile, who had followed Jack into Kris's flag quarters.

"It's through my night quarters," Kris said, and the Secret Service agent disappeared to return a moment later with two cups, no doubt manufactured for him by Nelly.

Jack took one and emptied it in a quick series of gulps. Beside him, Foile was doing the same. Both collapsed into the nearest chairs.

"You want a refill?" Diana asked. She was already out of her chair and reaching for their empty cups.

"Yes, thank you so very much," Foile said.

Captain Ajax arrived, took one look at the two men from the ground party, and asked "Would you two like a sandwich or something?"

"It's been a long time since breakfast," Jack admitted.

In a few minutes, a second class steward's mate arrived with a cart loaded with sandwiches and desserts as well as urns of coffee and tea. Kris found that Jack wasn't the only one hungry. She split a sandwich with Diana; the two older men also split one.

Only after they had all caught their breath did Kris lean back and fix Jack with a jaundiced eye. "You want to tell me what happened?"

"We got ambushed on the expressway between the space-elevator terminal and the Palace," Jack said simply.

"Why would they attempt to kill the security team?" Chief Mediator Fu asked.

"I don't think they were out to kill *all* the security team, Mr. Fu," Jack answered.

"Oh, must we be so formal," the mediator said, eyes sparkling. "We all know each other here, and I've heard your wife call you Jack and you call her Kris. I'm Alfred. Al if you want to talk fast."

"Okay, Al," Jack said. "Sal, show everyone the contents of that truck."

The rolling torture chamber appeared on one wall. "That was following behind our attackers. From the looks of it, I think someone wanted to capture yours truly and send me back to Kris one pound of flesh at a time."

"Damn," Kris whispered. "I do hate kidnappers."

"I'm developing a distinct distaste for them myself," Jack admitted.

"Okay, my fine brain trust, I want some opinions on what we do next. Any that put Jack at risk down there again are not acceptable."

"Or you, honey. Remember, I can lock you up." When the look from Diana took on horrible proportions, Jack quickly added, "There's a law that says the security chief of a serving member of the blood may take whatever measures he deems necessary to keep said member out of harm's way."

"As the only member of the blood serving in uniform, I take umbrage at that law," Kris drawled.

"Oh. Okay, so I'm not going to witness a case of spousal abuse," Diana said.

"Don't be too sure," Jack said. "She may put *me* in sick bay if I try to corral her."

"Definitely," Kris said, but with a loving smile.

Enough of that.

She quickly swept her eyes over those at the table. "We were invited to mediate between the Emperor, the Empress, and the Grand Duchess. Is there anyone outside those three that might be trying to kill me or suborn me by torturing my husband?"

The room grew serious. Unfortunately, it also grew silent. Kris didn't much care for it when her brain trust grew tongue-tied. She turned to Diana. "Do you want to nominate anyone else?"

"I can't think of any other movers than those three in this messy Empire."

"Al?"

He shook his head.

"Do you want to be called William Pierce or just William?" Kris asked Gladsten.

"Bill will do, or WP," he answered, "and no. All three of us have been watching the media intake the tech people have swept up. Whether you consider the Empress the mover, or her father the power behind her, those three you named are it for this place. I should tell you that we think there may be others, call them mice within the walls, who could come forward, but not now. No one will risk raising their head too high. Getting noticed is deadly in this place."

"But the Grand Duchess did raise her head," Kris said.

"Say rather that she became the final drop into the liquid that caused it to become supersaturated and precipitate out some interesting particulates," Al said.

"So it's not just Vicky," Kris said.

"Not just Vicky," Diana agreed. "Although we aren't sure whether she's moving them, or they're moving her. I suspect it may be either of those depending on the day of the week."

Kris chuckled. "God help anyone who thinks they can control Vicky."

Bill shrugged. "That may not presently be the case. We have a source from inside the Empire who says Vicky has become more open to learning new ways of late."

"Who?"

The three exchanged glances. "We would prefer to keep our source to ourselves," Diana said for the three.

Kris scowled. "Even from me?"

"I'm quite interested in seeing your impression of your friend Vicky," Diana said. "That may tell us a lot about what's actually going on."

Kris shrugged. "Okay. I am looking forward to meeting her again. She owes me for that interview she gave right after we got back from our little jaunt around the galaxy."

Diana raised her eyebrows in a question. Kris smiled and ignored her.

Two can play this game of I know something you don't know.

Kris eyed her three brain trusters, but they had nothing more to add. "Okay, if we don't think someone else is out for my hide, which of those three should we assume is looking to mount my head over their fireplace?"

"I'm not sure we can assume that," Bill said.

"Really," Jack said. "I don't know about you, but I'm getting a really strong hunch—"

"We prefer not to play hunches," Al said.

"Hmm," Kris said. "Okay, just for chuckles and grins, let me examine this situation out loud. Vicky is not on Greenfeld and likely has few friends here. Do any of us think she could have put together a rolling ambush dirtside accompanied by its own torture dungeon, then followed it up with that bot assault Jack just fought his way through to get home?"

"It would seem unlikely," Diana admitted cautiously.

"The Emperor invited us here to mediate this situation," Kris said. "I find it hard to believe that he would turn around and try to kill me before I can help him close down this civil war."

"Assuming he really wants to end this war," Bill said.

"Everyone knows there has been bad blood between the Peterwalds and the Longknifes going back to the Iteeche War, if not longer," Al put in.

"Hmm," Kris said. "You folks really are allergic to the assumption word, aren't you?"

"We prefer our conclusions to be firmly based on facts," Diana said.

"So," Kris said, her temper on a slow burn, "do you have any idea what we do next?"

The three just shook their heads.

What does it take to get these people to say anything?

Kris turned to Jack. "If we're not going down there, I guess we'll have to invite Harry up here."

"Harry and his blushing bride," Jack added.

Kris eyed the three.

"That does appear to be the next step," Al said. "I would certainly hate to attempt an intervention via screen hookup."

"I tried that once," Bill said. "Bad all around."

"I've kept children in the next room and asked them questions by hookup, but I think that would be our last option here."

Ah, I actually got one to say "option."

"Okay," Kris said, moving quickly to exploit the agreement before it evaporated for lack of hard facts. "It is time to call the Emperor and invite him up here. Nelly, get me a line to Harry."

34

It was a full fifteen minutes before the screen in Kris's quarters filled with a view of Emperor Henry, the first of that name. No surprise he was seated on his throne, a golden affair that glittered in the light. Beside him, on an equally golden throne, if a half meter lower, sat the Empress.

"We thank you very much for taking our call, Your Imperial Majesty," Kris said, laying the royal "we" on not with a trowel but more like a shovel.

Shovels of pure horse manure.

"*We* were *expecting* a visit from *you* in the near future, Your *Royal* Highness," the Emperor answered, with just a bit of a bite in it. Maybe more than a bit.

Beside him, the Empress fairly boiled with rage but managed to keep a lid on it. For the moment.

"Yes, about that," Kris said as diffidently as her anger would allow. "Have you been informed that *our* security team on their way to meet and coordinate our visit with *your* security team came under gunfire?"

The Emperor frowned. "No, we have heard nothing of such a thing. Have you, Your Imperial Highness?" he said, addressing his wife oh so formally.

"That could never happen on *our* peaceful Greenfeld," she said, with ever so lovely a frown.

"We *cannot* believe such a thing. You *must* be misinformed," the Emperor said, offering Kris a chance to back down.

Kris was not interested in backing. Down or anywhere else. "We are *afraid* it is true. Our consort, Prince John, led our team and witnessed the gunfire. We are informed that it left quite a traffic backup on your capital's main expressway. We also had to send one of our injured Marines to your nearest hospital."

Kris would have to do the paperwork when they got back. For now, they'd just have to fake it.

Now the Emperor allowed himself a serious frown. "Martin? Where is Commissioner Martin?"

A man in severe black quickly stepped up to stand behind the Emperor.

Talk about the power behind the throne.

Martin and the Emperor exchanged words silently for a long moment, then the Emperor turned back to Kris. "It would seem that there *was* some sort of fracas on the expressway this afternoon. Truckers are always exceeding our speed limits and causing no amount of trouble. However, *we* are told that there was *no* shooting involved. Certainly not," the Emperor said, shaking his head.

"Hmm," Kris allowed. "It seems that we are informed differently on the matter. However, we fear for our safety on your roads after what happened to our Prince consort. You have asked us to mediate these unfortunate affairs taking place in your Empire. We are afraid that we must respectfully ask and invite you to visit us on our flagship, the frigate *Princess Royal*."

"*You* want *us* to visit *you* on such a tiny vessel," the Empress snapped.

"Dear," the Emperor said, resting a gentle hand on her bare shoulder.

"Honestly, Harry, you would go hat in hand at the beck and call of a *Princess*?"

"Now, dear."

"Next thing you know, you'll go barefoot in the snow to Canossa."

BAREFOOT TO CANOSSA, NELLY?

A REFERENCE TO A HOLY ROMAN EMPEROR, HENRY IV, BEING HUMILIATED BY POPE GREGORY VII IN 1077, KRIS.

OKAY, GOT IT.

"Your Imperial Majesty," Kris put in. "We do not seek *anything* more than is necessary so that we can give you what *you* have *asked* of us."

"Must we go to you?" Harry said, frowning.

"We fear for our safety, Your Imperial Majesty. Certainly, you will be safe on your own roads and space station."

"Of course."

"But a tiny vessel like a frigate," the Empress put in.

"We assure you, Your Imperial Majesty," Kris put in quickly, "Our frigate is made of Smart Metal. It will be no problem for us to expand it to provide you accommodations appropriate to your honors."

"I *have* been wanting to see what is being done with Smart Metal in your realm," the Emperor said, slowly.

"We can give you a full tour of my flagship, Your Imperial Majesty."

The Emperor paused for only a moment as his face took on the look of a boy who had been invited into the candy shop with unlimited credit. "We shall *certainly* accept your *generous* invitation to tour your flagship, young Princess, and if we should *happen* to spend some time discussing these unfortunate developments in our Empire, that will just be all for the better."

"Very good, Your Imperial Majesty. When should we expect you?"

"Tomorrow, say around eleven."

"We shall be ready, Your Imperial Majesty, to give you a full tour."

"Good-bye until then."

"You are so gracious, Your Imperial Majesty," Kris said, pouring it on with a fire hose.

The screen blanked, and Kris took in a deep breath.

NELLY, IS THE LINE DISCONNECTED AND THE MICS OFF?

"Yes, Kris. I've even disabled the landline to the pier. They can't hear us anymore."

Kris blew out a breath and with it some of the tension. "Did the Empress look to you like she was ready to explode?" she asked Jack.

"I'm glad she's no longer pregnant, or we'd have witnessed the birth right there."

"Yeah," Kris said, still taking deep breaths and letting them out slowly. "From the behavior of Harry, I don't think he knows anything about the attack."

"Or anything about what's going on in his city, much less his Empire."

Kris rolled her eyes, but only said, "I tend to agree. Now, about the Empress. I would love to get her attached to a lie detector."

Jack nodded. "She, I can see sending me back to you a piece at a time with orders to do exactly what she said."

"Ugh," Kris said, shaking her head. "Okay. I suspect we will be saying 'Your Imperial Majesty' a lot tomorrow."

"No doubt," Jack said. "With them deriding you as just Your Royal Highness. Now, dear Admiral, just exactly what have you committed us to?"

Kris turned to her brain trust. "Okay, we've finally got a meeting set up. What do we do with it?"

35

Next morning, Kris found herself alone with the more mundane duties of the day. After breakfast, Jack changed to his best dress blue-and-red uniform and left to make sure that the Emperor's visit passed peacefully and with a reasonably low body count.

Kris ate, then dropped in to get a final briefing on what the tech people had stripped off the Greenfeld net. That continued to be painfully slim.

"We've got enough to tell us something is very wrong," the head data specialist, Runda Fairsight said. "Too much of what we've found just doesn't add up. There's something missing, and that missing stuff is what's encrypted up to its eyeballs. So far, we're unable to read any of it. The fact that nearly a quarter of the net is that highly encrypted tells us a lot."

"So tell me what that 'lot' is, please," Kris said.

Runda rolled her eyes. "Someone is willing to put up with a lot of slow traffic to make sure it's unread. On Wardhaven, about five percent of the net is this heavily scrambled. Bank transactions and critical military messages. Your grandfather Alex Longknife is about the only one who encrypts this much of his traffic."

"We know he's around the bend, paranoid," Kris muttered.

"Exactly. A huge chunk of this planet is as around the bend as your grandfather Alex."

Kris shook her head. "That does not bode well."

"Nope. We'll keep working on it, but the truth is, those other three better get ready to pull a real miracle out of their hats, ma'am, because we can't give them the normal hints from what we've dredged up."

"Thanks," Kris said, and left to find her three miracle workers. They were in the Forward Lounge that, at the moment, had been moved from the bow to amidships, only two decks down from the quarterdeck. Those three decks had now been expanded to be a thousand feet across.

They were eye-droppingly luxurious and spacious enough to match any palace in human space. They shared two glorious spiral staircases in shining wood, plush red carpets, and elbow room. They were arranged so you came down one from the quarterdeck, walked across a foyer covered in luxurious wallpaper of red and gold with delicate inlaid wood, festooned with classical statues, most of them nudes, Kris noted. From there, she descended a second magnificent staircase right into the middle of the lounge.

"Nelly, get me Ajax."

"Yes, Your Imperial Highness," came quick.

"Nope this is just Your Royal Highness."

"Sorry, I've been thinking too much about our visitors," Captain Ajax admitted.

"I guess you have. I'm standing at the foot of the staircase down from the quarterdeck and looking at something right out of a madman's dream of a palace. There's another staircase that leads down to the Forward Lounge which, I take it, today is not so forward."

"No, Your Highness. The general asked if I could shorten the distance from the brow to the lounge, and maybe get my bridge off the direct path. Defense came up with all the Smart Metal necessary to give you those thousand feet across decks."

Kris glanced around and did not see a thousand feet. Then she remembered that quite a bit of the space behind the quarterdeck was behind a wall presently covered with several huge murals of battles lost and won.

"How'd you fill up the space?" she asked.

"Well, Admiral, the Forward Lounge is a full thousand feet in diameter with a very high ceiling. The middeck that you are on has been assigned to the Marines. They've got really spacious quarters now. There's one hell of a workout area and a track that covers the full circumference of the deck."

"That's nice. What about the quarterdeck?"

"It's right where it was, only now much of that deck is Admiral's Country, ma'am. While you've been at breakfast and busy otherwise, we moved your quarters, and those around you, including the special advisors, to that deck."

Kris sighed and rolled her eyes at the overhead. "Will I recognize my space?"

"Not likely, Admiral. You can play handball in your new quarters. Your night quarters will make even an emperor jealous. Your bath has a tub that can seat ten. I really hope you'll extend me an invitation."

"I hope no one on the ship is stuck in a cubbyhole."

"No, ma'am. Even Ruthie's nannies will be quite comfortable although their rooms are arranged around the nursery. We kept that baby's space small so people can reach Ruth in a hurry. That chief warrant officer of yours was quite clear on that."

"Never argue with a Gunny. Are the Sailors going to be upset?" Kris didn't want any of her crew to feel left out.

"No, ma'am. We blew out quite a few decks, not out to a thousand feet, but the *Princess Royal* now makes the most luxurious space liner look downright poverty-stricken."

Kris let that thought run and quickly saw where it took her. "And the rest of the squadron?"

"They are all quite comfortable now though none of them got a Forward Lounge, Admiral. I have been asked by several of my captains to point out that with you not allowing any shore liberty . . ." left a whole lot in Kris's lap.

"Good point, Captain," Kris stalled. "I'm a bit busy preparing for the coming Imperial visit. Let me get back to you. If I don't, raise it at dinner tonight."

"Will do, Your Highness."

Kris noted the use of the royal rather than the Navy. As an admiral, the only answer to alcohol aboard ship was no. Better yet, Hell No! As a royal . . . things were more up for grabs.

"Nelly, how much booze does the Forward Lounge have in stock?"

"A lot, Kris, but not nearly enough for the entire squadron."

"Okay. Nelly, examine how you might order up a supply of beer, wine . . . oh hell, a bit of everything . . . without the folks you order from knowing it's headed here. Then could you redirect it in transit?"

"I've already studied that option, Kris. No problem doing it. Can I bill it to the Palace's account?"

"You sure can't bill it to a Wardhaven credit chit. When would such a bit of chicanery arrive pier-side?"

"If I do it now, say, three o'clock."

"Make it happen. We'll debit it against the Imperial visit."

"It is done."

Kris hoped she wouldn't live to regret it.

Down the next staircase, which Marines could march in ranks twelve wide, Kris found an establishment that beggared the mind. The Smart Metal™ walls appeared to be wood or golden wallpaper or more murals, some of battles, others of magnificent landscapes or classical paintings. The huge space was divided by banks of mirrors. They gave the vast rooms a near agoraphobic element that shrank the puny individual down to almost nothing. The furnishings mimicked styles from different ages of human existence with a strong bent toward wooden chairs and marble-inlaid tabletops. Others were already covered by snow-white linen, delicate china, and shining silverware . . . some of which was golden.

Kris found her mouth hanging open. She swallowed her awe and snapped it shut.

"Astonishing," Judge Diana Frogmore said, coming up beside her. "I'm amazed at what that computer of yours can do with Smart Metal."

Kris shook her head. "I'm just glad I dropped down here. I'd hate to see this place for the first time with Harry."

"Yep. That's why we have our teams down here. I've heard of a need to acclimatize troops to a new environment. This sure takes that cake."

"And eats it, too," Kris added.

"I assume you've come to ask if we are prepared."

"Yes," Kris said.

"Well, we're prepared as much as we can be. No doubt, Runda told you this place is a hard nut to crack."

"Unfortunately."

"We propose that we let the Emperor, and, no doubt, the Empress talk. None of us have ever met people who think overmuch of themselves who were not most willing to fill the air with their verbosity."

"Will that help us?"

Here Diana shrugged. "It has never hurt."

"There is always a first time."

"Yes," she said ominously.

"I've about run out of time," Kris said, "so if you'll excuse me, I've got to get ready."

Diana looked puzzled.

"Getting ready with an infant at the breast takes a whole lot more time than it took when I was carefree and single, or even newly married."

"Ah, yes," Diana said, enlightened, then her eyebrows dropped. "I can't help but wonder. Why did you choose to bring your infant on this mission?"

"Let me give you the quick answer. I enjoy nursing Ruth. If I leave her, even for a month, I can't get that back. Also, my mom and dad were what your profession calls emotionally unavailable for me after Eddy was kidnapped and allowed to die. I want to be as close to my kids as possible. I believe it's called wanting to have it all. And if all that is not enough, can you assure me that if I left Ruthie home that someone wouldn't kidnap her and hold her for ransom?"

Diana nodded. Kris went on.

"Here, she is safe with the same Marines and Sailors that protect me. While she can be as exhausting as any infant, I am not like other women. I cheat. I've got a staff of six to take care of Ruth and my dog robber to take care of the minutiae of my job. If I can't do this I guess it really is impossible."

"And, as an admiral, you can make your ship accommodate your expanded needs—"

Kris chuckled. "Without Smart Metal, I'm not sure even I could pull this off."

"See you in"—Diana looked at her wrist—"an hour."

36

Kris's hour disappeared in a blinding flash despite everything she did to catch it. She fed Ruthie from one breast while pumping milk from the other. If the meeting went long, she didn't want Ruth getting hungry—or her mother sitting at the negotiating table leaking milk through her dress whites.

A quick shower, and she found herself standing beside a fresh-faced Ensign Longknife, who was a study in puzzlement.

"Ma'am, I've managed to put on most of your fruit salad, but I have no idea where some of this stuff goes."

The boot ensign had done a good job with the medals that met Wardhaven's standard uniform regs. The Olympic Humanitarian Award was mounted above the pocket of her white dress coat farthest to the left with its V for valor. Next came the Turantic Medical Expeditionary Medal, also with a V to show Kris had won it in a fight. She often had trouble explaining how she managed to earn a Valor commendation during what were supposed to be humanitarian missions. Even Kris's Society of Humanity Devolution Service Medal had a V. She wasn't allowed to explain that one. The Navy and Marine Corps Medal, the one that started Kris off and which Mother wanted to encrust with diamonds and turn into a broach when Kris got out of the Navy, stood in the shadow of the Wardhaven Defense Medal. There was no V for that one. Valor was assumed for all those who volunteered for that bloody fight.

It always took place of honor on the breast of anyone who had lived past earning it.

It was the other gewgaws that stumped Meg. In truth, they also stumped Kris, but with a shrug . . . who could gainsay her, really . . . Kris dived in.

"Three go around the neck. Greenfeld's *Pour la Mérite* has the smaller choke chain. I think it's supposed to be worn right at the throat. Nelly, can you find out if it goes inside or outside the choke collar?"

"The chain goes inside the collar, with the cross hanging out."

"Good. The next two likely have no regs to follow. The Almar Medal of Highest Honor has the shorter ribbon." It was bright red and gold, with a triangular gold medallion. "We'll put it on second."

"What's this one?" Meg said, holding up a large golden globe suspended from a light blue ribbon.

"That is Granny Rita's bad conduct medal."

"Bad conduct?" Meg said, raising a doubting eyebrow.

"Bad conduct or just plain dumb conduct," Kris amended, quickly. "If you have the honor of tackling and destroying an alien mother ship, you get that honey in bronze. If you haven't learned your lesson, and mess with a second one, Granny adds bronze oak leaves. Third time and the metal is silver, with silver oak leaves if you need a fourth lesson. Those really slow learners can get a gold one for their fifth learning experience, with gold oak leaves for six."

"Do everyone's have cross swords at the top?" Megan asked.

"Seventh," Kris muttered.

"Is that a diamond in the middle of the mother ship on the medallion?"

"Eighth," Kris breathed.

"Eight!"

"What can I say, I'm a very slow learner. Poor Ruthie has two really dumb parents."

"Jack was there for eight, too?"

"Yep. Most people quit at six. Okay, moving right along, we've got these three starburst-type things."

"Four," Meg interrupted. "This arrived from the Palace early this morning."

"What is it?" Kris said, staring at the starburst in the red box.

"It's the Greenfeld Order of St. Christopher, Star Leaper, for those who circumnavigated the galaxy. Or not. I'm told there are posthumous tombstones for those that died before they got back."

"Hmm," Kris said, and talked herself through her problem. "The Order of the Wounded Lion is Earth's highest award. We'll put it upper right on my left chest, a few millimeters below the normal medals. Since we're on Greenfeld, I'll put St. Chris to its left. The Helvetican Golden Starburst came with no explanation, but it's likely for winning the battle that Harry's son died in, so let's put it lower left, and maybe no one will notice it. That put the Order of the Rose and Thistle from the kitties of Bizalt close to the buttons. Are we missing anything?"

"Only time," the ensign said, starting to affix the golden stars to Kris's dress white coat while Kris got into her pants and shoes. Kris would never have gotten the gold buttons on without Meg's help, or the awards around her neck.

Done, Kris asked, "Where's a mirror?" and one appeared almost before her eyes. It took Kris a dozen steps to get close enough to check herself out. She imagined a lot of the ship's company was enjoying the space they'd gotten today. Still, you could get too much of a good thing.

"The Emperor and his entourage are disembarking from the space elevator," Nelly informed Kris.

"And I'm ready to face him," Kris said, breathlessly. She was grateful the quarterdeck was just outside her quarters' door, though in the new, expanded *P. Royal* that was still quite a hike.

"Meg, go find out where we're meeting in the Forward Lounge," Kris said, as they marched for the door.

"I know where it is," Nelly said.

"Okay, Ensign, stay handy in case I need you."

"Aye, aye, Admiral."

On the quarterdeck, Kris's Navy band was tuning up; it

looked quite diplomatic in a spiffy kind of way. Eight sideboys were deployed, ready to render honors. Kris might have her own doubts about Harry's lack of honor, but he was going to be full of it by the time she pumped all this into him.

Or not.

A worried look on his face, Jack waited for Kris as she took measured steps up to his place on the quarterdeck.

"How are things?" she asked.

"There are way too many bots waiting outside the Smart Metal covering we've got up blocking access to the quarterdeck."

"I take it you've tried killing them or suborning them."

"Nelly and Sal have been working full-time with the Marine and Navy tech. We kill off two, three more arrive. We suborn five, eight show up."

"You've got a Marine Honor Guard out there for the Emperor to review. Are you going to let Major Henderson take the escort honor?"

"No, I have to do it, but you stay here behind the clear hatch covering. He can see you, and none of that crap gets near you."

Kris didn't like that, and her face, no doubt, showed it.

"Admiral, I will throw you over my shoulder and lock you up in your quarters if I have to."

Kris scowled and glanced down at all the fruit salad. "It would make a mess of my uniform."

"And, no doubt, I'd be gouged by all those prickly things. Good God, woman, where did they all come from?"

Kris glanced at all the salad on Jack's chest. "You're missing one. Meg, did a Star Leaper thing come in today's mail for Jack?"

The young woman took off at a gallop.

"Star what?" Jack asked.

"The Order of St. Christopher, Star Leaper. Harry awarded it to all the folks that survived the trip around the galaxy. Or not. Most got it posthumously."

"Maybe they forgot I was there."

"Maybe. What's taking Harry so long?"

"I have no idea. I got from the station to the quarterdeck in ten minutes, and I was fighting bots all the way."

Captain Ajax arrived to greet the Emperor. She took one look at Kris and whistled. "I'd heard that the King considered you his fightingest admiral, but I've never understood why. Did you get all that fruit salad at the produce section?"

"Catch me some evening when I'm feeling mellow, and I may tell you the stories. Tell you the ones that aren't classified."

"I'll do that. By the way, the Emperor's procession is making its way up A deck. They've got him in some kind of electric cart. We sent a nano out to get a good picture of it.

"Captain, we've got a feed coming in," the Officer of the Deck announced.

"Put it on the nearest screen."

"There is no near screen," Nelly pointed out. "I've got it coming up on the bulkhead beside the hatch."

A bit of bulkhead became a screen, showing a confused line of Imperial Guards, police, station security, and half the dogs and cats on the station. In the middle of them was an enclosed electric cart. The clear and likely armored plastic looked like a recent addition.

"So even Harry himself doesn't feel safe on his own station," Jack observed.

"Interesting, that he's afraid of the horde of bots filling the air."

"Kris, we're identifying a whole new batch of nanos. They're tiny, and they don't belong to us," Nelly reported. "I've tried to suborn them, but they are proving rather impossible to establish contact with."

"The Empress comes to call, and suddenly we're facing the worst infestation of nasty and small critters that we've seen," Kris observed.

"How do we handle it?" Captain Ajax asked.

Jack stared through the hatch, worrying his lower lip. "Captain, how much spare air do we have?"

"Let me get you that," Ajax said, raising her wrist unit to her mouth.

"We've got enough air to empty the quarterdeck five times," Nelly provided.

"We can't subject the Emperor and Empress to vacuum, Jack," Kris pointed out.

"Not vacuum," Jack answered, "but even they can survive a bit of wind. How about wind and infrared."

"Boil the tiny things and blow them out," Kris said.

"Exactly," Jack answered.

Kris turned to Captain Ajax. "Ma'am, would you please suck as much air from the outside as you can manage to strain, then superheat it. I'd suggest you keep it separate from the air you now have in storage. We could use the new stuff first, then do the final flushes with the air we brought."

"Good idea, Admiral, and Nelly, thank you for having the information at your fingertips."

"You're welcome, Captain. I'm always glad when I can help you humans make good snap decisions."

A quick call to the XO got that process started.

When Ajax finished, she cleared her throat. "I don't mean to be asking questions above my pay grade, but I understand that we've got interceptors out there. Why haven't we ordered them to destroy the offending nanos?"

"A very good question, Captain. Thanks for raising it," Jack said. "I haven't ordered war on the station nanos because they are on the station. That is not Wardhaven territory. Also, if we start a war now, who knows what reinforcements they could bring in. No. Let's bring Harry and his harridan aboard, isolate them in yonder air lock, sanitize them for all they're worth, then turn loose the interceptors to get what's left."

"Right. Politics," the captain said.

"It's always politics," Kris said drolly. "Jack, how are we fixed for nanos?"

"With the ship blown up way more than you'd ever dare do a balloon, I'll have to be careful just where Nelly grabs Smart Metal to make nanos. We've already taken down some of the walls in Marine country. A lot of the privates now have one huge barracks bay. We've promised them their walls back as soon as we get rid of Harry. Oh, Kris, if you decide to take the Emperor through Marine country, go to Enlisted Quarters 1. We kept one normal. Those other bays really look silly."

"And might be mistaken for space to transport an invasion force," Kris observed dryly.

"Yeah, that, too," Jack said.

"If you need more Smart Metal, pull it out of the wall between our day and night quarters."

"I would suggest not," Jack put in quickly.

Kris gave him a sour glower.

"I would think you're very likely to take the Peterwalds through our quarters."

Kris winced. "Right. Good catch, my wise husband."

"We'll take it out of the nannies' space," Nelly said.

"Okay, Nelly. Give them my apologies and explain what we're doing in case we have to do it real sudden-like, and someone's in the shower."

"I'm doing it now, Kris."

Jack glanced back at the band. It was turned up, and its commander looked ready to parade it across the quarterdeck and down onto the pier to take up its place next to the honor guard. Jack shook his head.

"We've already got too much nano bait on the pier. Captain, would you mind telling your band leader he's to honor our fine guests from here on the quarterdeck."

Captain Ajax eyed the pier, glanced back at the band, then went to see that they kept themselves behind the quarterdeck hatch cover. The band leader didn't look at all happy, but he obeyed his orders.

On the quarterdeck screen, the Emperor's procession arrived at the area above the *Princess Royal*'s pier. There, it came to a roaring halt.

No matter what your rank, you can't ride an electric cart down an escalator. *Looks like I'm not the only one making allowances today,* Kris thought.

There was a lot of shouting and carrying on until several freight elevators were located. Then there was more shouting and thumping of chests as they figured out who rode down on the elevator with the Emperor. It was worse deciding who got to ride down on the other two elevators and who got stuck hustling for the escalator, then struggling to find their place once more in the parade.

It was a mess.

Jack saluted Kris, then passed through the air lock and made his way down the gangplank to stand at the head of his Marines and make the official greetings. He glanced around,

got a thoughtful look, then marched the honor guard closer to
the escalator.

Then things got crazier.

Emperor Henry I refused to dismount his cart to take the
inspection of the honor guard.

Jack made a snap decision. He saluted the Emperor and
Empress in their cart and said on Nelly Net, RUFFLES AND
FLOURISHES, IF YOU PLEASE.

Kris nodded. Captain Ajax gave the band leader his cue,
and, with a shrug, his band belted out the proper honors. That
was followed by the Imperial Anthem, a quite bellicose march.

Musical honors rendered, Jack stepped forward and
escorted Emperor, Empress, and cart down the forward rank
of Marines.

Then he did a smart turn and led cart and occupants right
up the brow, onto the quarterdeck, and into an enlarged air
lock that Nelly had just expanded so that Jack, Emperor,
Empress, and their cart fit in it quite cozily.

The wall closed behind them just as Jack thought, RUFFLES
AND FLOURISHES AGAIN, PLEASE, AND THAT MARCH, EVEN
LOUDER.

Thoroughly puzzled, the band did as it was told, slamming
into the garish march, this time with added blaring trumpets,
hammering drums, and clashing cymbals.

NELLY, WHAT'S GOING ON?

KRIS, WE'RE GOING TO PLAY THAT NOISE FOR HOWEVER
LONG IT TAKES US TO STOMP ON ALL THE NANOS THAT TRIED
TO SLIP ABOARD ON THE IMPERIAL COATTAILS.

VERY GOOD, NELLY.

Meanwhile, everyone stood stiffly at attention, saluting.
The Imperial Guards were not happy at what Jack had pulled
off on them. They finally organized themselves to march up
the brow. There, their officers found they could do nothing
more than salute from outside the barrier, while staring daggers at anyone who would meet their eyes.

Kris was careful not to.

In the air lock, the Emperor asked Jack about the delay. He
explained the problem with the nanos and asked the Imperials'
indulgence. Nelly kept Kris up to date on what was going on.

NELLY, HOW IS THE EMPRESS TAKING ALL THIS?

Not well, Kris. Sal thinks she's steaming, but it's kind of hard to tell.

The Emperor got curious about the substance of the air lock.

"It's transparent Smart Metal," Jack explained, then had to help Harry out of his cart so he could touch the stuff. He rapped his knuckles on it and invited his Empress to come take a look.

She smiled coyly at Jack and asked for his help.

Kris had been eyeing her dress. The bottom was flounced out to fill up most of the cart. The bodice was a lot less.

A whole lot less.

As Jack helped the Empress from her cart, she gave Kris an evil smile . . . and stuck her practically bare boob in Jack's face.

You enjoying yourself?

Not really, Kris. There's enough silicone in there to just about knock me out.

Kris shook her head. The men will be missing half their IQ.

With a sigh and an effort, Kris pulled her mind out of the catfight it so wanted to get into and prepared to meet the Emperor and Empress.

37

The Emperor eyed Kris. "Transparent Smart Metal; what will you Longknifes think of next?" he said through the airlock.

NELLY?

TWO NANOS ARE STILL ELUDING US. GO AHEAD AND BRING THEM ABOARD.

The air lock vanished around them. Kris saluted and stepped forward, concluding Harry would prefer her smile to eight sideboys.

"Welcome aboard, Your Imperial Majesty," she said, then, holding her salute, turned to face the Empress. "Your Imperial Highness."

Kris dropped her salute and the loud racket from the band cut off.

"Why are you separating us from our Imperial Guard?" the Empress demanded.

"Ah. Yes. Just what is going on?" the Emperor asked.

"You'll pardon us, Your Imperial Majesty," Kris said, "but we have discovered that your station is suffering an infestation of bots and nanos. Do you know of this problem?"

"No," the Empress huffed.

"Yes, dear. Remember, that is why we were confined to that damnable little cart. They wanted to protect us from whatever it is that's buzzing about. Still, I must have my guards," Harry went on.

"And you shall, Your Imperial Majesty. However, could you limit the number to the essentials and have the others wait outside? Then, if those you want could hurry aboard quickly so that we only have to keep the outer air-lock hatch open for a brief spell . . ." Kris hoped he wouldn't press the question further.

So, of course, he did.

"Some of these pesky things are bound to get aboard, though. Some may already have gotten in when you opened that thing to let us in. By the way, how did you do that?" he said, pointing at the clear Smart Metal™ of the partition across the open hatch of the quarterdeck.

"My computer is able to make that, and, as you saw, create an air lock when we need it."

"That must be nice, and clear, no less."

"Yes, sir," Kris said, hoping Harry had forgotten about his first question.

"So," he said, turning to Kris, "how will you keep those buggers from infesting your ship?"

"As you can see, Your Imperial Majesty, the quarterdeck is isolated by more clear partitions at all passageways into the ship. We will board as many of your subjects as you require into an enlarged air lock. Once they are here, we will subject that space to weak infrared light that doesn't bother us but does effect tiny things. Then we will run a major ventilation through that lock. We expect it will blow the little things right back where they came from. Bots and things are challenging devices, but they don't have the power to tack long against the wind."

At least these bots couldn't. Kris had been offered a batch of nano prototypes superpowered by the strange plant from Alwa. She'd declined to take them into the belly of the beast. If she lost one, it might or might not be retroengineered. You could never tell how good Greenfeld technology was.

The Emperor considered Kris's answer and seemed happy with it.

The Empress wanted to know more. "And what if all the pesky buggers aren't blown away?"

"I have Marines prepared to go after them . . . with butterfly nets," Kris said.

That drew a laugh from the Emperor and several of the unused sideboys and other Sailors standing by for the OOD's orders. A scowl from the JOOD, who this watch was a grizzled old chief, and the only laughter belonged to the Emperor.

"Very good. So very good. Well, you must tell the general commanding the Imperial Guard that he and two dozen of his best men may protect us. We guess we'll have to let all our advisors in. Love, I know you'll want to include some of your advisors."

"All of them," brooked no alternative.

"That will make for five, ten . . . Oh, ask my prime minister who we need."

In five minutes, twenty-five guardsmen and twice as many advisors stood on the brow. Half the guardsmen were first, prepared to charge to the immediate defense of their Emperor. The other half were at the rear, ready to put speed on any slowpokes and provide a wall against those still arguing that they needed to be included.

A chief bosun's mate's pipe announced, "All hands, prepare to receive visitors. Civilians on the gangway, shake a leg."

Kris noticed an increase in air pressure; nanos would have a hard time flying against that wind. Harry eyed the clear partition. His eyes grew big, as a much larger air lock, one that was comfortable enough to hold all his guards and advisors, appeared.

The Imperial Guard charged aboard at the double. The civilians made their way aboard, squawking like a bunch of old chickens and hurried along by the last of the guardsmen.

Those who raced along to get aboard if there was the slightest chance found themselves staring into the blank faces of Royal US Marines with rifles at port arms.

That ended that noise.

The chief bosun piped again. 'All hands on the quarterdeck stand at ease while we take care of a minor problem."

Red lights came on. Kris wondered what other wavelengths were bathing the quarterdeck, but said nothing. The pressure on her ears increased slightly, and she could hear a whooshing sound as air poured into the air lock and leaked out through small holes in the partition. Five different times the air lock went through a complete change in its atmosphere. Five times there was a wait, encouraging any tiny rider holding on to clothes, hair, whatever, to drift away.

KRIS, THE AIR SWAPS ARE DONE. WE COULD USE SOME TIME TO LET OUR NANOS ATTACK ANY THAT ARE STILL HERE.

I'LL SEE WHAT I CAN DO, Kris thought, and, while the seventy-five still in the clear air lock made impatient faces, she turned to the Emperor.

"So, Your Imperial Majesty, what would you like to see during your visit to the *Princess Royal*?"

"Is there any chance we and some of our advisors might see your engineering spaces?" he said. "We've been told you no longer use magnetohydrodynamic generators to derive your ship's electricity."

"That is hardly something I know anything about," Kris said with as much of the airhead as she could muster. Wardhaven's ships were now generating electricity directly from the reactor's fusion plasma. It gave them a major advantage in combat and was something she had no intention of letting the Peterwalds get a look at.

That Harry had not asked about the improved power generators the US had gotten from the Iteeche spoke volumes for how much Greenfeld had fallen behind in the spying game. More reason to call the *Princess Royal* a frigate and make sure no one got a good look at how many lasers this battlecruiser carried.

"The Grand Salon where we will be meeting to discuss what you called me here for is only two decks down," Kris said, renaming the Forward Lounge. "This deck not only has the quarterdeck where we now stand, but also Admiral's Country. That includes our quarters and the nursery and quarters for the nannies we took aboard before we left Wardhaven."

"Nursery?" Harry said. "Nannies? This must be very recent. I heard nothing of such a thing."

"Yes, we and your lovely wife share the great joy of having recently presented our husbands with children. We brought our daughter with us. I'd hate to be separated from Ruth."

"I am so proud of my newborn son, Henry Smythe-Peterwald the XV," the Emperor said, and gave the Empress a loving hug. She kissed the side of his neck. "That's wonderful. You have a girl. I have a son. We might do a bit of matchmaking. Arrange an alliance around our children."

A look of rage and horror flitted across the Empress's face, but she immediately suppressed her visage to bland, and said to Kris. "You must be very proud."

"I never suspected the joys a woman might know before Ruth came into my life," Kris said. "Now, may I offer you refreshments in my quarters while everyone sorts themselves out?"

"Why thank you, we'd appreciate a drink," the Emperor said.

"And we might see the baby?" the Empress added.

"Yes, yes. Of course, dear."

So they adjourned to Kris's day quarters.

Which had grown even more opulent since she had left less than an hour ago.

Now the bulkheads were polished woods in delicate patterns that formed pictures of Wardhaven's hills, seas, and farmland. The wood shared the walls—Kris could hardly think of anything this extravagant as a respectable Navy bulkhead—with velvet red wallpaper covered in golden *fleur-de-lis*. The burgundy carpet under their feet was lush. They sank into it much as Kris remembered sinking into the mud of Olympia.

Don't go there. There be dragons . . . and memories of Harry here trying to drown me.

The conference table and chairs, as well as Kris's desk, had disappeared, some, no doubt, into nano interceptors. There was a conversation square, two very overstuffed chairs and a similar number of couches, in front of a roaring fire.

"You have a fireplace aboard your ship?" the Empress asked.

"It reminds me of home," Kris lied. It reminded her of a borrowed cabin where she and Jack had finally managed to discover the pleasure of each other's touch. "It helps me think," Kris finished.

And the imp in her came up with a really bad idea.

"If you'd prefer to eliminate the fireplace, Nelly, remove it," and the fireplace melted into the wall, to be replaced with more wood paneling.

Harry about dropped his uppers.

"Oh no," the Empress said, not at all thrown by the technical marvels before them. "Harry and I love a good fire, don't we, honey?"

"Of course, love," the boggled Emperor managed to get out.

"Nelly," was all Kris had to say before the cheery fireplace flowed back into place.

"Also, Nelly, there are only the four of us. We hardly need couches."

"Yes, Your Highness," Nelly said, and quickly there were four large overstuffed chairs and the rectangular coffee table between them shrank into a square.

"Your computer, Nelly?" the Empress said, "is quite intuitive."

"Nelly is quite unique among computers," Kris said, leaving out Jack's Sal for the moment.

KRIS, I'VE MANAGED TO KILL THE HANDFUL OF NANOS THAT GOT INTO YOUR QUARTERS WITH HARRY. WE'RE STILL CHASING A FEW ON THE QUARTERDECK. PLEASE STALL.

"What may we offer you?" Kris asked the Emperor. "Tea, coffee, something stronger?"

"I'll have a Manhattan," the Emperor said. "A double please."

"I'd love a strawberry daiquiri," the Empress said. "It's so nice to be able to drink again."

"I'll have iced tea," Kris said, and Jack asked for the same.

"I don't have a wet bar," Kris admitted, "but the artists of the Grand Salon should have them ready in a moment. So, how was your trip up the space elevator?" Kris asked, space offering little chance for small talk about its weather.

"Not really a bother," the Emperor said. "I so rarely get out of the Palace."

"It's a lovely day in Anhalt," the Empress added. "So pleasant for a drive. We really must thank you for inviting us up here."

Kris had to struggle to keep her face bland as the Empress put a new turn to events.

At that moment, their drinks appeared on the right arm of most of their chairs. Since Harry had his elbow on that arm, his came out on his left.

"Damn!" escaped the Emperor's lips. "This stuff *is* damn near magic."

"You must pardon my computer. We are still experimenting with new things we can do with Smart Metal. We must admit that we have never seen something like this."

"I wanted to get the drinks here before the ice had any chance to melt, Your Imperial Majesty," Nelly said, then added to Kris, AND WE'RE STILL CHASING A FEW PESKY NANOS ON THE QUARTERDECK. IF A WAITER HAD TO BRING THE DRINKS, ONE OF THEM MIGHT HAVE GOTTEN OUT.

WELL DONE, NELLY. I THINK YOU REALLY IMPRESSED HARRY.

HE BETTER BE IMPRESSED. HE'S GETTING THE FULL-COURT PRESS.

They sipped their drinks and talked of inanities. Then the Empress asked if she might see the baby. Thus, Ruthie was called for.

A moment later, the infant appeared in the capable arms of Fede Radko, with Li O'Maley walking sternly by her side looking every bit the Gunny, ready to make sure that the world was right.

And woe be to him who dared upset her world.

Fede handed Ruth to Kris first, and Kris realized this was a horrible idea. A baby and dress whites, complete with medals and decorations, were never intended to mix. Kris always held Ruth with her left arm. Today, she cradled her in her right. That kept the little one away from being poked by this order or that.

Still, Ruthie's eyes lit up at the sight of all those dangling sparklies at Mommy's neck. Her pudgy fingers were just learning to reach, and she managed to grab the Almar Medal of Highest Valor and pull it right into her mouth. She slobbered happily as she teethed on it.

Well, at least she didn't start pounding on my breasts to be fed.

Kris let Ruth chew away happily on metal brought from far across the galaxy, then said, "Okay, Gunny O'Malley, what do we trade her for my medal?"

The retired chief warrant quickly produced a teething ring, and while Fede carefully removed the baby from Kris's arms, O'Malley slipped the teething ring into Ruth's mouth and the award out before Kris was pulled away by its ribbon.

"Would you like to hold her?" Kris asked the Empress.

She glanced down at her exposed breasts with a knowing smile. "I don't think my gown would survive the attention of such strong hands that weren't my loving Emperor's."

That ended with her sharing a smile with the Emperor that left him gobsmacked and looking in need of a room.

"Your advisors are waiting for you in the Grand Salon," Nelly announced.

"Then I guess we should be going," the Emperor said.

And they went.

38

The short walk down two decks was not without its comments.

"You have done magnificent things with Smart Metal," the Emperor said as he eyed the statues and paintings that surrounded them as they crossed from one wide staircase to the next.

"This is Marine country, isn't it, Jack?" Kris said.

"Yes. Each Marine has his or her own stateroom. There's a movie stadium, bowling alley, rifle range, and exercise room that would beat any health club from here to Earth, with a three-kilometer track that circles the hull."

"You let your Marines live in such splendor," Harry marveled. "The commander of my Imperial Guard is always after me to provide better quarters and places the troops can relax and be entertained. Please don't give him any idea what you've done."

"Certainly not, Your Imperial Majesty."

They passed four Marines, rifles at present arms. Two were women with sharpshooter's badges.

"I keep forgetting," the Empress said. "You Longknifes give your women a free rein to attempt any job that they think they might succeed at."

"Yes, Your Imperial Highness," Kris said, wishing things were half as good in Wardhaven space as the Peterwalds gave them credit for.

"Do you aspire to the kingship?" was said evenly, with a slight rise of an exquisitely made-up eye.

Kris paused as if to give that question serious thought.

Hell no, I don't want the job.

But she answered the Empress with a vague, "I haven't actually read the final signed version of the Constitution. I've been rather busy elsewhere, you know."

That got a nod from both of the Imperials.

"But I understand that when Grampa Ray's twenty-five years as King are up, we Longknifes are barred from all political offices, including the purple."

"I find that hard to believe," Harry said.

"But I heard that was the intent," Kris answered.

The Empress said nothing, but for a moment she lost the placid face she wore. What flitted across her face left Kris uneasy at best. Scared at the worst.

And on those thoughts, they were down the stairs.

Someone had been making improvements since Kris was last here. Candelabras and chandeliers now gave the rooms a soft glow, reflected back by the mirrors. The circular bar in the center of the Grand Salon looked like it was made of marble with a bronze rail for the feet. Behind the bar were more mirrors, pictures of nudes, or arrangements of bottles.

Classy.

Each of the divided spaces had a different motif. One was red and gold, another blue and silver. The room Nelly directed them to was a cold and severe white. Lush white carpet, white, patterned wallpaper, stark white cloisonné tables and chairs. Here, the mirrors were edged in chrome.

The tables and chairs had been arranged loosely in a square around four large, comfortable armchairs. They alone added color: two were red, the other two blue.

THE RED ARE FOR THE IMPERIALS.

Kris ushered the Emperor and Empress to their chairs. Their lackeys immediately jumped to assure that their raiment was arranged properly, and they were totally comfortable.

Two drinks, identical to the ones ordered in Kris's quarters, immediately appeared out of the chairs' arms.

"I hope I did not presume," Kris said.

"No. No. This is perfect," Harry agreed.

Kris and Jack took their places. To Kris's and Jack's back were two corners of the square, tables drawn up two rows deep. Her main staff of advisors had taken their places. Farther back, the lesser specialists sat in comfortable chairs closer to the walls. There was no fuss or bother as to who belonged where.

On the other side, behind the Imperials, it was much more unclear. Many of the men in fancy doublets, breeches, and hose also carried swords and at least for a while, it looked like duels might be fought for seats at the table. In the end, the left half of the space, that behind the Emperor, went to people in fancy dress in every color of the rainbow. The right half, behind the Empress, filled up with men in more somber clothing, darker blues, purples, and blacks. They were still in doublets and hose with befeathered hats. Oh, and swords.

Kris wondered if she should have added her Navy-issue automatic to her dress today. She hadn't forgotten her spider-silk underarmor.

And Jack had plenty of Marines at the ready. Although only twenty-five stood against the wall, balancing the same number of Imperial Guardsman, her backup was a lot closer than the Imperials.

There will not be any problems today.

After the commotion died down, Kris waited for Emperor Henry I to say something. Instead, he just sipped his Manhattan. The Empress sipped her daiquiri. Kris took a taste of her tea and put it back on the arm of the chair.

How LONG ARE YOU GOING TO WAIT? Jack asked on Nelly Net.

NOT ANY LONGER THAN THIS.

Kris leaned forward and cleared her throat. The two Imperials continued to lean back, sipping. "You called us here, Your Imperial Majesty. May we ask what you require of us?"

The Emperor of everything that resided under the Greenfeld flag . . . maybe less . . . huffed out a sigh. "My daughter, the Grand Duchess Victoria, seems to be in rebellion against me. I was hoping you, as a good friend to both of us, might get her to stop this nonsense and come home."

Kris noted the loss of the Imperial "we." A father was speaking to her, not an Emperor.

"Really, I don't think it's the girl's fault," the Empress put in. "I really think she's fallen in with a bad bunch who are urging her on to this, ah, defiance of her father."

Kris tested those words, and, as much as she didn't want to, found them sincere.

"How did all this happen?" Kris asked.

The Empress cast her husband a glance. When he imperceptibly nodded, she began, "I don't know if you've been keeping up to date with current Greenfeld events," she said, and paused for Kris to respond.

Kris chuckled. "Actually, I haven't been keeping up on *any* events this side of the galaxy."

The Empress considered that for a moment, almost allowed a frown to slip onto her face, then went on. "Well, there has been much economic distress here. The economy has contracted. What started as minor economic adjustments on some planets have spiraled down to worse and worse. *Some* elements have chosen to take advantage of *our* trouble, and while Emperor Henry here and others have been as gentle as possible in their efforts to secure the safety of our many distraught people, some have taken to using these times for their own profit.

"Previously, when rebellion raised its ugly head, my gentle husband relied on State Security to properly chastise those involved and preserve the tranquility of the Empire. However, no doubt you may recall that State Security attempted a coup of its own and would have killed my loving Emperor while he was hunting on Birridas. You saved his life, and I thank you from the bottom of my heart." That was done with a hand to her heart that somehow managed not to put what little she wore into disarray.

"I don't know what I would do without my Harry in the center of my life." The Empress interrupted her story to send a kiss her husband's way, and he returned one to her.

She turned back to Kris with a loving smile on her face, sighed, and continued. "The rooting out of the cancer in State Security left the place little more than a shell. Thus, when some elements incited people to riot, there were few options open for us to prevent the civil unrest."

"Who were these people inflaming your subjects?" Kris asked.

"The Navy," the Empress spat. "They have betrayed their sacred duty. They had been allowed to found their own colonies, supposedly retirement communities. We've found that to be a traitorous lie. Would you believe it, when we had to cut the budget and decommission ships, captains took their ships off to those same Navy colonies and joined in open rebellion."

The two Imperials exchanged angry glances.

"You know that my Vicky has spent the last four years with the Navy," Harry said. "I thought they might instill some discipline in her. She was a most willful girl to start with."

Kris nodded. *Willful? How about murderous?* Still, she said nothing.

"We think," the Empress went on, "that some of those elements in the Navy brainwashed her into spouting their propaganda. When last I saw her, she was strutting around in a uniform. What was her supposed rank?" she asked, glancing over her shoulder.

"Vice admiral," the field marshal commanding the Imperial Guard provided.

"Vice admiral, would you believe. She's hardly been in the Navy four years."

Kris had to admit that four years to vice admiral was cutting it mighty short. She'd taken five.

She did not tell Vicky's stepmother that.

"So what do you want me to do?" Kris asked again, dropping her royal "we" since they had dropped theirs.

Now the Emperor leaned forward earnestly in his seat. "Go to her. Those rebels wouldn't dare fire on the US flag. Tell her I love her and all will be forgiven if she'll just abandon those traitorous elements and come home."

"I tried to bring her home," the Empress put in.

"I took a major fleet to St. Petersburg to get our Vicky back from their clutches. They had the audacity to resist me and even fire on some of the ships with me. I couldn't believe it. I would have gotten through to the ship she was being held on, but we received a message from my loving husband announcing that he wanted to bring you into the resolution of this problem, and I announced a general cease-fire. Badly outnumbered, the rebels were only too happy to grab this chance to withdraw and regroup. They still refused to let me have my daughter back. They refused me, her loving mother."

Kris nodded, doing her best to remain evenhanded and listen, really listen to the Empress. Still, in the back of her brain was a clear memory of Vicky's sharing the uptick in assassination attempts that started just about the time her stepmother announced she was pregnant with a boy.

Kris blinked. The silence after the Empress's last word was growing.

"Your Imperial Majesty, I will accept your charge. You mentioned that the Grand Duchess was last seen at St. Petersburg."

"Yes," the Empress provided.

"Then I and my squadron will depart for there immediately and do our best to retrieve your daughter from anyone holding her hostage. As a Longknife, I detest kidnappers."

Of course, it was rumored that the man seated across from her had paid to kill Kris's grandmother Sarah and arrange the kidnapping of her brother, Eddy.

Without so much as blinking an eye, the Emperor said, "I knew you would answer my call. Can you take a fleet out to St. Petersburg and bring back my Vicky?"

"I will most certainly try, Your Imperial Majesty; however, I don't have a fleet," Kris pointed out.

"What do you have?" the Empress asked.

"The squadron you see here, eight frigates."

"Good God, young woman, they will blow you to bits," the Empress put in. "I saw the fleet they had. And the admirals organizing this rebellion are smart fighting men. We can't seem to find anyone of that high caliber."

"I've won a few battles of my own," Kris said, modestly.

"Well, if you think so," the Emperor said.

"As you mentioned before, Your Imperial Majesty, I fly the US flag. I do not expect to have to fight my way in or out."

"But how will you get your hands on her?" the Empress demanded.

"All I need to do is get her onto US territory, and I will do it the same way there that I did here to bring you to US territory."

"Oh," the Emperor said.

"Oh," the Empress said, glancing over Kris's shoulder at the Marines standing stiffly against the wall. A quick glance over her shoulder and the face that came back to face Kris was most thoughtful.

"I am very grateful for your coming," Kris said, standing. "Now, if you will return to the station, I have a squadron I would like to get under way as soon as possible."

It took much less time for the Imperial mob to exit the *Princess Royal* than it had to get them aboard. As they gathered on the quarterdeck, Nelly formed an air lock around them and sent them on their way with only a minimal loss of air.

The returning Marine guards quickly paraded into the now-empty air lock and began their decontamination.

Four hours later, the squadron was in its last preparations to close locks and depart. Several large containers were towed up to the seven other ships of the squadron. It seemed that Nelly had indeed arranged for the delivery of certain libations.

"Ma'am?" Captain Ajax asked.

"Nelly, are those loads paid for?"

"The requisition chit has been submitted to the Palace. If it is to be audited, it won't happen until we are well away from the pier."

"Jack?"

"You've gotten away with treating Sailors like grown-ups so far. Why not try it again? You will, no doubt, maintain the limit of no more than two drinks or beers an evening."

"And if anyone renders themselves unfit for duty, I will reinstate keelhauling and see how long they can hold their breath."

"Keelhauling?" came from Captain Ajax.

"Nelly, you explain it to the captain when you have a chance. Get the beer trucks taken aboard first. Make sure they're decontaminated."

"How long do we keep this love-boat configuration?" Captain Ajax asked.

"No later than when we come within double 18-inch-laser range of a jump. We still go through the jumps at Condition Zed and battle stations."

"Aye, aye, Admiral.

With no further problems, they headed out to get Vicky's side of the story.

39

Jump after jump, as they made their way out from Greenfeld, passed with no surprises. They seemed to have space all
to themselves. When they jumped into the Pozen system, they
were nervously hailed.

Kris personally took the comm to inform the planet that
they would not approach them. "We are US ships on a diplomatic mission. I am Princess Kris Longknife."

That seemed to mollify the station . . . and the battleship
and two cruisers docked to it.

A few jumps later, they entered the Presov system, only to
find the light cruiser *Emden* holding fifty thousand kilometers
out from the jump.

"We have been detailed by the Grand Duchess to assure the
safety of your last few jumps."

"We're deep into rebel territory," Kris pointed out. "Can't
you control your own shipping lanes?"

"Usually, yes. We've blown up or captured quite a few of
the so-called pirates. Still, the black-hearted Empress occasionally gets the odd ship deep into our territory by using the
minor jumps and barren systems."

"Well, we are grateful for your help," Kris said. "Nelly, cut the commlink." Then she turned to Jack. "Well, what do you think of that?"

"I'd say it puts a bit of a different twist on the Empress's opinion."

"The Grand Duchess can order ships to meet us. That doesn't sound like a hostage situation to me," Kris snapped.

"Let's hold our horses," Jack said. "The skipper of a light cruiser may not know anything about what is taking place at the high-command levels."

Kris scowled. "Yes. Yes, I know. Still, I can't see the Vicky I know letting anyone use her. Her use them? No question. Them use her? Nope. Not going to happen."

"I won't argue with you, wife. But I would suggest the admiral pass along that communication to her brain trust with a request to assess it and the Empress's side of the story to see what we can make of the two."

Kris sighed. "Okay, my ever-cautious husband. I will refrain from my usual exercise of jumping to conclusions."

She slipped close to Jack, and whispered, "But I would dearly like to jump your bones."

"Hon, I'm scheduled to lead my Marines in a run. Every time we expand amidships back to huge, we Marines get our track back. It's exactly three point two seven kilometers around the waist of the ship."

"You could get your exercise jumping my bones," Kris pouted.

"Or we could both get our exercise, first a ten kilometer run, then a roll in the hay."

"You really want me to work off my baby fat, don't you?"

"Nelly, can you rerun my last few comments for Kris. Was baby fat mentioned by anyone but her?"

"I assume that is a rhetorical question," the computer said.

"You win, husband, but you can lead from the front. I will pull up the rear where I shouldn't be too embarrassed by any-one's noticing my finishing time."

A few more jumps, and Kris was almost able to finish right up with the rest of the Marine detachment. And with Ruth skimming the top off the fat she ate for her milk, Kris wasn't doing too badly tightening up her mommy body.

Still, the entire squadron was at battle stations, ships at

Condition Zed, as they made the jump into the St. Petersburg system.

Kris stood before the main screen. "This is the US frigate *Princess Royal*, and I am Admiral, Her Royal Highness Kristine of the United Society in a diplomatic mission. I have come to talk to Grand Duchess Victoria of Greenfeld."

The message went out at light speed. They would have a long wait before Vicky could reply . . . if she was permitted to.

The sensor crew quickly developed a picture of the St. Petersburg system. The station hardly had a vacant pier, what with freighters coming in and going out.

"There's a lot more trade going on than we saw around Greenfeld," the tech specialist advised. "There are also a whole lot of warships. I've made out an even dozen battleships, another dozen cruisers, heavy and light, and twenty or so destroyers. I think some of the merchant ships are armed cruisers, but all the merchant ships are armed. It's hard to draw a line between armed merchant ship and ship loaded with heavy armament to make them merchant cruisers."

"No doubt we'll get a better picture once we're on approach to the station."

"Ma'am, several of those battleships are honking big dudes. One has sixteen 18-inch lasers and a whole lot of secondary guns."

"And to think, just a few years ago, we'd be worried about such a monster," Jack whispered to Kris.

She had to chuckle at how things had changed.

Kris met with her brain trust and found them still unwilling to make any commitments. She found she got more out of time with Ruth and her nannies than she got from those ninnies. Kris had paperwork to keep up with. She'd requested a report from all her captains about how they were handling sailing ships blown up like balloons and with their own public house aboard.

Each ship had at least one chief who did not like the idea of booze aboard. However, it was universally agreed that the gripe came from the chief who operated the still in the goat locker, and since everyone else seemed to be getting along, the change in situation was deemed acceptable. Those who couldn't hold themselves to the two limit were few and given counseling. They were in line for more if the first session wasn't enough. Several ships had established a policy that those on probation for breaking the two limit would not be allowed in the bar without a buddy who was responsible for them.

Kris liked that policy and sent back a well-done to those ships that had established it and a suggestion to the others to do likewise.

The day turned out very busy, and Kris had just collapsed into bed with Jack, Ruth fed and a spare bottle of milk for her so Kris could sleep through the night. She was edging into Jack's arms and wondering if she was really exhausted or might she have a bit of reserves for her and Jack when Nelly announced, "A message has arrived on the bridge from Vicky Peterwald."

Kris said a most unprincesslike word, which was seconded by Jack, and the two tumbled out of bed and hastily pulled on shipsuits.

"Nelly, have the message sent down to flag plot and advise the three heads of my brain trust to report to my quarters immediately, as in five minutes ago. You might tell them why."

"I have the message ready to play in your flag plot and all of your brain trust had left messages to alert them when a message came back. They're already on their way here."

That was one advantage of letting the ship balloon out. Flag Country and the brain trust were just about next door to each other. Jack opened the door, and Kris stepped through from her bedroom to her work.

It is, it is a truly glorious thing to be a pirate Princess.

Judge Diana Frogmore was already there, waiting, though her attire was a bit informal, a tank top and gym shorts. "I hadn't gone to bed yet, so it was easy to rush over."

Senior Arbitrator Bill Gladsten arrived a moment later, in sweats. "Am I late?"

"Al's still missing," Diana told him.

The clock ticked off three minutes and Kris was edgy enough to start without him when Al Fu, the chief mediator, walked in wearing a dressing gown, a hair net, and showing where he'd missed some skin cream when he hastily wiped it off his face. "Okay, okay, sorry to be late."

"Now we'll start," Kris said, but the door opened again, and Runda Fairsight trotted in, wearing light blue slacks and a badly wrinkled but brightly embroidered shirt that Kris remembered her wearing that morning.

"Sorry, we were looking at the data take from St. Petersburg. It's not nearly as encrypted as Greenfeld's. I think we're making up a good picture of the economy."

"Good, now, let's see what Vicky has to say, assuming she was allowed to talk to us at all," Kris said.

The screen lit up and there was Vicky in Navy blues showing the stripes of a vice admiral. "Kris, I'm so glad to see you," she squeed. "Boy, have I got dirt to dish with you. You wouldn't believe all the stuff I've done in what, the last two years is it?"

Vicky paused to take a breath. "I don't know how you've managed to do all you do, but I've tried my hand at a few things, always wondering what Kris Longknife would do. Not that I've turned into someone who's all for democracy and stuff. Though, this guy, you remember him, Mannie Artamus, the mayor of Sevastopol, he's kind of making it easier for me to think we need to get more people involved than just we Peterwalds in deciding what needs to be done."

Vicky's attention was drawn offscreen. "Oh, Admiral von Mittleburg says I should tell you that I did a pretty good job myself when we were fighting off the Empress's fleet. Well, fighting off several of the Empress's fleets, but she was only out here for the last, big fight. Anyway, he wants me to tell you that my three stars aren't just window dressing. I earned them. Hard to believe that, huh? I wish Admiral Krätz were here to see me now. I think about what he'd do at least as often as I think about what you'd do."

"Does that woman always talk this much?" Diana asked.

"And this fast?" Al added.

"What's she been smoking?" Bill wanted to know.

"I think she's just excited," Kris said, "though I have to admit, I have never seen her on this kind of a jag. Still, remember, it's been the better part of two years since we've been together."

On the screen, Vicky was still talking.

"Kris, you wouldn't believe what we've done out here.

There were planets that were breaking down. Total civil collapse, cannibalism might even have been in the cards. We've managed to get food out to those that were really bad off, and get trade going so planets could get their industrial sector back up and give people jobs."

Again, Vicky glanced offscreen. "We have figured out how the Empress and her father's cronies managed to collapse everything. I thought it was cutting off credit, but there was more. Admiral von Mittleburg is shushing me. I don't think he wants that identified on an open channel. And maybe I should stop talking, but I've missed you, Kris. Really missed you. We so need to talk."

Vicky paused and got a fay grin on her face. "I know how you got the Order of the Wounded Lion," she almost sang. "Signing off for now, Kris, but hurry down here. You really have to see what we've done."

The screen went blank.

The six of them looked at each other.

"Vicky is something," Kris said.

"Something else," Diana added, again staying vague.

"Well, we now know that she can access the net," Bill said. "She had an admiral of some sort with her, but I could see no gun at her head."

"She was talking too fast to be reading a script," Al observed. "I don't know how much control she actually has, but she really believes that she has been significantly in command of her fate and of planets."

"Did she say that she could claim some of the credit for resisting several invasions?" Kris asked.

"Yes she did," Nelly replied. "Would you like me to replay those parts of the message?

"Do, Nelly," and the screen lit up and Vicky talked again.

"Yes, she was in on the fight," Jack said. "Note that Admiral von Mittleburg, whoever he is, wanted her to take some credit for the victories."

"Which is not to say that she deserves such credit," Diana pointed out.

"Are you going to stay the doubting Thomas?" Bill asked.

"Someone has to," Diana said. "She may not have been waving her boobs around for every man to see, like the Empress did, but that girl is drop-dead gorgeous, and I don't trust you guys not to think with the wrong head."

"Diana, I'm a bit old to let a pretty face run away with my hardheaded logic," Al said.

"I'll believe it when I don't see it," Diana said.

"Have we done enough for the night?" Kris said through a yawn.

"I think we'll have our work cut out for us in the morning," Bill said, "but we're done here."

"Then shoo. Get out of my house," Kris said.

The others left, and she and Jack found themselves once more in bed.

"Jack, I'm sorry, but I don't have anything left for us."

"Don't be sorry, I'm running on empty, too."

"Will you at least hold me?"

Jack rolled over, and she scrunched her way until her back rested against him. He put an arm over her. Kris breathed a soft sigh . . . and was out like a light.

40

Kris sat as comfortably as she could in dress blues with all the required fruit salad. Surrounding her in her flag bridge was Jack, in full dress blue and reds, as well as her brain trust. Commander Ajax, on her bridge, brought the plus-sized *Princess Royal* smoothly up to High St. Petersburg Station. The rest of the squadron followed at thousand-kilometer intervals at Condition Baker.

All hands had been advised that their ships might go to Condition Zed with no notice. Kris's lifesaving paranoia was once more bubbling to the surface. Still, the chance to put on a display of what her frigates could do was not to be passed up.

Ahead, there had been a lot of juggling of pier assignments. Without any request from Kris, eight piers had been opened up for her squadron, all next to each other.

The pier assignment for the *Princess Royal* would have her sharing with that honking big battleship.

"Nelly, who are we tying up next to?"

"That large battleship squawks as the Imperial battleship *Retribution*, Kris."

"They still claim to be Imperial?" Jack asked.

"All of them are squawking as Imperial ships, Jack. They

have added a second line to their identification, though. They all report they are part of St. Petersburg division of the Greenfeld Imperial Navy Reserve Fleet.

"St. Petersburg division of the Greenfeld Imperial Navy Reserve Fleet?" Jack echoed. "That's quite a mouthful."

"Any comments?" Kris asked her brain trust. They stared blankly back at her, contributing nothing.

Kris ran a worried hand through her hair. "It does appear they are doing their level best to claim to be loyal subjects of their Emperor and part of the Greenfeld Imperial Navy," she said, breaking the silence.

"However, the Empress claims that the Imperial fleet is in rebellion," Jack pointed out. "The words mean nothing. They could be a cover story to make the Sailors think they are still loyal."

Kris sighed. "Agreed." She had thought that facing several gigantic alien mother ships was the worst of all possible fates. It seemed that humans with their ways of obfuscating a situation had come up with something worse. With an alien, you knew where you stood; they wanted you dead. You had to kill them.

Kris knew someone in the Greenfeld Empire wanted her dead. Those two battleships ambushing her at that jump told her that. The try at killing Jack and the nano assaults screamed something. Someone was out to kill her and hers, but who?

Easy to know. Not so easy to figure it out.

"Do we know anything about that big battlewagon, the *Retribution*?" Kris asked, hunting for something concrete.

"Not much," Nelly said. "It's got those sixteen 18-inch lasers. Lots of secondary and tertiary guns. Oh, Kris, it just changed its squawk. They've unfurled a three-star flag, so to speak, and are reporting that they are the flagship of the Vice Admiral, the Imperial Grand Duchess, Her Grace, Victoria."

The room was silent for a long moment.

"I wish they'd done that a bit earlier, like from the time we first read their identification, friend or foe," Jack said.

Kris nodded. She could think of a dozen reasons for that late addition to their information At least half of them were not good.

"We're coming alongside the pier now," Nelly reported.

Kris heard the solid "thumps" through the hull as Commander Ajax caught the four tie-downs and ran her bloated ship smoothly along the pier, giving up the last bit of momentum.

The 1MC reported a minute later, "All hands secure from underway stations. Set the in-port watches."

"The brow is in place to the quarterdeck," Nelly reported.

Jack added to that a minute later, "My Marines have established a pier-side watch with no problems.

"I have feed from the quarterdeck," Nelly reported.

"Put it on screens," Kris ordered.

The first screen showed a lieutenant commander standing as Officer of the Deck at the lip of the brow. Beside him, a young JG had on the JOOD brassard. He waited patiently, if a bit anxiously, for his senior to tell him what to do.

Kris remembered all too well having that duty not so long ago and smiled.

A dozen Sailors stood at ease along the bulkhead, ready to render honors or serve as runners or guides.

Commander Ajax ran a right and tight ship.

A second camera covered the pier. At the foot of the brow, four Marines stood at ordered arms. Beside them, a sergeant, sword in hand, stood by to render honors.

"Their rifles loaded?" Kris asked.

"Nope," Jack answered. "Only the sergeant's automatic. They have orders to withdraw at the first sign of something going ass over teakettle."

More screens showed the go-down to the pier from the station's A deck. Nothing moved. A camera focused on the brow across the pier from them showed four Marines in Imperial black-and-green dress uniforms, at order arms with a sergeant, sword in hand, standing by. A mirror image of the *Princess Royal*'s guard.

"Any nano problems?" Kris asked.

"Not so much as a buzz," Nelly reported.

Kris glanced at her brain trust and raised an eyebrow. They remained as unmoved as statues.

"Do you think we ought to give her the full treatment, honor guard and all, like we did the Emperor?" Jack asked.

Kris shook her head. "I don't think Vicky wants all the fancy stuff. If I read her right, she just wants to talk."

"Good," Jack said. "If the word gets back to the Empress, it will probably work better if we didn't."

"Kind of my thoughts, too."

One screen caught the sound of a bosun's pipe. "Grand Duchess departing. St. Petersburg Reserve Fleet departing. Battle Squadron Two departing."

The camera focused on the other gangplank caught a young woman rendering honors and hurrying down the brow, followed by two older men. Between them, they carried enough gold braid to outfit a circus.

"I think we've got company coming," Kris said. "Let's go, Jack."

"Can we come, too?" Diana asked.

"Why don't you stay here," Kris said. "I'll bring that herd of elephants to you."

That would cut down on the mob at the quarterdeck. Besides, Kris didn't want civilians messing up the time-honored dance of a well-ordered quarterdeck.

Straightening her dress blue coat with all the spangles that Ruthie could ask to jam into her mouth, Kris left to see just what had become of the junior officer she once knew.

41

Kris stepped directly from her day quarters to the quarterdeck. The band had just finish their tuning and was going to parade rest with their instruments. Captain Ajax and the OOD had their heads together, whispering earnestly. Kris joined them.

"How many sideboys do we give her?" Ajax asked, bringing Kris into their dilemma.

"Eight," Kris said. "She's the heir apparent to the Imperium. Alternately, she's the leader of a rebellion. That qualifies for eight in my book. Oh, and make them all girls if you will, Captain."

A nod from his skipper, and the OOD went to assign eight women to sideboy duties.

Kris looked around the quarterdeck. "Nelly, please add my flag next to the US ensign. Also, put a Greenfeld flag on the forward bulkhead of the quarterdeck, and when the bosun pipes Vicky aboard, make a three-star flag appear."

"Glad to," Nelly said, her voice holding pure delight, as a blue flag with four white stars appeared to the left of the US ensign.

The sidegirls paraded into their place beside the gangplank; Kris, Jack at her elbow, took her place across from

Captain Ajax and her OOD and JOOD. With a deep breath, she prepared for what would come next.

Vicky was leading the charge up the brow. She took in the zoo on the quarterdeck with a glance . . . and blanched. She whispered something to the Vice Admiral trailing her. He only had to glance at what lay ahead of them before he smiled and took over the lead.

Someone doesn't know how to accept formal flag honors, Kris thought, and swallowed a smile.

The chief bosun's mate of the watch had been paying attention to how this pack of circus elephants had conducted their exit from the *Retribution.* Without batting an eyelash, he piped honors, and announced, "St. Petersburg Reserve Fleet arriving."

A vice admiral in dress blues turned to salute the Greenfeld Imperial ensign, then did an about-face and saluted the Royal US ensign. He held his salute as he turned to Kris and her collection of officers and stepped past Kris before turning again. Now he saluted his arriving Grand Duchess.

Vicky squared her shoulders and took her first step. Behind Kris, the band went into ruffles and flourishes. Four sets of them.

Vicky paused; her mouth hung open just a smidgen. Then she took a deep breath and marched to the top of the brow as ruffles and flourishes segued to the Imperial March.

The chief bosun's mate piped, "Grand Duchess arriving." Vicky earnestly went through the same process as the first admiral, not missing a step, despite a tremble on her lower lip. Her eyes went wide as her three-star flag unfurled beside the Greenfeld Imperial flag.

The trailing rear admiral kept his distance so as to not step on Vicky's official greetings. That done, he marched forward to be piped aboard as "Second Battle Squadron." Once he'd saluted everyone, the saluting was over and introductions began.

"Wow, Kris," Vicky said. "Just wow."

"It's your due, Admiral," Kris pointed out.

"I guess it is, but . . . wow. Oh, right, I'm dropping the ball. Kris, I'd like you to meet Vice Admiral von Mittleburg, who was kind enough to give me refuge when I thought I was lost beyond hope. Beside him is Rear Admiral Bolesław. He's been my flag captain and saved my butt more times than I care to count."

Kris shook hands all around, and introduced Lieutenant General Juan Montoya and Captain Ajax before inviting her guests to join her in her in-port quarters.

"Right this way," and in a few steps they were there. Since the time Kris had left, Nelly had made it over into the lush digs that had greeted the Emperor and Empress.

"Nelly, my flag quarters do not need to look like an over-priced whorehouse for these people. They work for a living."

"Sorry, I thought you'd want to lay it on equal for her as we had to do for the Emperor and Empress."

"This was what Dad wanted?" Vicky asked, looking around to take it all in. "And how did you do all this, Nelly?"

"Easily. We've discovered a lot of new things we can do with Smart Metal," Kris's computer answered.

"Down, girl, or should I say girls. Nelly, give us enough comfortable chairs for the mob I've got here and get rid of the statues, paintings, and woodwork."

They began to melt into the deck, bulkheads, and overhead.

"You might keep those nudes, Nelly," Vicky said with a chuckle. "Is Kris really loosening up in her old age?"

"I'll have you know, I'm an old married woman, with a kid to boot," Kris announced, not managing to keep the pride out of her voice.

"You've got a baby!" Vicky squeed.

"You want to see her?"

"Of course. I've always wanted to meet a Longknife I was smarter than."

"Don't be so sure," Kris tried to growl, but there was way too much smile on her face to carry it off.

So Ruth got brought out and passed between Kris and Vicky. The two admirals took two steps back when it looked like they might be offered the tiny human. Kris gave Jack the stink eye when he joined them.

Guys against the gals, huh, she thought, apparently too loudly.

I DON'T WANT THEM TO FEEL UNSUPPORTED, Jack answered on Nelly Net.

Once Ruth was taken off to get an aromatic diaper changed, Kris introduced her brain trust.

"Do you think you can really figure a way out of this mess we're in?" Vicky asked them, and got the same noncommittal mumbles Kris had had to put up with so far.

"Yeah," Vicky said into the silence, "it's a mess. We've had quite a few years to get into it, and it's going to take quite a few years to get out of it."

Kris eyed Vicky. The Grand Duchess met her eye to eye.

"Yeah, I'm not the stupid little girl you left on High Chance, and Kris, I want to apologize for hanging you out to dry in that interview. I was alone. I was scared, and I wasn't thinking straight."

Kris canted her head to one side. "I didn't see that coming."

Vicky nodded. "I've done a lot of growing up . . . fast. It was either that, or my stepmother would have killed me."

"Can you prove that?"

Vicky was shaking her head before Kris finished the question. "Could you ever prove that my dad was trying to kill you?" she shot back.

Kris winced. "Some Peterwalds are very good at not leaving fingerprints. So, ignoring the personal for a moment, what can you tell me about the situation here in the Empire?"

"What did they tell you?"

Kris shook her head. "This is your time to talk to me. I'm listening."

Vicky looked at Vice Admiral von Mittleburg. He nodded to her, and she took a deep breath.

"I knew things were crazy when Rear Admiral Gort picked me up on High Chance. He had three options for my delectable body. First"—a finger went up—"deliver me to my loving father at the Palace, as per his orders. Second"—and another finger went up—"he had been given a very large bribe to deliver my very lovely, but very dead body to the Palace. The last option was accompanied by a smaller bribe and involved handing me over to other people, unknown, to be used to raise a rebellion against my father."

Kris eyed the two admirals. "Such as these two?" she said.

"No! No," Vicky said, shaking her head emphatically.

"Whoever that group was, they've vanished. I really don't know a lot about the last two options because Admiral Gort took a bullet intended for me, and what he knew died with him."

Kris studied Vicky. The death of the admiral actually moved her.

Not at all the old Vicky I knew.

"We took the admiral's body home to Bayern, a Navy retirement colony where I was introduced to a batch of retired admirals and some wives who weighed the decision to kill me or send me back to the Palace."

"Not start a rebellion?" Diana asked.

"No, Your Honor. None of us saw any chance to get a revolution going. Things were bad but not *that* bad."

Vicky sighed. "They sent me back to the Palace, kind of like a spy. I thought I might be able to find something out. Stupid me."

Vicky's eyes got lost in the distance. When she spoke again, it was softly. "I dodged three or four assassination attempts a day for three, maybe four days before they got me. The Marine captain escorting me was killed. I was raped, but I got the drop on them and killed my kidnappers." For a moment, her eyes focused on Kris.

"You'd have been proud of me, killing my kidnappers and getting away before the Empress, or whoever, came to kill me. The Navy helped me get away from Greenfeld but had no idea what to do with me. Some thought I might hide out in a Navy colony, but my new Navy escort wasn't so sure someone wouldn't turn me in, not with the size of the price on my head. He thought I might hide out in one of the new US colonies, but I knew the money would make no place safe for me. The final option was to make a run to Wardhaven and throw myself on your King Ray's mercy."

Vicky shook her head. "That would take me out of the game. The only way I'd be able to come back would be at the head of an army provided by your great-grandfather, and that stank."

Vicky shrugged. "So I came to St. Petersburg and threw myself on the locals' mercy. It hasn't worked out too badly, has it?" she said, eyeing the two admirals.

"It certainly hasn't been boring," Vice Admiral Bolesław said through a grin.

"It never is boring around us, is it, Kris?"

"Nope," Kris agreed.

"The Empress tried a couple of attacks. I stopped one by driving her appointed commander into a heart attack," Vicky said with a chuckle, then glanced at the junior admiral beside her. "Admiral Bolesław stopped another one by scaring the Navy officers into killing the Empress's terminally stupid commander. We've done our best to avoid letting the slaughter get out of hand. Most of the young Sailors on both sides are just following their officers."

Vicky glanced at her two admirals. They nodded their agreement.

Kris liked what she was hearing. Of course, Vicky was telling her what she must know would bring Kris over to her side. Kris knew her hardheaded brain trust needed more than just happy words.

Kris cleared her throat and redirected the conversation. "Okay, it looks like you've got a major opposition movement going here. Tell me, Vicky, in your own words, just how did this mess get started?"

Vicky took a deep breath, eyed the admirals, and leaned toward Kris.

"I thought it was the banks run by the Empress's family, Kris. Credit suddenly dried up. With no money flowing around the Empire to support trade, the wheels of commerce crumbled. People lost jobs. The unemployed went into the streets, and riots made a wreck of things. The Empress's family sends its 'security consultants' into the streets using machine guns for crowd control, and suddenly another planet is totally owned by the Empress's family. Wash, rinse, repeat. That was what I thought. Then Admiral von Mittleburg did his own analysis."

Now it was the turn of the other vice admiral to lean toward Kris. "Really, it was the Grand Duchess here that got me wondering. She arrived with a report that a small mining colony a few jumps away was running low on spare parts and soon would be out of food as well. If they couldn't produce enough product to pay their taxes, they'd be bought up for pfennigs on the mark. By exactly who, I didn't feel a need to question."

"I passed through that system, Kris, when I was running

away from my stepmother's assassins," Vicky added. "I just wanted to help, but there was more to it."

"There are only two planets in the Empire that produce raw crystal," von Mittleburg continued. "The largest one is wholly owned by the Peterwalds. The newer and smaller one is just a hop, skip, and a jump away from here. The Peterwalds didn't own it. Officially. But as demand grew, the supply shrank, and as it did, planets began to lack for a critical chunk of their industrial economy. The price of crystal shot through the roof. The Peterwalds made a fortune. It all happened because production from the mines out here was going down the tubes."

"I tried to help those mines," Vicky said, "but next thing I know, the guys running them are doing things that just don't make sense. I charged them with fiduciary malfeasance and hauled their asses back here to St. Petersburg for trial. Once I put some of the second-level managers in charge, the production at the mines shot up. We're meeting the need for crystal for all those planets allied with us and growing our economies. My stepmother and her family are going unhinged as I get our economies back on the right track even while we're spending more than we should have to on an Army and Navy to protect us from her goons."

Bill jumped on that. "Can you document any of this?"

"I have a copy of my analysis right here," Admiral von Mittleburg said, and aimed his wrist unit at the screens in Kris's day quarters. They lit up as data cascaded across them.

"Nelly, can you evaluate what you're getting?"

"Yes, Kris. I'll need to verify this against other data, assuming I can find any such data from Greenfeld, but it is internally consistent with his words."

"Pass it along to Runda's data hounds, Nelly, and see if this makes some of the data they picked up on Greenfeld more comprehensible."

"I will work with them, Kris."

"I'd like to talk to these other two admirals about how they saw this revolution getting started," Chief Mediator Alfred Fu said, and was quickly joined by the other two leads of Kris's brain trust.

"Why don't we adjourn to my office on the station," Admiral

von Mittleburg said. "I've got access to a lot more information there than I have on my wrist unit."

A moment later, the three leads were gathering up the members of their own teams, collecting a few data and electronic specialists from Runda's support group, and heading off to the station.

Soon, Kris found herself alone with just Vicky and Jack. He seemed to test the air, found it overloaded with estrogen, and dismissed himself to check on security.

"Well, what's been going on with you two?" Vicky asked with a salacious smirk on her face. No doubt, she wanted every detail of Kris's sex life.

"Some of this. A lot of that," Kris answered, intentionally vague.

"And a baby."

"You won't believe how that happened," Kris said, shaking her head.

"I know where babies come from," Vicky said slyly. "Don't tell me that you and Jack didn't."

"Oh, we did, but I had a bit of help from an unpleasant direction."

"Oh, do tell, but first, I have to tell you that I got access to the information they allow the top admirals to know."

"Yes," Kris said cautiously.

"I know the story about your Order of the Wounded Lion," Vicky singsonged.

Kris tried to frown, but Vicky was just so full of herself. Still, she grumbled, "That's supposed to be a secret."

"Not from me it isn't."

And the evening took off for points unknown.

42

Kris never had a sister. She'd tried a few times to find a substitute among some of the girls at school or daughters of Father's cronies.

It had never gone well. Girls can be hurtful and untrustworthy. Just as Kris's first try for a boyfriend had ended in a disaster, her attempts to have a girlfriend had also crashed and burned. Not as bad as the boyfriend thing, but not nice either.

As the hours went by, and she and Vicky talked and talked, Kris found herself discovering a girl that needed a friend almost as desperately as she had. Vicky talked about Mannie, the mayor of Sevastopol who had somehow managed to stay out of her bed, and Kris talked about Jack and how Granny Rita had finally forced them to take time for each other, then given them the push to rush at each other and into marriage.

The heavy dress blue uniforms seemed too stiff and thick for the intimacy that was growing between them, and Kris invited Vicky back to her quarters. The uniforms came off, and Kris settled into a pair of sweatpants and a T-shirt.

There was little in Kris's closet that looked to fit Vicky, but Kris was not about to have Jack come in, late at night, to see Vicky in the nonregulation and very skimpy bra and thong the Grand Duchess revealed as she slipped out of her blues.

Kris hunted up a pair of running shorts that she'd used to exercise in when baby was bulging all over the place. There was also a Marine T-shirt that she'd stolen from Jack when she felt like a blimp. Even in the last months of pregnancy, it had hung loose on her. On Vicky, it revealed every curve.

There is no justice in the universe.

But Vicky was in awe of Kris and Ruth when Sally Greer and Li O'Malley brought Ruth in for her lunch.

"So that is what boobs are really for," Vicky breathed.

"Yes," Kris said, "but don't try this at home. There's a whole lot of stuff they don't tell us about pregnancy and nursing." And Kris and the nannies dumped all the horror stories they could think of on the impressionable young woman.

"Maybe it will be easier with a uterine replicator," Vicky said.

Once Ruth was taken off to a nap, Vicky began to unload on Kris just what it had been like for her for the last two years. Kris found herself shaking her head, time after time. Vicky might not have been facing down huge alien mother ships, but she'd been tackling a lot more human horror than any young girl should have to wade through.

Kris ordered pizza in for lunch from the Forward Lounge. Its popping up on one of the empty chairs scared Vicky, and Kris discovered just how loud the gal could shriek. When they still hadn't stopped talking by suppertime, the Lounge provided Chinese takeout.

"Pizza, Chinese, what can't your Forward Lounge do?" Vicky demanded.

Kris shrugged. "I don't know. I've never asked for something they didn't have."

"You Longknifes. You're so spoiled."

"You're the ones with the Empire. Remember, we've just got a King."

"My dad may be the Emperor, but he married the Empress from hell," and Vicky told Kris what it was like to wake up naked, handcuffed to a bed, and not a drop of water in sight. She ended the tale with Mannie's being the one to rescue her.

"Really, Kris, you have just got to meet Mannie. If anyone is going to make a democrat out of me, it's him."

"Democrat, hell, Vicky. Can he make an honest woman out of you?" Kris took the opening offered.

To Kris's surprise, Vicky got serious. She grabbed a pillow from the next chair over, pulled it to her lap, and huffed. "I sure hope he will. I think he will. Kris, how do you get a man?"

And Kris found herself offering matrimonial advice to the sexpot who'd once used all her wiles to get a long line of men to do their best to kill her.

I can't believe I'm doing this.

But she did. As the evening went along, Kris shared stuff with Vicky she'd never told another soul. Jack had never asked Kris what it felt like . . . really felt like . . . to order the fleet to fire on the aliens that screamed they wanted to surrender while they just kept steady on a course for Alwa.

"I thought I'd finally taught them to surrender."

"But they were saying one thing and doing another," Vicky whispered softly.

"Yeah. Was there something wrong with the instructions we were sending them? I don't know, but I couldn't let them get through that jump. They could park on the other side and blast us out of space as we came through. Then they could bombard Alwa at their leisure. They had to disarm, but it didn't look like they were going to."

"You had to kill them," Vicky whispered.

"Yes, I did. Still, I wonder how long it will be before I have a chance to take another surrender."

Vicky shrugged, then changed the subject. "I've got to tell you about the time I drove one of the Empress's high lord commissioners so far around the bend that Admiral Bolesław, he was a captain then, got the entire squadron on the other side to surrender. We were trying to open up trade with Brunswick . . ." and the Grand Duchess was off on her way to another story.

Were they tall tales? Kris listened to them, wanting to believe that her erstwhile friend just might have changed her stripes. The stories all held together, and they tumbled from Vicky's mouth with no time at all to concoct them. When Kris tossed out a question about this or that, Vicky had an answer without taking time for reflection or construction of a lie. Only where Mannie was concerned did Vicky slow down. Only when Vicky talked of the mayor did she get circumspect and have to search for words.

*She really has it bad for that guy. She likes him enough
that she really doesn't want to screw it up.*

It was edging toward midnight when Jack showed up with
the strangest foursome in tow. Two were the tiny ninjas whom
Vicky had taken with her to circumnavigate the galaxy. They
studied Kris and the room as if some assassin might drop from
the overhead light fixture or one of the nudes still standing
against the wall might come alive.

One of them actually pinched each of the statues as Kris
tried not to stare.

The third was a commander who looked very official, kind
of like Jack five or six years ago.

But it was the fourth who caught Kris's eye. Or rather,
didn't. He looked so bland that Kris had to work at making her
eyes not slip past the fellow without taking note of him. She
focused her eyes on him and stared.

"Don't I know you?" Kris asked.

"I was aboard the *Wasp* for her last trip," the fellow said.
Jack had introduced him with a hint of a smile and a cryptic,
"This is Mr. Smith."

"I thought I remembered you. What was your job?"

"Officially, I was an Able Spacer. Actually, I was there to
keep you alive. There were a half dozen or more of us. Some
of us knew each other and worked together if we needed to.
There were others we didn't know."

Kris frowned. "Why not?"

"If we all were chasing the same duck, we might miss the
swan behind us. I'm sure you were worth the extra coverage.
Every one of us I knew about was kept busy, saving you, then
taking up the slack on the Grand Duchess. There were some
really good people who wanted her dead and getting her, they
might get lucky and get a twofer."

"I hired him," said Vicky, jumping in. "He came to me
when Jack was giving me the bum's rush off the *Wasp* for that
stupid stunt I did with the newsies. I was broke, but Mr. Smith
was willing to work for me on consignment. He's been worth
every penny I've paid him."

Vicky pulled at the spidersilk-armor bodysuit Kris had
spotted when they changed into something comfortable. She
had said nothing then.

"He got your Gramma Trouble to arrange for these to make it through Wardhaven customs."

"She is a very helpful Gramma," Kris admitted.

Vicky shivered. "And she didn't even mention the time I had her kidnapped. Wonderful woman."

The two diminutive assassins collected Vicky's blues and were clearly ready to lead her out the door.

Vicky gave Kris one more hug. "We've got to do this again. I'm not half-done."

"I want to, too," Kris said. "Let's make it soon."

With a few more good-byes, Kris found herself alone with Jack. She leaned against him and sighed. "I really think she's telling the truth. I feel it in my bones that it's the stepmother, her father, and that family that is causing all this trouble."

Jack let out a sigh that was almost a rumble. "Did any of what she told you tonight rise to the level of evidence we can use?"

"Not a jot or a tittle."

"You can plan an assault on an alien base ship based on one of your hunches," Jack said. "God knows, you've gotten away with it enough times. You won't be allowed to settle this mess on a hunch."

She hugged him. "Do you have any idea how we're going to solve this?"

"Not a clue."

"Take me to bed and make me forget about tomorrow."

"I thought you'd never ask."

43

Kris was not allowed to sleep in. Ruth was hungry, so Kris tried to serve her breakfast in bed, hoping the nannies would take Ruth off to points unknown without her really having to wake up.

That didn't work.

"Kris, your brain trust would like you to have breakfast with them in the Forward Lounge," Nelly informed her.

"How much sleep did they get last night?" Kris asked through a yawn.

"A lot less than you did, honey," Nelly answered, sounding very much like Kris's former maid. Abby, in full 'tude.

Kris rolled out of bed, took a quick shower, put on the undress khakis Jack had laid out for her, and went through the high points of her in-box while Jack finished dressing.

"There anything there from the brain trust?" he asked as he tied his field scarf.

"Nothing, which leads me to fear they're holding on to some really nasty stuff for the sole purpose of ruining my breakfast digestion."

Jack finished, delivered a peck on her cheek, and said, "I will defend your digestion to the death. Mine, too."

There were still two very spacious, if a bit less decadent,

circling staircases down to the Forward Lounge. The place still looked like an insane King's fevered dream, but to the right was something more like a classical O club. A turn to the left led into a comfortable English public room. Beyond that was something French. A Marine waitress waited for them.

"They've got a room to themselves in the six o'clock position from the stairs, Your Highness, General."

She led them through the O-club portion past walls decorated with classical military art. Double doors of apparent oak opened into a more utilitarian quarter of the pie that was the Forward Lounge's circular deck.

It was not at all plain. No, Nelly had arranged for finely polished wooden walls and marble columns supporting ceiling beams. Interspersed around the room, and taking up at least half of the wall space, were screens filled with numbers and equations that were gibberish to Kris. No doubt, she'd know more than she ever wanted to know about them in a few short hours. The furnishings were tables of rich mahogany. Around them were comfortable chairs, with thick red brocade padding on the seats and armrests.

Al spotted them standing in the double doors and opened his arms as he made his way to them, the affable host incarnate.

"In here, it's easier for our teams to work side by side," he said, resting a hand on Kris's elbow and steering her toward a couple of linen-covered tables close to a table laden with every possible breakfast food. "It's easier for people to float from one group to the next without having to wander around the ship. Also, if someone needs you, they have only to holler."

At that moment, someone hollered, "Hey, Judge," and Diana's head popped up. A hand waved her over to a table halfway across the room. She excused herself from where she'd been and headed for where she was wanted.

"We eat when we can. Your wardroom has been kind enough to keep all of our coffee urns filled."

"Have you been here all night?" Kris asked.

Al rubbed his eyes, and Kris now saw past the amiable host to the exhausted elder who had gone without sleep for too long. "I've kept negotiating teams up for two days running. It's amazing the concessions you can get when folks are looking out the window at their third sunset without a minute of sleep."

Kris felt very guilty for her night's rest even if it hadn't been nearly long enough.

"Now, why don't you two get yourselves some breakfast? We are getting the best food I've ever tasted. Listen as you eat, and we'll see if we can put together a briefing for you once you're finished. I might keep people up for days at a time, but I never interfere with their first cup of coffee come morning," Al said, and chuckled at his joke as he left them to respond to his name and a waving hand.

Kris and Jack eyed the choices laid out before them. There was everything Kris had ever seen on a breakfast menu: crepes with a half a dozen fruit fillings; quiches; pancakes and waffles of assorted embellishments; eggs prepared several ways; a breakfast burrito; potatoes of several sorts, including little pancakes; oatmeal with quite a few berry, fruit, or sugar toppings close at hand; a tray of assorted sweet breads. A chef stood ready to make an omelet to her specifications.

"I didn't know Mary Finten had brought aboard either the chef or the produce to lay out something like this," Kris said.

"Oh, we know how to make all this," the woman who stood ready to make the omelets said. Her name tag said Song, so this would be Mary's wife. "We just had a delivery from St. Petersburg that we didn't order. Seems someone wants to thank a Kris Longknife for getting his town a charter or something like that."

"This is all from Mannie?" Jack said, mouth hanging open.

"Mannie or Mike. Mary told me, but I forgot," Song agreed.

Kris felt her mouth watering and loaded a plate for a long and pleasant breakfast.

As she and Jack settled down at a table, Song brought a tray full of glasses of milk and juices. Kris took the large milk, it was clearly intended for her, and fresh-squeezed orange juice. Jack took apple juice and coffee.

"Clearly, St. Petersburg is not going hungry," Kris said. "Song, did you or Mary try to order fresh meats or produce while we were at Greenfeld?"

"Funny you should ask, Your Highness. We were told that the bug infestations meant we didn't dare take on fresh supplies. But we didn't get that word until we tried to order some fresh meats, fruits, and vegetables. The prices being asked from the station suppliers were just outrageous. Mary tried to contact some suppliers dirtside, assuming we'd pay for transport up the beanstalk ourselves, but their prices weren't any better."

"Hmm," Kris said. "Song, if there's no one asking for you to cook something at the moment, would you go over to that tall woman, Diana? Tell her Kris Longknife sent you, and she needs to hear what you just told me."

"Yes, ma'am," the cook said, and made her way to where Diana was bent over a table. Kris munched her crepes while the two talked. Done, Song headed back to her place behind the table.

Diana gave Kris a knowing nod and went two tables down to talk to someone else.

"They can't even keep food flowing into their capital," Jack said, shaking his head.

"I remember when I was campaigning for Father for the farm vote, Jack. Farming has come a long way from plowing a field and tossing out some seed. They need spare parts for their equipment: hundreds of thousands of dollars of equipment. They need fertilizer, bugs to keep the bugs down, a whole lot of things. You start trouble over here, and the supply chain to over there frays and breaks. If it gets bad enough, you get famine, and people start dying," Kris finished softly.

After a minute, she shook herself. "It's not smart to mess with a complicated mechanism like a modern economy. If things really did get as bad on some planets as Vicky claimed, then she's done some herculean lifting to get it going again."

"We didn't hear a word of this from the Emperor or Empress."

"Nope," Kris said, "just a lot of complaining about rioting in the streets and a kid that won't do what Papa wants."

"Do we have any proof that someone is out to kill Vicky?" Jack asked.

"Kris, I have found information to verify at least one of the assassination attempts."

"Talk to me, Nelly."

"I've located a news story from Savannah about the Grand Duchess paying them a short visit. Very short, unannounced visit. A bit more than two days in system. The story recounts the death of a Rear Admiral Gort, shot by a bystander who was herself killed. The murder is carried on Savannah's books as unsolved. This took place only a bit more than a week after we were hauled off that wreck of a *Wasp* at High Chance."

"Good God," Jack whispered. "Somebody wanted Vicky dead, and they could reach very far and grasp for her that fast."

"She said her 'Mr. Smith' had been earning his pay," Kris pointed out. "Nelly, please pass that along to our brain trust."

"Yes, Kris, it is done. Judge Diana says they are close to having a report ready for you."

Kris and Jack finished their delicious breakfast and self-bussed their table. Just as she turned around, Kris was presented with all three of her brain trust with their heads together in the center of the room.

As Kris and Jack walked toward them, the three turned to meet them.

"We're ready to brief you, Your Highness," Diana reported.

44

The room began to change around Kris as she wound her way to the three leaders who were there to advise her on matters less mortal than her normal business. Tables that had been scattered around the room started moving, following the people who had been working on them. The room reformed itself into a triangle with five comfortable chairs in the center. Several new tables appeared in the triangle as other cluttered tables moved to form a loose second row behind the first. Chairs that had sunk into the floor as the tables began their perambulations reappeared as the tables settled into their places. Quite a few of them were easy chairs.

God, you have to love this Smart Metal, Kris thought as she took one of the chairs in the center, Jack at her right elbow. The judge, the mediator, and the arbitrator settled into place in front of her.

For a long minute, as the migration of the tables finished up, the three across from Kris sat, apparently lost in some quiet meditation.

Kris, who was used to action, forced herself to try some deep-breathing exercises to keep from taking the floor and telling them what she wanted.

These people are here because a whole lot of folks thought this new challenge might not be amenable to my usual solution of blowing something up. Let's let them have their say.

I can always blow stuff up later, Kris thought, and made no effort to suppress what was, no doubt, a fey smile.

Across from her, Al, Bill, and Diana exchanged glances, then Diana cleared her throat.

"I think, as a judge, I should be the one to explain this."

"Explain what?" Kris said, jumping in the moment Diana paused for a breath. Kris clamped her mouth shut. *Listen, don't talk,* she ordered herself.

"Your Highness," Diana went on, "we think there is something that really must be at the forefront of our conversation here today."

Kris gritted her teeth and did not venture into Diana's second pause.

The judge seemed surprised at Kris's silence. Surprised and pleased.

"Many people would think that we are gathered here to determine guilt and innocence. Who is in the right and who is wrong? I may have the honor of being called a judge and have a courtroom, but determining the guilty is not the purpose of my court."

Kris continued to keep her mouth shut, but she couldn't avoid a puzzled frown.

"So you want to know what my court *is* about?" Diana said.

This time, Kris allowed herself a "Yes."

A tight smile flitted across Diana's face as she nodded thoughtfully. "When I sit in robes, my purpose is to find the best path for the children. I want to examine every option that my associates can dig up, then decide which one is best for that young person's future. I *cannot* waste my time searching for who might be the guilty party who brought on this situation. I. Am. There. For. The. Child. I am there to find a way forward out of a mess."

Kris leaned back in her chair, and, for once, didn't have to clinch her jaw to keep words from dropping out of her mouth. What Diana had said was not at all what Kris had expected. In all the time she had spent with these three and their supporting staff, this rather peculiar idea had never crossed her mind.

It did not go down easy for Kris.

All her life, she'd been looking for the right way. Campaigning for her father, the whole idea had been to convince people that his party was the right one and the other parties were wrong. In the Navy, Kris had always looked for the best way. The one that left her enemy defeated and her victorious. That left as many of her people alive as possible.

Worse, as Kris listened to Vicky last night, she'd found herself wanting the Empress defeated and all her ambitions left in the dust.

When Kris began speaking, her words kind of fell out of her mouth. "You don't want to prove who's right and who's wrong? You want me to look at this civil war and ignore who's responsible for starting it? For creating all this havoc? Causing all these deaths?"

"Strange as it may seem, you are correct," Al, the mediator, said softly. "We can't afford to waste our time and effort on that. We came here to end a civil war. It will take everything we have, every bit of our experience and skill, to end this war. Any effort or time we waste seeking out the guilty and trying to devise punishments for them is effort taken away from ending the war and restoring this Empire to peace and prosperity."

"That doesn't seem fair," Jack said. "Someone *deserves* to be punished for what they've done to the people of the Greenfeld Empire."

"Maybe someone will," Bill the arbitartor said. "But. It. Can. *Not*. Be. Us."

"We can try to end this civil war," Diana said, "or we can try to punish the guilty. Your Highness, please say again what your purpose for coming here is."

Kris took several deep breaths as she considered her mission before she spoke softly. "Before a few minutes ago, I would have considered punishing the guilty and ending this civil war one and the same." Kris paused. "I don't like the idea that they are not. Tell me why we can't do both."

The three looked at each other for a moment, then Al faced Kris. "For a moment, let us say that the Emperor, or was it the Empress who said it. Anyway, let's say that we tell the Grand

Duchess that her actions here have been in the wrong and that the right thing for her to do is return to her father's loving arms at the Palace. How do you think that would go over?"

"Other than that she would be dead within a week?" Kris asked.

"There is that likelihood," Al said. "But before she actually boarded a ship for Greenfeld, how do you think our conversations would proceed?"

"You tell her that," Jack said, "and she'll tell you to go to hell and this mission will get no more cooperation from her side of this civil war."

"Precisely," Al said. "The Emperor's, or is it the Empress's, solution is a nonstarter from the Grand Duchess's perspective."

"We haven't gotten quite so specific a proposed resolution to this civil war from the Grand Duchess's side," Diana said, "but I suspect it would go something like this. The Empress abdicates and divorces the Emperor. Her family, as well as herself, is banished from the Empire and may leave with only the clothes on their back. All properties that have changed hands in the last three or four years are returned to their rightful owners, and all cases involving murder and rape are referred to courts established by the Grand Duchess's new regime. Have I about got it right?"

Kris nodded. "Pretty much. Vicky was quite reserved when talking to me yesterday, but I could feel the rage and need for vengeance."

"Do you see the Empress's faction agreeing to anything like that?" Diana asked.

Kris just shook her head.

"So you see our challenge," Diana said. "We need to find a solution that is acceptable to both sides. Hurling condemnations and anathemas around is not productive."

"No matter how satisfactory it may feel for the moment," Bill added.

"So where do we go from here?" Kris asked.

The three looked at each other a bit sheepishly. It was Diana who first smiled, shrugged, and leaned toward Kris.

"Having just won your support to our viewpoint that we are not here to determine the guilty party, we must now determine what the true circumstances are in the Empire. Doing that will, no doubt to some skeptics, look like we are hunting for the guilty."

Kris had to chuckle. "So you've spent the last fifteen minutes stampeding me off in one direction, and now you're going to take me off in the other?"

"It may look that way," Al said.

"Well, lead on, and I will follow," Kris said.

45

Bill took the lead on their presentation. "For what it is worth, we have been able to develop more information in support of the Grand Duchess's side than the Empress's. Admittedly, the Empress gave us nothing more than her narrative, and quite a bit of the message traffic on Greenfeld was heavily encrypted, but what we have gathered here has allowed us to put what we dredged up there into a perspective that is not very supportive of the Empress."

He glanced over to a woman seated at a table in the inner triangle and nodded. She stood and walked over to a large screen on one wall. Kris's chair moved to face that direction.

Bill continued. "The Grand Duchess's people have been fully cooperative with our staff. Assuming we are not looking at a perfectly choreographed lie, it is persuasive. Iba, would you please brief Her Highness on what we find persuasive to a reasonable person."

"Yes, sir. Your Highness, there have been three attempts on the Grand Duchess's life here on St. Petersburg, assuming we ignore the attacks on the entire planet. In one, she was left chained to a bed in a remote cabin. In another, a car bomb failed to kill her but slaughtered innocent bystanders. A third took place along a country road in the hills above Sevastopol.

We chose to investigate the first two. We had limited staff for
field trips yesterday," she explained.

A picture of a decrepit farmhouse beside a burned-out barn
appeared on the screen. "This site had been investigated previously but was pretty much undisturbed. We found the Grand
Duchess's DNA present, as well as traces of her blood. Her
bare footprints showed where she had walked away from here.
All this fitted the story we were given."

Now a city street filled the screen. Bodies lay strewn on the
ground; cars were burning. "The scene of this car bombing
had been cleaned up. We talked with several of the survivors.
They truly believed what they said. We talk not only to those
witnesses provided but also to random subjects in the surrounding buildings. The variations in their stories were reasonable and within the expected range."

The young woman paused. "It is our conclusions that, even
out here where support for the Grand Duchess is readily
voiced, there have been serious attempts on her life. Unfortunately, none of the perpetrators lived to testify. They either
escaped or died resisting arrest."

The screen changed to show bags being stacked for transport. "These are standard famine biscuits. These pictures were
offered in support of the story that the Grand Duchess led a
major relief effort to the colony on Pozen. In support of this
claim, we stripped off the net orders, transit invoices, and even
letters to pen pals from fifth graders. It appears that some of
the biscuits were baked by the kids from grain they grew
themselves. We found too many references to this in private
mails to doubt the actuality of this event."

"A Peterwald really tried to help people. Who'd have thunk
it?" Kris said.

"The private e-mails had quite a few references to just that,
Your Highness. Even some of the youngsters didn't hold the
Imperium in much regard. But of the Grand Duchess's efforts
to feed the hungry and defend the planet, there are just too
many public and private comments to doubt that the people
really believe this and participated in it. Oh, and we found
archived media reports of Vicky, they actually called her
Vicky in some press stories, handing out ribbons at city fairs.
The kidnapping occurred while she was visiting a carnival.

She'd just won a little girl a huge stuffed bear when all hell broke loose."

The young woman allowed herself a slight shrug. "I couldn't make this stuff up."

"I don't think you are," Kris said. "It seems at least one Peterwald has changed her stripes. What about the space battles?"

An older man stood. His crew cut and ramrod-straight back hinted strongly that he had come to this vocation as a second career. The screen changed behind him to show a map of the Imperium. The planets were divided into two groups that showed red and blue.

"Vice Admiral von Mittleburg cooperated completely with us in examining the fighting that has been going on in the civil war. He walked us through the strategy they are presently using. It involved fixing a major part of the Empress's fleet here, in front of St. Petersburg, while several of their fleets nibbled around the flanks, cutting planets out of the Empress's holdings. He credits the Grand Duchess for the basic idea although it is plain that it was the Empress that chose to concentrate her fleet in a thrust directly at St. Petersburg."

"Is this where Vicky has operated from?" Kris asked.

"Yes."

"So the Empress was going for the Grand Duchess," Kris said. "Something tells me that she knows that Vicky is nobody's patsy."

"The data is open to that interpretation by a reasonable person," Bill said.

When have I ever been called a reasonable person?

When the silence grew, the briefer continued. "The admiral had nothing but praise for the Grand Duchess. He's found her courageous, creative, and flexible. He repeatedly mentioned how well she listened although she can be quite headstrong at times."

The briefer chuckled. "I think Vice Admiral von Mittleburg views the Grand Duchess like a daughter. Oh, both of them are vice admirals. I was very surprised when von Mittleburg told me that Vicky is senior to him by a few seconds."

"How's *that* worked out?" Kris had to ask.

"Apparently well. Even during the big battle with the Empress, it was she who decided to call back their destroyers from a torpedo run on the opposing battle line. The tin cans weren't as supported as they needed to be, but they were so close. She made the call, and he obeyed."

"Interesting," Kris said. "This is all nice, but we're looking at an Empire bleeding to death, pfennig by pfennig. That admiral, von Mittleburg, said it was crystal taking the economy down. Did you find out anything on that front?"

An eager young man rushed to the screen to take over the briefing. "They had archives stored here from St. Petersburg, Metzburg, and Brunswick as well as two dozen less industrialized planets in the rebel union. All show that three to four years ago, the availability of crystal plummeted as the price skyrocketed. In the middle of that problem, credit suddenly dried up to finance trade. As if that wasn't enough, the insurance rate for merchant hulls and cargos shot up. It seems the Navy couldn't keep pirates from hijacking honest merchants."

Kris and Jack exchanged glances. They'd had some experience with Greenfeld's pirate problem before Kris took off to explore the galaxy and discovered what lurked under its bed.

"Did von Mittleburg have any explanation for the Navy's failure to control pirates?" Jack asked.

"The Navy has been driven from pillar to post, if I may say so, sir. First, they were ordered to planets to root out State Security, then, a bit later they were ordered back to maintain order when unemployment or food riots started. He had me talk to a few Navy officers who were there when the Security Consultants organized by the Empress's family showed up. The Navy had orders to get out immediately, but they saw the first sweeps. State Security's trigger-happy thugs were never as bloodthirsty as this bunch was. Their uniforms are red, by the way. That kept them from showing the blood they waded through, according to one of the bitter stories that ran through the fleet."

"So it's ugly," Kris said.

"Apparently very ugly," the briefer said.

Kris turned to the three heads of her brain trust. "Do you feel like you have a solid enough handle on what the real situation is here in the Empire?"

The three nodded.

"Okay. Now what do we do about it?" she asked.

"That will not be at all easy," Bill said.

"Not easy at all," Al agreed.

Diana just nodded.

Leaving Kris with nothing but a frustrated sigh.

46

An hour later Kris had Nelly invite Vicky to the *Princess Royal*.

A half hour after that, Kris watched from her day quarters as Vicky led a line of civilians and officers up the gangway. Vicky rendered honors without hesitation.

Behind Vicky, sandwiched between her and Admiral von Mittleburg, was a civilian.

"Nelly, is that the much-mentioned Mannie?"

"Yes, Kris."

Kris studied the man Vicky talked so much about. She'd met him two years ago. His hair showed a bit of gray now; he looked worn but chipper. Kris looked forward to meeting him again.

What surprised Kris was the last civilian following Vicky across the brow. She had brought Mr. Smith to this meeting. Interesting. Hopefully, Mr. Smith would not prove to be as slimy as Admiral Crossenshield, but only time would tell.

Which left Kris wondering who her Crossenshield would be.

There was little time for introspection before Kris was being introduced to a small mob of people. Beside the two admirals and Mr. Smith, whom Kris had met previously, there was Mannie as well as the mayors of Kiev and St. Petersburg.

Right behind them came three civilians who proved to be a banker, an industrialist, and a rancher.

Kris and her team were ready for some serious bargaining, and so, apparently, was Vicky.

Nelly arranged comfortable armchairs side by side for Kris and Jack, with two long rows facing each other in front of those. At Kris's side were three leaders of her brain trust. After seeing Mr. Smith in Vicky's lineup, Kris had invited Senior Chief Agent in Charge Foile to join them, both to even up the sides and to bring his insight.

Vicky and Mannie took the two chairs facing Kris from the other end of the lineup of chairs. It was interesting that Mr. Smith sat at Vicky's right hand and Vice Admiral von Mittleburg at Mannie's left. The other five were comfortably, if unevenly, spaced down the two lines toward Kris.

Kris opened the meeting. "I'm glad to see more people brought into our discussion," she said, eyeing Vicky.

"I've learned to value the input of a lot of people. We wouldn't be here, and I wouldn't be alive, without the aid and advice of these and a whole lot more."

"Can you speak for the rebellion?" Kris asked.

"Please Kris, don't call us rebels. I'm a loyal subject of my father, the Emperor, as is everyone here in the room and on more than three dozen planets that stand together against the tyranny that the Empress and her family have imposed on the Empire."

"You'll stipulate," Kris said, "that the Emperor and Empress don't see it that way."

Vicky looked around her group, then nodded to Mannie.

He said, "Yes. We will stipulate that the Empress has pulled the wool over the Emperor's eyes and that he accepts her totally wrong version of events."

Kris chuckled softly as the mayor of Sevastopol agreed with her while getting in the rebels' twist on the situation.

"It is clear there is a major disagreement as to the facts on the ground and what should be done," Kris said.

"I think that is what has brought us to this crossroads," Vicky said. She seemed to want to say more, but she closed her mouth and eyed Kris "We can continue the war until one side wins or both are exhausted, or we can resolve the issues peacefully and leave a strong Empire to face any alien base ship that can show up in our skies at any moment."

There, the major problem was now on the table. If one of those huge mother ships showed up in Greenfeld space in the future, they would find planets wrecked and defenseless. While the US and other alliances were building up their fleets, Greenfeld was blowing theirs apart in fratricidal warfare.

What's the female equivalent for fratricidal?

Kris took a deep breath. "Okay, Vicky, but how do we stop the war?"

"Kris, I was hoping you'd come in swinging with a way we could all end this and live happily ever after."

"You've been reading too many fairy tales."

"I've been reading the Longknife legend," Vicky shot back.

"Sorry, Vicky, but I'm fresh out of rabbits to pull a hat out of."

The room fell silent for a long moment as that thought sank into a lot of people's minds.

"Then what *do* we do?" was finally voiced by the mayor of Kiev. "We can't keep burning our production and sending our children off to die in some distant fight."

"It's better they die in some distant battle than do it defending our cities as they are blown to rubble." That came from the industrialist.

Kris figured the room was dark enough. She stepped in with a light.

"I have been given one suggestion by my advisors," Kris said.

"What?" Vicky shot back immediately.

"It's not a solution in and of itself. Rather, it's a path to a solution."

"You've got my attention," the Grand Duchess said.

Kris took in a deep breath and let it out slowly. "All of my advisors agree that the only possible way forward is to bring all the principals together in one room to talk this out."

Vicky eyed Mannie, and they shared a small smile.

Maybe I wasn't the first to come up with this idea.

Meanwhile, all those around Vicky mulled that thought over for a long moment. Mannie was the first to shake his head.

"If Vicky went to Greenfeld to meet with the Emperor and Empress, she'd be dead within a week."

"Even under my protection?" Kris asked.

Vicky shook her head. "Kris, I know you mean well, but if I went to Greenfeld without my battle fleet, the Empress's ships would blast me out of space. And if I went with my fleet, I can't believe she wouldn't scream 'invasion' and I'd end up fighting on her home ground. I don't see that working any way you cut the cards," she said. Beside her, Mannie joined her in shaking his head. All her associates did the same.

"You could come on my ship. I have a squadron with me," Kris said.

Vicky didn't need more than a second to form her reply. "Kris, your frigates look beautiful the plush way you have them fitted out. No doubt with Smart Metal you could shrink them down into something more combative, but not even a Longknife could win with eight dinky frigates against the Empress's battle fleet. I may have shaved some very nasty ships out of her fleet, but it's still one big fleet."

Kris considered for a moment letting Vicky in on the secret of what the new battlecruisers could do to old-line ships, but swallowed it. She didn't need to let that secret out of the bag. Not yet.

And she had a different card to play.

"You could invite the Emperor and Empress to St. Petersburg."

Vicky barked a laugh. "Excuse me, Kris, but if I'm unwilling to go to Greenfeld, I expect the Empress would be twice as quick with her 'I'm not going there.' I've learned the value of paranoia from you, Kris. The Empress is way past paranoia and deep into full insanity. Sorry, Kris, neither one of those ideas is going to happen."

"How about some neutral ground?" Kris asked. Her brain trust, who had been getting antsy, finally relaxed as Kris put their idea on the table.

Vicky took a moment to consider before she asked. "Where would we find neutral ground? Neutral ground we would all agree upon?"

"Both my mediator and arbitrator have a suggestion for that," Kris said, and opened her right arm in their general direction. Bill, the arbitrator, took up Kris's offer of the floor.

"Her Highness has already given you some idea of how we

would do this. Let's say we make up a list of five planets where we might hold such a meeting with, say, Greenfeld at the top and St. Petersburg at the bottom. No doubt, you would strike one and they would strike the other as a nonstarter. But what about the other three? Those in between?"

"I guess that would depend on what those three were," Vicky said.

"My brain trust has three to suggest," Kris said. "The next two would be Brunswick and Dresden. Both of those planets are fully developed and have space stations that would meet our needs. One is yours while the other is theirs, but both are only a few jumps from the other's territory. Again, it's very likely that you would strike one and they the other. That brings us to the fifth planet. The one between the other planets that have already been struck."

Kris paused to take stock of Vicky's advisors. None of them looked ready to storm out. All were leaning forward, listening intently.

"We looked at several possibilities. Bliven meets our needs. It has a space station. It was in the Empire until recently. It did not join your rebellion, but it did petition the US for acceptance into the union and is now a full member of the United Society. It also is easily reached from both your territories. That's one choice.

"The second one is also US. Pandemonium. Its new space station is a bit on the small and primitive side. Still, the amenities available on the planet will meet all essentials though its spirits are limited to beer. They have yet to start a vineyard. I'm told they do produce a moonshine with quite a kick, but it might not please refined tastes."

So far, none of the planets named had gotten any reaction from Vicky or her associates. Kris continued.

"There is one last planet we considered. Cuzco is a well-established planet that has managed to maintain its independence since the Society of Humanity broke up. It's industrialized and has a large space station. It's about an equal number of jumps from both Greenfeld and St. Petersburg. They kowtow to no one, but I think they'd be willing to let us park a few ships at their station if it would resolve this war and increase their trade with the Empire."

For a moment, as the silence grew and stretched, Vicky eyed Kris. Then she nodded "Can you give me a few minutes to consult with my advisors, Kris?"

"That will not be a problem. Nelly, could you raise a wall to give them their privacy."

"As you said," Nelly replied, "that will not be a problem." A wall began to grow out from the bulkhead and also slowly from the deck. There were a few looks of dismay from Vicky's team, but when it quickly became clear that no one would be sliced in half, dismay turned to awe.

"Why don't we have something like this?" the banker asked.

"Because we're too busy blowing up the stuff we can make and don't have enough time or money to research this and get it in production," the industrialist growled.

The Empire had Smart Metal™. Hank, or someone else, had used some of the stuff to try to kill Kris. They had the basic stuff but hadn't made nearly as much progress as the rest of humanity.

Just shows the price of civil war.

"When you're ready to talk to us, just have your computer contact Nelly. Nelly, no listening in on the other side of that wall, okay?"

"I have disabled all devices on that side of the wall," Nelly said.

SPOILSPORT. I WAS SO LOOKING FORWARD TO SEEING HOW A DIFFERENT BATCH OF HUMANS HANDLE SOMETHING LIKE THIS.

YOU WILL WAIT LIKE THE REST OF US TO SEE WHAT THEY COME UP WITH, NELLY.

And that settled that.

47

Kris was quite surprised at how long Vicky and her advisors took.

The first couple of minutes were busy, filled with comments on how well Kris had done in presenting their ideas. The troika of advisors had been busy watching the faces of those seated down the line from them. Al, Bill, and Diana were quite excited by this or that twitch or fleeting expression that they thought bode well for developments.

All Kris had seen were blank faces.

I'm not that bad at reading people, am I? Kris wondered.

After about five minutes, they ran out of things to talk about.

As time stretched, Al, the experienced mediator, produced a deck of cards and asked if anyone played bridge. The other two admitted to that addiction, and Foile added himself to the necessary four. Nelly produced a table, and they quickly lost themselves in the game.

Which left Kris and Jack the odd couple out.

YOU WANT TO SLIP OUT TO OUR NIGHT QUARTERS?

IT IS TEMPTING.

Nelly interrupted. "O'Malley wants to know if you're available for nursing duty, Kris."

Thus Kris found herself only half-undressed in her night quarters, and Jack looking down at the fussy miracle at her breast. Ruth really wanted to fuss and ignored the offered breast. Kris ended up walking the floor with her, letting her gnaw on her finger.

Those teeth really are coming in.

Only after Ruth chose to settle down would she allow herself to be fed.

Halfway through draining one breast, she fell asleep.

O'Malley removed the sleeping princess. "Thank you. She had all of us pulling our hair out. We offered her the bottle you filled last night, but she wanted nothing of us. Sometimes, a baby just wants Mommy and nothing else."

"Yes," Kris said, with a satisfied, motherly smile. She got herself put back together. "Sorry our time got redirected."

"I could watch you and Ruth for hours," Jack said, sporting a very satisfied, fatherly smile.

They returned to the Forward Lounge where the card game was still going on. The four played energetically to the point of rowdiness but with good humor.

NELLY, CAN THEY HEAR THIS ON THE OTHER SIDE OF THE WALL?

KRIS, I CAN'T ANSWER THAT. YOU HAD ME DISABLE ALL MONITORING DEVICES ON THAT SIDE OF THE ROOM.

OKAY, BUT CAN YOU DO ANYTHING TO KEEP THIS ON OUR SIDE?

KRIS, THE FIRST TIME THINGS GOT ROWDY, I PUT IN A SECOND WALL AND LEFT A VACUUM BETWEEN THE TWO. I'M PRETTY SURE NOTHING IS GETTING THROUGH TO DISTURB THEM.

THANK YOU, NELLY.

Every once in a while, Nelly still managed to put Kris in her place.

The wait stretched further. Much further than Kris liked, but the cardplayers didn't seem disturbed by the length of the time.

"They're talking," Al, the mediator, said during a short time as dummy. "We dumped a lot on them. It's no wonder they're taking their time to vent and process all they heard."

Kris had Nelly start calling the length of the break at

five-minute intervals. She'd just said, "Fifty-five minutes," when she added, "And they are ready to rejoin us."

In a flash, the cards disappeared into Al's pocket, the card table and chairs sank into the deck. Six comfortable, over-stuffed chairs were again where they'd been for the discussions. As they settled into their places, Kris said, "You may take the wall down, Nelly."

Again, Kris's computer let the wall melt away slowly and in an unthreatening manner. Vicky's advisors were just taking their places. Kris's waited patiently. Glances from her advisory troika seemed to hint strongly that she should keep her mouth shut.

Vicky finally cleared her throat. "Have you considered offering all seven planets to me and my father to choose from?"

Kris watched her advisors make ever-so-slight nods. Slight smiles might even have snuck out for brief seconds.

Have I been played? Did they have me mention seven planets so Vicky's team might get an oar in the water on this decision? We're going to have a little talk when this is all done.

"I don't think that would be any problem at all. We've already composed a letter to the Emperor and you. Nelly, would you please expand the choices of planets to seven."

"I've already done it. A formal letter to the Grand Duchess is printing out now."

Jack was up and returned quickly with two pages in his hand and a pen.

Kris glanced over the letter one more time. She almost had it memorized; she and her advisors had been over it time and time again. Nelly added a flat writing board to Kris's chair and she signed it.

Diana produced a stamp and notarized her signature before carrying it over to Vicky. Her computer scanned it, and sent copies to all her advisors. For several long minutes, heads pored over their screens.

"It's good," the rancher muttered. "Too good for that damn Empress, but I guess if we want this, we got to hand the same to them. I still think you should have blown her out of space when you had the chance."

Vicky studiously did not hear that.

Kris smiled. The girl she'd first met would not have avoided hearing that. Hell, the girl she first met would never have accepted an order to stand down and not kill the Empress—assuming she could actually have pulled it off.

From what Kris had found out about the Second Battle of St. Petersburg, Vicky might really have had a chance to kill the Empress. A better chance, at least, than Vicky had the couple of times she tried to kill Kris.

"How do you want us to do this?" Vicky asked.

Al raised a finger, and Kris nodded to him. "Usually we have the two parties in a room. A flip of a coin determines who scratches first. Then they take turns scratching through one name at a time. The name left after they've scratched off two, or in this case, it would be three, is where we'd go. However, this time we would suggest you put a one beside the first planet you'd scratch out. They will do the same. When we get these back, Bill and I here, with the judge looking over our shoulders, will scratch them out. Number one from your list, then number one from theirs. Number two, then number three. If your next choice has already been scratched, we go to the one after that."

"And we'll probably wind up at Cuzco," Mannie said.

"Likely, but I suspect it could be any of the middle three," Al answered.

"Nelly, is the letter on its way to the Emperor?"

"Yes, Kris. The moment you signed the letter, I dispatched it, highest priority, to the jump point. I've routed it nine different ways, assuming communications might not be as smooth as they once were. I'm sure one copy will arrive. I also sent the letter in the clear. Is there any problem with that?"

"I certainly don't have one," Kris said.

"If you will allow us," Mannie said, "we'll distribute this throughout our area of control. I think everyone will be happy to hear this."

That brought nods of agreement all around from Vicky's advisors.

"So we relax while their letter gets to them and their answer gets back to you," the banker said.

"Kris, a message just came in from Captain Jack Campbell," Nelly announced. "I think we may have a problem to add a bit of excitement while we wait."

"Shall we wait outside?" Vicky asked.

"Does it concern Vicky and this civil war?"

"It concerns the Empress and those delightful alien raiders, Kris."

That drew expletives from Jack and Vicky both.

Kris sighed. "Vicky, do you want to ask any of your advisors to leave?"

The Grand Duchess glanced around the room. "No, if they can stomach it, they can stay."

Several looked green or pale as a ghost, but none made for the door.

"Okay, Nelly, have at us."

The bulkhead to Kris's right turned into a star map. Most of the stars were unblinking white.

The Empire was in red or blue, depending on who held what. The US planets were golden. The area that Kris's Patrol Squadron 10 had policed out beyond the Empire was sprinkled with tiny, flashing, red dots.

"The flashing red area," Nelly explained, "is the patrol area for Captain Campbell's cruiser squadron. They've been nipping off pirates and other unsavory types that try to use that no-man's-land for nasty things. Campbell just reported, and hotwired to you, about a cruiser he boarded. The skipper of this formerly Greenfeld Navy heavy cruiser demanded to be left alone. He said he was on a diplomatic mission by order of the Empress. He might have been left to go on his way, but Jack didn't think all that added up. What kind of diplomatic mission would an ex-Navy cruiser be doing out in the middle of nowhere? The Iteeche Empire was not even close, and the guy didn't mention anything about them."

Nelly paused. She'd learned to do that recently to allow humans to catch up with her.

"Campbell found the skipper of the ship as easy to get talking as a block of granite, but the navigator was all twitchy. His word, not mine. He took the navigator aside and asked to see his charts and his destination. The guy crumbled. Kris, the Empress had sent them out to find what you call the bug-eyed monsters and get them to come into the civil war on her side."

"That has got to be the stupidest idea I've ever heard," Kris exploded.

Around the room, some people said a lot worse, while others looked puzzled, and asked, 'What?' When they were brought up to speed about the alien raiders, there was more profanity.

"Okay. Okay," Kris said, trying to bring order. The room settled down but did not go quiet.

"Kris," Nelly said in her professorial voice, "back on old Earth, there were a lot of times when a failing rebellion or even an anointed sovereign called in help from outside his borders. It often ended with bad things happening to both the original sides, but it worked enough times that it happened many, many times."

"I seem to remember something like that from school, Nelly. Now, what does Captain Campbell have to say about this instance?"

"He's holding the ship and crew while he passes the buck up the chain of command. He wants you to know that he suspects the buck won't stop until it lands on the King's desk, so he's not expecting orders anytime soon. However, he knew about the mission you're on and figured you'd like to know what he'd stepped in."

"Is that all, Nelly?" Kris growled.

"Yes, Admiral."

Kris leaned back in her chair. What the hell could she do with this? What the hell was the Empress up to? Had they stopped the only one of her "diplomatic missions"?

"Ah, Kris," Vicky said cautiously.

"Yes, Vicky."

"Admiral von Mittleburg just told me of something you might want to hear."

"Admiral," Kris said.

"We have been picking up rumors of this kind of thing, but we didn't put much faith in them. That might have been a mistake. I didn't bring the Grand Duchess into the loop on this because, well, she had her plate plenty full and didn't need to be bothered with what everyone took for a minor distraction."

Kris nodded. A human could only juggle so many buzzing chain saws.

"I asked for more information about this," the admiral said. "It is possible I may get a reply soon."

"Or not," Kris said.

"Or not, if it is still viewed as unbelievable by the senior staff."

"Nelly, get the address of the admiral's higher-ups, compose a letter for his chop with an information copy of this attached to them from him, marked personal and most secret, addressee's eyes only, unless he's out of town, then his second immediately. You willing to sign that?"

"No problem, Your Highness," Admiral von Mittleburg said.

"Kris, I also got the cipher for admiral-to-admiral communications from Admiral von Mittleburg's computer. The message is ready to go if he's willing to sign it."

The admiral glanced at his wrist unit for a long moment, then nodded. "Put my chop on it."

"The message is on its way," Nelly reported.

Kris leaned back in her chair. "Now what?"

"I guess we wait," Jack said.

"Kris, the Marine guard at the brow report that there is a runner coming aboard with message traffic that Admiral von Mittleburg needs to see soonest," Nelly announced.

48

"Have the OOD send him here immediately," Kris ordered before allowing herself the luxury of a deep breath. Several deep breaths.

Don't things ever slow down?

There were advantages to having her day quarters on the same deck as the quarterdeck; the runner had less distance to cover. Apparently, he'd run all the way because he was out of breath as he entered Kris's quarters and sprinted to his admiral.

The messenger was a lieutenant, j.g., and he was under arms. Not a good sign.

The admiral thanked the young officer for his speed, then dismissed him while he glanced at his message traffic. Only after the door closed behind the exhausted JO did Admiral von Mittleburg speak.

"Does anyone want to leave the room? If you don't, I will have everyone sign the State Secrets Act, and I assure you, I will have you shot if you divulge any of what you hear here."

The Greenfeld subjects paled at the serious tone the admiral took, but none headed for the door.

"Fine. Vicky, could you have that fancy computer of yours sync with Her Highness's computer and print out"—here he looked around the room—"ten copies of the Act."

"Ten?" Kris said. "You don't intend to have *my* King's subjects sign *your* act?" Kris asked, pointedly.

"Then you print out *your* Secrets Act and have *your* people sign it."

"Jack and I already have," Kris said, eyeing her team.

Senior Chief Agent in Charge Foile rummaged in his wallet and pulled out his Ident Card and handed it to Kris. "I've signed it."

His card did indeed have the necessary endorsement, among others.

Kris eyed the three leaders of her brain trust as well. All shook their heads no.

"Three copies, Nelly, unless you want to leave the room."

Diana again shook her head. "I'm guessing that this involves the Empress. We have to be in the know."

A printer appeared and began spitting out paper. Jack trotted over to it and returned with six copies of the Greenfeld Imperial State Secrets Act printed in a dark, blocky, and threatening format. He brought those to Admiral von Mittleburg, who handed them out to his people.

Jack then returned to pick up the US version. It was much longer but at least was nicely calligraphied.

The banker, industrialist, and rancher quickly read the two-page Greenfeld Imperial State Secrets Act and blanched.

"But we're rebels," the rancher said. "Do we really have to sign this?"

"If you want this rebellion to succeed, we have to keep a few secrets," Vicky pointed out.

The banker shook his head. "Your Grace, there is no way in hell I'm going to sign this."

"I understand, Bert, but I must insist if you want to stay."

"I guess I'll be on the next shuttle down," Bert said, handing back his copy. The industrialist and rancher quickly followed his example. Both the mayors from Kiev and St. Petersburg also stood.

"Mannie, can you look after St. Petersburg's interests. I won't expect you to brief us when you get back. Just tell us what you can and what we need to know," one mayor said.

"If I can tell you anything, I will," the mayor of Sevastopol said, and signed the Secrets Act with a flourish.

The room quickly emptied. Nelly rearranged it, bringing up a conference table and converting the easy chairs into station chairs around the table, still comfortable, but more utilitarian.

"How do you get used to having your chair change and move around while you're still sitting in it?" Vicky asked, glancing down and making a face at her chair.

"I've made chairs vanish from underneath people who were sitting in my place, but I don't think Nelly has ever done things like this until the last couple of days," Kris said.

"But I've wanted to," Nelly said.

"So, Admiral," Kris said, getting down to business, "what hot potato do you want to dump in our laps?"

"There have been reports, none of them creditable, that the Empress was trying to put together a battle squadron for exploration."

"That sounds silly in the middle of a civil war," Kris said.

"Yes. That was why the reports were not creditable. But we now have information." The Admiral glanced at his message flimsy. "One of our 'loyal' stay-behinds got one of their loyal officers drunk. The guy bragged that he'd be navigating eight battleships out to find the aliens and *they* would make contact for the Empress where even Kris Longknife couldn't."

Kris swallowed hard but said nothing.

"We even got a sailing plan. The ships they've pulled out of the Reserve Fleet are eight battleships of the Deneb class. They pack twelve 15-inch lasers."

"The aliens blew Admiral Krätz's four battleships out of space even though they packed the most up-to-date 18-inchers," Vicky breathed. "The Empress is out of her mind."

"No. The Empress is desperate. You nearly killed her the last time you met," Admiral von Mittleburg said. "She wants to make sure she kills you the next time you two face off."

"And she's willing to get all of humanity killed if she has to," Kris growled. "What's the sailing plan? Do you have it?"

"It is attached," Admiral von Mittleburg said. "The Navy General Staff would like us to go after them, but it would mean stripping St. Petersburg of most of our battleships."

"Nelly, have you got the sailing plan?"

"Yes, Kris. They're heading out deep, and they aren't going

near US territory. It will be a long, stern chase for any of the Grand Duchess's ships from here."

"Would any other planet's ships have better luck?" Kris asked.

"Brunswick is closer, but they only have four battleships," Admiral von Mittleburg said.

"Kris, we could overtake them without too much trouble," Nelly said.

"Have you figured out a course?"

"Yes, Kris," and the screen that had the star map suddenly had two lines: one red, the other gold. The red line showed a series of short jumps. The gold one was a lot fewer jumps, but they were long leaps going far out before returning to intersect at a system well away from the Empire.

"I think the *Princess Royal* can handle eight obsolescent battleships," Kris said. "We can have the *Intrepid* at the next pier spin off a pinnace and have it squawk as the *Princess Royal*."

"Will you be leaving Ruth behind?" Jack asked, voice level as a plain.

Oops. "No, Jack. I will be taking Ruth with me. I said I was going to nurse her for at least the first year, and I will. Besides, there have been three assassination attempts on Vicky while she was on St. Petersburg. I don't trust Ruth out of my sight."

"Then how about four ships spin off pinnaces, and we take four frigates with us?"

"You don't think the *P. Royal* can take eight old battleships, Jack?"

"I expect she could, but this intel is as squishy as it comes. Will more ships join them? Will they have tied in with a couple of honking-big alien warships by the time we catch them? Will we have to take all of them out before they go home to Momma and bring all their brothers and sisters back?"

"You want a larger safety margin, my paranoid security chief."

"At least four. I'd prefer all eight, but you're probably right. We have to maintain a presence here. Someone has to stay and respond to the letter we sent the Emperor."

Kris eyed her brain trust. "Folks, you won't be all that

helpful if we get into a fleet engagement. Do you mind staying behind?"

"I was afraid you'd never ask," Al said, looking relieved. "I remember signing on to help you make peace, not blow shit up."

"I have a bad habit of doing that," Kris admitted.

"Which ship do we transfer to?" Judge Diana asked, hurrying their exit along.

"Let me talk to my flag captain." Kris said. "Sad to say, she knows more about this squadron than its commander does."

"Kris, I want to go out with you," Vicky said.

Kris eyed the Imperial side of the table. She'd almost forgot they were here.

"As much as I hate to miss the fun, I must stay and maintain the fleet," von Mittleburg said.

"I think I will go with the Grand Duchess." Admiral Bolesław said.

"Mannie, you should go ashore," Vicky told the mayor.

"I was just thinking I would like to go along with you. This might be as much fun as the last time we sailed into battle together."

"Mannie, I have to go to accept the surrender of any ships that decide to throw in the towel. You aren't really needed."

Mannie gave the Grand Duchess a half shrug. "Since when have I needed an excuse to go where you go?"

"Mannie, this crazy Longknife is taking four small frigates and chasing after eight or more huge battleships. No one in their right mind would go along with her."

"If you are not in your right mind, neither am I. Who knows, I might come in as much handy as you."

"Assuming we can get a few to surrender, I have a job."

"Vicky, I'm not moving unless Her Highness here throws me off her boat."

"Ship," Vicky corrected, and turned to Kris with a shrug that was a mixture of hopelessness and delight. "Do you have room for one more crazy?"

"Always room for another in this insane asylum I run," Kris said, "especially a guy as implacable as my Jack."

Who leaned over and gave her a quick peck.

"Well, time's awasting. I have a division of frigates to get away from the pier. Admiral, I may need to top off my tanks and refill the larder."

"I'll get right on that," Admiral von Mittleburg said, saluted, and exited.

"As much fun as you three and your people have been," Kris said to her brain trust, "you need to get ashore as fast as you can."

"We're going."

"So, Vicky, you want to shadow me for the day?" Kris asked her occasional friend. "If you think you saw everything we can do that the Empire can't while we were gallivanting around on the *Wasp*, wait until you see what I've got up my sleeve now. Let's go."

49

Vice Admiral, Her Imperial Grace, the Grand Duchess Victoria of the Greenfeld Empire, and in rebellion against the same, stood as Kris Longknife led a division of four frigates away from the High St. Petersburg Station. It had taken the Wardhaven Princess exactly five hours from the time she ordered go to the minute they were gone.

How does she do these things?

Vicky remembered the last time she'd shared a ride with Kris Longknife. A lot of water and spilled milk had flowed under a lot of bridges since then.

They'd fled in the old *Wasp* across the galaxy, first with enraged aliens after their blood, then in a ship run just about dry of reaction mass, fearing they lacked enough to slow down and refuel. Kris had gone to heroic levels to pull them through.

Vicky had gotten drunk and mouthed off to Kris, the best friend she had, then thrown Kris under the bus the first time she had a chance for an interview back in human space. Vicky shivered in embarrassment.

Back then, she'd been a terrified little girl with a target on her back painted there by her stepmother. She'd had no idea how she'd survive from one day to the next.

Vicky squared her shoulders. The last year had been an

education for her. She'd learned a lot and done a lot, often asking herself "What would Kris Longknife do?" She and the people around her had pulled themselves up by their bootstraps and gotten a lot of worlds walked back from the brink of disaster.

Here she was, once again, following Kris around. Only now, she was no confused little kitten. She had made of herself the leader of a cause and half an Empire. It was good to have Kris's help, but it was only possible for Kris to do anything because Vicky had first done a whole lot more.

Today, Vicky spent most of that time shadowing Kris. It was still educational and a lot of fun watching how Kris made things happen.

Early into the count, Kris ordered Nelly to call Vice Admiral von Mittleburg. "About that reaction mass and fresh meat and produce. Ya'got any to spare?"

"Reaction mass, no problem. Fresh produce, not so much."

It was Mannie who placed a call to his contacts in Sevastopol. They found two shuttles waiting on cargo and leased them. In an hour, they were stuffed with the best Sevastopol's hinterland had to offer. Kris had sent Vicky off with a Supply Corps lieutenant to see how easy it was to resupply a Smart Metal™ ship. Clearly, the Wardhaven Princess had a few things to do that she didn't want a Peterwald looking over her shoulder at.

Kris is such a stickler when it comes to some things.

Then again, I'd hate to have Stepmommy dearest know some things I saw on the old Wasp *as we shot around the other side of the galaxy.*

Vicky's jaw dropped as station trucks drove right into the *Princess Royal*, through holes that suddenly opened into the ship. They off-loaded crates directly into storage rooms. The meat was parked in an open space. A minute later, a refrigerating unit had grown up around it, complete with a door warning DO NOT LEAVE OPEN.

Vicky, Mannie, and Admiral Bolesław were in Kris's much-reduced flag plot as the *P. Royal* backed away from its pier. The next frigate spun off a pinnace that quickly ducked in to fill the vacancy. It expanded to look hardly smaller than its mother ship and began squawking as the *Princess Royal* at the exact same moment that Kris's ship went silent in space.

Perfect.

Even Admiral Bolesław nodded with respect at the smoothly run evolution. He rarely had anything nice to say about the Longknifes. Then again, he'd been raised on Greenfeld propaganda.

All done, three frigates followed the *Princess Royal* as she ducked down toward St. Petersburg, then accelerated toward the jump point that had coughed up the Empress not so long ago.

Vicky had overheard enough to know that the next system over had one of those fuzzy jumps that Wardhaven ships could see and Greenfeld ships were totally blind to.

Kris turned from observing her Captain Ajax do her job perfectly to eye Vicky and her small team. "I've decided to keep Admiral's Country down here in amidships. It means traffic will be routed past us, but it also means we'll have the strongest protection, both against radiation and lasers for the nursery. I had my brain trust of helpful conflict solvers bunking close to me. Their space is now vacant. Do you have a problem with us keeping Admiral's Country together for all three admirals aboard?"

Admiral Bolesław silently shrugged.

"I'm fine with that," Vicky said.

"I assume you'll want the mayor to have quarters next to you?" Kris asked.

Vicky nervously glanced toward Mannie. "Whatever you want," she said.

"Whichever way you want. I have no problem," the mayor said.

"So it's that way," Kris said. "Well, your quarters are going to be next to each other. What you do about it is in your hands."

But the embarrassing problem was not solved just yet. Mr. Smith arrived with Kit and Kat as well as all their gear.

"Do you want us to bunk on either side of your quarters?" Mr. Smith asked.

"They tell me we can have a door directly into your quarters," Kit said hopefully to Vicky.

"Ah, I was thinking Mannie might have one of the rooms next to me. Is that okay with you, Mannie?"

"Ah, I have no problem with anything you want," he dodged, again.

Kris and Jack looked ready to split a gut. *Well, they're married and have a baby, no less.*

Kris stepped forward and quickly redrew the staterooms around the outer circular passageway. "Kit and Kat, Mr. Smith, Vicky, Mannie, and Admiral Bolesław, in that order. Okay?"

"Fine," Vicky mumbled, trying not to blush.

Me. Blush! No.

Then why is my face all warm?

It must be hot in here.

In a moment, Vicky was being led to her quarters for the cruise by a chief and a Sailor who carried her luggage. Her quarters were not quite as spacious as those on the *Retribution*, but nothing to sneeze at.

"If we get in a fight," the chief started, then corrected himself. "Rather when being more likely with the Princess in command, the ship will shrink down to Condition Baker, then Charlie, and lastly Zed. By Condition Zed things are quite cozy but we're all at battle stations so it doesn't really matter if our quarters are stowed away into nothing but a few lockers. After the battle, we stretch out again. By the way, Your Grace, there's an app that lets you make adjustments to your quarters. If you want more space in your day quarters, you can make your night quarters shrink to nothing. If you need even more space, you can open up a door to one of the rooms next door or, if those next to you have been warned and are willing, you can make either bulkhead go away."

"You can?" Vicky said, glancing at the bulkhead between her and Mannie. She quickly shook her head at the thoughts that tumbled into her mind.

"You can. Would you like the app?"

"No," she said, but she was nodding yes.

"Which is it to be, Your Grace?" the old chief said.

"Let me have it," she said, not looking at him as she spoke. "If I never use it, it will never matter."

"Yes, Your Grace," and Vicky's computer beeped happily.

A moment later, the door closed on her quarters as the two enlisteds left.

And another moment after that, there was a knock at her door.

"Enter."

And Mannie cautiously stepped in.

"Are your quarters this good?" Vicky asked.

"Not quite. I think you got extra room so you could hold meetings. Are your sleeping quarters through that door?" he asked.

Vicky found her eyes were fixed on the deck. It looked to be nice carpet. "Yes."

"Wasn't it fantastic the way they moved walls all over the place to load supplies," Mannie said. "I bet your Sailors would love something like that."

"Ours will, once we get this into the Greenfeld fleet."

"Um," Mannie said. "I understand there are all sorts of apps. You can make your own easy chair. Widen or lengthen your bed. All kinds of things."

"What did you think of the way Nelly made entire walls appear and disappear?" Vicky said, finding she'd kind of rushed breathlessly into that thought.

"It must be nice what Nelly can do," Mannie was quick to point out, then added, "I understand that there are apps that Sailors can use to do the same."

"You heard about that, too," Vicky said, feeling excitement in places she'd ignored for a very long time.

"Yes."

"I was offered one of those apps," Vicky offered.

"So was I," Mannie said softly.

"It's something you'd want to have around if a ship were damaged, or other things," Vicky said, leaving her words vague.

"Did you take the app?" Mannie asked.

"Did you?"

There was a pause, before both of them blurted out, "Yes."

Vicky turned toward Mannie and found his arms open. It was only two steps before she was in them. His kiss was so soft, just a brush of her lips that shot electricity down her body and left every nerve ending tingling.

She pressed her mouth to his, claiming him. His hands came to surround her face, moving her ever so slightly so they fitted perfectly together. For a long time, there was only his touch and their kiss.

Then she broke away for air.

And her doubts.

"Mannie, aren't we supposed to avoid tumbling into bed until after the problems from my father's bedtime tumbles are straightened out?"

"It's been an awfully long wait," he said.

"It has," she agreed.

"And we are on a Longknife ship, and everyone knows the Longknifes have no morals at all."

"So I was told growing up," Vicky agreed again.

"And four small frigates taking on eight huge battleships could leave us dust, and think of what we'd have missed."

"It would be sad to miss kisses like that one," Vicky found herself once more agreeing.

"And we can make the wall between our night quarters vanish, but still be able to dash into the front room if we have to."

"Yes. Yes, we could. You are a most persuasive politician," Vicky said.

"So kiss me again, and we'll figure out how to run the app later."

"Oh, yes."

50

Vicky felt herself gain weight the next morning as the *Princess Royal* changed its acceleration from 1.5 gees to 2.5 gees. *For the third time this morning!*

"Kris, why the different accelerations? I don't see the pattern."

"There's a pattern. I'll tell you, if first you tell me why you're so chipper. You look like the cat that gorged itself on cream."

Vicky glanced around, startled. None of her entourage was close by. "I don't look chipper." Then she hunched down, and whispered, "What do I look like?"

"Well, if you were a normal person, I'd say you got laid. You, I'm not so sure."

"Kris!" Vicky said, but kept it low.

"So, have you and Mannie figured out how to work the app?"

"Leave it to you Longknifes to come up with something as disgusting as that."

"Don't say Longknife. Some Sailor figured it out and passed it around. It was only a slight modification to the one to move walls for loading supplies. What's a skipper to do?"

"Well, it certainly beats hiding out in the paint locker," Vicky finally allowed herself to admit.

"Did you figure out how to get one king-size bed?"

"Kris!"

"Well, did you?"

Vicky sighed and gave in to the inevitable. "After about five seconds of trying."

The Wardhaven Princess had the ill humor to laugh . . . outrageously. When she sobered up, she leaned in close to Vicky. "I take it that you and Mannie haven't been, ah, huh."

"No, we haven't been either ah or huh. It's the longest string of celibate days I've had since I got my first monthly."

"Can I ask why?"

"Policy. Politics," Vicky said, spitting the words. "All this trouble started when my dad tumbled into bed with a whore. Mannie was afraid that if any other Peterwald tumbled into bed, even if the he was a she and the he wasn't a whore but a politician. Is there a difference? Anyway, either way it might not go over so well. Would you believe it, for the good of the rebellion, he walked out of my hotel room?"

Kris had gotten very serious while Vicky talked. Now the Princess nodded along with her words.

"As hard as it has been, I think he's right," Kris said. "Your father is a selfish, thoughtless fool who looks out only for himself. If you want to get the people behind you, you have to look a whole lot better. Mannie's a good advisor."

"I'm hoping we'll marry as soon as this mess is over."

"You likely couldn't chose a better consort," Kris said. "I'm not trying to make Greenfeld over into some Longknife democracy. I know your feelings on that. But your Empire is going to need a lot more transparency than it has had. It also has to include a lot more perspectives as well."

Vicky let out a big sigh. "I hear the same talk from Mannie. I was raised, as you would say, to be autocratic. Well, not so much me to be autocratic but to accept that autocratic Peterwald men were ordained by God to rule, and if God had any problems with that, He'd better get with the program."

Kris laughed. "My father's never quite put it into those words, but I suspect he'd agree with the sentiment. As for Ray, he *is* god."

Vicky laughed along with Kris but quickly sobered. "Do we have to become gods to make things work?"

Kris shook her head. "Do you really think things work because our fathers and my great-grandfather think they're Zeus on Olympus?"

Vicky's shoulders slumped. "A few years ago, I think I would have believed them."

"Now?" Kris asked.

"Not so much," Vicky said, and thought for a moment. Then rethought herself. "Hold it. You were supposed to tell me why our acceleration varies. You told me I had to answer one question. That was a dozen questicns ago."

"Okay, I'll let you in cn a secret. We go 2.5 gees when Ruth is napping on a high-gee station. We cut down to 1.5 gees when she's up and wants to bounce around. I tell you, that kid is going to have legs that any high-school track coach will die for."

"Ruth is setting our course?" Vicky said, almost in a shriek.

"No, not our course, but maybe a bit of our speed," Kris said. "Nelly, you want to explain this to Vicky."

"Not really, Kris. Let's just say I'm juggling my assumptions of when Ruth naps and what accelerations and decelerations we need to make our jumps. Ruth's nap time is a major unknown in my sailing plan, but she's woken up or gone to sleep within fifteen minutes of my estimates. A six-month-old is nothing if not free willed."

They exited the St. Petersburg system at 50,000 kph and accelerated almost constantly to the next jump. Vicky and Admiral Bolesław were in Kris's flag plot as they approached the jump out.

"We'll be using the fourth jump," Nelly informed Kris.

Beside Vicky, Admiral Bolesław scowled, but only after covering his mouth with his hand. "There are only three jumps in this system," he whispered to Vicky.

She covered her mouth, and around a cough said, "Long-knifes see jumps we can't. Both us and the aliens."

"Oh," Bolesław rumbled, and watched as Nelly threaded a needle through space that he would never have guessed was there.

"Nelly's taking the indirect course to catch your Empress's diplomats," Kris announced after the jump was done, and Nelly reported it was good. "They'll be about ten jumps and three hundred light-years out from Greenfeld when we catch up with them. We will have made six jumps and gone out two thousand light-years in a most erratic course when we run them down. But it will have taken us less time to cover our distance than they will have taken to cover theirs."

Admiral Bolesław ran a hand through his hair and shook his head. "The fools. The fools."

"Which fools?" Vicky asked.

"Anyone who thought we might stand our ground in a fight with the Longknife King."

"I don't know," Vicky muttered. "We're still chasing after eight big, bad battleships in four small frigates." She gave Kris Longknife a dour frown.

The Longknife Princess glanced her way and returned her a soft, knowing smile.

Did she hear what I just said? Or worse, could she figure out for herself what I just said. Damn you, Longknifes, and the democracy you rode in on.

They were now outside the Empire and deep into unknown space. Vicky watched as Kris began to make the division her own. Even as they went on their way, she had them practicing battle evasion drills. At all hours of the day or night, Vicky got use to the bong of General Quarters and the announcement "Battle Stations. Battle Stations."

Yes, despite the battle preparations, the journey to the next jump was still at different accelerations and decelerations. When Ruth was awake, it was 1.5 gees. When she napped, it jumped to over two gees.

Vicky just shook her head, then thought better of it.

What will I do when I have a baby at my breast?

That brought a whole lot of thoughts Vicky wasn't ready to contemplate. She did ask Kris about the small army of nannies on board.

The Wardhaven Princess just shrugged. "I'm trying to have it all. If I can borrow reinforcements, I'm good to go with it."

The nannies weren't the only ones who looked after Ruth. It looked like half the young women in the Marine detachment spent some of their spare time playing with Ruth.

"That infant has this ship wrapped around her little finger," Admiral Bolesław muttered, but he was smiling softly as he muttered.

"It's nice that the ship is Smart Metal." Vicky grinned back. "It makes it easier to bend the ship around her tiny finger, don't you think?"

"I was going to say I was rethinking having women on a warship," the admiral growled, "but I think one woman on my ship is quite enough . . . for a lifetime."

Vicky enjoyed the laugh, and the admiral soon joined in.

They were deep in unknown space, headed for a near jump that would take them back toward human space, when Nelly told Kris, "We have signal traffic in this system."

Kris sat bolt upright in her chair. "What kind of signal traffic?"

"They are conventional radio and TV traffic. There are no fusion reactors operational in the system."

"Thank God for that favor," Jack muttered.

"Record all the message traffic, Nelly, and try to triangulate on the source of the signal."

"We are doing that, Kris."

Kris was up, nervously pacing the length of her flag plot before turning back. "Whatever it is, we keep going. If it's another sentient race, we'll have to come back later."

"We come back?" Jack asked, leaving a lot hanging unsaid.

Kris paused in her pacing and turned beet red. "*We'll* send someone *else* back to look it over," she corrected herself.

What is that all about? Vicky wondered but said nothing.

Kris slumped back into her chair, she and Jack still holding aggressive eye contact.

Maybe Kris Longknife is not the one I want to ask about how to keep a husband happy.

As soon as they were out of the system, Nelly reported on what they'd found.

"It is a primitive civilization. They have radio and television but no atomics. I think I made out some small satellites with weak transmitters. None were communications satellites. A few years ago, I would have suggested that they bear watching. However . . ."

Did Nelly just leave it to us to figure out where the data leads? Maybe her attitude is worth putting up with, not that Kris would ever allow me such a computer.

"Yeah," Kris growled. "We can't leave them hanging out

there for the bug-eyed monsters to sniff out. Nelly, log your findings and forward them to the King as soon as we are back in communications with the US net."

"Yes, Kris."

Kris turned to her husband. "I wonder how Sandy's making out with the cats."

"Better her than us," Jack answered.

"The cats?" Vicky asked.

"Another race we stumbled across," Kris said, but added nothing more to that bit of vagueness.

"Greenfeld isn't the only place we're trying to protect," Jack said.

"I hope we can protect ourselves," Vicky said. "I expect that once this war is over, we will need to continue building battleships."

"Or something," Kris said, and again left Vicky with more questions than answers.

Now the division of frigates turned back toward human space. For several days, it decelerated more than it accelerated, slowing until it took the last jump at a mere fifty thousand klicks per hour.

They jumped into the target system to find it empty.

"Either we're early, or we missed them," Admiral Bolesław said.

"We're early," Kris said, with all the definiteness in her voice that admirals and ship's captains were wont to muster.

Admiral Bolesław raised a questioning eyebrow to Vicky, but she just shrugged. "I trust Kris," she mouthed silently to him.

Now both of the admiral's eyebrows went up, but he said nothing.

Ten minutes later, the debate ended. Eight Deneb class battleships began jumping into the system. Nelly reported them, one after another.

"*Aldebaran, Arcturus, Sirius, Rigel, Leonis, Ursae, Vega,* and *Alpha Ceti*. All present and accounted for, sir," her computer said, and seemed to finish with a proper English foot stomp.

Vicky wasn't the only one trying to squelch a grin.

"Thank you, Nelly. Is that what they're squawking, or is that who they are?"

"Kris," had hurt in it. "I've checked their registration against their reactors and capacitors. They are Denebs right down to the moonshine stills in the goat lockers. And may I point out to the doubting Thomases among you that my readings are off ships that jumped into the system two hours ago. Right when I expected them to."

"Yes, Nelly. You are magnificent," Kris drawled.

"Kris, I find your attitude unbecoming one of your nobility," Nelly said with a sniff.

"Nelly, I don't have time for this. Save it for later when I do."

"Kris, you never have time."

"Trust me, I will after this is over."

"I don't think Jack or I believe you."

"Nelly, what are the battleships doing?" Kris said, cutting off further complaining by her computer.

"They are on course to the nearest standard jump in this system. It will be a while before they discover we are here. You don't really think I would be having this much fun giving you lip if everything wasn't under control, do you?"

"I never know with you, Nelly. Not anymore." But Kris was now grinning. "What do you say we do something to prepare for the coming battle?"

"Okay, Kris."

"All ships, go to Condition Charlie. All hands should be dismissed into high-gee acceleration stations in rotations. We will go to Condition Zed at any time after we close with the hostiles to four hundred thousand klicks. Captain Ajax, set an intercept course for the division."

Acknowledgments came back immediately.

"Okay, folks," Kris said, cheerfully, "now we make this happen.

Vicky and Admiral Bolesław just shook their heads. Mannie looked from her to the Wardhaven Princess and back to Vicky, clearly puzzled.

"Eight battleships," Vicky whispered to him. "Four *frigates*. We're doomed."

"Watch and learn," Kris said. "Watch and learn."

51

The four frigates closed inexorably on the battle line. Vicky watched the screen on Kris's flag plot as the lines representing the two of them closed, heading for a single point.

Before any of them arrived at that point, there would be mayhem and death.

Vicky had already been dismissed back to her room to find two Smart Metal™ high-gee stations: one for her and one for Mannie. Kris had told her that she'd likely want to strip before she got in the station. "They fit you like a second skin."

Vicky and Mannie did strip, but only after taking a few moments for themselves did they take their seats in the stations and order them to close up.

Kris, you are so mean, to lead a poor girl into temptation when she knows she's going to be blown to dust.

Still, it was nice to have the scent of Mannie on her as she prepared to face whatever death wish Kris had for them all.

Strange. None of the crew seemed at all worried about what's ahead. Does Kris know something she's not telling?

"Range is four hundred thousand klicks," Nelly announced.

"All ships, go to Condition Zed," Kris ordered.

Vicky had been told her quarters would disappear when the

ship shrunk to this. Still, she was surprised as Kris's flag plot shrunk to half its previous size.

"If I need to pee, can I use the bathroom in your night quarters?" she asked Kris.

"My night quarters are boxed up, too, Vicky. If you need to pee, do it in your high-gee station. It was made for that. Late in my pregnancy, when I was peeing all the time, it was kind of nice to go into a battle and have the high-gee station take care of that for me." Kris actually chuckled at that.

"You've got to be kidding."

"Nope. Trust me, when you've got a little one bouncing on your bladder, you'll think time in a high-gee station is worth a fight or two."

"*I* will use a *uterine* replicator," Vicky spat, and gave Mannie the evil eye.

"That sounds great by me," he said, edging his station a bit away from Vicky's.

"Kids, we've got a battle coming up here," Nelly said. "Kris, when do you want to tell those battleship folks they ain't going anywhere?"

"I was figuring on two hundred thousand klicks."

"Okay."

"Are we going to start shooting then?" Jack asked.

"Nope. I don't want to fire first."

"Two hundred thousand klicks?" Admiral Bolesław asked before Vicky got her mouth around that huge number.

"Yep," Kris said.

"Those battleships' 15-inch lasers can reach out eighty thousand klicks. Your pulse lasers, even if they're 24-inchers, don't have that range," the Greenfeld admiral pointed out.

"Yep, it would be a real pain if we were only packing pulse lasers, now wouldn't it?" Kris answered with a question of her own.

"So?" Vicky said, when Admiral Bolesław proved to be speechless.

"Do you want me to tell you now, or wouldn't you rather see how this all ends up?"

Vicky blinked several times as she took that in and parsed the sentence. "Can you tell me if we'll be alive when this is over?"

"Most definitely. You will live to enjoy tonight," Kris said with one of those smiles a newlywed bride tends to give the gal who caught her bouquet.

Vicky settled back in her station and prepared to see the rabbit this Longknife was clearly intent on pulling out of a hat. She hoped the poor thing didn't mind being held by its ears. Whatever Longknifes did, they did with a flourish.

The battleships stayed silent, intent on their course and ignoring the small combatants approaching them. At two hundred thousand klicks, Kris stood up from her high-gee station.

"Hold it, you're in uniform," Vicky snarled.

"Yep, I figured I'd better be. Who surrenders to a gal in the nude?"

"I'm supposed to take their surrender!" Vicky snapped.

"We can focus the camera on just your face and keep the station out of the picture."

"I'm getting in uniform," Vicky grumbled, and got her station in motion.

"Your quarters are all folded up," Mannie pointed out.

"Unfold them," Vicky growled.

"I can do that," Nelly said helpfully.

"Do it," Kris said. "Oh, Vicky, you don't want to wear ribbons or anything with sharp corners. I did once when we went to high-gee maneuvering, and one of my boobs was black-and-blue for a week."

Mannie followed Vicky out the door. They found themselves in a very small space that had Vicky's uniforms and a chair. Quickly both were out of their eggs and a delightfully naked Mannie was helping Vicky into a shipsuit of Navy blue with the proper loops to feed her vice admiral's shoulder boards through.

With a glance at a mirror that suddenly materialized, Vicky decided she was properly dressed to attend a funeral or accept the surrender of part of the Empress's fleet. Done, she gave Mannie a quick kiss, settled back into her egg, and motored quickly back to flag plot.

"You ready?" Kris asked.

"Yes," Vicky answered curtly. She had a bone to pick with Kris. A whole pile of bones, really. She'd just have to wait until things slowed down.

Yeah, right.

Again, Kris stood up. "Open a hailing frequency," she ordered.

A bored lieutenant filled the screen. "Yeah."

"We are Admiral, Her Royal Highness, Princess Kristine of the United Society commanding Frigate Squadron 22. We will speak to your captain."

"Admiral Dirk's busy. You can leave a message," was surly to the core.

Kris gave the lieutenant the look. The look that Admiral Krätz had and that Vicky had done her best to learn. The junior officer should have been crawling under his workstation to get away from it.

But, then, he wasn't meeting Kris's eyes.

"Sorry, lady. Don't bother us," he said, and cut the comm.

Kris sat back down into her egg.

"That didn't go very well," Jack said.

"It went exactly the way I expected it to," Kris said. "Nelly, tell me when we hit the hundred-thousand-klick mark."

It wasn't long before Nelly announced they were there.

Again, Kris stood and ordered hailing frequency open.

The screen remained blank.

"We know you are listening," Kris said in a voice that was measured and cold as death. "Know this, if you do not vent your reactors to space, discharge your capacitors, and prepare to be boarded, you will all die."

"That's a laugh," came from a screen that suddenly showed a pudgy man in an Imperial Navy's vice admiral's uniform. "*You're* threatening *me*? I got your piss pots outnumbered two to one. Let me tell *you* this. *You* turn around and run away home, little girl, and *I'll* let *you* live, okay?"

"You have been warned," Kris said, but she was talking to a blank screen.

"Do you think it would help if I talked to them?" Vicky offered.

Kris shook her head. "I doubt it. Well, at least my message got through to all the ships. We'll see how things work out after I blow the flagship to hell."

Vicky found that both of her eyebrows were up so far they were about to the back of her head, but Kris only gave her that fey smile and turned to her screens to watch the developments in the two fleets.

"They've armed their lasers," the Wardhaven Princess muttered to herself. "I guess it's time to load ours. Nelly, advise Captain Ajax to charge the *Princess Royal*'s capacitors."

"What about the other ships?" Nelly asked.

"No. Tell them to stand by but not load until I give the word. Our other three ships are not weapons free until I order them free."

"Yes, Admiral," said the computer.

Admiral Bolesław glanced at Vicky. Consternation flooded his face. Eight battleships against four frigates was suicide. Eight of them against one frigate!

It boggled the mind.

Vicky just shrugged. *It's way too late to get out of this now.*

"We're coming up on eighty thousand klicks to the flagship," Nelly announced.

"Is the armor solid and tight in place, Nelly?"

"Now you ask, Kris? Of course it is, or I would have mentioned it sooner."

Had the great Kris Longknife actually shown a bit of nervousness?

"We're coming up on eighty thousand klicks between us and the last ship in the battle line. Kris," Nelly said. "Should we be jinking or something?"

"Nope, we let them plant one on our chin," Kris almost whispered.

"The hostile battle line is firing on us, Kris. All ninety-six 15-inch guns at little old us," Nelly reported.

"Is our hull overheating?"

"No, Admiral," Nelly said. "We're radiating the laser energy back into space. No burn-through. Quite a few missed. I don't think they've got their lasers bore sighted all that well."

"Thank you, Nelly. Captain Ajax, you may fire on the flagship. All the forward battery if you please."

Around Vicky, the *Princess Royal* swung quickly but smoothly to bring herself bow on to the battle line. The light didn't even dim, but Vicky spotted a representation of a ship on Kris's board. One of four. Only this ship showed twelve beams leaving it.

"You've got twelve pulse lasers?" Vicky asked in a whisper.

"No, I've just hit the *Aldebaran* with twelve 22-inch lasers at well inside their normal range. I'm afraid that battleship is toast."

On another screen, said battleship was indeed toast. Its ice armor boiled off it, making the lasers piercing through it visible. The huge battleship looked like a butterfly mounted by a pin-happy six-year-old.

And then the battleship was no more. Where it had been was a boiling, roiling ball of fire and gas; and then there was nothing. Only a few bits and pieces were visible in the light of the lasers exciting the steam that had once been ice armor.

Then the lasers cut out.

"Holy Mother of God," Admiral Bolesław said. "What just happened?"

"The battle line fired on the *Princes Royal*," Kris said. "Our new crystal armor took their light in, diffused it around the hull, and radiated it back into space before it could do any damage. Then my battlecruiser returned fire on the *Aldebaran* with its forward battery of twelve 22-inch lasers. You saw how well its old-fashioned armor stood up to those new lasers."

"Longknifes have all of that?" Vicky asked, her voice a strained whisper.

"The US does, and quite a few other alliances who have joined us in defending the Alwa system against the aliens. Two years ago, I would have considered an 18-inch laser the top of the line. We expect to have 24-inch lasers in the near future."

"Our battleships are like dust to your frigates," Admiral Bolesław whispered.

"Battlecruisers," Kris corrected. "Your Grace, please see what you can do to get those other poor doomed souls to surrender before I have to slaughter more of them."

Vicky stood and addressed the screen. It was amazing how quickly the other ships vented their reactors to space, emptied their capacitors, and dropped all acceleration to drift in space.

Vicky quickly negotiated a formal surrender with the rear admiral commanding the second division. US Marines boarded the remaining seven ships and found their crews quite docile. Vicky asked for the loan of the Marines to keep them that way, and Rear Admiral Bolesław volunteered to take command of the squadron and see that they turned around and headed back for Brunswick.

"I'll loan you the *Resolute* to serve as sheep dog," Kris offered, and Vicky was glad she didn't have to ask. As much as she expected the fear of the Lord that Kris had put into them to last until they got to rebel territory, it was still good to have a ship on standby if things got rowdy.

"I thought you were crazy when you said you were ready to take on a battle squadron with one frigate," Vicky said. "You weren't crazy at all, were you?"

"Nope, one battle line, one battlecruiser. Even odds. Right, Jack?"

"Yes, love, but I'm still glad, Admiral darling, that you took along reinforcements. It could have gotten so much worse. If they'd had a couple or a dozen of those alien warships of five hundred thousand tons and a whole wad of lasers, it could have gotten a bit out of hand even for you, my dear."

"You notice how he lays the love on with a trowel," Kris said to Vicky. "He knows we were both right, but he's apologizing nevertheless. Smart husband."

"Mannie, are you taking notes?" Vicky asked her mayor.

"Copious notes. Copious and enlightening," he answered.

"Now, Captain Ajax, are you ready to go back to Condition Able?"

"How about we stay at Condition Baker until we see what these docile hostiles do for a day or two?"

"Sorry, Captain, but we need to be heading back to St. Petersburg as fast as we can. I would suggest you avoid making the jump out of here that we came through until these folks jump out themselves, but then we need to beat feet for home."

"Aye, aye, ma'am. As soon as we are out of their range, I will return the ship to Condition Able—Royal Plus Size, but not until."

Kris sighed. "Sometimes it's hard to remember that you might be an admiral, but aboard ship, you're just a passenger."

52

The trip back took a bit longer. Ruth had to put up with less than two gees and that only when she slept. Vicky found herself wishing the voyage would never end.

On the way out, Admiral Bolesław studiously did not notice or comment on Vicky's being, as Kris put it, chipper. Mr. Smith and the assassins did not make any effort to enter Vicky's quarters. Even Kat refrained from rolling her eyes and talking in salacious French.

She and Mannie could be themselves, and Vicky very much liked what they could be when it was just them. Mannie was neither so athletic nor so "creative" in his lovemaking as some Vicky had shared her bed with. Instead, she found herself in a place she'd never been before. Loved. Yes. Relaxed? Definitely. Satisfied? Totally.

Could something like this last forever?

I sure would like to try.

Her idyllic interlude didn't last much past their jumping into the system one jump out from St. Petersburg. A message was waiting for them.

The Emperor had accepted Cuzco as the neutral ground for the negotiations and set the date for three weeks from his date of acceptance. Time had been lost getting the message out to St. Petersburg, and more before Vicky got the message.

"Can we make it?" Vicky asked Kris.

"Nelly?" she said, passing it along to her computer.

"Ruth ain't gonna like it, but we can make it."

"Then let's put pedal to the metal and get things moving."

It hadn't been as easy as that.

Kris had to pick up the three ships still at St. Petersburg; *Defender* had gone on ahead with Kris's brain trust. The three frigates rose from High St. Petersburg Station looking like strangely swollen fish. Then Kris let Vicky in on another one of her secrets. The swollen ships were in tanker mode, bringing up reaction mass to refuel the ships with more miles on them.

They also brought a load of fresh meat and produce, which was transferred over by the pinnaces when they brought the reaction mass.

"We got to get some of this stuff," Mannie whispered in awe.

Vicky just shook her head. The Empress had destroyed so much of Greenfeld, and what she had left was rapidly becoming little more than a series of start-up colonies.

Kris had insisted that killing the Empress was not an acceptable negotiating position. More and more, Vicky wanted to offer it as her starting position . . . and then negotiate *back* from there.

Like throw in torture before finally killing her.

Mannie had been teaching Vicky negotiating techniques. It seemed you needed something to do in bed between doing what you were in bed to do. He'd taught Vicky about how you were supposed to bargain. You stated your opening position. They stated theirs, and you bargained *toward* each other. It wasn't considered kosher to bargain *away* from your opening position.

Vicky was ready to make special allowances for her stepmother.

They pulled up to High Cuzco Station with a cranky Ruth and an hour to spare before negotiations were supposed to start.

"Supposed to" were the operative words.

Both parties had sent advanced teams to Cuzco to prepare for the actual bargaining. So far, Vicky's advanced team had dodged one bomb and several drive-by shootings.

Someone on Wardhaven must have been following developments. Several crates of Spidersilk body armor had arrived; so far, they had saved three lives.

Was Vicky the only one who found it strange that all the assassination attempts were on her advance team?

When Judge Diana took a bullet to the heart that was stopped by Spidersilk, it became clear that no one was safe.

Even at the risk of life and limb, the negotiations were going depressingly slow.

The Emperor had reserved a resort hotel in the hills beyond Machu Picchu, Cuzco's capital. He, or maybe the Empress, insisted negotiations take place there. Vicky's advance team had started with a location on the High Cuzco Station where all the principals could retreat to their ships after each bargaining session.

When the Imperial side rejected that option, Vicky's team had fallen back to using the *Princess Royal* for the negotiations.

That had also been rejected.

The Emperor insisted he needed the open air the resort allowed.

"I don't think it's the open air, so much as all the places assassins can hide," Vicky told Kris with a frown.

Kris turned to her brain trust, who had greeted the *Princess Royal* when she docked. "Okay, how do we arrive at an agreement to end this civil war when we can't even agree on where we talk?"

The three exchanged glances, then Al shrugged and spoke, apparently for all. "You make a concession to get the bargaining going and assume that he will accept that he owes us one."

"I don't think the Empress will ever concede that she owes anyone anything," Vicky snapped.

"You are probably right," Diana said, "but nothing ventured, nothing gained."

"Assuming someone doesn't blow us all to kingdom come," Jack pointed out.

"There is that," Bill conceded.

Kris ran a worried hand through her hair. She needed a haircut, but her hair had still not recovered from her pregnancy. *Thank you very much, Ruthie.*

"Okay. Jack, get your Marines down below, and go through

every inch of that place up to ten thousand meters in the sky
and down a thousand or so in the dirt. If you say it's safe, we'll
assume we can keep it safe and risk it."

"And Ruth?" Jack asked.

"Stays up here safe and sound. I'll pump milk for her nannies to give her. That acceptable to you, oh my ever-cautious
security chief?"

"I would rather you and Ruth Marie were both safe up
here," Jack said. "Whatever happened to telecommuting?
Can't we do this thing via screens?"

"You need to see each other's body language and inflec-
tions," Diana said.

"As well as the trust matter. If you don't trust them enough
to meet them face-to-face . . ." Al left hanging.

"But I don't trust them," Jack pointed out.

"Yes. Maybe we don't either," Bill said, "but we still have
to show we are willing to trust them."

With a scowl, Jack stood and started talking into his
commlink. "Give us a day to see what we can do down there.
We'll meet again this time tomorrow."

"Very good," Kris said.

A day later, Jack was back. "There are no surprises underground. Each building has its own power supply, so there are
no conduits. Even the sewage is treated in each cottage and the
main lodge. All that is underground is a network of water
pipes. I have to admit, the place is secure underground. It's
aboveground that worries me."

"How so?" both Vicky and Kris asked.

"Trees. Lots of trees. All of them tall, so there aren't a lot
of bushes; still, there are a lot of trees. Then there are the
mountains. There are some serious mountains around that
place. Someone with a rocket launcher could do a lot of damage fast."

"Can you stop that?" Kris asked her husband.

"Nelly, can you make us an aerostat out of Smart Metal?"
Jack asked.

"Yes. Do you want it powered?"

"I want it tethered, but with enough power to handle any
strong winds. Make that two of them. We can use one to rove
the area."

Judge Diana was looking on, having gained a new respect for security since her spidersilks stopped a bullet. "We may have to include reps from the Emperor on board your balloons, Jack, if we're to get him to agree to a balloon out his window."

"That's your job," Jack said with an impish grin. "It must be a whole lot harder than my simple job of keeping you all safe.

Diana snorted and left to talk to her associates and arrange for a new meeting.

Vicky frowned. "I like your idea of balloons looking for trouble, Jack. But if we have to put some of the Empress's assassins aboard, will they be any good?"

"You let me worry about that," Jack said. "Nelly, I'm going to need some really tiny eyeballs in the gondolas of those balloons with a tight beam link to the *Princess Royal*."

"I think that can be arranged," Nelly said, and you could almost hear a proud chuckle in her voice.

It took three more days of haggling, which Jack put to good use securing the resort, but in the end, Kris's and the Emperor's negotiators all agreed to where they'd be. Who got what quarters, when and where they'd actually sit down, and how the room would be arranged for that sit-down.

"I can't believe it's taken you this long just to agree how you will talk to each other," Vicky said to Kris and her troika when they reported back.

"We expected it would take longer," said Bill, the man with experience arbitrating between different sides.

"So we can start now?" Vicky asked.

"Nope," Diana said. "Now they tell the Emperor that everything is ready for him and the Empress."

"They aren't here?" Kris snapped.

"No. They're back on Greenfeld waiting to see if we can agree to meet."

Kris shook her head. "When will the Emperor and Empress arrive?"

"Not for a week, at the least," Diana said.

Vicky blew out a breath as if she'd been punched in the gut. Shaking her head, she said, "More and more, I'm coming to wish I'd just finished the Empress off when I had the chance."

"You think it would have ended the civil war?" Kris asked her.

"I don't know," Vicky admitted. "So much of this mess comes

from her family. If she'd died, my best guess would be that my father, our Emperor, would somehow die, oh so sadly, and the Bowlingames would put their little baby on the throne, with Grandpapa Bowlingame the all-powerful regent. Hmm, I hadn't actually thought that through until you asked, Kris. Thanks."

"Sorry. That's not a pretty picture."

Vicky sighed. "But it is the picture my father has allowed to be painted. So, do you play bridge? It looks like we've got plenty of time on our hands."

53

Admiral, Her Royal Highness Princess Kristine of the United Society didn't find time to play bridge with Her Imperial Grace, the Grand Duchess. The two of them were juggling too many porcupines.

It seemed like everyone who was anyone had heard about the negotiations and wanted in on the fun. Admiral Waller arrived from Bayern with a battleship full of staff and a whole lot of retired admirals and wives who didn't look to be into shuffleboard for their golden years.

A woman from Metzburg showed up with a small army of business associates to make sure their interests were fully considered. To make sure Metzburg didn't get overly considered, right behind them was a young man from Brunswick with a similar mob to assure their concerns weren't lost in the shuffle. St. Petersburg brought in reinforcements, and those were only the three largest delegations. Just about every planet that had sworn fealty to the Emperor through Vicky wanted someone sitting at her elbow on Cuzco.

Thus, one morning, Vicky stormed into Kris's quarters in somewhat of a panic. "How do you democrats handle all these people with all their competing agendas? Hell, half of them don't know what they want." Vicky came to a halt in front of

Kris, shaking her head. "No. No. No. First problem. Kris, do you have any idea where I put them all?"

Kris had no clue how to answer either question, but Nelly did know where Judge Diana lived. A few moments later, Diana walked into Kris's quarters on the *Princess Royal*.

Vicky was bringing the judge up to date on her growing list of problems before she even sat down.

"Hmm, and I thought we were just bargaining for half the cottages and rooms in the lodge to keep down the number of courtiers and courtesans following in the Emperor's wake. Okay, we do have half of the space at the resort. How many people do you have asking for rooms?"

Vicky had her computer transfer the list to Diana's computer.

Of course, Nelly picked up on the transfer. "Would you mind if I tried my hand at matching people to space?"

"Please. Go right ahead. But remember," Vicky said, "some of the older and wealthier will expect that their status gives them better accommodations than those less privileged."

"I am well aware of human vanity," Nelly answered dryly.

"Is she always like this?" Vicky whispered to Kris.

"Only when a human fails to remember they're dealing with the Magnificent Nelly," Kris said, no hush in her voice.

"So you're actually learning, Kris," Nelly observed.

"I'm learning," Kris said. "I just never know what you've figured out about the world and what you haven't gotten to yet."

"Harrumph," came from Nelly, but no further comment for a moment, then, "I think we can accommodate most of the ones who will be walking around with their noses in the air, assuming they're willing to double up or take in some of those lesser mortals to fill their spare rooms. The rest are going to be a problem, and it will likely get worse. Vicky, the representatives present only account for about half of the planets fighting on your side. If more show up, you will need more quarters. A lot more quarters."

Vicky turned to Kris. "Any more rabbits left in that hat of yours?"

Kris hollered, "Jack, how are the Marines set for tentage?"

"I was planning on using them for Marines," Jack said,

only slightly cranky as he glanced up from a screen he'd be intent on.

"Ookaay. Nelly, who on Cuzco rents tents?"

"I already have that information. Kris. Jack had Sal check on that yesterday."

Kris raised an eyebrow at Jack.

"I want to cover the four main entrances to the lodge with some sort of tent, either with sides or extended sloping roofs so no one would have a good long-range shot at you."

"Okay, Vicky, this is a job for your advanced team. There must be a Navy supply type who can wrestle this problem to the ground."

Vicky tapped her commlink. "Admiral Waller, have I got a problem for you."

Diana looked like she might take this as a chance to step out; Kris rested a restraining hand on her shoulder. "I think we've only tackled the easier half of her problems. I suspect the other half is a whole lot more intractable."

"That could be very true. May I call in my associates?"

"Please do."

A few minutes later, Vicky was off the phone, and Kris's troika was seated around a conference table that had suddenly become round. Beside Kris, a lovely cloisonné teapot appeared with five delicate white-and-gold teacups and saucers.

"Is Nelly going to turn this into an honest-to-God English afternoon tea?" Diana asked.

"Give me a moment," Nelly said. "The cook in the Forward Lounge is still cutting the crusts off the cucumber sandwiches."

"She's not!" Diana exclaimed.

"She is," Nelly said, as a plate of scones with clotted cream and several fruit marmalades appeared on the table. A moment later, Nanaimo bars, tiny pecan pies, and sweet lemon bars followed. It was a minute more before the cucumber sandwiches on thinly sliced bread finished up the presentation.

Kris began pouring tea, while Diana got the different plates of goodies circulating around the table.

"Am I being fattened up for the kill," Vicky said warily, "or is this already my last meal?"

"I assure you," Kris said, passing Vicky a teacup and saucer, "we would not have gone through all we have only to knock off one of the two principals in this civil disturbance."

"Aren't we a war anymore?" Vicky asked, taking a sip. "This is delicious tea."

"The proprietor of the Forward Lounge procured it," Nelly sniffed. "Of course it's delicious."

"Want a sip?" Vicky offered, impishly.

"I assure you, if Kris and Jack rutting around has not tempted me to take on flesh and blood, tea and clotted cream haven't a chance."

"Nelly!" Kris half shouted.

Nelly didn't answer Kris, but the entire table was laughing. Vicky and Bill spewed tea from their noses and were gasping for breath, grasping for napkins and still laughing.

"Nelly, I'm fingering the button."

"Kris, I apologize," Nelly quickly said. "I should not have shared your intimacy with anyone beyond you and Jack. Now, can I please stay and do what I do best, like finding ways out of the messes you get us into?"

The speed with which Nelly went from contrite supplicant to hard bargainer gave everyone whiplash, but Kris found herself taking a deep breath and bringing the room back to the matter at hand.

"Okay, my brain trust. Vicky has a mob. One might even call it a jungle. None of these people have any experience at give-and-take or at maintaining transparency while negotiating their way from A to Z. How do we help them get the skills they need, the practice with those skills, and, in the process, manage things so that they don't kill each other? Or worse, slip out in the night to conduct their own negotiations with the Empress. We can still be stabbed in the back."

"I hadn't thought of that," Vicky said.

"We had," Al said. "You have the north side of the resort, cabins, and lodge. They have the south side. You share the swimming pool. I suggest you hire lifeguards from the local economy to assure those drowning are actually rescued and not loaded down with stone so the body won't be found."

"You make this sound like war," Vicky said.

Bill moved to answer her. "I believe an ancient wise man

back on Earth said, 'Warfare is the continuation of diplomacy by other means.' You must learn to consider diplomacy a continuation of war by more peaceful means. Both are ways of resolving your conflicts. Hopefully, diplomacy will have a lower body count."

"So how do we do this?" Vicky asked.

Quite a few hours later, Vicky brought in several key representatives from her most important planets. Their talk went long into the night. Next morning, tents as well as a large pavilion were delivered to the resort grounds. Hired locals began to lay down floors, unroll rugs, and put up canvas.

That morning, Nelly also published the first issue of *The Grand Duchess's Imperial Gazette*, recording for all to see just what had been going on in Kris's quarters the day before. The paper included no videos but did have attached articles selected by Kris's brain trust on how to get to yes with helpful hints on how not to kill anyone while doing it.

Nelly's *Gazette* was downloaded over a thousand times. Apparently, Vicky's allies weren't the only ones interested. Quite a few people in Cuzco wanted to know what was going on, likely with hopes on how they might make some money on the visitors.

Ten of the Emperor's advance team downloaded copies as well.

At least four of those were known to be in the Empress's pocket.

Kris just shook her head when Nelly told her that. Then Nelly added that she and Jack had come up with their own idea of how to keep Kris safe in the negotiations. "A week ago, we sent off to Wardhaven for ten thousand tons of Smart Metal™."

"Isn't that a bit much, Nelly?"

"Jack intends to present you your very own castle; outlandishly palatial with plenty of space and security every which way you look."

Kris thought about that. "I still won't take Ruth down there."

"I'd never suggest it."

Someone, likely King Ray or Mac, had assigned a Royal US courier ship to stand by at High Cuzco Station even before

Kris's squadron arrived. She'd wondered when it suddenly left. It must have made some fast jumps; the newly commissioned battlecruiser *Dauntless* soon showed up sporting quite a big bump around her middle.

She carried thirty thousand tons of Smart Metal™ for Kris and orders to join her squadron.

Riding as passengers on the *Dauntless* were quite a few architects and engineers. They messaged ahead from the jump some draft plans for a proposed castle. From the looks of it, it had to be based on the mad dreams of some insane prince from old Earth. Still, it was sure to impress.

Kris and Nelly made a few mods under Jack's cautious eye and sent them back. Even as the *Dauntless* went into orbit, it spun off a lander that converted to a glider once it finished entry into Cuzco's atmosphere and came to a dead stick landing in the parking lot next to the lodge, light as a feather.

Next morning, presto, the castle was ready for occupancy. Oh, and the *Imperial Emperor and Empress* had jumped into the system.

"That oversize barge was the *Golden Empress* last time we laid eyes on it," Vicky snarked. "I guess under my father's eye, even she has to admit that she's not what she wants to be. At least not yet."

"You want to come see my palace?" Kris asked Vicky.

"I've already seen pictures of it. It looks like a castle to me. That curtain wall around it is sure to keep the average assassin out."

"Only the average one, you think."

"My dear darling stepmum can afford to hire the best. After all, it's only my father's tax money," came out with pure Imperial Grand Duchess hostility.

Despite her attitude, Vicky was only too eager to see Kris's new digs. They took the beanstalk down with a company of Marines and most of the staff of the Forward Lounge. A heavily armed motorcade was already at the station to whisk them off to the forested hills above Machu Picchu. There, waiting for Kris, was an amazing sight.

A hill, just beyond the north edge of the lodge's parking lot, had been cleared of trees to provide a spectacular view for the restaurant on its third floor. Now its view was of a fairy castle, complete with spiraling towers along a curtain wall.

"We'll post sentries in the towers, but the real watch is the sensor suite," Jack pointed out.

Their limo drove straight through the gate and up to a covered portico. Jack opened the door for Kris and Vicky, and the Royal Wardhaven Princess led the Imperial Grand Duchess through huge double doors that appeared to be heavy oak but swung open as if they weighed nothing.

"The magic of Smart Metal," was all Kris had to say to get an awed "Wow" from Vicky.

The massive foyer showed a plush red carpet underfoot. The walls were a bright cream satin wallpaper with gold and silver patterns running through it that somehow formed a vision of fields and mountains. Lit sconces added a soft glow. Overhead, a vast crystal chandelier sent dancing rainbows around the room.

"The Empress is going to be so jealous of this," Vicky said, her mouth hanging open. She shut it to grin at Kris. "And Dad won't believe you did this."

"Oh, he will," Jack said. "You've seen how the *Princess Royal* could be decked out. So have they."

"Oh, right."

"There's more," Kris said. She pointed to the left. "Those three lovely arched doorways lead to a banquet room. To the right, you have three more doors and a ballroom. Diana told me that much of the work of a conference like this is done over drinks while socializing. We will be entertaining in something a lot fancier than a rustic dining room and great hall with the heads of horned animals hanging on the wall, don't you think?"

"Very much," Vicky said. "What's up the spiral staircase? I can't wait to see you and Jack make an entrance down it. I do hope that you brought a few ball gowns."

"Hmm, that's interesting," Jack said with a loving leer. "A ball gown with miniature medals and all your orders on it."

"With the weight of all that, I'd be risking a wardrobe malfunction?" Kris said.

Jack gave Kris a hopeful look.

"Down, boy. Down," Kris said, and changed the subject. "The staircase leads to the upper floors that are reserved for bedrooms and essential services, like the Marine barracks and nano defense center. If you try to go up the staircase but aren't an authorized person, you will be warned at the first step. If you keep going, there are autocannons covering the stairs halfway up."

"You really don't want to go where you aren't wanted," Jack said.

"Kris, can I visit you for some girl time?"

"Have your computer talk to Nelly, and we'll see about it."

Vicky rolled her eyes but didn't voice any objections.

"What's through those four double doors beside the stairs?"

"Those lead to the Hall of Mirrors, where we'll be meeting. Beyond that are the quarters for my brain trust and their people. Diana said they needed to be able to come and go freely. Jack swears they can."

"But no one who doesn't have their biometrics better try to follow them home. Again, I've got autocannons covering their entrances."

"I've heard about a Hall of Mirrors somewhere," Vicky said. "Wasn't some war back on old Earth settled in such a hall?"

"I copied it though I've made it larger, and there's more marble and fancy lighting to go with the mirrors," Nelly said.

"You've got all this from thirty thousand tons of Smart Metal," Vicky said, still in awe.

"Actually, we did it with twenty thousand tons," Nelly reported.

"Only two-thirds of your metal? What will you do with the rest?" Vicky asked.

"We could make the castle walls higher and more intimidating," Kris said, but she'd spotted the envious way Vicky eyed the castle. "Or we could loan you some to build your very your own castle."

Vicky thought on it for a long moment, and then sadly shook her head. "I've got a very fancy pavilion on order. Huge. Big enough for a throne room, without a throne, just a receiving area. There's enough space for me and my immediate team, and a third bay for a meeting room. I think it would be better if I didn't look too Longknifeish."

"I have to agree," Nelly said. "I don't think the brain trust would like you to give Vicky Smart Metal so obviously. However, Vicky, it might be nice if I slipped some of the Smart Metal between the threads of the canvas of your pavilion. Just enough to make its wall impervious to the usual cutting tools, bullets, or rockets. You know, that sort of stuff."

"Could you do that, Nelly?"

"Of course I can do it. If I do it right, I can cover Admiral Waller's pavilion as well as the St. Petersburg circus tent."

"Circus tent?" Kris asked.

"There were only so many pavilions available," Vicky said. "Mannie's got his people in a tent they got from a local circus. It's quite a big tent. They're providing space for representatives from several of the planets in St. Petersburg's immediate trading zone. Mannie says having all of them under one roof gives them plenty of time to get organized and try to present a common front."

"If Mannie's doing that, I suspect the other major planets will be doing the same if they're smart," Jack said.

"I think a lot of them learned from that little get-together of yours," Vicky said. "We've spent the last two days getting our ducks in a row. We're ready for the Empress when she gets here."

"Nelly, see how far you can stretch the Smart Metal without spreading it too thin," Kris said.

"I'm working on it with Sal," Nelly said.

"One thing," Vicky said. "Could you give me a Smart Metal bed? It's either put up with a rental or buy one, and prices are though the roof."

"I think I can do that," Nelly said.

"Kris, do you plan to borrow any Smart Metal from the squadron's ships?" Jack asked.

Kris thought on that for a long minute, then shook her head. "That is something I will *not* do. I don't trust *anyone* here at the table not to slip a fleet in so they can get their own way. Vicky, I'm not looking at you, but can you honestly tell me that you have control of all the elements of your alliance?"

Now Vicky shook her head. "I'd like to think my people aren't that dumb, but I can't swear to it. As for the Empress, no way would I trust her. Not with so much as a bucket of sand on a long and sandy beach."

"It was a good question, Jack, but I think you got the answer you expected."

"I did. It was a question that needed raising and a policy that definitely needed to be made and locked in place."

"Now, Vicky, why don't you go check out your pavilion while Jack and I see just how decadent Nelly made our bedroom."

"And bath, and parlor for receiving guests," Nelly added.

"You two go have fun," Vicky said.

"An Imperial Grand Duchess just told us to have fun," Jack whispered to Kris as they mounted the stairs.

"Then we must follow the Imperial order."

54

While the Imperial couple made their way to Cuzco at one gee, Kris put the time to good use. Each night, she gave a banquet that then adjourned to the ballroom for dancing and talk.

There was a lot more talking than dancing.

The day was filled with meetings followed by more bloody meetings. Jack insisted Kris not leave the castle, so most of the meetings were in her lovely, first-floor conference center.

Having a huge banquet hall, ballroom, and conference hall with breakout rooms for smaller discussions was impressive. Very impressive.

And very effective. Kris had everyone at her palace, getting them used to the palatial surroundings.

Kris even invited the Emperor's advance team to the banquets, balls, and some of the conferences. Jack assured that they were heavily monitored by security, but it wasn't necessary.

The Imperial advanced team was shunned like lepers by the delegates from the rebel alliance.

Kris eavesdropped on the Imperials' small talk. The more they saw of her suddenly appearing castle, the more they were in awe of it.

Vicky's brain trust did convene one negotiation session with the Imperials to adjust the venue for the formal meetings. They proposed that half still be held in the resort's Great Hall but that the other half be in Kris's Great Hall of Mirrors. Kris expected some objections, so she offered to give up all the rooms in the lodge.

The Imperial advanced team caved like bats.

"The Emperor may even prefer the better amenities of the Hall of Mirrors. Your chairs are a lot more comfortable."

"The chairs adjust to the persons sitting in them," Kris said.

"Yes," the leader of the Imperial team said, leaning back in his chair and having it conform to his every move. "Can all the chairs give a massage?"

"Some can. Some won't," Kris said.

"I'd be willing to use my good offices to encourage the Emperor to meet here more often if you could arrange for him, the Empress, and me to always have massage chairs."

"I think that can be assured," Kris said. "A lot of the chairs can be massage chairs. It's just if there are too many requests, the computer may not be able to meet demands."

"Just so the Imperial couple and I get our rumps taken care of."

"I can assure that," Kris said.

NELLY, YOU HAVE MY PERMISSION TO MAKE THE CHAIRS QUIT WORKING FOR THE EMPRESS AND HER FAMILY WHEN-EVER THE MEETINGS GO LONG.

I'M SO GLAD YOU TOLD ME, KRIS. I INTENDED TO DO IT ANYWAY, BUT IT'S NICE TO HAVE PERMISSION.

The Emperor and Empress arrived at High Cuzco Station and immediately took the next ferry down the elevator. Nelly reported that the entourage filled up the next four drop ferries and totally screwed up the change of shift. There were fist-fights for places on the four o'clock ferry, and the overflow had to wait for the four thirty.

The problem, complete with video of the fistfights and swords being drawn with tired and irritated workers in the background, made the evening news and was repeated on the late-night news as well. The Emperor's visit was not off to a good start as far as the people of Cuzco were concerned.

The Emperor wasn't too happy, either. But it was the Empress's reaction that warmed Kris's heart. The Imperial couple was sharing the two best suites the lodge had to offer. They were large and comfortable, but, in keeping with the ambiance of the resort, quite rustic.

And they had a lovely view of Kris's castle.

Kris knew exactly what the Imperials thought about their accommodations. She had a nano hovering just outside their window transmitting every shout and scream. In the end, the advanced man was banished to a small room on the top floor. The only reason he kept his head was because the prime minister suggested that he might be helpful if there were any questions about the ground rules Kris Longknife and Vicky had agreed to with him.

The man actually crawled from the Imperial presence on his hands and knees.

Kris waited a few minutes to allow the couple to get control of their rage before sending Major Henderson, dressed in formal blue and reds and with an honor guard, with an invitation to a reception and formal dinner Kris was throwing in honor of the Imperials present.

The Empress quickly spotted that the careful wording, "Imperials present," could well mean both them and Grand Duchess Victoria.

That put her in another rage, but she could not vent it on a Royal US Marine. Before she might try, the Emperor dismissed Major Henderson with a promise that a response would come later.

When the Empress calmed down, they, with the second man from the advanced team, went down to see what facilities were available for proper Imperial entertainment.

That rocketed the Empress into another rage.

"Why did you agree to Cuzco and why *ever* did you think that a resort like this woodland slum should be where we met with the little whore?"

"There, there, honey, remember, the doctor says you must stay calm. Your blood pressure," the Emperor said, taking what sure looked like the woman's side of this cliché of a conversation.

"This place is barbaric. Will we have to use outhouses for

toilets? I expect a bear to wander by any minute and start eating people, like that worthless advance team of yours."

There was a pause in the rant. Kris suspected it was for the Empress to get a breath and the Emperor to roll his eyes, but Harry got the next word in.

"Really, honey pie, the Imperial Guard will shoot any bear that shows its face."

The Empress changed the conversation. "Well, I can hardly entertain in such a place as this," she said, wheedling him.

"We can accept Princess Longknife's invitation for tonight. Tomorrow, we can rent one of those huge tents like they have out there. Can we get one of them?"

The advanced man mumbled something that Kris's nano missed.

"Those are theirs! Didn't *you* rent *anything*? Why have an advance team if they're going to sit on their hands and do nothing?"

"Your Majesty, our money is no good." Kris did catch that. "Edgard had to sign a mortgage on the ship bringing you here to assure that we would have either hard cash or trade goods to cover the cost of goods and services here at the lodge for you and your court during your stay."

"He had no such power," the Empress screamed, heading into her fourth rage of the afternoon. *Maybe it was her fifth.*

NO, KRIS, IT'S THE FOURTH. I'M KEEPING A TALLY.

Back in the Imperial presence, the poor number two in the advance team was trying to explain their problem. "Edgard and the resort owner's lawyer do believe that your commission to him to speak in your name did give him enough authority. The owner has already gotten a lien on the *Emperor and Empress*. You'll need to have something like crystal or other trade goods brought in to meet our debts. Your debts," he quickly corrected himself.

"They intend to hold us hostage! I tell you, Harry, *this* is a Longknife plot. I *told* you it was."

"Sweetums, you knew our money is no good outside the Empire. I just assumed that our signature was enough to handle matters for now, and we'd settle up later."

"Ray Longknife will have us thrown into debtors' prison,

and you'll have the devil's own time settling up later with your hands chained to the dripping stone wall of some dungeon."

"You exaggerate, honey pot. We can always leave the ship and book passage on another."

"Leave my ship! My lovely ship! You gave her to me, Henry. You fitted it out as an anniversary present. You would just *give* it away? Would you give *me* away?"

Kris eyed Jack, who had come in halfway through all the drama. He silently mouthed, "I would" to Kris.

"Me, too," she mouthed back, then thought how silly it was to be so quiet on a one-way hookup.

Kris figured she'd heard enough. She'd be getting an RSVP from the Imperials in an hour or so. Vicky had already replied. Diana and her friends were carefully arranging the seating. The banquet today would have to be carefully arranged with the primaries as far from each other as possible. They might or might not mingle on the dance floor, but their seating would be separated by the locals who had been invited. Likely, the two groups would not mingle; still, the brain trust was carefully weighing just who should be seated close to the locals. They might get some movement there.

They would have to be careful that it was in their direction, not toward the Empress.

"So you've decided that the problem is the Empress," Kris said.

"We have decided that the Grand Duchess and her alliance are more willing to work with us, and we like the options they would be willing to accept to end this conflict," Diana said.

"And the Empress?" Kris asked.

The three looked at each other, then Diana continued. "Her opinion of the facts on the ground are quite divergent from the facts as we see them. Her stated objective sets a very high goal for her side and . . ." Here Diana again checked with her colleagues. She was met with sad shakes of the head. "We do not expect much flexibility from her in moving away from her initial demands. Put the way a Longknife would want to hear it, she is a problem now and likely to be a problem in the future."

"Hopefully, that will change," Al said.

"We will just have to see how negotiations go," Bill added.

"Yes, we will," Kris said, "but I was taught long ago that hope is not a strategy and hope appears to be all we have at the moment."

"Kris," Nelly interrupted, "a colonel of the Imperial Guard has presented the Marines at the front gate with the Emperor's RSVP. He will be glad to dine with you this evening."

"Then I better get ready," Kris said, and headed for her bedroom. There, Nelly had put a totally new twist on palatial.

55

Nelly had really outdone herself with Kris's bedroom. Several chandeliers cast rainbows on walls half-marble with gold and silver veins running through them. The rest of the walls were covered in lush velvet wallpaper with gold and silver trim. Set strategically around the room were classical statues and paintings, most of them not suitable for work.

"You're tying up a lot of Smart Metal with this erotic statuary, aren't you Nelly?"

"Not really Kris. Try picking one up."

Kris strode over, and easily hefted a large statue of three nude women.

"The statues have little more substance than a balloon, Kris. I have to lock them down, Smart Metal to Smart Metal, to keep them in place. I recovered the Smart Metal from the plush carpet underneath the pedestals. That about makes the statues a wash."

"Do you plan to put a few of these in the Banquet Hall and ballrooms?"

"Likely, Kris. Only in those, I'll mount antennas for nano tracking and bugs for listening."

The bathroom was all Kris could dream of. The walls appeared to be marble with inlays of gold and sparkling jewels. She soaked in a tub large enough for a small party as jets did their best to relax the tension in her shoulders and back. She had to wash her own hair, then rinsed off in a shower with a dozen rotating heads for both front and back.

"I almost don't miss Jack," she muttered, missing Jack.

"Now, what do I wear?" Kris asked herself.

Ensign Meg Longknife was waiting for her as Kris returned to her bedroom with one towel wrapped around herself and a second vigorously drying her hair. Meg had become Kris's *aide-de-camp*, dog robber, and all-around maker of things to happen.

"You may be surprised, Admiral, by what's in your closet."

"Surprised?"

"Yes, ma'am. The *Dauntless* brought in a rather large wardrobe full of ball gowns. Someone wanted you to have a wide choice."

"Good Lord, please tell me it wasn't my mother."

"I think there's a note in there from one of your great-grandmothers."

"Gramma Trouble?"

"I do believe so, Your Highness." And so saying, Meg walked Kris over to a closet bigger than her night quarters aboard ship. Several lovely gowns in the traditional pattern were hung out for Kris to choose from.

"But will they fit?" Kris asked. Ruth had not been kind to Kris's body. Well, maybe she hadn't been all bad; Kris now had a decent pair of breasts for the first time in her life. If only she'd had something more like these all those miserable years in high school and college. No, it was Kris's waist that caused her to tremble in fear.

"Help me into my spider silks," Kris said. "I will not get dressed and have Jack insist I get undressed and pull this armor on." Kris did dress in the essentials, like a nice support bra and some lacy undies over her armor.

That brought Kris face-to-face with the ball gowns. She picked out a lovely floor-length, royal blue gown with a bodice of brocade and a billowing skirt of silk and lace. It would match her eyes and offset her skin and hair perfectly.

To Kris's delight, the waist was relaxed from what it might have been a year and a baby ago. The bodice, however, fit perfectly, showing more décolletage than Kris had ever presented to the world.

"Gramma Trouble has an eye for details," Kris said, "or a hidden laser that took my measurements. I'd bet on the laser. She was taking lots of pictures of me and Ruth and Jack and just about everyone. You sneaky but nice old lady."

"What do you want to wear for jewelry?" Meg asked.

"I don't need pearls or diamonds," Kris muttered. "Let's show them what we've earned." She turned to her awards drawer; Nelly had them laid out quite nicely.

"Let's put the Greenfeld *Four la Mérite* at my throat." And Meg did. "Hang the Almar Medal of Highest Valor next. With any luck, Granny Rita's Hammer of Enlightened Ones will fall right where Jack will enjoy it, if he notices it at all."

"That pretty much covers up everything that dress was showing off," Meg pointed out.

"I'm sure Vicky and the Empress will be showing enough skin for all of us. But they've got nothing to show like these," Kris said. "Now, I want the sashes and badges of the Order of the Wounded Lion from Earth, Order of St. Christopher, Star Leaper from Greenfeld, and Order of the Rose and Thistle from the cats, too. I don't think the colors will clash too much, do you?"

"Whatever you say, Your Highness."

"They clash, huh?"

"That orange sash of the Order of St. Christopher, Star Leaper would clash with just about anything but your birthday suit."

"We are not wearing that," Kris said, thinking fast. "St. Chris is from the Emperor, so we have to include it. Let's go with just the starburst. Now, how about my medals?"

"Miniatures, right?"

"Well, we'll want to slip Chance's Golden Starburst somewhere near the middle of the bodice, but the medals should be up close to the top," Kris paused, "of this strapless gown. Hmm."

Meg put the line of miniature medals just a few millimeters down from the top of the bodice. "Ah, ma'am, I feel that I must warn you that any rapid movement, and maybe just enough gravity, and I can't assure you that you won't be showing everyone what Ruth likes to suck on."

"Hmm," Kris muttered, doubtfully.

"Feel yourself up, and see for yourself," Megan suggested.

Kris did. Her aide was right. "Ookaay, there's got to be some tape or putty or super glue that can keep dress and boob together for an evening."

"And not take an inch of skin off when you take the dress off?"

"Nelly?" Kris called.

"Abby had just that kind of tape," Nelly answered.

"But she's on the other side of the galaxy."

"If you will quit interrupting me, I will finish telling you that she left it behind, and it should be appearing in a moment on your bedside stand. Happy?"

"Ecstatically," Kris said.

"Don't sass me, Kris."

"I wasn't. I really meant it."

Meg put a strip of double-sided tape inside the dress above where the medals went. Kris worried the top of her dress for a moment with results that might please Jack but did not meet with Kris's approval. They took that strip off and added three strips. One below the medals, one where they were pinned to the dress, and a third between the pins and the top of the dress.

"Those puppies aren't going anywhere," Meg said.

Kris was not so optimistic. She was a bit more experienced. If she took off running or did a drop and roll . . .

Kris weighed the matter, decided she wanted the medals on display, and accepted the risk.

While Meg was putting Kris's hair up, Jack dropped in, remarked again on the palatial nature of their palace, to Nelly's vain delight, and took a quick shower before pulling on his spidersilks.

Kris held the top of her armor away from her neck for Jack to see. He nodded and quickly put on his formal blue and reds without saying a word.

Kris credited herself with one in the win column.

"How are our guests doing?" Kris asked Nelly.

"The Grand Duchess arrived early," Nelly said. "You were in the shower for her fanfare. You may have heard the fanfare for the Emperor and Empress a few minutes ago. We played the Imperial March for both of them, but the Empress didn't hear

Vicky's honors, so she hasn't flown into a rage yet this evening. At least not at your reception. Our bug outside their window caught quite a bit of shouting while they were dressing."

"Can that marriage be saved?" Jack muttered.

"I don't know what kind of game she's playing," Kris said, "but it doesn't seem very smart to me."

"She is the mother of the Emperor's only living son," Nelly pointed out.

"Well," Jack said, offering Kris his arm, "you look stunning this evening, Your Highness. Would you care to make a spectacular entrance?"

"How could it be anything less than spectacular on the arm of such a dashing lieutenant general?"

And with that, Kris let herself be led so daintily to the charge, diplomacy being the continuation of war by silk and satin means.

56

At the top of the staircase, Jack and Kris paused. The room below was aswirl with people, but it only took a second for Kris to spot the pattern.

The Emperor and Empress and their people occupied the third of the room to the right of the front doors. The Grand Duchess and her people held down the space to its left. Mingling in the center with occasional forays into the factions were local government officials, businessmen, and academics from Cuzco.

Kris's brain trust had arranged for their invitations. They would serve as neutral observers who Diana hoped would be a calming influence to the gala tonight. With any luck, they would also serve as potential sources of experience as to how the give-and-take of bargaining went. Hopefully, they'd share some stories with the attendees from the warring sides.

After a moment standing there, observing the start of their party, Nelly announced them in a voice that carried over the babble of the hall.

"Admiral, Her Royal Highness Kristine of the United Society and her consort, Lieutenant General Juan Montoya."

Kris stood in place for four ruffles and flourishes, then took her first step down as a royal fanfare recently composed for

King Raymond and any other US royalty blasted the hall with brass and percussion. That continued until Kris was about halfway down the stairs, to that area covered by autocannons, when the music softened only a bit as it segued into the Royal US anthem.

All of this was new to Kris. The music hadn't existed when they shipped her off to exile on Madigan's Rainbow, and she certainly hadn't been met with a fanfare when she snuck back to Wardhaven. She'd taken off for the other side of the galaxy none the wiser about the royal trappings Ray was taking on.

Now she was marching . . . albeit carefully . . . down thickly carpeted stairs to their strains.

Below her, the fine and independent citizens of Cuzco bowed though some of them did it ever so slightly. Vicky led her alliance in a deep bow. The man next to her in formal civilian dress bowed lower, and most of her followers took their guidance from him. On the Emperor and Empress's side, the Imperial couple did little more than nod, and their huge entourage of dandies and half-dressed ladies did no more than that.

Kris schooled her face to Navy bland and glanced again at the Empress.

NELLY, ARE THE LADIES OF THE IMPERIAL COURT ACTUALLY TOPLESS?

KRIS, IF YOU LOOK CLOSELY. AND I AM SURE ALL THE MEN PRESENT ARE LOOKING VERY CLOSELY, YOU WILL FIND THAT THE DRESSES DO REACH UP TO COVER THE NIPPLES WITH A BIT OF SPARKLE AND THIN CLOTH.

WHAT IS THE EMPRESS TRYING TO DO, WAVING ALL THAT PULCHRITUDE AROUND HER HUSBAND?

I HAVE STUMBLED ACROSS SOME CORRESPONDENCE FROM THOSE ON VICKY'S SIDE. THEY SUSPECT THAT THE EMPRESS AND HER BOWLINGAME RELATIVES HOPE THE EMPEROR WILL TUMBLE INTO THE BED OF A WOMAN WITH A JEALOUS AND EASILY INFURIATED HUSBAND WHO WILL HASTEN THE EMPRESS INTO AN EARLY WIDOWHOOD. I HAVE NOT BEEN ABLE TO CONSTRUCT A BETTER EXPLANATION FOR HER BEHAVIOR.

Kris had to work hard to keep any reaction off her face. Diana waited at the bottom of the stairs. "We are ready to see if we can get this reception line going. We'd planned to have just the Imperial couple and Vicky with her plus one with you and

Jack between them. However, the Imperial couple insists the prime minister and his wife be included. The Empress insists, as in demands, that the Grand Duke and Grand Duchess of Greenfeld and the Duke of Anhalt, to whit her dad, mom, and oldest brother, be included as well. Her brother left his wife behind on Greenfeld and insists we include his mistress of the moment at his side."

"Is that allowed?" Kris asked.

"I can find no reference to it, but he is a showstopper for the Empress, and he won't get in line without his latest interest. We're doing it the way the Imperials want."

"That's starting on the wrong foot," Jack muttered.

"But at least it's starting. We three and our plus ones will be beside you two. Vicky has identified three more couples."

"Then I guess we're ready to see if we can make this work," Kris said. "Lay on, Macduff, and damned be he who shouts too loud."

It took only a moment to get everyone into their places in the receiving line. Kris and Jack were insulated on both sides by her members of her troika. The Emperor and Empress took the head of the line followed by the two Grand Dukes and their ladies. The prime minister and his wife were left to stand beside Diana and a male member of her team.

Past Kris and Jack, Bill and a young woman from his staff stood beside Al and a young man. That led to Vicky's four. Admiral Waller stood grimly at the head of the rebel section of the receiving line, an aggressive young Marine lieutenant colonel beside him: her left hand rested on a sword, her right was on a holstered sidearm.

Kris took one look and saw trouble.

NELLY, WHAT'S GOING ON THERE?

GRAND ADMIRAL WALLER IS THE NAVY CHIEF OF STAFF. HE GOT OUT OF ANHALT ONE STEP AHEAD OF AN ASSASSIN SQUAD. HIS WIFE WAS CAUGHT. THE EMPRESS PERSONALLY SLIT HER THROAT AND SENT THE VIDEO TO WALLER. HIS YOUNGEST DAUGHTER IS HIS PLUS ONE.

NELLY, KEEP AN EYE ON THEM. JACK, CAN YOU GET A PAIR OF MARINES IN CIVVIES TO FLY WING ON THOSE TWO?

I ALREADY HAVE.

OOPS. SORRY. JACK, IF YOU CAPTURED SOMEONE'S WIFE,

WOULD YOU SLIT HER THROAT OR HOLD HER HOSTAGE FOR HER
HUSBAND'S GOOD BEHAVIOR?

KRIS, I DON'T MAKE WAR ON CIVILIAN WOMEN.

WELL, THE EMPRESS IS. AND SHE'S NOT ACTING VERY
SMART.

YA'THINK?

The reception line started. Ensign Longknife called out the
first couple's names, a Baron and paramour.

PARAMOUR, NELLY?

THAT'S WHAT THE CARD SAID. MEGAN READ IT RIGHT.

DEAR GOD. THAT PALACE MUST BE A BURNING LAKE OF
SEWAGE.

IT SURE SMELLS THAT WAY FROM WHERE I STAND.

But Kris quickly found herself with worse problems. Said
Baron went down the line, got to Al's boyfriend, and turned
his back on the rebels in the last third of the line and blatantly
stomped away.

Kris was shaking a countess's hand. She caught the uncivil
developments out of the corner of her eye. A moment later, the
next couple in bright Imperial dress did the exact same thing.

The rebels, who had been looking reluctant to shake the
Imperial hands, now formed into their own line. The elderly
woman from Metzburg cut right through the Imperial line to
smilingly present herself to Diana and shake her hand. The
Imperial went for his sword, but the next rebel in line was a
Navy officer with a dress sword at his side.

*Which begs the question, are they both cake cutters, or have
these two brought seriously sharp steel to my reception?*

JACK?

ALREADY ON IT.

Out of nowhere, Major Henderson appeared, he of both
sword and sidearm. He interposed himself between the Imperial line, and let the rebel pass, then he switched lines, blocked
the next rebel couple and let an Imperial pass. He spent the
rest of the hour, functioning as school crossing guard for some
very rowdy kindergartners.

Imperials went down the line of Imperials and Kris's section . . . then turned their back, shunning the rebels. Rebels
started at Kris's segment and continued until the end of
Vicky's four couples.

Somehow, no blood ended up on the floor.

Dinner was an equally cold affair. The Emperor and Empress were invited in first. That meant they'd have to pass through the rebels who had collected around Vicky. Jack arranged for a Marine Honor Guard to form a double line down which the Imperials sashayed.

Once in the Banquet Hall, more Marines escorted the Imperial couple to their table. Kris's troika had arranged for the Emperor and Empress to be seated close to the far right corner. There were name tags at each place, but those nobles following in the Imperials' wake quickly moved to take the places closest to the Imperial couple, ruthlessly displacing others.

When all the tumult ended, Kris had Nelly check. Most of those surrounding the Emperor and Empress were of the Empress's faction.

Interesting.

Now the Marine Honor Guard paraded into the Banquet Hall and just happened to form a riot-control line down the middle of the small dance floor. Almost there was a riot, but not quite.

Jack maintained a Marine bland face through this all, but Kris noticed that he did allow himself a deep breath when the last of the two sides settled at their dinner table.

YOUR MARINES WERE GREAT, JACK.

AND THEY DID IT WITHOUT PRACTICING THE DRILL, Jack added.

Vicky's rebels had at least obeyed their table assignments as they took their seats to the left-hand side of the Banquet Hall. Kris's troika had worked hard to distribute the representatives from all the different rebel planets around that third of the room. Hopefully, that would get them talking, sharing, and maybe help them see the others as allies rather than competitors.

Kris and Jack, along with her brain trust and the locals who had wrangled invites, filled up the space between the two warring sides. Kris had hoped that the locals might mingle with the two belligerents. It seemed to work with Vicky's side.

The Empress's father and brother made it plain that they were not interested in talking to the locals, and the rest of the courtiers and courtesans quickly followed their lead.

While this nothing was going on, Nelly reported that the

first-step trip wire on the staircase to the second-floor quarters had been tripped.

WHAT SAY WE SEE WHAT WE CAN SEE? TURN OFF THE AUTOCANNON, THOUGH, Kris said, and eyed Jack. He looked to be following this development as well.

WE HAVE A LONE MARINE AT THE TOP OF THE STAIRS, LURKING IN AN ALCOVE WITH A SUDDENLY MUCH SMALLER STATUE AND NO LIGHT.

FINE, JACK.

KRIS, I'M GOING TO PATCH YOU THROUGH.

WHAT HAVE WE HERE? Kris heard. The question was followed by a feminine yelp.

YOU ALMOST SCARED ME TO DEATH, SOLDIER.

AND WHY WOULD LITTLE OLD YOU BE UP HERE?

IT'S BORING DOWN THERE. NOTHING TO DO. I THOUGHT I MIGHT POWDER SOMETHING. NOW, YOU AND ME, I THINK WE COULD REALLY HAVE SOME FUN. I BET I COULD SCREW YOUR EYEBALLS OUT OF THEIR SOCKETS. WE COULD USE THAT ROOM RIGHT OVER THERE. I BET IT'S EMPTY.

IT LIKELY IS SINCE IT'S HER ROYAL HIGHNESS'S ROOMS, BUT I KIND OF LIKE MY EYEBALLS WHERE THEY ARE.

WHAT'S THE MATTER WITH YOU? SHOULD I SEND MY BOYFRIEND UP HERE? DO YOU PREFER BOYS?

ACTUALLY, I PREFER BEER AND PIZZA. NOW WHY DON'T YOU GO POWDER YOUR BOOBS SOMEWHERE DOWNSTAIRS?

KRIS, I THINK THAT LAST WAS PUNCTUATED WITH A SWAT ON HER BACKSIDE.

NELLY, I THINK YOU MIGHT BE RIGHT.

HOW BEASTLY.

IF HER MOTHER HAD PATTED HER DIAPERED RUMP A FEW MORE TIMES, SHE MIGHT NOT BE RUNNING AROUND HERE WITH ALL HER CHARMS HANGING OUT, Jack put in.

Kris decided to skip the debate about the proper way to raise children for a few more years and turned back to the challenge at hand.

The Emperor did not seem to have noticed how the Empress's family was leading his court around by the nose. He had his head on his wife's bosom as she fed him from her own plate.

Diana shook her head halfway through the meal. "This is going to be harder than even I thought."

After dinner, there was light music, but no one attempted to dance on the floor that separated the two factions. People did mingle. Locals and rebels at least. Kris and her troika tried to talk with some of the Imperial entourage.

She'd never seen so many people turn their backs on her.

She did manage to make her way to the Imperial couple's table.

The Emperor looked up from between his wife's naked décolletage. The sparkles that had covered her nipples were now shining in his hair. "Thank you for inviting us to this wonderful banquet," he said. "I hope we can dispense with the receiving line next time. It was so tedious."

"I think we can arrange that," Kris agreed.

"Well, we really must be going," the Empress said. "I can-*not* believe our advanced team agreed to start at *eight thirty* in the morning. That is disgusting," she said, eyeing Kris.

Kris smiled blandly, refusing to make any concessions to the agreed-upon ground rules by simply refusing to notice the question not actually asked.

So the Imperial couple led the exodus of their court, the Emperor's head solidly resting atop the Empress's bare boobs. The Duke of Anhalt had raised the skirts of his paramour and was pawing her bare ass as they followed the Imperial couple. He looked back to leer at Kris.

Jack took a sharp breath in, then slowly let it out.

"You sure I can't kill those bastards?" he muttered low to Kris.

"I'm sure we can't. We've got to end this civil war."

"Wouldn't killing them all end it?"

"I'll have to ask Diana about that," Kris said.

"She'll never agree. What do you say we do it and then ask forgiveness?"

Kris chuckled. "It's worked for me plenty of times."

"See?"

"Plenty of times when I was the subordinate, Jack. Remember, we have seven stars between us and a darling little girl we want to make a better world for."

"This being a grown-up isn't all it was cracked up to be. You think if I warn Ruth Marie now, she could avoid it like her parents didn't?"

"Jack, what do you say you take me to bed, and we pretend we're grown-ups and do that thing that grown-ups do?"

"Raid the ice-cream locker?" he asked, brightly.

"Think harder, Jack. You must remember something we can do?"

"Harder, huh?"

Kris managed to exit the Banquet Hall without being way-laid by anyone. By the time they got to the top of the stairs, it seemed that Jack had remembered something fun that grown-ups could do . . . and was eager to do it.

57

The morning did begin bright and early.

For some.

At 0815, when Kris and Jack walked into the Hall of Mirrors, Vicky and a major portion of her party were already there. They had the tables and chairs down the left-hand side of the conference room. Kris's brain trust, with two comfortable chairs for Kris and Jack, held down the far wall of the room.

There was a line of tables down the middle of the room where local court stenographers and other people with recording gear had set up shop. It was in the middle of the room in the hopes of delaying an attack from either side of the room against the other.

The right-hand side of the room was reserved for the Imperials. It had tables, several comfortable chairs, and like the other two sides, a podium where one person could stand and address the room.

There were two squads of Royal US Marines standing against the wall. Marines had stood guard through the night to assure that no bomb was placed in the room, their presence balanced by two squad of Imperial Guardsmen. Other than them and the prime minister bumbling around the podium, the Imperial side of the room was empty.

Totally.

Kris and Jack walked to their chairs at the other end of the room and stood. Kris bowed respectfully to Vicky, who returned it. She bowed respectfully to the Emperor's first minister, an elderly man in a dark, conservative vest coat. His doublet fell all the way to his hose. It seemed like it took a moment for him to decide if bowing to Kris was a career-ending decision, maybe even life-ending, but he did return her bow.

That done, Kris sat down.

Diana came up behind Kris. "It's quite possible that the Emperor is waiting for you two to get here."

"It is possible," Kris allowed.

Fifteen minutes later, as the minute hand on the clock above the door swept past the bottom of the hour, Diana was back. "Maybe he wants to be fashionably late?"

"Possibly," Kris allowed, and settled her gaze on the prime minister.

He took Kris's hard eye contact for a full minute before folding. He signaled to the captain of the guard detail. He came to the prime minister, was given some instructions, and hurried out of the room. The prime minister sat down to await the results of his, no doubt, gentle query.

Kris checked the clock.

It was fifteen minutes later that the guardsman returned. He bowed to the prime minister's ear and whispered something.

The poor old fellow turned around in his chair to eye the young officer. "No. No," came in too loud a whisper and with a cracking voice.

The guard captain nodded emphatically.

The prime minister shook his head ever so slightly and cleared his throat. "I am charged by my master to begin the proceedings of the day," he said, standing.

"These proceedings will not open," Kris said firmly, staying seated.

"But Your Highness . . ." was not finished.

Kris stood. "Your Imperial Master requested of our liege lord our assistance in resolving a difficulty he was having ruling his Empire. We are here at his request. We have reached an agreement on how to proceed. Your Master has agreed to proceed in that fashion. He charged some of his subjects to meet with me and agree on precisely how we will proceed. That agreement has been signed." Kris knew her voice had been rising. That her rage was showing through.

She didn't care.

"You may tell your Master that it is 8:29 in this hall, and it will remain 8:29 in this hall until your Master is prepared to meet his solemn commitments."

Without a word from Kris, Nelly backed the clock above the door to exactly 8:29 and froze its hands in place.

THANK YOU, NELLY.

THINK NOTHING OF IT, KRIS.

The prime minister looked about to have a heart attack. He reached for his cane and hobbled from the room.

Kris took her seat and prepared to wait however long it took.

58

Slightly less than an hour later, a flood of courtiers and courtesans heralded the imminent arrival of the Emperor. His entry was somewhat hurried. And harried.

The Empress's entrance was in full snit. Clearly, she didn't want to be here nor think Harry should be. Apparently, she had lost the argument and was not happy about it. Maybe more so.

She glared at Kris as she plopped herself down in the easy chair reserved for her.

Kris ignored the drama from that side of the room. She stood; the clock above the door made a loud click and buzz before flipping over to half past eight.

Kris made her way to the podium in front of her central party. "According to the agreed-upon ground rules, each side shall have an hour and a half to make statements or ask questions each morning and each afternoon. Who will go first each day will be determined by a flip of a coin. I have a Wardhaven silver dollar here. Would you both please provide a representative to check the coin and see it flipped?"

The Emperor waved a languid hand, and the prime minister huffed his way over to Kris's podium. Vicky said a whispered word, and Mannie hurried there, too.

"Heads," Kris said, showing Lady Liberty. "Tails," was a

stylized example of the rocket that had brought the first land-
ers to Wardhaven.

Here Kris found the ground rules had failed to determine
who made the call. She let the prime minister call the toss. He
called tails and won.

The Emperor and Empress would address them first. The
prime minister returned to his podium and shuffled the papers
he had prepared. However, there was a commotion around the
Imperial couple. It ended with the Empress stamping her way
to the podium and shoving the prime minister aside.

What followed was ninety minutes of the worst harangue
that Kris had ever had the misfortune to sit through. Kris had
stood through the ranting of the mad Great Guides of Xanadu
that aliens were coming who would boil her eyeballs in her
blood. She'd listened to the interminable harangues of the alien
raiders' Enlightened Ones, unable to understand a word but
shaking with the hatred and murderous intent behind them.

The Empress started with the calm and smooth reasoning
that she had used when she first told her side of the story to
Kris. But it only took her a few minutes to take a hard turn
down Insanity Lane and dive into Crazy Lake. She never quite
got around to foaming at the mouth, but she was most definitely spewing spittle.

The people seated at the central tables right in front of her
got up and moved to seats away from the spray.

Without moving her head . . . the last thing Kris needed
was to be seen exchanging glances with Vicky . . . Kris did
cast her eyes at the Grand Duchess.

Vicky was pale as a sheet. Mannie rested a hand on her
thigh. Vicky had one of hers on top of his. Her eyes narrowed,
and her face took on a hardness as the Empress's rant went
longer and longer. The two of them put their heads together
and soon were making use of their computers.

KRIS, I HAVE GAINED ACCESS TO VICKY'S COMPUTER.

NELLY, WHAT ARE YOU DOING?

I THOUGHT YOU MIGHT WANT TO KNOW WHAT VICKY AND
MANNIE ARE DOING.

Kris squelched a scowl. AND WHY WOULD I WANT TO
KNOW THAT?

BECAUSE SHE AND MANNIE ARE DOING A VERY GOOD JOB

OF GETTING AT THE TRUTH TO ALL THE LIES THAT THE EMPRESS
IS TELLING US.

LIES?

FOR EXAMPLE, SEVERAL OF THE RIOTS THAT SHE SAYS
VICKY INCITED TOOK PLACE WHILE SHE WAS STILL SAILING
WITH YOU. YOU DID NOTICE THAT THE EMPRESS WAS NAMING
A LOT OF PLACES BUT NOT TOO MANY DATES.

I HAD NOTICED THAT LACK.

THE EMPRESS ALSO SAYS THE REBELS ARE RESPONSIBLE
FOR ALL THE PIRATES THAT THROTTLED COMMERCE.

SHE SURE HAS.

THE GRAND DUCHESS JUST GOT A LIST FROM ADMIRAL
WALLER OF ALL THE "PIRATE SHIPS" THAT THE NAVY FOUGHT
AND CAPTURED THAT HAD BEEN SOLD OUT OF THE NAVY FOR
SCRAP, DELIVERED TO COMPANIES OWNED BY THE EMPRESS'S
FAMILY, AND ENDED UP GOING APIRATING.

DO TELL.

YES, KRIS. I THINK THE GRAND DUCHESS'S REBUTTAL
WILL BE A THING OF BEAUTY.

Kris began watching the clock after it passed 9:30 "conference time." This demonstration of mad intent would not go
one minute past the ninety minutes the agreed rules allowed.

At exactly ten o'clock, Kris stood. "Your time has expired."

Stopped in midsentence, the Empress drew herself up to
her full height, and said, haughtily, "I am not finished."

"If you feel the need, you may use the ninety minutes allot-
ted to your side in the afternoon," Kris said evenly.

"I want them now!" she screamed, eyes shooting daggers
at Kris.

"The Emperor and the Grand Duchess have agreed to these
rules. Do the two of you agree to unanimously suspend the
rules?"

The Emperor sheepishly would not meet the Empress's eyes.

Vicky made no bones about it. "We decline to suspend the
rules on the first day that we are working under them. Later,
we may find it to our mutual interest to adjust the schedule.
Not today."

The Emperor looked truly relieved.

The Empress stormed out of the Hall of Mirrors, hurling
invectives in every direction.

"It is within my powers to suspend the meeting for a fifteen-minute break," Kris said, after the door closed off that noise. "Would you like to get some tea, coffee?"

"Scotch," came from somewhere in the room.

Vicky stood up. "I am prepared to answer the Empress's comments of this morning. Then, I would propose that we yield the remainder of this session's time to Your Highness, so that we can go to lunch before all our stomachs are rumbling too loud."

"You may address those assembled here," Kris said.

As Vicky made her way to the podium, Kris changed gears in her head.

JACK, THE EMPRESS LOOKED DOWNRIGHT DERANGED AS SHE STORMED OUT OF HERE.

YEP, KRIS, AND YES, I HAVE DOUBLED THE GUARD. IF WE FIND ANY UNEXPLAINED SMALL OBJECTS, WE WILL TREAT THEM AS BOMBS. WE ARE DOUBLING THE NUMBER OF NANO INTERCEPTORS WE HAVE ROVING OUR CASTLE. SO FAR, THEY'VE FOUND NOTHING.

THANK YOU, JACK. Now Kris could relax back into her chair.

Vicky stood at the podium. For a long moment, she rested her eyes on her father.

"Dad. I love you," she said into the hush of the room.

"I have always loved you, and I will always love you."

"Then why are you leading a rebellion against me? Or letting these others use you in their rebellion?" the Emperor said, waving a hand at those behind Vicky.

Kris knew she should gavel the Emperor out of order, but Vicky shook her head ever so slightly, and Kris held her hand.

"Dad. I'm a Peterwald. No one *uses* a Peterwald. *We* use people. They *never* use us."

The father smile was proudly paternal at the daughter's reply.

Vicky glanced over her shoulder. "But Dad, I have found that people can be quite helpful, especially if you help them. I'd love to tell you some of the things I've done over the last two years. I think you'd be amazed and delighted. I've taken famine biscuits to starving kids and brought law and order back to planets where it had totally collapsed. I've opened trade between planets where pirates and other bad things had totally clogged up the arteries of commerce. Dad, I've learned a lot, and I've done a lot, and never, during any of it, have I done anything that would place myself in rebellion to you."

Vicky waved to the right and left of her podium at the people seated behind her. "None of these people have stood up in rebellion to you. Every one of them, just like me, stand in full fealty to you, our Emperor."

"I don't understand, daughter. I was told you fired on Imperial Navy ships."

"Say rather, Father, that I fired on ships going about the destruction of the Empire by doing the Empress's will."

That let the cat out of the bag and a full-fledged riot loose in the Hall of Mirrors.

The Empress might be gone, but her father and many of their party had not left. Now they were on their feet, shouting "Liar!" Traitor!" "Take that back, foul whore!" and much worse.

Swords were drawn and waved over heads. The poor working stiffs at the tables down the middle of the room beat a swift retreat for the door, though many of those on the Imperial side crawled under the table to make their run for it with the table between them and the waving swords.

Kris let the demonstration go on: she'd attended political conventions before. Then it started to get serious. The Imperial Guardsmen were ordered forward. Jack and Nelly ordered the Royal US Marines forward from their place against the wall. Others, part of the detachment billeted on the third and fourth floor, arrived at the double and reinforced the thin blue line standing at attention along the far side of the tables from the Imperials.

Kris hammered with her gavel but to no effect. Nelly captured the clash of wood on wood and amplified it.

Suddenly, everyone was reaching to cover their ears. To the eternal honor of the Corps, the Marines stood in their line, rifles at parade rest, ears not quite bleeding.

Into the silence, Kris announced in her command voice, "Your Imperial Majesty, please withdraw to the lodge. May I suggest that you take your lunch at its facilities. I will send a representative when I am ready to reconvene this afternoon."

"After what was said about my daughter, you can reconvene in hell," the Grand Duke of Greenfeld bellowed.

"She said worse about our Grand Duchess," came from the other side, and Kris was again hammering with her gavel.

Nelly didn't have to resort to a mass sonic attack. The Imperial side emptied quickly.

Once they were gone, Kris stood, and Vicky quickly joined her.

"That didn't go too well, did it?"

Kris worried her lower lip. She really couldn't say a word, not without ruining her role as mediator.

"I would suggest that you use the Banquet Hall for your lunch, Vicky."

"What about you?"

"I've got a mess hall for my Marines on the fourth floor."

"It's a shame to roust you out of your fine Banquet Hall for us."

"Yes, but we both know your people would be shot if they tried to go up the stairs."

Vicky glanced around. "I think the Empress would love that."

Saddened, Kris took the measure of the room. Some of the Imperial chairs had been knocked over in their haste to leave. She had entertained hopes that they might actually be able to do something. Kris sighed and answered Vicky's question. "I'm not in the business of doing what the Empress wants, much less loves."

"I'll see you after lunch," Vicky said, glancing back at the clock. "We'll be back in an hour and a half, negotiating time."

"Yes, and we'll see where we go from there."

59

Kris was ready to hike up four flights of stairs, but not everyone on her advisory teams was as fit as a Marine. Al and Bill moved with caution. One of the data miners used a wheelchair to get around, and one of Diana's advocates had twisted her foot in a pickup football game yesterday and was on crutches.

Nelly manufactured an elevator and ran people up the outside of the castle keep from the ground floor to the fourth.

Lunch was warm ham, beef brisket, barbecued pork, and roasted turkey with several cheeses and breads on the side and at least a dozen kinds of salad. Robin Song supervised it, but most of the food workers were local hires. At least Kris was doing something good for the Cuzco economy.

"I'm sorry. All we have is what we could quickly throw together. We figured the lodge's Great Hall for lunch and another banquet in our hall for supper," Robin said. She'd come down from the Forward Lounge with her wife, Mary Fintch, and most of their cooks to run Kris's kitchen dirtside for both the Banquet Hall and Marine mess.

"I don't see anyone turning up their noses," Kris said, then went down the line with Jack when everyone had been served.

At the troika's table, two seats stood empty, expectant. Kris joined her team leads.

"On a scale of one to ten, how bad does today stack up against what you've sat in on?" Kris asked after she'd swallowed her first bite of a delicious sandwich of ham and turkey on rye.

"I must admit," said Bill, "I've never had swords waved about at any of my arbitration sessions."

"That is an original for me, too," Al agreed.

"I've seen some pretty bitter words," Diana said, "though not between parent and child. It's usually the parents."

"So where do we go next?" Kris asked.

"We go back to the hall and talk some more," Bill said.

"We cannot get to a resolution of this matter if we cannot get the sides talking. Yes, they will start out venting like this morning, but over time and more sessions, the words will get softer and more constructive," Al said hopefully.

"It always goes that way," was Diana's contribution.

Kris looked around the room, spotted Major Henderson, and waved. He immediately came to stand by Kris.

"As soon as you finish eating, please carry my respects to the Emperor and tell him we will reconvene in the Hall of Mirrors at one thirty."

"Yes, Admiral," he said, and immediately left.

It was a good thing Kris sent that request so quickly, because the major was back in ten minutes with a reply. "The Emperor wants this afternoon's negotiations to take place in the lodge's Great Hall."

Al shook his head. "We're not set up for the Great Hall. We have the recording devices over here."

The major shook his head. "The Emperor was quite definite. If I may offer an opinion, although the Empress and the dukes said nothing, I got the feeling that they were the push behind this, and the Emperor was doing his best to please his wife."

"Is someone trying to arrange it so that there is no afternoon session?" Kris asked her troika.

They nodded. "Most definitely," Diana said.

"Ookaay," Kris muttered. "Jack, get a security team over there and go over that place with a fine-tooth comb."

"On it," Jack said, and had Sal ordering an officers' call even as he stood.

"Nelly, get me Ensign Longknife."

The eager young ensign was at Kris's side in a blink.

"Tell the people with the recording equipment that they've got to move their setup to the Great Hall of the lodge."

"Yes, Admiral," and Meg was off at a trot.

Ensign Longknife returned as Kris was watching her troika enjoy their second cup of coffee. She watched them longingly since she hadn't had a cup in over a year. Caffeine in the breast milk led to Ruth's bouncing off the walls.

"They're moving their gear, but the lodge is scrambling to find tables and chairs to outfit the Great Hall for the session. I really don't want to pass this along, but I have a request from the lodge manager for some Smart Metal to make tables and chairs."

Kris was pretty sure what her answer was going to be, but she passed the question to her brain trust with a raised eyebrow.

"I don't know about you," Al said, "but I like meeting in the Hall of Mirrors. I hate to say it, but I don't trust the Imperials. I think the Emperor is sincere, but the Empress, and even worse, her family . . ." He just shook his head.

"But if we let them cancel this session, when will we get things going again?" Diana said.

"You willing to trust the walk between here and there?" Bill asked.

"We always knew we'd have to do it," Diana countered. "Half here, half there, switching every day."

"Nelly, tell the fine gentleman who runs this resort that he better get some rental tables and chairs out here pronto."

"He'd figured that would likely be your answer, Kris. The necessary gear is already being loaded in town. The first truck is on the move."

"Thank you, Nelly," Kris said. "And no," she added to her troika, "I was not going to let any of the Smart Metal out of my sight. Besides, I think once the Emperor has to sit his backside down in a chair for three hours that isn't the comfortable Smart Metal chair that he's enjoyed with us, he might have a different idea about where he wants to do his listening."

Two hours later, Kris opened the next session. The Empress was conspicuous by her absence. This time, the prime minister took the podium and read a long statement in a painfully boring monotone. Kris did her best to follow it, but she kept either getting lost in the crazy twists and turns of the verbosity, or she'd nod off, hopefully for only a moment.

Kris would have thought the uncomfortable chairs would have made a nap impossible, but there were soon snores coming from several places in the hall, including the Emperor.

NELLY, ARE YOU GETTING ALL THIS?

YES.

CAN YOU MAKE ANY SENSE OF IT?

NO, KRIS. IT DOESN'T MATCH WHAT WE'VE MANAGED TO CAPTURE OF GREENFELD'S RECENT HISTORY. IT DOESN'T EVEN HAVE INTERNAL CONSISTENCY.

THANK YOU. I WAS STARTING TO THINK IT WAS ONLY ME.

Ninety minutes later, Kris ended the torture in midsentence and called for a fifteen-minute break. Several of the Imperials had to be woken. Even some of Vicky's had fallen asleep although she, Mannie, and a couple of others had been taking copious notes.

KRIS, WE'LL BE READY TO GO WHEN YOU CALL US BACK, suddenly came over Nelly Net.

I DIDN'T KNOW YOU COULD TALK TO ME THIS WAY.

I DON'T WANT TO BE SEEN TALKING TO YOU TOO OFTEN, SO I ASKED MY COMPUTER IF IT COULD ACCESS NELLY NET AND, *VOILA*, HERE I AM.

NELLY?

I AGREED WHEN VICKY'S COMPUTER ASKED NICELY. I'VE HAD A LOT OF OTHER ATTEMPTS TO BREAK INTO MY NET. NOT NICE. I'VE BROKEN A LOT OF NETWORKING GEAR. IT'S FUN.

OOKAAY. THANKS FOR THE HEADS-UP, VICKY. I'LL GET US BACK TOGETHER RIGHT ON TIME.

KRIS, WE'VE BEEN MAKING NOTES AS HE TALKED. WE'VE HEARD MOST OF THAT BEFORE. WE'RE READY TO GO WITH A FULL REBUTTAL.

60

Kris did not get the meeting under way when the fifteen-minute break was up.

It seemed that the Imperial side was more than a little slow to return to their seats. They had taken their break in the lodge's Banquet Hall. Even though the Grand Duchess's allies had returned to the castle for their break, they were back a lot sooner than the Imperials.

WHAT'S GOING ON, NELLY?

MY NANOS SHOW THE EMPRESS HAS THE EMPEROR DEEP IN HEATED DISCUSSION. OTHER IMPERIALS SEEM RELUCTANT TO FINISH THEIR COFFEE, BEER, OR STRONGER BEVERAGE. THERE ISN'T MUCH MOVEMENT THIS WAY.

There was a short pause, then, KRIS, WE'VE FOUND A BOMB. WHERE?

IT'S BURIED IN THE WALL BEHIND THE GRAND DUCHESS'S SIDE OF THE ROOM.

Kris considered her options. Clearly, Jack was playing it quiet. She should follow his lead. She considered several outcomes from this, both the bloody ones and the political, and made her call.

"Folks," Kris announced in the calmest of voices, "it appears we have a bomb in the room. May I suggest we all walk, not run, to the nearest exit. I see four in the room. Two are on the farthest walls from me," Kris said, and motioned with both her hands to the two exits in the front of the room, "and two behind me," and she spread her hands to point to those on either side of the hall.

Among the rebels, there was a quick exit. The few Imperials made a frantic dash, with people pushing and shoving. One fell and was trampled under feet.

"Kris, would you please get out of here," Jack said, coming up to her.

"Did you see me?" she asked excitedly. "I've been wanting to do the exit talk since I was six years old and saw it on an airplane."

"Fine. Fine, You've done it, now follow your own instructions and get gone."

"Are you going?" Kris said, eyeing Jack.

"Ah, there are the bomb experts," Jack said, moving Kris aside so three people in well-padded gear could waddle by. "We are out of here," he ordered, and led Kris by the elbow out the door.

NELLY, HOW'S THE BOMB?

IT'S QUIET, AS YOU NO DOUBT HAVE NOTICED.

Exasperated, Kris went on, NELLY, WHAT TYPE OF BOMB IS IT? HOW DANGEROUS?

IT APPEARS TO BE A BANGALORE TYPE. FROM THE LOOKS OF THE MOUTH, IT'S LOADED WITH ANTIPERSONNEL FLÉCHETTES. VERY NASTY FOR UNPROTECTED FLESH.

WOULD THEY LIKELY CARRY TO THE OTHER SIDE OF THE ROOM?

NO, KRIS. VICKY'S SIDE WOULD BE SLAUGHTERED. FEW ON THE OTHER SIDE WOULD EVEN BE HURT.

Kris scowled at Jack. "You getting this?"

"I heard it before."

"How come we didn't spot the bomb in the sweep before we came over here?"

"It's plastic, and its electronics were inactive," Jack said. "It would not have been noticed, but one of the sleepers leaned back against the wall. He didn't notice the wall caving in behind his head, but a guy coming back from the break noticed it and started widening the hole, and, bingo, we've got a bomb."

Jack walked Kris farther from the door they'd just walked

out of. It soon opened, and the people in the big suits walked out, pulling a little wagon behind them with a large barrel on it.

"You going to blow that up?" Kris called to them.

"Yes, ma'am," came back to her through a speaker.

"See if you can get any evidence off it."

"If we can, we will."

"Pardon me," said a man of middle height, middle weight, and middle appearance. "You may not remember me. I'm Mr. Smith. The Grand Duchess would appreciate it if I could join your bomb-examination team."

"They're going to blow it, but feel free to look at the pieces," Kris said.

"Often the pieces say more than you'd expect."

He went after the bomb-disposal team, and Kris set about restarting her meeting. It seemed like an impossible task, but it got easier when the Emperor appeared. He went straight to Kris.

"I understand there was a bomb aimed at my daughter."

"Yes, Your Imperial Majesty," Kris said.

"Why wasn't it found?" he demanded.

"It was put deep into the stone wall where it had crumbled with age," Jack explained. "It was made of plastic, plastered over into the wall, and apparently its electronics were silent until it was time-activated. There was no way our sweeps could have caught it."

"Had it been there for a long time?"

"No way to tell, Your Majesty," Jack said.

"So there could be another bomb behind her or even one behind me," he snapped.

"During the break, my Marines and your Imperial Guard went over the walls of the Great Hall with nails and hammers. We found nothing. We think the stones are stones."

The Emperor rubbed his ear. "I don't like this. I don't like this at all."

"Your daughter, the Grand Duchess, says that there have been quite a few attempts on her life," Kris mentioned.

"So some have told me. Others say it's her own fault for associating with lawless thugs."

"You've seen the people who are following her, Your Imperial Majesty," Kris said.

"Yeah. Now I've seen them." The Emperor rubbed his chin and eyed the Grand Duchess's followers filling up their chairs, if looking a bit askance at the painted stones behind them, now showing a lot of chipping from where they had been hammered. Several of those seated against the wall made their own inspection.

"Interesting. Very interesting," the Emperor said, and turned to his seat. A dozen courtiers followed closely behind him.

The Grand Duke of Greenfeld had come in and taken his place on the Emperor's right hand. An empty chair waited for the Empress.

Kris banged her gavel, and those who hadn't found their seats rushed to them. When she felt the last few deserved what they would no doubt get from those whose toes they stepped on, Kris said, "Your Grace. You have the floor for the next hour and a half."

"Thank you. Your Imperial Majesty," Vicky said with a nod to her father, followed by one to Kris, "Your Highness. I cede my time to Steve Rojek," and she turned and sat down.

A young man in conservative business dress came not to the podium but to a table that had been placed beside it during the break. A young man and woman, again in professional dress, came forward, their arms full of readers. They took the seats beside him and spread their electronic gear out in front of them. Steve, however, had only one tablet in front of him.

Again, he started with bows. "Your Imperial Majesty, Your Grace, Your Highness, other noble ladies and sirs, ladies and gentlemen. For the last several years, our beloved Greenfeld has been through some very troubling times. Earlier this afternoon, we heard one version of those troubles. At least those of us who managed to stay awake," he said with a near-comical shrug of his shoulders.

That brought loud guffaws and soft chuckles; several of those who had slept through the prime minister's boring and rambling statement got elbowed in the ribs.

"Now, I would like to offer a different perspective of how all this came to pass." So saying, the young man began to lay careful groundwork for where the Empire had been and how it managed to sink from there to its present low.

His words were soft, but firm. His facts were, wherever

possible, backed up with citations. Where they were not, he allowed for differences of opinion, or offered to bring forth witnesses to give sworn testimony. Between his soft words and simple-to-follow rhetoric, he had most of the room intently listening to him.

There were the occasional outbursts, inevitably from the Empress's faction. They grew fewer as those on the Imperial side of the room took in their Emperor's demeanor. He was leaning forward in his chair, eyes intent on Mr. Rojek. His right elbow rested on the arm of his chair, and his chin rested on the knuckles of that hand.

He did not nod along with Steve. However, though he showed no agreement, neither did he object to his words. As the time wore on, the Emperor never took his eyes off Steve. Vicky's spokesman, rather than wilting under that pressure, faced his Emperor and spoke his words calmly and gently, right to his face.

Kris watched the two men and felt like she was watching a conversation like two gentlemen might have seated next to each other in their club.

Has Vicky finally found a way to get inside the Emperor's bubble? The Empress is not playing her cards right. If she doesn't want her man to get his eyes opened for himself, she needs to be down here, rubbing those oversize mammary glands of hers in his face.

But the Empress stayed gone, and the Emperor stayed intent on Vicky's spokesman.

With twenty minutes left to go in his time, Kris began to worry she'd have to gavel him to silence in midsentence. She'd done that to the Empress; she would do that to him but hated to treat his logical presentation like she'd treated the Empress's tirade.

With exactly five minutes left to go, Steve brought his presentation to a perfect conclusion. He rose, and said, "I yield the remainder of my time back to Her Grace."

Vicky stood, but for a long moment, she said nothing. Then, someone among her people blew a clear perfect note on a pitch pipe, and Vicky began to sing.

NELLY, WHAT'S THAT SONG MEAN?

THAT, KRIS, IS THE IMPERIAL ANTHEM.

Vicky only had to sing the first line solo. Quickly, people around her rose to their feet and joined in the song. On the Imperial side, confusion reigned. Should they stand? It was the Emperor's anthem. But rebels were singing it.

Some stood, not looking around for instructions. It was their anthem. Some even began to sing along, though softly at first.

The Grand Duke, father to the Empress, stolidly sat in his chair, mouth firmly shut.

Then the Emperor turned to him. It was just a look, but it was *that* look.

Shamefaced, the Grand Duke stood and began to mouth the words. That was all it took. Soon everyone in the hall except the Emperor, or the citizens of Cuzco or Royal US citizens, was standing and singing. Kris had to remember not to join in on the refrain, especially the catchy one, "Greenfeld, ever verdant, ever ours."

When the song came to an end, there was silence for a long moment. Kris hated to break it, but it was her job. She tapped the plaque of wood on the arm of her chair with the handle of her gavel to get a softer sound.

"I close this session now. We will meet again tomorrow morning at nine o'clock in the Hall of Mirrors."

"About that," the Emperor said, coming up to Kris's chair. She stood to meet him. "I don't know about your ass, young woman, but mine is damn near numb from sitting in that chair."

"I was told that these were the best chairs in the resort."

"No doubt they are. Leastwise the best chair in my suite isn't any better. Oh, and about that bomb. Do you think anyone could put a bomb in your Smart Metal walls?"

Kris shook her head. "We've had those walls under continuous observation since they were constructed, Your Majesty. There is no way anyone could make a hole in those walls and secrete a bomb inside them without our knowing."

"Yeah, that's what I thought. Between your comfortable chairs and tighter security, I think we should continue to meet in the Hall of Mirrors."

"Your Majesty," said the Grand Duke of Greenfeld, coming up on the Emperor's other side, "it is a matter of equity.

They host some meetings. We host some. A balance must be struck."

"Equity, hell. We had a bombing here, and my ass is asleep from that damn chair. Here's the equity I'll give you. If anyone gets bombed in their hall, or my ass gets tired, then we come back here. That okay with you, kid?"

Kris nodded. "Is that acceptable to Your Grace?" she called, as Vicky's immediate team walked by on their way out the door.

"Of course, Your Highness, Your Imperial Majesty," was accompanied by the appropriate bows.

"Good. That's settled. Vicky, I'll see you tomorrow. Your guy had a lot of things to say. I can't say I agree with all of it, but it wasn't some of the bullshit I hear too often in the Palace."

"Thank you, Father," Vicky said, but added no more, not even a smile that might be mistaken for gloating.

61

The morning schedule that Kris had sent around to the delegates, and not followed all that much, did include an invitation to another banquet at nine o'clock that evening. She'd asked for RSVPs so they might know how many they would be feeding.

Vicky's side were definitely available for free food. All of them had responded before the first session started that morning. Only after the Emperor returned to his room following the last session did he reply in the positive. Within half an hour, Mary Fintch had heard from every Imperial.

"Thanks for promising to pay for a meal for everyone the first three days," Mary said in a quick note to tell Kris the Banquet Hall would be full. "Otherwise, I never would have ordered enough food for this many."

Kris just smiled. *Maybe I am getting the hang of this diplomatic thing.*

She quickly pumped milk for Ruth while watching her on-screen as she played with her nannies. They tried to get the infant to look at Kris, but though they said she was smiling at her mommy, her mommy wasn't feeling the love.

I have got to make a trip up the beanstalk to visit Ruth, she swore.

Dinner went much better that evening, partially because Mary was late serving it. Kris arranged for an open bar in the vaulted entrance, and people circulated a bit more than they had the night before. The Empress had a headache and didn't attend. Her older brother hadn't been seen all day, apparently unable to leave the bed of his paramour, but most of the Imperials were there with the Emperor.

That included several young women with heaving, minimally covered bosoms, who orbited around the Emperor until they caught his eye, then, smiling coyly, closed in for his closer attention.

"Someone is definitely not playing her cards right," Jack muttered. Kris could only nod in agreement.

The Grand Duke was there at the Emperor's side, scowling at those bearers of such visible pulchritude, but they ignored him and continued basking in the Emperor's attention.

Emperor Harry was only too happy to encourage their basking.

Not all of the femininity around the Emperor was in Imperial bare. Several of the young women were locals, and not a few were from Vicky's faction. Vicky didn't seem to notice their waywardness, or if she did, she shrugged off her father's wandering eye with easy aplomb.

"What must it have been like for Vicky, growing up in that Palace, even if it wasn't officially a Palace yet?" Jack asked softly.

"I thought she was bad when I first met her," Kris said, "but after looking at this, I wonder how she managed to survive to be the person she is now."

"She put on quite a show, first answering her stepmother's tirade with gentle words, then handing the lead over to that Steve fellow. What he did . . ." Jack just shook his head.

"I suspect he was operating from a lot of notes given by Vicky and her Mannie."

"You're proud of her. Busting-buttons proud."

Kris swirled her tonic water and lime twist. "I'd like to think I had something to do with who she's become."

Soft chimes announced dinner. It went well and progressed smoothly into after-dinner drinks in the ballroom. The conversation showed the sides mixing a bit here, a bit there. Some of the locals managed to bring people from both sides together.

Kris's brain trust had noted which Imperials listened more intently to Steve. They worked hard to get those people talking with locals. Then they would smoothly add one or two from Vicky's faction.

Kris allowed herself to traipse up the stairs to bed early, hoping the next day might show more progress.

Next morning, the Emperor arrived five minutes early and stood at Kris's side, facing Vicky, as Kris flipped the coin. Vicky allowed her father to call the toss. He lost, but she invited him to go first.

Kris soon wished Vicky hadn't.

The Grand Duke of Greenfeld quickly took the podium and began to defend his daughter and family's necessary actions to bring law and order back to the planets being stalked by rebellion and sedition. "Factions seated across from us. Factions making groundless accusations against our moderate efforts to keep the peace and see that Greenfeld's business was business," he said, turning to the Emperor.

Emperor Henry nodded as his own words were fed back to him.

The Grand Duke's rebuttal was loud and proud. He mentioned a lot of planets, but usually in the context of rooting out the State Security traitors. That always got the Emperor's nod. But when he addressed other planets and other outbreaks of lawlessness, he got vague. And the actions of the Security Consultants were always appropriate and no more than were essential to restore peace and the rule of law.

The Emperor nodded along every time the Grand Duke said, "Restore peace and the rule of law."

The Grand Duchess's factions sat stony-faced but silent through it all. About half of the Imperials, the faction Kris was coming to recognize as the Empress's lackeys, cheered and whistled whenever the Emperor appeared to approve of what he was hearing.

There was another faction, though. Dressed in the colorful fashions of the Imperial court, they nevertheless did not react when the Empress's faction did. Slowly, it became clear to everyone in the hall that there were a lot of people on the Imperial side sitting just as silent and stony-faced as those on the Grand Duchess's side.

It started as a few gentle digs in ribs as the Empress's faction tried to get a rise out of the silent ones in their midst. Then it escalated to serious jostling. When someone called out "Stop that," Kris brought the gavel down and two shamefaced men traded seats with the men next to them.

The last forty minutes of the Grand Duke's speech was interrupted by more and more of Kris hammering her gavel. She finally resorted to an appeal to the Emperor.

"Your Imperial Majesty, please restore order among your delegation."

"Cut the crap, or I'll have the Imperial Guard escort you out of here."

"And you'll go to bed without any of that whore's nice supper," someone added.

Kris locked eyes with the Emperor. He owed her an apology. He owed her one, but would he give it to her? He broke eye contact first.

"Bruno, I think you've made your point," the Emperor said. "Your Highness, I yield back the remainder of my time to you so we can have a nice, long break to let things calm down."

"I think that would be a very good use of that time, Your Imperial Majesty. I propose we meet back here in forty minutes." That was a bit longer than the remaining time and the break time added up to, but Kris needed some time to calm herself down from that last anonymous remark.

"Your Majesty, we have refreshments for your delegates in the ballroom. Nelly, would you open a passageway there?" Kris didn't want anyone sniping or tossing real grenades at her guests.

"Yes, Your Highness."

"Your Grace, there will be refreshment in the Banquet Hall for you and your associates. Nelly, open another passageway."

"Done," said Nelly

"Thank you, Your Highness," said the Grand Duchess with a gentle bow.

"What about us?" Jack asked.

"I guess we use the Marine mess. Nelly, see that there is an open bar in the ballroom."

"Not in the Banquet Hall?"

"Nope. Unless Vicky asks for it, don't offer it."

"You trying to get the Imperials soused?" Jack asked.

"Jack, do you doubt the Imperials will want something stronger than tea, and yes, if they want it, I'll let them get as drunk as they want."

While Kris and her immediate team headed up the elevator that had suddenly appeared, most of her brain trust followed the other two factions. The data miners and technical staff went with Kris, but Al, Bill, and Diana, along with their staffs, looked more interested in doing additional work rather than taking a break.

Kris took part of the break to off-load some milk and watch Ruth play up on the *Princess Royal*. That took some of the pain out of her breasts, but none of the pain out of her heart.

After the break, an Imperial Navy officer took the podium. "I am Admiral Bolesław, and I had the honor of being captain of several ships that carried the Grand Duchess. I was at the conn when my heavy cruiser went through a jump to find a schooner with 18-inch pulse lasers waiting for us. We blasted it out of space, but it damn near blew us to kingdom come."

"What does this pirate ship have to do with anything?" the Grand Duke shouted out.

The admiral was unfazed. "We wish to make the point, Your Imperial Majesty, that those who have contributed to the breakdown in law and order in the Empire have also stalked your daughter, Grand Duchess Victoria."

The Emperor cocked his head to one side and seemed thoughtful though he said nothing.

Kris rapped the handle of her gavel. "I find this attack interesting, Your Imperial Majesty. On our voyage to Greenfeld, my squadron also was ambushed. The ships involved were old Greenfeld battleships, left over from the Iteeche War, but they still packed a punch though not very accurately," Kris said, wanting to avoid just how she'd managed to handle them. "We captured quite a few of the crew, including one officer. I think those assembled here might well benefit from his testimony. If it pleases Your Imperial Majesty, Your Grace, I would present that witness tomorrow."

Vicky nodded agreement. The Grand Duke was busy bending the Emperor's ear. Said Emperor began slowly shaking his head, but the Grand Duke didn't give up. The head shaking got more and more vigorous until, finally, the Emperor scowled and shoved the father of his Empress away.

"Did you identify these rogue battleships, Your Highness?" Emperor Harry asked.

"Yes, we did. They were the *Hephaestus* and *Poseidon* of the Mars class, Your Imperial Majesty."

"You can call me sir, Kris. Otherwise, these sessions are going to go on forever."

"Yes, sir," Kris said with a gentle smile.

Do not start to like this bastard. Remember, he wanted you delivered naked to him for torture just a few years ago if the brags of one of his people can be believed.

"Where were the *Hephaestus* and *Poseidon* assigned?" the Emperor asked.

That brought silence from those around him.

Vicky nodded to Admiral Waller, who sat in her entourage. He stood up. "Sir, the *Hephaestus* and *Poseidon* were assigned to the Greenfeld Reserve Fleet. When I left the capital, they were still trailing the reserve station with no crews aboard."

"You can't believe a word that man says," the Grand Duke shouted. "He broke his oath to you to run away and join the rebellion against you."

Kris was torn. Vicky had let her father talk during her time. Should she allow this cross talk? Cross talk, hell! That bastard was shouting.

The admiral handled the interruption like a gentleman. "Your Majesty, may I answer that question?"

"Go ahead, Rolf."

"Your Majesty, I left the capital one step ahead of an assassination squad." The admiral paused here, and you could see his jaw tremble. "My beloved wife was not so lucky."

Oh, no. Kris had heard that his wife had been caught and delivered to the Empress. She had personally slit the woman's throat and sent the video of it to her husband on Bayern.

This is about to get so ugly.

Kris got a good hold on her gavel.

The admiral went on, his voice low and trembling with emotions. "My wife was caught by the assassins and murdered."

Kris and the Grand Duchess's side of the room breathed a sigh of relief.

The Grand Duke scowled. *Did he want the full accusation?*

"I'm sorry, Rolf. I didn't know," the Emperor said, then turned to one of his courtiers. "Utz, you're supposed to have a handle on our Navy. What do you know about those two battleships?"

A young man, dressed even more flamboyantly than the rest of the Emperor's retinue, if that was possible, began talking to the red-and-silver box he carried.

"My Emperor, according to my files, they are still in the Reserve Fleet."

Harry turned to Kris.

"According to my *experience*," Kris said, "they are dust around a certain jump in the direct course from Wardhaven to Greenfeld."

Harry made a wry face. "So we add one more thing to the list of what one side thinks is true and the other says is false."

"So it would seem, sir."

The Emperor did not look happy, but the scowls he was throwing around were not meant for Vicky's side. Now, they were aimed at his own.

Finally, he shook his head. "Vicky, do you have more?"

"Yes, Father."

He waved a hand for her to continue.

Vicky put her head together with several of her team, and Mannie was the next to take the podium.

"I was with the Grand Duchess when she was kidnapped. Later, I saw the bed that she was handcuffed to and left to die of thirst on. I was with the team that rescued her and shot down those who were trying to recapture her. They would not surrender but died resisting arrest. It was my investigators who traced the assassins back to the ship they had arrived on and followed their trail back to when they crossed from territory controlled by the Empress to Vicky's sworn planets."

Having said that, Mannie began to provide full details of everything he had outlined in his opening statement. Kris knew the attack had occurred; her team had investigated it and verified every fact Mannie was now providing the Emperor. He listened intently, smiling when the mayor described how Vicky had struggled to get herself free of the bed's iron embrace.

"How long did it take you?" the Emperor asked his daughter.

"Too long, and I got a splinter in my right boob."

"And I wasn't there to kiss it and make it well."

"Sorry, no."

Kris wondered just how much information she was getting about this father/daughter relationship but refused to speculate further.

When Mannie finished, the Emperor asked Vicky, "So that was why you didn't come to court when I called you?"

"No, Father. I admit I wasn't quite as debilitated as the video made it seem. I was afraid for my life if I returned to the Palace and the assassination squads that seemed to dog my steps when I was there."

Kris had seen the video of the enraged Empress threatening Vicky that was piggybacked on the Emperor's message calling Vicky to court. Strange that the Grand Duchess made no attempt to enter that into the record for her father.

Then again, as the morning wore on, the relationship between father and daughter had warmed quite a bit.

At eleven thirty, Kris gaveled the session to a close and offered the two sides the same arrangement for their lunch.

The Emperor stood. "I would like to share my lunchtime with my daughter. You did say that you had done quite a lot of things you wanted to tell me about."

"Yes, Dad."

"Your Majesty," the Grand Duke interjected. "This is not proper. It just isn't done during these kinds of things."

"Bruno, last time I checked, I was the Emperor, and I do believe I can do what I damn well please."

Bruno turned and stomped out. Several of his faction followed him. Others looked around, saw the Emperor heading for the other side of the room, and followed.

"Nelly, tell Mary to change her luncheon arrangements. You might help by magicking up more tables in the Banquet Hall."

"Already doing it, Kris. I made the suggestion to Mary right after the Emperor opened his mouth."

"Good girl," Kris said. She considered joining the Imperial couple for lunch, but saw Diana was edging her way through the crowd around the two and decided to give herself a break. She and Jack enjoyed their lunch and relaxed for a bit in their room. Nelly opened a window, giving them a gorgeous view of the forested hills with snow-covered mountains in the distance. The gentle breeze wafted the scent of pines into their room. Nelly really had the room open.

The afternoon session proved to be interesting. For one thing, the Grand Duke as well as the Empress were not present. There were quite a few missing from the Imperial side.

In fact, the Imperials had no one to take the podium when Kris gaveled the session open. It was an Imperial, dressed more as a businessman than a courtier, who finally stood. "Your Majesty. The Empire has been suffering inflation and severe scarcity of critical items needed to maintain production and employment. Might we ask the Grand Duchess what answer she can make to the claim that *some* people have been waging destructive economic warfare against our beloved Greenfeld?"

The Emperor looked around his delegates, checking for anyone either raising an objection or offering a better use of their time. When he saw none, he shrugged toward Vicky.

"Daughter, what have you to say to these charges?"

"Father, neither I nor anyone who has sworn fealty to their rightful Emperor through me have had anything to do with such matters. In truth, we have suffered the same fate. Suffered it so harshly that some planets have been reduced to starvation and have been taken over by bandits. During lunch, Father, I told you about my efforts to bring food to Poznan and restore commerce to them. I would like to introduce a business leader from that planet to tell you how they were reduced to such devastation."

The Emperor nodded, and Vicky called up Mr. Arnsvider. He quickly, with broad brushstrokes, described how the loss of credit and the depredation of pirates reduced his planet's access to critically needed raw materials and spare parts.

"The people who wiped out State Security somehow forgot to take their guns and ammunition with them when they left. A group of bandits got their hands on them, and from there, it was all downhill. Only the arrival of your daughter, the Grand Duchess, pulled us back from the brink of cannibalism. For that, we thank her and you."

He then went on to tell how matters had improved as trade opened up again, first with St. Petersburg, then with more planets.

Through all this, the Emperor nodded along, occasionally resting his eyes on Vicky with a proud, fatherly smile.

Mr. Arnsvider was followed to the podium by a long line of people from various planets. They described how they had been reduced to less desperate straits and walked back from them with the help of the Grand Duchess. She had secured the space lanes, then increased trade, first by barter but more recently with the help of banks and a respected currency.

The afternoon went this way, with people from the Imperial side also going to their podium to tell their own stories. The Emperor's face grew stormier by the minute. There were fewer and fewer members of the Empress's faction present, and none of them were objecting to any of this.

Then a man from Dresden came to the podium on the Imperial side. Like those before him, he described the destruction of the State Security apparatus. Economic dislocation soon led to strife as hungry people took to the streets. "And then the red coats arrived. The so called Security Specialists. These were led by Giorgio Topalski, now the Duke of Radebuel. To us, he will forever be known as the Butcher of Dresden."

The story went long. The man was reduced to tears well before he finished. The Hall of Mirrors became quiet, then silent as a tomb. Someone dropped a stylus; it resounded like a bomb.

When the man finished, he sat down. The people on both sides of him scooted closer and put their arms around him as he gave himself up to wracking sobs.

No one stood to claim either podium.

Kris put her gavel down quietly, stood, and left the Hall silently. Slowly, others followed her.

The man, with his description of the horrors he had experienced and the sharing of his grief had succeeded where the best of intentions and skills had failed.

He had united both sides in their shared grief.

62

The banquet that night was a totally different affair. The Emperor said he wanted to be seated by the Grand Duchess. "Oh, and that guy that's always at her side. Something tells me I better get to know him."

Nelly did away with the dance floor; they no longer needed neutral territory between the two sides. Without its taking up space, they spread the tables out, leaving more room for people to circulate. Other than the two tables, one for Kris and the other for the two Imperials, there was no assigned seating. People found someone they knew, or people they didn't, and sat down to share a meal.

For the first time since this started, Kris got to relax and enjoy eating without fearing it might end in bloodshed. When dinner finished without a boom, and people began to adjourn to the ballroom to share more drinks and talk, Kris leaned close to Jack.

"There were a lot of empty chairs. Definitely no Empress or Grand Duke in evidence. Do you know where they are?"

Jack shook his head. Before he could open his mouth, Nelly answered.

"You remember that superhigh tech we've been waiting for them to kick off using?"

"Yes, Nelly,"

"Well they kicked it off hard this afternoon. They put up some sort of electromagnetic barrier around the main lodge that will fry any nano that gets within five meters of the place. I tried hardening a few but got nowhere. Whatever's going on inside that lodge, we don't know thing one about that."

"Jack?" Kris asked.

"I tried to get a few Marines. Even tried to slip Mary Fintch into the kitchen to ask for a cup of sugar. No joy. There are Imperial Guards at every door turning away anyone not an Imperial."

"Hmm," was all Kris could say to that. "Any idea what they're up to?"

"Not a guess, but they are certainly up to something. Since lunch, they've also been running limos, SUVs, and vans in and out of the lodge basement and circulating them into town. We tried following them, but they damn near ran our trailing cars off the road, and there are some pretty sharp cliffs on the drive into town that you don't want to get knocked over. We've got cars in town, now, but it's like some sort of snipe hunt."

"It looks like they might be doing what we've done a few times," Kris said, remembering how she'd got out of Nuu House and up to the *Princess Royal* after the sniper attack.

"Don't you hate it when the bad guys and gals get as smart as you," Nelly said dryly.

Kris frowned as she puzzled this through, and at the pain in her breasts. She raised first one, then the other. They were heavy with milk.

"Listen, no one seems to have any idea what the Empress is or is not doing. Things here seem to be pretty laid-back and don't need us. I really could use a baby fix. I've had enough of pumping these jugs dry. I'd love to hold Ruth for a bit while she does the service for me."

"Can I go along, too?" Jack said. "I've missed seeing you and Ruthie together."

"Ensign Longknife, tell them to hold the next ferry up to the station for one Wardhaven Princess who desperately wants to see one tiny princess," Kris said, standing.

"Done, Your Highness," came back at Kris only a moment later.

Jack took no time at all to arrange a guard detail; the caravan was small. "I think it ought to be good enough, what with this being so spur-of-the-moment."

In no time, they were at the space-elevator station and on their way up. A call ahead to the nannies revealed that Ruth had been asleep for a while but would likely be awake by the time they got there.

Kris and Jack managed to spend the ride up talking to each other about nothing that was world-ending. They were only a few minutes out when Jack called Security Central on the *Princess Royal.*

"How's everything tonight?"

"Fine, General. Quiet watch. We've been getting some static on the cameras covering the pier tie-downs, though. I was about to dispatch two technicians to check Tie-down Number Two, the one that has all our housekeeping connections."

"How many Marines do you have covering that one?" Tie-down Two was the only one big enough for someone to walk aboard.

"Two Marines, sir. They are reporting every quarter hour."

Jack looked at Kris.

"Call them. *Now!*" Kris shouted into Jack's commlink.

"Yes, ma'am. Wait one."

They didn't have to wait a full minute. "I got their usual report. When I tried to talk to them some more, I got the same report."

"We are Code Red," Jack said evenly. "We are Code Red."

The five minutes until the ferry docked at the station were the longest years of Kris's life.

63

Kris and Jack stood right behind the hatches as the ferry rumbled and bumped to a stop, their service automatics out, ammo set on deadly. Safeties were off and full auto was selected. Behind them, Meg and the Marine guard detail waited, their weapons locked and cocked.

The hatch had hardly begun to open when Kris wiggled her way through it and hit the station at a dead run, Jack right behind her. The rest did their best to keep up, but Kris was going for the three-minute mile.

She already knew that the two Marine guards at the pier tie-down were dead, shot through the eyes. Kris had ordered the nursery doors sealed, but any effort to raise them on net had failed. Now she took the escalator stairs three at a time down to their pier. The OOD got out of her way as she shot up the brow.

I'll render honors twice next time.

The quarterdeck was still large. Her day quarters were a lot smaller. She slowed as she approached the door to the nursery.

Behind it, Ruth was screaming like she'd never screamed before.

She and Jack approached the door, Meg right behind them, automatics up in a two-handed stance.

"Nelly, make the wall disappear on one."

"Yes, Kris."

"One."

The wall went away.

Kris's blood froze.

A man in station working clothes held Ruth suspended by the back of her onesie. He had a gun aimed at her tiny head.

Beside him, another man, dressed alike but showing the signs of a tough fight, had a gun aimed at the top of Sally Greer's head. She had one arm around his leg; another was a fist ready to slug him in the balls. If she could have killed the man with her eyes, this guy would be fried.

The last Kris noticed was Warrant Officer, ret. Li O'Malley. She lay on her back, four bullet wounds weeping on her chest, eyes fixed at the overhead. Somebody had wisely gone for the center of his target's mass.

A service automatic was still grasped in Li's dead hand.

"Put the baby down, and we will let you live," Kris said through clinched teeth, not letting her gun waver from its lock between the eyes of the guy threatening Sally.

Jack was the better shot. He had his automatic aimed at the arm of the man holding Ruth.

"No, I got a better idea. You give us safe passage to the Imperial Courier Ship *MC-410*, and we'll leave the baby on the pier."

"You know you won't do that," Kris said. "As soon as that courier ship pulls away from the pier, there are nine battle-cruisers that will blow it to hell. No, you're going to keep the baby until it's no longer convenient, then you'll ditch her. Maybe she lives. Maybe she doesn't. It's no skin off your nose either way."

"So, maybe I promise that I'll make real sure she lives."

They were negotiating, just as they had been doing down in the Hall of Mirrors. These guys had expected to die a minute ago. Now they could see a way to live. They relaxed ever so slightly.

Kris gave her head a brief shake. "I don't think you'll have much control over what happens to her. I don't see you doing this for fun. It's got to be the money. Yet you're talking to one of the richest women in human space, and you aren't even giving me a chance to bid."

JACK, DO YOU HAVE A SHOT?

YES.

I'LL GO FOR THE BABY, Meg put in, putting her automatic down slowly.

GET READY EVERYONE TO MOVE WHEN I SAY SHOOT.

READY, Jack snapped.

ME, TOO, Meg added.

"How much you willing to offer?" sounded way too eager.

"How much is on the table now?" Kris answered.

The two thugs exchanged a quick glance.

THEY'RE GETTING SLOPPY, Jack thought.

GET READY.

"Fifty billion," the guy holding the screaming Ruth said.

"Fifty billion what?"

"Gold Imperial marks."

SHOOT.

Kris put two rounds into the center of her target's mass, then two more right between his eyes. He crumpled where he stood.

Jack put one round in his guy's pistol, knocking it into his chest and away from Ruth's head. The thug got one shot off . . . it hit him, creasing his chest. Jack put two between the guy's eyes next, then two more for good measure where his heart was rumored to be.

He dropped backward like a felled tree.

Ensign Longknife hurled herself across the space, sliding in under Ruthie and catching her before she hit the deck.

64

Kris managed to put her weapon down at the same time she swooped in to collect a screaming Ruth from Meg's arms. She kept going until she fetched up beside the rocker and sank into it. While one hand held Ruth, Kris pulled down the top of her strapless ball gown with a bit of help from Mai Tiamat. Shushing her darling softly, Kris slid Ruthie to her other side and gave her a breast to suckle.

"There, there, baby. Mommy's here. No one's going to hurt you. There, there."

Ruth was having nothing of that soothing stuff.

"Nelly, raise a wall between us and those bleeding corpses. This place stinks."

A wall appeared, blowers went to high, and the smell quickly dissipated.

Kris kept trying to soothe Ruth, but inside she was seething.

NELLY, WE NEED TO TALK.

JACK'S HERE, TOO.

THEY WERE PAID IN IMPERIAL GOLD MARKS AND WANTED AN IMPERIAL COURIER BOAT FOR THEIR GETAWAY. THIS CAME FROM INSIDE THE EMPIRE. NELLY, IS THERE AN IMPERIAL COURIER BOAT IN PORT?

NO. NOT OFFICIALLY. BUT THERE IS A PIER AT THE END OF

THE STATION. THERE ARE NO CAMERAS WORKING THERE, AND NOTHING IS OFFICIALLY THERE, EITHER. HOWEVER, THE WATER, AIR, POWER, AND SEWAGE USAGE HAVEN'T BEEN ADDING UP FOR THE LAST COUPLE OF DAYS NOW THAT I LOOK AT THEM.

CAN YOU GET ANY KIND OF READOUT FROM THAT PIER, NELLY?

NO, IT'S IN THE SHADOW OF THAT MONSTER, THE *EMPEROR AND EMPRESS*.

THAT DOESN'T MAKE ANY SENSE, TO HAVE NO WORKING CAMERAS ON THE PIER NEXT TO THE IMPERIAL FLAGSHIP, Jack put in.

JACK, I WANT A MARINE STRIKE TEAM DOWN TO THAT PIER FAST. CIVVIES AND CONCEALED WEAPONS.

It took a long moment before Jack was back on net. THEY'RE ON THEIR WAY. MEGAN IS LEADING THEM. SHE DITCHED HER BALL GOWN. SHE'S RUNNING BAREFOOT IN JUST A SLIP. Kris ignored the thought of Jack watching a half-naked version of her younger self. She gently stroked Ruth's cheeks. She was hungrily sucking down her mommy's milk, and her little tears seemed to be drying rapidly.

NELLY, WHAT OTHER SURPRISES ARE GOING ON AROUND HERE?

THE LONG-RANGE RADAR HAS BEEN ON THE FRITZ OFF AND ON FOR THE LAST COUPLE OF DAYS.

AS IN SINCE THE *EMPEROR AND EMPRESS* ARRIVED?

YEP. IT WENT TOTALLY DOWN AROUND NOON TODAY.

WAS ANY TRAFFIC LEAVING ABOUT THEN?

AN IMPERIAL LIGHT CRUISER.

Kris remembered Vicky telling how she and her second escort/bodyguard had slipped away from High Greenfeld Station when the long-range radar was down by snuggling up next to a light cruiser.

NELLY, HAVE CAPTAIN AJAX ACTIVATE THE *P. ROYAL*'S LONG-RANGE SCANS. FIND THAT LIGHT CRUISER AND SEE IF THERE ISN'T A FAST COURIER BOAT OUT THERE AHEAD OF IT.

SHE'S WORKING ON THAT.

Minutes passed. Kris found herself and Ruthie settling into their calm nursing routine. *I'll miss having you at my breast when it comes time to wean you.*

The wall went away, giving Kris and Ruth back the whole nursery. The blood and stink as well as the bodies were gone. Ruth didn't even notice the change, but Kris liked having Jack standing next to her.

"Kris," Nelly said softly "you will never guess what our Marines found at that pier."

"Don't keep me waiting, Nelly."

"There is a fast Imperial courier ship, *MC-410* by name, complete with crew and a whole lot of courtiers. I've already run them through facial recognition. They're the Empress's faction."

"Did we get the Empress or Grand Duke?"

"Nope, Kris, but the pilot said a courier boat headed out around noon today."

"And they stayed because?" Jack said.

"They were waiting for a 'package.' A certain count was to tell him when it was aboard, and they were to sail immediately."

"Did he mention the name of that count?" Kris snapped.

"He certainly did. He'll be in the first batch of prisoners Meg is bringing back."

"Jack," Kris said, "I think we have a good reason to send a strong Marine detachment to a pier very close to the Imperial flagship."

"Thank you, my love. You call the Emperor, and I'll get the Marines going and accompany them in case things get diplomatically challenging."

Kris made a call to the Emperor that took a while to be answered and when it was had no visual. She briefed him on the attempt to kidnap her child.

"That's unacceptable" he huffed, not sounding at all like the man who had paid for Kris's Grandmother Sarah to be killed or her brother, Eddy, to be kidnapped. "By the way, I have not seen the Empress since morning. Do you know anything of her whereabouts?"

"An Imperial courier boat left here around noon. We don't know who its passengers were. I can get you a list of who was on the courier boat that was supposed to carry Ruth away. I am told there were several of your retinue aboard."

"Say not my retinue but the Empress's toadies."

Kris ended the call and had Nelly pass along photos of those on the boat. Very quickly, she got a call back from neither the Emperor nor the prime minister. The fellow was middle-aged, just starting to gray, and his clothing was sober gray.

"I've looked at all the pictures you sent. They are fairly high up in the Empress's faction, but not the top. We've looked around, and none of the senior supporters of the Empress, her father, or her brother are here although we have found the Empress's mother, Grand Duchess Maude and her brother's girlfriend. The Imperial Guard are interrogating them now, but their initial claim is that they have no idea where the others are."

"So the dukes took off but left their ladies behind. Strange," Kris said.

"Past strange."

"Just a moment, I've got another call coming in. Will you wait?"

"For a short time."

"Admiral, this is Captain Ajax. We found the cruiser. It was harder to find the courier; it was stealthy as hell, but we've got it."

"Where?"

"The courier is boosting at four gees for Jump Point Gamma, the most direct one to Greenfeld."

"Thank you, Captain. Hell's a popping. Keep your eyes out for anything."

"Aye, aye, ma'am."

"Thank you for waiting," Kris said to the man she'd kept on hold, and filled him in on what her ship's sensors had to say.

"They're running for home?"

"That's their course."

"Bruno can't believe he can raise a rebellion with only the Empress and child as a power base."

"I'm not well schooled in these types of politics," Kris said, and left the fellow to his problems.

A few minutes later, Jack asked if he could frog-march a certain count into the nursery. Kris handed off the now-slumbering little one to Fede Radko and met up with Jack and

Megan. She really had stripped out of her ball gown to lead the Marines in just her slip.

I think I like this gal.

Kris left the count standing in the middle of her day quarters as she circled him, eyes hard.

He took one look at Kris and became very eager to tell his story even without her saying a word. He'd been left behind by the Empress and Grand Duke with orders to only leave when the package was delivered.

"I had no idea what the package was. They told me I'd know it when I saw it. I was told to shoot the messengers who delivered it, but I didn't really plan to do that," he insisted, groveling now at Kris's feet.

"That's pretty much what he's been saying since the pilot pointed him out," Jack said.

"Toss him in the brig," Kris ordered. "I'll talk to him some more while we chase down that other courier boat."

"No. No. Send me ashore. You don't want me messing up your boat. Look at me. I've wet myself."

"Why don't I want you on my ship?" Kris said slowly, studying this poor excuse for a human.

"Kris, Captain Ajax wants to talk to you," Nelly interrupted.

"Yes, Captain."

"The Gamma jump is spewing out ships like my brother's momma guppy."

"Ships?" Kris said, eyeing the count. He looked as if he wanted to crawl into the floor; he couldn't get any lower.

"First through was a destroyer squadron, say twenty strong. It was followed by squadron of heavy cruisers. Now we got battlewagons following each other through like elephants the day I saw the circus come to town. Oh, my! Sensors say that last one is sporting twenty-four 19-inch guns. I think I'm scared," was pure sarcasm.

"Captain Ajax, I assume our squadron has all hands aboard."

"Since your Sailors can get a beer without going ashore, you bet, ma'am."

"Order the squadron to be ready to sortie on one hour's

notice. I request your presence and that of your navigator in my flag plot in thirty minutes to plan our battle."

"Aye, aye, Admiral."

The count eyed Kris with eyes as big as saucers. "Will you put me ashore now?" he pleaded.

"Jack, see that this son of a bitch is locked up in the brig and throw away the key," Kris growled.

65

Kris gathered her truncated staff in her flag plot. No surprise, Vicky and Mannie showed up with Admiral Bolesław in tow and added themselves to the small group with Kris. They stood around a plotting table that now showed the Cuzco system.

Between Cuzco and Jump Point Gamma was a light cruiser accelerating toward the jump at 1.25 gees. Well beyond it was the courier boat still maintaining four gees.

"There must be a lot of water beds on that boat." Jack muttered. "Has the Emperor got back to us with a list of who he's missing from the Empress's faction?"

"Nope," Kris said. "I think we can assume at least the Empress, Grand Duke, and Duke are aboard with the closest of their cronies. Captain Ajax, what have we got headed in?"

The captain touched the battle board, and a list of ships appeared. "We've got quite an interesting collection. Pride of place goes to the *Terror of Space* and *Death to Traitors*. Both of them are sporting twenty-four of those new 19-inch lasers. I have no idea how powerful they are. Since they were knocked together recently, I doubt they're Greenfeld's finest. With them are six with twelve 18-inch guns and another four with twelve 16-inch. The rest of the battle line is made up of ancient ships dragged out of mothballs. Heaven knows what they've got for crews, but there are twelve 15- and 14-inch battlewagons trailing the big punchers. Add to that a dozen heavy cruisers, a half dozen light, and forty tin cans, and you have a well-balanced fleet."

"Who expect they are only up against nine frigates," Kris said with a broad grin she knew was pure evil.

Beside her, Vicky shook her head and shared a tight smile.

"I think they expect so," Captain Ajax said. "We're all there is in town. Cuzco maintains no fleet, counting on its central place among three different competing alliances who presently seem happy with her neutrality. The Emperor only brought two light cruisers, and one of them seems to be in the Empress's pocket."

"Let's talk to the Emperor," Kris said. It took a few minutes to get him. The fellow who talked to Kris earlier took the call and asked if he might help. When Kris said no, he explained the Emperor had asked not to be disturbed again.

"He has company at the moment," the man said with a soft cough.

Vicky scowled and rolled her eyes at the overhead.

Kris scowled, too, as she said, "He has a hostile fleet with twenty-four battleships headed for his bedroom just now. He might want to talk to me about it."

The Emperor was quickly on the line, again with no video. "What's this about a battle fleet?"

"There are twenty-four battleships headed for Cuzco led by the *Terror of Space* and another one just as mean. Do you know anything about them?" Kris asked.

The Emperor suffered a bad fit of coughing. Many soft feminine voices offered him several things to drink. It was a bit later before he could continue.

"The Empress kept telling me we couldn't trust a Longknife. That Vicky was going to do something treacherous. She insisted we station some ships close by, and I finally agreed. She didn't tell me how many ships she was going to haul out here or how close they'd be . . . and I didn't ask," he finished slowly, dawn coming up a lot sooner for him than most today.

"Well, we've got my nine frigates and one of your light cruisers between you and whatever those battlewagons intend."

Captain Ajax cleared her throat. "The courier boat just flipped ship and is now decelerating at four gees."

On the battle board, Nelly drew a line from the courier. It would put the boat dead in space soon enough that it could accelerate back up and match with the incoming battleships.

"It would appear that the Empress and Grand Duke intend to join those battleships," Kris told the Emperor.

"Should I run? I have one light cruiser. It's faster than that tub the Empress insisted on."

"I'd really prefer that you didn't, sir," Kris said. "I can't protect you if you're out there in just a light cruiser."

"But all you've got is nine little frigates," the Emperor said, his voice squeaking.

"Yes, Harry, but I've blown a couple of huge alien base ships out of space with ships like these. I think I can stand my ground against a couple of dozen battleships."

"Vicky?" he asked.

Vicky glanced at Kris, then said, "Father, I think we really need to trust Kris Longknife. She's been in a lot more fights than anyone on your wife's ships. If she says she can take them, I'd trust her."

"If you say so, baby girl. You think I should stay, Kris?"

"You're safer on the ground for now. Trust me, Harry," Kris said. If she was going to save the dumb bastard's life again, he'd better get used to her calling him whatever she wanted to.

The Emperor said nothing.

"Well, I have a battle to plan. I'll get back to you when it's over."

"Nine frigates against a battle fleet?" the Emperor squeaked.

"Remember, I took twelve mosquito boats up against six huge battlewagons and won." *That will teach you to keep doubting me.*

It was cruel of Kris to point out that mistake of Harry's, but she was fresh out of the milk of human kindness where he was concerned.

The Emperor said nothing. He was still saying nothing when Kris cut the connection.

"Is that off?" Vicky asked, nodding at the commlink.

"Dead as a brick," Nelly said.

Vicky rolled her eyes. "I can't believe my dad is still

calling me baby girl. I haven't wanted to be called that since I was five."

"Maybe he'll learn and give you the respect you deserve," Kris said, wondering when she, herself, would get a little respect from her elders. Kris shook that thought off.

"Now, folks, we have a battle to win. Let's see how we do it. Do we hang around here for a bit, then swing around the moon to take them down when they're on final approach? Do we swing around some planet and come back at Cuzco on a parallel course and hammer them all the way in? Or"—Kris grinned—"do we charge right at them like a bunch of fools and wipe out a whole lot of battleships in one pass?"

Kris eyed her staff. They were grinning back at her.

Vicky wasn't smiling. She blinked several times, then said, "As much as I hate my stepmother, many of those Sailors are loyal subjects of my father. I would prefer to give as many of them a chance to surrender as we can."

She glanced at Admiral Bolesław at her side. "Can we cut out the rotten part of the apple without making applesauce of the rest?"

66

Three days later, Kris's squadron sortied from High Cuzco Station.

As much as Kris had looked forward to winning this battle with the dumbest of attack plans, she'd dropped the idea. Captain Ajax pointed out that even if Kris did blast the flagship out of space and get the rest to surrender, they still might not get the results they needed.

With the hostile fleet in the final stages of decelerating toward Cuzco, they could hardly dump their reactor cores. Kris could never trust them to approach Cuzco except under her guns. This hour's surrender could too easily be followed the next hour by their zapping the planet from orbit.

It became even clearer when the Empress addressed her husband from the bridge of her new flagship, the *Terror of Space*. Her tirade against the Emperor and his stupidity was only balanced by her gloating over how she would kill Kris Longknife, then laser all of them, "That whole damn planet," from orbit.

Nope, Kris would have to match orbits with this bunch and make sure they surrendered and stayed surrendered.

The one delight Kris found while listening to the Empress's boring harangue was watching the admiral standing beside her. The *Terror of Space* rated an admiral for its captain, and that admiral was her old buddy, William T. Thorpe, former skipper of the Wardhaven corvette *Typhoon*. Kris had relieved him of his command back when she was just an ensign.

When Kris countered the Empress's spiel with a demand they surrender now or face the consequences, Billy Thorpe laughed in her face. "I'm so glad you command that collection of shrimp boats, Ensign Longknife. It would be such a joy to take your surrender, but please, please keep strutting around. I will so enjoy blasting you out of space."

Kris just grinned as if she knew something he didn't and cut the line.

Boy, do I know something you don't know.

"You know him?" Jack asked.

"He was before your time, but his time is up."

"Yes. Yes, I do think it is."

Kris studied how the enemy battle array had developed. The two super battleships were following one behind the other. Ahead of the *Terror of Space* were the six battleships with 18-incher lasers. Instead of being in a long line, they were stacked three high and two deep. The four 16-inch battleships trailing the *Death to Traitors* were stacked two high, two deep. The older battlewagons formed two blocks, one forward, and the other aft of the newer ships. Both were three high and two deep. Sixteen heavy and light cruisers made up four stacks of four, two in the lead, the rest trailing. The last two light cruisers and the forty destroyers formed two circles, one below the thick battle line, the other above.

"Somebody wants to concentrate his fire," Kris said.

"The last time I fought the Empress, I divided by battle force into two lines of seven and nine. Her admiral divided his battleships into four long lines of a dozen each, minus those with engineering casualties. It left the older BBs out of range while I smashed the newer ones as they came in range."

"This still has the battle line bringing its different guns to bear at different times," Kris observed.

"Assuming she keeps them that way," Jack pointed out. "Any idea who commands over there?"

Both Kris and Vicky shook their heads.

"The only admiral I saw," Kris said, "was Thorpe. Vicky, did you see anyone?"

"Nope, Admiral Bolesław, was there anyone familiar to you on that bridge?"

"Interestingly, no. Every officer's face I saw was that of a stranger, and the Navy is a small place. I would have expected to recognize someone."

"I think my stepmom brought in people to officer those big ships from anywhere but Greenfeld."

"The better to slaughter the Emperor," Mannie said.

"My father is nothing if not gullible." Vicky sighed, tiredly.

Kris pursed her lips and let that thought sink in, then began to issue orders. "We will stay in line ahead for the trip out to the moon. As soon as we have the moon between us and the hostiles, second squadron will close up even with the flag with a thousand-klick interval between the two columns. On my orders, we will open up the interval to five thousand, but I don't intend to do that until we are two hundred fifty thousand klicks from the hostiles. Any concerns with that?"

"They've shortened their battle line," Vicky said, "so you're shortening yours?"

"Yes," Kris said.

"Kris," Jack said, "who will we target with our first broadside?"

"You're thinking it will be our only broadside."

"I hope so," Vicky said.

Kris ran a worried hand through her hair. "The first division's four ships target the two big ones. The second division's five ships target five of the six 18-inchers. Immediately after that, all Imperial survivors will be dismissed from stations so they can toddle off to their quarters to change their underwear."

That got a laugh.

Kris turned to Vicky. "Your stepmother, the Empress, tried to kidnap my daughter. I stood in the nursery for an eternity before Jack got a shot and killed the bastard she hired. She's got a whole battle fleet aiming their guns down my throat. As far as I'm concerned, she's a dead woman."

Vicky took in several shallow breaths and let each out with

a huff. Finally, she shook her head. "I didn't kill her when I had a chance, but Dad was telling us to quit fighting. Still, I swore when I finally tore that bed apart and managed to get a drink of water that I'd had enough. I'd kill her. I think I would have if she'd been right there at that moment."

Vicky paused for a long minute, then fixed Kris with hard eyes. "Kill the bitch."

"All right, ladies and gentlemen, the squadron has its orders. Let's go do what the Grand Duchess ordered."

67

Kris came out from behind Cuzco's largest moon with all her ships at Condition Baker and her squadron in two parallel columns.

She wasn't the only one who had changed her battle formation.

It took the hostiles a bit longer to complete the reorganization, but when they did, Kris had to hand it to Thorpe. He'd come up with a very interesting way of defending the flag and bringing all his guns to bear . . . assuming he faced frigates armed with short-range 24-inch pulse lasers.

The *Death to Traitors* still trailed the *Terror of Space*, but it was the only ship.

Well forward of those two, but forty thousand klicks closer to Kris, the stacks of 18- and 16-inch battleships followed one behind the other. Well aft, but coming up on eighty thousand klicks closer, were the 15- and 14-inch battleships. From the looks of it, they'd form a column of four, three ships high. The cruisers appeared to be racing to form a similar column of stacks well ahead of the newer battlewagons. Most likely, they'd end up only eighty thousand klicks from Kris.

The destroyers, all forty of them, were already turning to begin a pulse-laser run.

"Thorpe's a very smart fellow," Kris said through tight lips. "He's put together a very nice trap . . . for a frightened bunny rabbit. Pity he's set it for one mean and angry momma bear."

Kris studied her board for a full minute, then asked, "Nelly, will we need to worry about those tin cans?"

Circles appeared on Kris's battle board. The red of the destroyers were well back when Kris's ships passed the two-hundred-thousand-klick range mark.

"Kris, we're coming up on the two-hundred-fifty-thousand-klick range mark."

"Thank you, Nelly. 'Squadron, open your intervals to five thousand klicks. Division 2, drop your distance to five thousand klicks below Division 1 on my mark. Admiral Longknife sends.'"

The ships board on Kris's wall all blinked twice as every ship acknowledged.

"Mark," Kris said.

The *Princess Royal* kept its course steady. Every battle-cruiser around it slowed or slipped lower, or both.

"Squadron, go to Condition Charlie now. We will go to Condition Zed when we come up on two hundred ten thousand klicks to the two big boys. We will dispense with high-gee stations for the moment. If we need them, we can order them out of the Smart Metal then."

Around Kris, flag plot got smaller. Kris, Jack, Vicky, Mannie, and Admiral Bolesław got closer to the table.

"Nelly, put me on-screen. Beam this to all the ships across from us." Kris turned to face a blinking red lens. It turned green. "This is Admiral, Her Highness Kris Longknife of United Society. I've slaughtered half a trillion aliens, so adding a few thousand humans to my blacked soul doesn't bother me."

She paused to let that sink in. "But you aren't subjects of my King. You aren't, for the moment, rebels to your Emperor. However, if you continue to follow the false orders of the Empress, you will be in rebellion to your sworn liege lord. Discharge your lasers and blast away from Cuzco, and mercy shall be yours. Maintain your present course with charged lasers, and I will begin your destruction in three minutes."

Kris turned the comm over to Vicky.

"I am the Grand Duchess Victoria. You are all loyal subjects

of my father, your Emperor, who is present on the planet of
Cuzco, where you are heading. In a few minutes, a lot of you
will be dead. If, after that, the rest of you choose to surrender, I
will accept it."

"You bitch," the Empress broke in screaming.

*I wonder what took her so long. I must have caught her
comm wizards napping.*

"Worse, you stupid bitch. I have more than two battleships for
every one of those luxury-liner frigates that Wardhaven whore
has, and you have the gall to demand my surrender? You're a
fool! You and that Longknife whore will be dead in ten minutes.
Enjoy your last few moments, 'cause they're all you've got."

"Nelly, off," Kris said, then turned to Vicky. "That woman
has serious anger-management problems and a very limited
vocabulary."

"We were discussing that during the last battle, weren't we,
Admiral Bolesław?"

"Yes. Her temper will be the death of her yet if she doesn't
learn to control it."

"I think 22-inch lasers will get her long before a heart
attack," Jack muttered.

"General, I think you just might be right," Kris said.

Kris paused, then said, "Attention to orders. Take the
squadron to Condition Zed."

Her flag bridge got smaller, and she and her team got more
chummy.

"*Princess Royal* and *Intrepid*, you will engage the lead
battleship of those most distant. *Courageous* and *Furious*, you
will engage the trailing battleship. Commander Division 2,
assign one of your ships to five of the 18-inchers. You decide
who the lucky son of a bitch is who isn't blown to hell in the
first salvo."

Kris let those targeting orders sink in before continuing. "As
we come up on two hundred thousand klicks, I will order weapons release. You may fire your forward batteries as they come
in range. If your target is still there, flip ship and fire aft batteries. You will be weapons lock after your aft batteries are empty.
Immediately begin to reload. If, however, this shoot is to continue, I will give you another weapons free. Any questions?"

"One point, Kris," Vicky said.

"Yes.

"We've had a lot of luck punching through armor when we aim two lasers at the same point. We've even grouped four together though I doubt your big lasers need that."

"Right, my mistake," Kris said. "That is standard practice on Alwa Station. That's the problem with being an admiral; you forget how to be a squadron commander. All ships, concentrate fire on your target by pairs of lasers."

The ships blinked their reply.

"You sure we want to blow all those ships away just like that?" Admiral Bolesław whispered.

"You remember that battle where we had a hard time figuring out which ship was the flagship?" Vicky said.

"Yes," he scowled.

"You really want to bet the Empress is on any ship smaller than an 18-inch battleship?"

He shook his head at his Grand Duchess's question.

"The big battleships die," Vicky said, her words harsh.

Kris was eyeing the two. "You couldn't identify the flagship?"

"Long story. I'll tell you later," the Grand Duchess said.

"Kris, we're coming up on two hundred thousand klicks," Nelly said.

"Thank you, Nelly."

68

Kris closed her eyes. She took a deep breath and let it out slowly. She took a second one and held it for a moment, searching for her center.

I'm about to slaughter a whole lot of people. Most of them innocent.

Not the Empress.

The Empress tried to kidnap Jack and torture him. She went after Ruth. She'll do anything to get her way, even slaughter a lot of innocent people on the planet below.

If only Harry was on that battleship with her, I'd consider my family finally even with the Peterwalds.

But he isn't. Just the Empress and most of her twisted family.

Kris opened her eyes, steeled her heart, and set her face to hard military bland.

"Squadron, prepare to fire one salvo. Fire."

The *Princess Royal* swung around, bringing the twelve 22-inch lasers of her forward battery to bear and throwing Kris against Jack. She grabbed hold of her battle table, and Nelly had it grow handles. She grabbed one and brought herself upright.

"I told you to get yourself into a high-gee station," Jack growled.

"I'm tired of going naked into those things, then needing to stand up and take someone's surrender," Kris snapped back.

"And no," she quickly added, "wearing a uniform is no better. It has all those buttons and sharp points."

"I agree with Kris, and I still do," Vicky said.

The *Princess Royal* flipped ship and aimed her aft battery of eight more 22-inch guns at the *Terror of Space*. They fired.

Kris looked down to see what the battle board had to say about how the shoot was going. Five of the 18-inch battleships were in trouble.

First, the forward top, then the aft middle battleship blew up. That was followed by the forward bottom and the aft top going together in the blink of an eye. For a moment, it looked like the forward middle battleship might survive. Then the aft end, where the reactors were, blew itself to gas, and a moment later, nothing of that ship remained.

Only the bottom aft battleship, the one not targeted, still existed as Division 2 shut down and began to reload.

"Come on, you two monsters, blow."

Was that Vicky or Kris? No, it was both of them.

For a breath, the two huge ships with twenty-four of the "new" 19-inch lasers and ice armor more than six meters thick just lay there in the center of the board.

Then the aft one vanished. It just disappeared. One moment it was there, the next moment there wasn't anything there.

The lead one, the one *Princess Royal* and *Intrepid* were aiming at, looked like nothing was happening to her. Suddenly, the aft end flashed out of existence, and a chain reaction of explosions raced through the ship.

In the blink of an eye, there was just hot gas where it had been, then nothing. Not a thing.

The heart of the hostile battle line, and very likely the life of the Empress and much of her family, had been snuffed out in less than a minute.

"Kris, the other ships have flipped and are boosting away from us," Nelly said. "They've emptied their lasers into space. We're checking them, but from the looks of it, none are recharging their capacitors."

"Are we getting any requests to surrender?" Vicky asked.

"Not yet. Right now, they're just trying to sort out what's

left of their chain of command, Your Grace. A couple of the vice admirals commanding battle squadrons have abandoned their bridges. One has shot himself, and it appears the others are drinking themselves blind drunk. Oh, they just called out a crash cart for one vice admiral. I don't know why."

The screen in front of Kris and Vicky came alive with a rear admiral's face.

"Hi, Ramiro," Admiral Bolesław said, "How's it going?"

"Good God, man, what happened? You weren't even in range of us, and suddenly seven of our biggest ships are just gone." His voice rose to a sharp screech.

"Calm down, Ramiro."

"Calm down, you say? Damn it, man, what have you got over there?"

"I'll let Admiral Longknife explain her battle squadron to you."

"Battle squadron?"

"Hello," Kris said softly. She'd made her point. If Vicky was to save the lives of her subjects, there was no need to hammer them. "I'm Admiral Kris Longknife. I've been away for the last two years, fighting alien raiders and their oversize base ships. We've pushed our technology. The broadsides that just took out seven of your ships were from my ships' twenty 22-inch lasers."

"Your frigates carry twenty 22-inch lasers?"

"We're reclassifying them as battlecruisers," Kris said modestly.

"I guess you would," the Greenfeld admiral murmured in agreement.

"Ramiro," Admiral Bolesław said softly, "what's happening over on your side?"

"Everything's gone to hell. One of the battlewagon vice admirals just OD'd on red heroin. I'd never have taken Spinosa for a user, but he's been in the Empress's pockets for a long time. I'm told they called out the crash cart for him."

"Most people don't survive that kind of a thing."

"Yeah. Well, the vice admiral commanding cruisers and destroyers is a jumped-up bank clerk who married some daughter of someone in the family bank. I hear he's locked himself in his cabin with a bevy of girls he brought aboard, and they're getting sloshed. That leaves me senior officer present outside the battle line. Our ships don't have all that extra reaction mass, so what do you want us to do?"

Vicky stepped forward. "A chief on one of the destroyers who surrendered to us at the last Battle of St. Petersburg smashed the buss to the mains that would reload the capacitors. Did I get that right, Admiral Bolesław?"

"Yes, Your Grace."

"Is that the Grand Duchess?"

"Ramiro, may I introduce you to Vice Admiral, Her Grace Victoria of Greenfeld," said Admiral Bolesław.

The admiral ran a nervous hand through his black hair. "I think I better take this chance to be the first of my fleet to swear allegiance to you."

"I am in allegiance to my father, your Emperor, as you are. We are gathered on Cuzco to resolve certain matters. I believe the Empress was intent on disrupting those talks between myself and my father, if not killing us both."

"We were told that the Longknifes had violated a parley truce and seized the Emperor."

"Kris, can you get my father on the horn, quick? That might settle a lot of this."

"Nelly," Kris said.

It was again night on Cuzco, but since a fleet was inbound, intent on lasing the Emperor to glowing magma, he was waiting up and still dressed in court garb.

"To all my people, I say that I am well, and free to come and go as I please," Emperor Harry began.

Strange how the Imperial "we" becomes "I" when it gets deadly and personal, Kris thought.

The Emperor continued. "It is the Empress who has by nefarious means attempted to do harm to my body. My daughter, the Grand Duchess Victoria, and her friend, Princess Kristine of the United Society, have done me good service. Are there any questions any of you may want to ask me to assure yourself that I am truly talking for myself?"

No one had a question.

Surviving battleships, as well as cruisers and destroyers, quickly rendered their armament unusable and docilely set their course for High Cuzco Station.

69

"It is said that victory has a thousand fathers, but no one ever said how many traffic controllers it needed," Captain Ajax said as she collapsed into a chair in Kris's day quarters. "It's a zoo out there."

"Is Cuzco's prime minister still demanding we keep half of the station's piers clear for commerce?" Kris asked, offering her flag captain a cup of soothing chamomile tea.

"He is, and we're insisting they follow the usual rule of first come, first served. Hell, Admiral Waller has got his ships rotating through the piers just as fast as they can load reaction mass. Oh, and Cuzco doubled the price of reaction mass. Again," Ajax said through a scowl.

"Even after we sent four pinnaces out to gather reaction mass for them?"

"Yes, ma'am. They're selling the reaction mass we brought in for free at four times the price it brought a week ago."

"I do not like people taking advantage of my generosity." For a moment, Kris stared at the overhead. "Okay. Send out all nine pinnaces this time and rig hosing so we can pass reaction mass to two ships at a time."

"You going to refuel the Peterwald fleet well away from the station?"

"If it gets them out of here, yes."

Captain Ajax put down her half-full cup of tea and headed up to her bridge.

Kris had already had a talk with Vicky and the Emperor about who paid for all the costs that had been going on Grampa Ray's royal credit chit.

"Oh, didn't I tell you?" Vicky said. "We brought raw and polished crystal as well as electronics. It may not be as fancy as Wardhaven stuff, but it still ought to have a market. We also brought along some of the latest artwork from our painters and sculptors. I'm sure some of it will find a buyer. I'll have that released immediately. With any luck, I'll be able to pay half the expenses of this conference."

"Harry?" Kris said. He still hadn't shown any negative reaction to being treated so familiarly by a US Princess.

He scowled. "They've got a lien against the *Emperor and Empress*. Would you believe that? Until I pay my own bills here, they won't let her go."

"You really want to keep a tub with the late, unlamented Empress's name on it?" Vicky asked.

Her father's lips took on a sly smile as he looked Kris's way. "I wonder what a fine yacht like that will bring on the open market, say above Wardhaven?"

Kris limited herself to a shrug. With Smart Metal™ all the rage, she doubted old, overblown scows like that one would maintain much of their popularity, or value, for very long.

"Vicky, could I manage a ride home with you?" he asked.

"Only if you'll send ninety percent of those worthless hangers-on and all of the Empress's lackeys home with the fleet."

"Done," he said.

Next day, Vicky told Kris that they'd found buyers for all of their crystal and electronics and a surprising portion of the art. "It seems there's a retro movement, and the Empire's art has been locked down by Dad and his grandfather for so long that we're right where the nostalgia crowd is going."

"You think the market will stay there?"

Vicky shook her head. "Not likely. If stuff comes flooding out of the Empire after we leave, it will likely be selling into a saturated market. But it was nice to us while it lasted."

The next day, the Hall of Mirrors was rather comfortable

and spacious for those who were still in attendance. A committee of five from each side had been working behind closed doors to hammer out a proposal that would be either accepted by Vicky and her father *in toto*, or rejected if either one of them objected to any part of it.

Vicky's five included Mannie, Steve Rojek, a woman from Metzburg, Admiral Waller, and a businessman from a planet Kris had never heard of. The Emperor had chosen the fellow who answered the phone that night when the Emperor was otherwise occupied, the man who brought the hall to tears with his telling of the slaughter on Dresden, and three other men just as sober in their dress.

Their proposal was simplicity itself.

Emperor Harry would remain Emperor of the Greenfeld Empire.

The Grand Duchess Victoria was acknowledged as his rightful heir and upon his death or abdication would become the Empress.

For the time being, the Empire would be divided into two economic zones: one made up of the territory presently acknowledging the Emperor through the Grand Duchess and the other the rest. Trade between both zones would not be limited or taxed. At any time, but no more than every five years, any planet could vote, by a majority of those over eighteen, to change zones.

Imperial taxes were set at no more than ten percent of a planet's GDP, with half of the money raised in Vicky's zone going into a budget that she would manage. Planets would decide for themselves how to raise the money and were free to raise more for their own purposes.

There were a whole list of other things. How much or how little could be spent on defense, to include not just a Navy but an Army as well.

The presentation, rather wisely, paused before it was more than a quarter done and everyone went to an early lunch. People gathered around tables to talk to the writers. Kris's brain trust, who seemed to know an awful lot about the proposal, were also in great demand.

Kris decided to go up the beanstalk and play with Ruth for the rest of the day.

The next day, she gaveled the morning session open, with each of the sides having ninety minutes to raise questions about the plan on the table. There was a rush from both sides to get the floor, so Vicky took the job of recognizing members of her delegation for five minutes, then yielding the floor to the senior writer from the Emperor's side, who seemed to be in line to be the next prime minister.

In this fashion, the talks went on for three long, long days.

After lunch the second day, Kris announced supper would be at five, and there would be a three-hour session after dinner.

The third day, the evening session went all the way to midnight. That was when Vicky said she'd heard enough. "Dad."

Someone had to wake the Emperor up.

"Yes, yes," he snorted.

"Do you feel a need to hear more?"

"Ah, um, not really."

"I'm willing to accept the proposal as it is before us. I'm also willing to meet with you and any interested party in two years to discuss changes. Your Highness, would you be willing to chair such a meeting?"

"Me?" Kris said, coming out of her thoughts of what Ruthie must be doing about now.

"Yes, you. Who else do you think would do it?"

"Anyone else," Kris suggested.

"Kris, I'm willing to outfit and send two squadrons of battle-cruisers to Alwa's defense using funds from my zone, assuming you will share with us the technology necessary to make them."

Kris frowned at Vicky.

"Come on, BFF. If we're going to be ready to kill any alien mother ship that shows up in our sky, we'll have to build battle-cruisers just like you do."

"She's got a point, Kris," Jack whispered.

Kris sighed. "Okay, but if I'm pregger with our next one, Bub, you got to carry it while I'm sitting here."

"We'll use a uterine replicator next time," Jack whispered. "No way I'm going through what you went through."

"Men," Kris and Vicky said, but they glanced at the men in their life with fond eyes.

70

A week later, Admiral, Her Highness Kris Longknife presented herself before Field Marshal McMorrison.

"Done already?"

"Yes, sir," Kris answered smartly.

"So, I imagine you want a job."

"Yes, sir. A desk job. One I can work at eight hours a day, five days a week, and go home to my daughter without taking the job with me."

"I've never found one of those."

"I've served my time in hell, sir. I think I deserve a little boredom, don't you?"

The field marshal scowled. "Any thoughts on where I might find a job for you? You are wearing four stars, Your Highness."

"And I'm not giving them back."

"I didn't think you would. So?"

"I noticed that the Battle Force and Scout Force are still arguing where the battlecruisers fit in. The battleship Sailors say they're ships of the line and belong to them and the cruiser type commander insists they fit right into his Scout Force."

"And they've been arguing over that since the first one was launched. You got any ideas, Admiral?"

"Yes, Mac. I want the job of type commander for battle-cruisers. That will make sure they get their own slot, not shoe-horned into someone else's hip pocket, where they can get lost, ignored, or misused."

"That sounds like a job for a miracle worker. You realize you'll be in the very middle of the budget battles. Spread-sheets at five paces."

That gave Kris pause, but not enough for her to walk away.

"Nope, I'll take the job. I've blown away alien base ships, I think a few entrenched bureaucrats shouldn't be all that much trouble."

Mac chuckled at that. "Kris, you can kill alien base ships. People will gossip at the watercooler if you kill your fellow admirals."

"That's a problem how?" Kris said with a straight face.

"I'm just saying."

"Mac, I want a desk job. This looks like the kind of desk job that's right down my alley. Unless you've got another nice *desk* job for me, I want this one."

"No ship duty, huh?"

"Been there, done that. Got the medical bills to prove it."

"You really think you can settle for a desk job?"

"Watch me."

"You know, they've already started a betting pool for how long you'll last. I've got the twenty-four-month slot," the field marshal said with a grin.

"Tell me who's holding the pot. I want the ticket that's forever."

Now Mac chuckled. "It will be interesting to see who wins."

71

Kris answered the door chime herself at Nuu House. Waiting outside were Mother and Father as well as Honovi and his brood.

Father frowned. "You look mighty formal, dress blues and all those gewgaws, for a quiet afternoon supper with your family."

Kris knew her smile was fay. "There are a few things to do before supper. Please follow me." No one took their coats as she led them through the width of Nuu House, out the back door, then across the cobblestoned esplanade and down into the garden.

"What's that?" Brenda didn't quite demand.

"A small family get-together," Kris said, as she led her parents down front to the chairs to the left of the aisle. The bride's side.

Kris exchanged a quick smile with Jack's mom and dad. He'd seated them and answered more of their questions than she had of her folks.

Taking a deep breath, Kris walked back up the aisle. Smiling and nodding at both those in the know and those still ignorant. Grampa and Gramma Trouble had managed to get Ray here. *Who's his plus one? I will need to get to know her.*

Brenda's own mother and father, he a professor at a university farther down the coast, had insisted on seats in the back row. Kris had always known her mother was a social climber. She rarely took her children to meet their grandparents on her side. *I'll have to make a special effort to build bridges there. It's not as if I'm going anyplace tomorrow.*

Kris smiled at that thought.

A few paces back from the chairs, Kris was met by Ensign Meg Longknife in dress blues. Beside her, in her very first formal, was Jack's sister Estella. She was so excited she looked ready to jump out of her violet sheath dress that modestly rose to her neck. Three-quarter sleeves showed where she clutched her bouquet.

Kris had won extra wifely points from Jack when she took Estella dress shopping and nixed the strapless gowns the young woman had done her best to talk Kris into buying for her.

Megan handed Kris her bouquet as she joined her bridesmaids. She turned to face forward; Jack and the two chaplains had just gathered at the front. It saddened Kris that Jack had no one to stand up with him as best man. She'd run him pretty ragged and left him with few friends at hand.

Then again, most of the women Kris wished were here were scattered across the galaxy, too. *Maybe we can learn to play bridge with couples our own age. Might even arrange some playdates with people who have kids Ruth's age.*

Kris was called out of her reveries when the organist began to play a march for the bridesmaids. The two began to process down the aisle.

Kris stared at Jack staring at her. *Does he actually look nervous?*

Heavens knows, they had enough to worry about just for this small, family wedding. Take the chaplains: one Catholic for Jack's mom, one Episcopal for her folks. Kris was pretty sure Mother would not have accepted just the Catholic chaplain, so she'd balanced that. And Jack had already explained to his mother as he ushered her in that the Catholic priest would be doing all those parts required for a proper Catholic wedding, but that the Episcopal priest would be assisting everywhere it was allowed.

Kris had to chuckle softly. *I managed to negotiate peace between the Peterwalds. I'm good for this, too.*

Yeah, right.

The bridal march began. Kris took a deep breath and began the longest of short walks. Strange, she'd felt better, more accepted, among the Alwar colonials than she did here.

But I'm not on Alwa. I'm home, and I'm going to stay home. I will mend my fences and build some more, so I can stay right here and enjoy it.

She came out of herself when Jack smiled at her like some love-struck fool. She found herself smiling back, just as love-struck and just as much the fool.

The ceremony went quickly. She had a gold ring for Jack this time. He again used the simple gold ring he'd bought for her at the BX on Hellfrozeover long ago, when both of them feared that they might never see each other again. It wasn't long before both the priests said, "You may now kiss the bride."

There were cheers as they did, and another as they began the walk back up the aisle, arm in arm.

At the end of the aisle, a line of uniformed officers had formed, swords crossed to form a passageway for the couple. She'd wondered where Mac got the collection of admirals and generals who helped him form two surprisingly long rows. Kris suspected she'd be deep in budget battles with many of them soon enough; she fervently hoped the swords weren't sharp.

She noticed that Mac had taken the last slot on her side. She eyed him, and mouthed, "I've already had my rump swatted," but he kept staring straight ahead.

"Ouch," Kris said, as Mac used his cake cutter to rap her on her backside. With intent.

She eyed him but then shook her head. Maybe she didn't deserve this whacking, but, no doubt, before long, he'd be wanting to whack her upside the head or other place. She'd let him have this one.

Kris turned back to meet those who now filed down the aisle behind her. Lotty had outdone herself with the dinner awaiting them.

After dinner, there would be a small family gathering in

the library, and the Catholic priest would baptize little Ruth Maria Brenda Anne Longknife. That would be her concession to both sides of the family. Maria got her granddaughter baptized, and Billy got another Longknife in the family.

What Ruth had to say about her name in eighteen years was hers to decide. She would have her mother's support no matter what she chose.

Kris looked around at Nuu House. Over seven years ago, she'd fled the place with no intent of ever looking back. Somehow, she had come full circle. But it was a full circle that held so much.

She remembered the old chief who'd asked her why she was in her Navy. Kris hadn't really known the answer then. Now she did.

This Navy was her Navy, too. And the Longknifes were her family, both the small one she'd made and the given one that milled around her today. She'd even made a dent in all of humanity, and even the galaxy.

All of it had brought her back to here.

Kris took a deep breath. She was home, and she liked it.

The End

Special Note to the Reader

Thirteen books ago, the Kris Longknife saga began as a coming-of-age story. Kris was a fresh-caught boot ensign, making all the mistakes you expect of a green JO. A retired Navy captain wrote me that in *Kris Longknife: Mutineer* I had captured the life of a junior officer and all the challenges a senior officer faces to properly lead and mentor that JO. That feedback made my day.

For seven more books, we followed Kris as she learned the ropes and came to be a qualified Officer of the Deck. There is only so long a writer can keep a good character like Kris in coming-of-age mode, so in *Kris Longknife: Daring* we changed the thrust of her story.

No longer was she trying to figure out where she fit in or who she was. Kris was ready to use all she'd learned and see what she could do. Certainly, the bug-eyed monsters were a worthy opponent for Kris.

Now Kris has fought her monsters, both the alien and the human ones. Kris is an admiral, a married woman, and a mother. It is time to write "The End" on the last page of this book.

I do this with intent. A fan wrote me that he was struggling with cancer and hoped that I'd reach the end of Kris's story before he reached the end of his. For him, if he's still reading, here is a very satisfactory ending for Kris, Jack, and Nelly.

For those of you who want to know how the lottery goes and what happens next, don't worry. As you're reading this, I'm turning in the next Kris book and very likely starting the one after that. Kris may have achieved flag rank, a ring on her finger, and a lovely baby girl on her hip, but you don't really think she's going to last long behind that desk, do you?

Which month did you pick in the lottery for how long she'll stay put behind a desk?

About the Author

Mike Shepherd grew up Navy. It taught him early about change and the chain of command. He's worked as a bartender and cabdriver, personnel advisor and labor negotiator. Now retired from building databases about the endangered critters of the Pacific Northwest, he's enjoying some fun reading and writing.

Mike lives in Vancouver, Washington, with his wife, Ellen, and close to his daughter and grandchildren. He enjoys reading, writing, dreaming, watching grandchildren for story ideas, and upgrading his computer—all are never-ending.

Despite what you may think, Mike is already hard at work on Kris's next story, *Kris Longknife: Emissary*, coming from Ace in October 2017, as well as other exciting tales in Kris's universe.

You may learn more about Mike, his projects, and his books at his website mikeshepherd.org; you can e-mail him at Mike_Shepherd@comcast.net or follow Kris Longknife on Facebook.

From *New York Times* Bestselling Author
MIKE SHEPHERD

. . .

The Kris Longknife Series

MUTINEER
DESERTER
DEFIANT
RESOLUTE
AUDACIOUS
INTREPID
UNDAUNTED
REDOUBTABLE
DARING
FURIOUS
DEFENDER
TENACIOUS
UNRELENTING
BOLD

. . .

"A whopping good read . . . Fast-paced, exciting, nicely detailed, with some innovative touches."

—Elizabeth Moon, *New York Times* bestselling author of *Crown of Renewal*

mikeshepherd.org
facebook.com/acerocbooks
penguin.com

M905AS0815

Connect with Berkley Publishing Online!

For sneak peeks into the newest releases, news on all your favorite authors, book giveaways, and a central place to connect with fellow fans—

"Like" and follow Berkley Publishing!

facebook.com/BerkleyPub
twitter.com/BerkleyPub
instagram.com/BerkleyPub

 Penguin Random House